THIRSTY
GHOSTS

THIRSTY GHOSTS

EMER MARTIN

THE LILLIPUT PRESS

DUBLIN

First published 2023 by
THE LILLIPUT PRESS

62–63 Sitric Road, Arbour Hill
Dublin 7, Ireland
www.lilliputpress.ie

ISBN 9781843518631

10 9 8 7 6 5 4 3 2 1

The Lilliput Press gratefully acknowledges the financial support of the Arts
Council/An Chomhairle Ealaíon.

Set in 10pt on 15pt Hoefler Text by Compuscript
Printed in the Czech Republic by Finidr

The O Conaill Family Tree

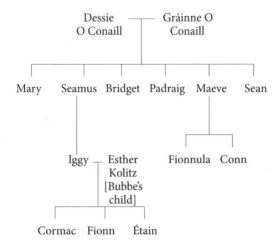

Dessie O Conaill —— Gráinne O Conaill

Mary Seamus Bridget Padraig Maeve Sean

Iggy — Esther Kolitz [Bubbe's child]   Fionnula Conn

Cormac Fionn Étain

The Lyons Family Tree

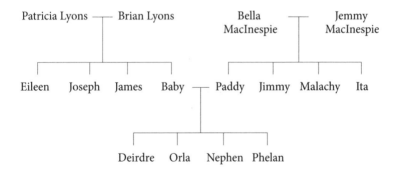

Patricia Lyons —— Brian Lyons   Bella MacInespie —— Jemmy MacInespie

Eileen Joseph James Baby —— Paddy Jimmy Malachy Ita

Deirdre Orla Nephen Phelan

PART I

For all the bold and bad and bleary they are blamed, the sea hags.
    – James Joyce (*Finnegans Wake*)

Hag

The Seed of All Stories

The stories mean the pain will not always kill you. The seed of all stories was coded deep in the first thought. Just as with your children, you began to destroy me as soon as you named me. God became small through you. Vulnerable Gods will do anything. We are inside each other. And all I've seen, I have seen through your eyes. We spiral in the beginning of endings.

Before you, endless winter kept me calm and silent and still. It was only ten thousand years ago that you clambered noisily off your boats. But I am not oblivious to the slaughter that you have scrawled on my body. Hate might not be solid to touch but yours has left a fossil trace.

You came from the restless sea. I have seen everything you built fall to ruin.

As millennia pushed on, you shunted me away in corners, froze me into rocks on the shore. And I never stopped feeding you, never stopped washing you clean. Even when you no longer said my name. When you thought you could buy and sell me without seeing me.

The war on me was a battle you never thought to record.
There is never justice when the victim is your only witness.

I am the hag. I am Ireland. I stretch my sinewy arms wide. I open my toothless mouth. Spread my rocky legs. My openings licked and eroded by the salty sea. In them you sheltered shivering. You had to hide from each other in me. Gulping like blind eels up my crevices, crawling through to the womb of the world back to the first thought. Thoughts that became sounds, the sounds that came before songs. A wailing that began when you were only dreaming of beauty.

The first word was a warning, and you were no longer free. Calling danger to your tribe. A sharp wild sound that encased thought like a shell. Wordshells threaded into stories. Your mind adorned – it was beautiful, but it was a weight. Because you loved – you feared. Because you feared, you screamed. Because you screamed, you spoke. Because you wanted a shape to outlast you, you told a story. To send messages to those not yet born. And those stories mean the pain will not always kill you.

Dymphna

I Won't Go Down to the River Again
(1968)

I was born in Gestapo Ireland in the 1950s – where men weren't allowed to think and women didn't exist. My name is Dymphna. Patron Saint of the Mad. Yeah. I've heard all the jokes. I came to the Laundry at fourteen years old. The others all called me Little Poet, on account of me writing me own poetry when I was little and walking barefoot by the River Dodder.

I used to put me feet in and let the river soak me and I'd suck up the spirit of the water to give me strength.

Ma was told I was always sitting by the River Dodder with me eyes closed. And she found all me poems, scribbled on the backs of bits of paper. Sure, I can't remember even one of them now. They had always been telling me that if I didn't behave, I'd go to the Magdalenes and that's what they done – and they never came looking for me after. All the blame went on them nuns but they didn't have to come looking for us, it was our own famblies who shoved us in for the most part. Of course, the nuns were there to suit them, and the Guards to send us back if we ran. What a racket. Me uncle was a small man with a red face. He would disappear on the lash for days and then come back to kip at our house even though he had to squeeze into the other bed with all me brothers. He was a cute hoor and always came back at dinner time, buttering me ma up with his auld plámás and throwing shapes. Me ma adored him, me da was never home. In anyways, me ma sent me to do the messages and, after I'd done them, I went to the Dodder to sink me feet and write some poems in me new notebook. It wasn't new, but me teacher had seen that I wrote poems on pieces of paper and given me one of her notebooks that was a bit used. I tore them pages out and had it all to meself. Me uncle followed me and bellowed like a bull. I told him he was a dosser and did nothing for us anyway.

Back at the house, he told me ma that I was at the river. She grabbed the basket off me and started rummaging around in it; she was livid that the bread was wet at the bottom. She found me notebook. Me sisters were screaming at me and me brothers pushing. 'She's a feckin eejit,' they said. 'The bread is soaking.' They all crowded in on me, pulled out me notebook of poems. 'What's she writing?' 'Who does she tink she is?' I was mortified, and me uncle started to read them, and two of me brothers came at me.

I took up a chair and held it up like I'd seen a picture in a book of a lion tamer do. 'That's it!' me uncle said, 'I'm going to the Cruelty Man.'

'The Artane Man?' me brother said, swinging his arms like an ape, dancing in front of me and me chair held up.

'No, that's for ye. The nuns will take the girls for the Laundry,' me uncle said, as if it was all decided.

I was gobsmacked and shouted, 'What did I do?'

Me uncle said it to me ma, who was already turning away, looking like a tired sack as always, 'She's always acting the maggot. And her going down to the river and with the writing of the poetry. She'll bring disgrace to us one day. Only a matter of time.'

Me ma sighed, 'Yizzer all wrecking me head.' She turned to me and it was as if she couldn't see me, as if I was already gone. That's when I knew I was done for.

Me uncle marched out of the house on a mission. I set the chair down thinking I was safe. I saw where me ma had put me notebook, on the top shelf beside the Virgin Mary, so I made me mind up to get it back as soon as I could.

In anyways, the Cruelty Man was only too delighted to come back with me uncle. He had short grey hair and loomed in the door like a mountain. He and me uncle tore me out of the house – dragged me barefoot down our street, women leaning against their doorways with children teeming all over them, childer at their feet, in their arms, growing in their bellies, stray and starving. The Cruelty Man stopped at the corner – he and me uncle were having a disagreement as to where I could be brought.

'I won't go down to the river again,' I pleaded. Looking around thinking I could leg it. 'I'm only always taking off them shoes because they don't fit any more. Me toes are turning black in them and me nails are sore.'

Me uncle grabbed hold of me arm. It was as if I didn't exist, a piece of shite to be scraped off their shoes. I don't know why me uncle wanted me gone. I shared a bed with me sisters and ate the same as the rest of them. Which wasn't much.

The Cruelty Man said he would take me to Golden Bridge, and I liked the sound of that. I imagined a bridge like those I had seen on a blue-and-white china plate in a shop window on Clanbrassil Street. I liked to wander there where the Jews were because it was just that bit different to the other streets and the people had dark eyes and hair and more of the world in their glances. Some had foreign accents and softer ways, and the men weren't all drunk like me da and me uncle. The Cruelty Man and me uncle decided on the Laundry instead.

I squirmed away from me uncle when I heard that, I wasn't as green as I'm cabbage. The Cruelty Man grabbed me by the wrist and tightened his grip. He looked at me for the first time and said, 'Steady on now, pet. You'll have food where yer going and they'll straighten you out. You have no idea what could happen down by the river.' But there was no concern or kindness in his voice.

'And they'll clear out them notions of yours,' me uncle laughed. So they dragged me to the Laundry; I left me family and the wet bread behind forever. The nuns opened the door and eyed me uncle and the Cruelty Man. We were poor and they could smell that off us. I didn't know much about money, but I knew it changed the way people looked at you. A beardy nun called Sister Paul asked if I could work and they said I could.

'She can read and write,' me uncle said, almost with pride. 'She can write in rhymes.'

'The only rhymes she'll need here are her prayers,' Sister Paul said and pointed to another room. I walked in and I turned around quickly, but the door slammed shut and I never saw me uncle again. They shaved me head and gave me new clothes. They said Dymphna was a good saint's name. The Patron Saint of Mental Illness and all. You can keep your name, they told me, that was the first real shock I got. I had thought I would be punished for a day or so and have to do a job but come home at nights. Why would they want to take me name?

That night I sat at a long table with the Laundry women. Half of them were baldies and the other half had wispy hair under their bonnets. There was one who stood out. She had glowing blue and grey and green eyes and looked as if she had been waiting for me. The nuns and everyone called her Teresa, but she said it wasn't her real name. When I told her I was writing poems and putting me feet in the river she called me the Little Poet, and everyone started calling me that. I liked that. In the night she told one of the old stories of the childer who were turned into swans and banished for hundreds of years on wild seas and cold lakes. She crawled into me bed to hold me when I cried for the world. I didn't cry for me family, cos they sent me there, but I cried for the long wet friend of a Dodder who would suckle me feet and settle all the thoughts in me head. Once, when we were together, she told me a poem that she said was written a thousand years ago and was why we were all here.

I am Eve, great Adam's wife,
I that wrought my children's loss,
I that wronged Jesus of life,
By right 'tis I had borne the cross.

Bogman

Yestreen I Went Under
(1000 BCE)

Yestreen, this night was my last night, onion-layered dark and tight around me like a thousand eye-stinging cloaks of fright. Moon drowned, I sat bound and shivering on a stone chair. The hag was watching. The only one waiting.

I was gasping. My foster parents dissolving with grief. I don't remember being given to them as a small boy, but they had raised me with affection. Children were swapped from tribe to tribe to quell the constant warfare. For who would go kill their brothers?

For this ceremony everyone had come. My blood father's eyes were black holes, obscure as the starless gloom. I barely knew him. Was he proud? Repulsed?

Trembling men held my arms. The hoods up on their cloaks. Iron knives glint in fire. They stutter-danced towards me. Faces painted, straw hair. I couldn't tell who was who. I played with one of them as a child. I'm sure. We hunted over the bare mountain, through woods full of wolves. A poisonous roar of wind whipped into the stone circle. The men descended on me, they pulled my head back and sliced off my nipples. My blood flowed. I saw the whites of their eyes – wolf-eye white. Stars were sucked back into the flesh of the nothing sky. The drums went inside me drumming. A bloody slit opened in this world, and I slipped in through. It is worth something – this sacrifice.

Yestreen, breath stolen, heart surged, stomach lurched, one starless deep night slowly slid to an ancient cypher. This frantic solemn pummelling to protect the world. Embedded in the folds of the old hag's bog skin.

I was brave. I was willing to go down. To live beneath you, to feel your feet pounding on the roof of the underworld. I agreed to this. I longed for it. Do you even know I'm below you? That something is holding you up?

Oh, hollow hag, I sink into your wound and it closes over me until I'm sealed, trapped like a stone in a scar. Yestreen my blood river in the grasses, drowned underground. They sink me down. Over before I was over.

I had to become nothing for you all.

Dymphna

A God Who Became So Small
(1972)

Teresa, she was a pet, she took me under her arm, she was only
thirty-nine when I went in but she looked older – they all did. Worn
out from work and starvation. She weighed about six stone and she
was tall too. But she was a real darling to me. She protected me.
I would have been at the mercy of them bitches, them nuns. The
other girls were all a bit soft in the head, or at least they'd gone
soggy with the washing and drying. Their minds steamed out of
them. Outside people had got washing machines of their own and
we weren't so needed except for the big orders from the state, like
hospitals and prisons and orphanages and all that.

Am I rabbiting on too much?

One of them girls padded after Teresa like a little lost duckling
down at the Dodder. The nuns called her Bridget, but Teresa made
everybody call her Bright. Bright was a divil for the stories. She would
moon after Teresa and only came to life when Teresa was telling us

all about the swans, or the princess who looked into the mirror of all wishes and demanded to marry a bull, or my favourite one about the fairy queen Etáin who was turned into a fly. Bright had it out daggers for me since I was Teresa's new pet and she wanted her for herself, but there was no self there. And there were no mirrors for us, no wishes for us, but we had Teresa who, to tell the truth, the nuns tried to tame but couldn't. She had a streak in her and a mad rough laugh. She moved fluid like the Dodder.

Once, Teresa and I plotted an escape in the laundry van. She had got in with the dirty fella who drove it. But Bright would live in yer ear and she slimed off to them nuns and ratted us out. Teresa said it was all her and didn't squeal on me. Swore till she was blue in the face that it was her only. They beat her with a hairbrush in front of us all. We all stood in a line, wincing from every wallop. After that Teresa never spoke to Bright. Bright sat on the side with a face on her like a pig licking piss off a nettle, and a longing that only settled when Teresa told them stories at night. Bright would lick her lips when she listened, eating up the words, wringing her hands and giving out small grunts now and then at the parts that would make the rest of us weep for our own sorrows.

'Two men have to sign you out.'

'Your family has to come and get you and they have to be your brother or father.'

'The family has to go to the priest who goes to the bishop to get you out.'

I knew no one would be coming for me. Me sisters were probably glad of the extra room in the bed. Me ma for one less mouth to feed. Me da wouldn't notice when he fell in from the pub. I was sure me uncle got some kind of deal from the Cruelty Man. I didn't know what the Cruelty Man got. I had not been told how the world worked but I knew it wasn't working for me.

Teresa was a tonic. She was me guardian angel, all she wanted from me was that I'd listen to all her bleedin' stories, and sure

I was only delighted. There was nothing else to do. She told me her name was once Maeve and that she'd be Maeve again when she got out, but in here she was Teresa. Them nuns loved St Teresa and let us read her stuff. They had put up a poster on the wall with a picture of Baby Jesus in his crib and the words: '*A God who became so small could only be mercy and love –* St Teresa.'

Them nuns had a telly. But do you think they'd let us look at the yoke? Ya must be joking. But we loved the telly because once *The Riordans* came on every nun in the place would scarper off. We could do what we liked during *The Riordans*.

Then one day they came rushing into us and told us to stop work and come look at the telly. The whole flock of auld nuns were crying.

'Wha, has the pope died or something?' I asked.

It was the first time I seen telly.

'The Brits, I mean the British Forces, shot dead thirteen unarmed marchers in Derry,' the Superioress said, her face flushed.

'Civil-rights marchers,' Sister Benedict said slowly, testing the phrase.

'What's that when it's at home?' I asked. And she shut her gob – she wouldn't have known a civil right if it crawled up her leg and into her knickers.

We were told to get down and pray in front of the television, and we saw people running around screaming and bleeding and the army coming on all heavy and murdering away to their heart's content. Ye'd think them nuns were going to get out the hairbrushes and go tearing up the North to free Ireland once and for all.

This was when Teresa pulled me out the door, with poor Bright looking helplessly at the two of us. I'd give her a right puck in the gob if she so much as looked sideways at me.

'Come on quick.'

'What? Are we off to fight the Brits?'

'Don't be a thick. At least the Brits don't lock their women up for writing poems by the river. That's where ye have to go. Get to England and never come back here. The van is coming from the prison and the fella there owes me a favour.'

They usually watched Teresa like a hawk, but with all the commotion, the nuns were now kneeling and wailing in front of the telly. We ran out the back, and sure enough the van was unloading the last stuff. And getting ready to close the doors.

'Mickey!' Teresa said.

A man turned around. He wore a cap and had two front teeth missing.

'Jaysus, haven't seen you in years, wha?' He scratched his head and gave me the once over with his eyes. 'I can only take one of ye.'

'Why?' Teresa hissed.

'I'm not codding ya. One can fit into the empty hamper at the back. The others are all packed in.'

'I'll ride with ye up front,' Teresa said.

'Ya will in yer hole. I can't afford to lose me job. I don't know if this is even worth it.'

'Ye got your payment.'

'That was years ago, love. An old grope every now and then wasn't much.' He looked at me. 'There's not much to ye now, Teresa. But she's a fine thing. How old is she?'

'She's seventeen now. Been here three years, but she still has some life in her. Get her out and don't mess with her.'

'I, I, I haven't got any of me stuff.' Me tummy was doing loops and panic vomit was rising in me throat.

Teresa grabbed me. 'Get out of here before you become like one of them in there. You'll end up like poor wee Bright. Scared of her own shadow. Not knowing what life is without walls around you. Never speaking to anyone except a hairy nun and Laundry girls. If I escape, I can go to my sisters, but then there's no one to rescue you. My sister knows the priest, and the family she works for will help her. If I get out, I can't help you. But you can go to my sister, and she'll get me out. I know she will. Mary would do anything for any of us; she'll sort you out too.'

'I'm scared of him. He seems like a right bollox.'

Teresa glared at me. 'Get in the back, just suck him off or something or let him feel your tits. Don't let him put his thing in or you'll end up back here before ye know it.'

She pushed me up into the truck and he opened a smelly basket and I climbed in.

'Janey Mack, Teresa, I don't know about this ...'

'Don't come back here or they'll have yer guts for garters,' Teresa warned. 'Listen to me, Child of Grace. Don't let me down.' She was peering at me with her hand on the lid of the basket. 'You're to go to Kilbride in Co. Meath, just beyond Trim, and ask for Mary O Conaill. She's in a house with the Lyonses, the local schoolteacher and a solicitor. She'll help ye, and tell her to come get me. Mary in Kilbride. Then get yerself out of the country on the first boat to Liverpool.'

And that's how I was bundled off from the Laundry.

435

Only You Can See This Light

She was gone. The one we called the Little Poet, on account of her being put in by her uncle because she wrote poems. Teresa lost something then and a weariness seeped into her, from waiting for the Little Poet, from waiting to go to her sister and her sister to come. The waiting dragged her down like the dirty wet water from the river of a floor we worked on. Not because they beat her, they didn't this time. Instead, when they suspected she had helped with the escape, they made her stand on a stool till she fainted, so they did. She stood in the steam under the glass roof of the laundry. When she fell, none of us dared to run to her. She lay in the torrents of suds always swirling at our feet – her bottle-green uniform soaking up the water, until two nuns dragged her out, her cropped hanging head. And years suddenly gathered. Though she became even thinner, her body moved with an unseen weight. The stories still told but heavy. Her swan wings clipped. Behind the steam, the iron, the water, the heavy detergent, the dryer, the row of beds, she grieved for a child, for a dark daughter – even though she boasted that it was she who had freed her from this iron trap. And the tiny bit of hope was draining from her.

I had never been outside. Teresa's cold eyes looked through me – I'm still here, tell me the tale. I couldn't go because I was scared, and she couldn't go because I told them she was going to escape and so now they watched her like hawks. What could I do? I had kept her here for me. After that she wouldn't talk to me. But I knew what love was. I knew. But she didn't know that's why I done it. I like to think back to the first evening I came to the Laundries. They marched me through a tunnel from the Industrial School into the church and then another tunnel that led to the Laundry. I never had to go out into the air. My name in the school was 435. That was my real name. The nuns said the Laundry girls could have actual names and they named me Bridget. Teresa said a poem to me, a poem about Eve. Teresa named me Bright, and only she could see this light, so she could.

Prince Alfrid

The Tongueless Bell
(ACE 680)

I, Prince Alfrid, travelled throughout Ireland looking for teachers. I spoke to the famed poet Ruman, the vegan St Fintan – who smashed the vessel with my offering of milk as the monks hoed the land and touched no flesh nor dairy. Ita, the foster mother of all the saints, told me the tales of Brigid.

Respectfully, I, Alfrid, took instruction from thin and soft-spoken ascetic monks, living among them as they made their fine books. I rose with them at the strike of the tongueless bell. The dry stone beehive huts with a simple cross over each door. The school, the refectory, the small oratory. I was thirsty for knowledge; I sat with my fellow travellers from England, people of noble and of ordinary birth all wanting to understand. They taught me to transcribe. Finally, one of the monks told me I had learned enough formally and advised me to go wandering deeper into the woods.

I, Alfrid, traversed the dark woods where hermits lived with animal flocks. I met the humble monk, Mochua, who had no wealth but a cock, a mouse and a fly. I heard the cock wake Mochua to pray in the morning. I saw the mouse lick Mochua's ears if he slept more than five hours without praying. I watched the fly walking each line of his book of prayers as he sang the psalms; this fly would wait upon the line so he would find his place again.

Later I learned that Mochua's three friends died and that Mochua had written to Colmcille in terrible grief. Colmcille wrote back: 'My brother, marvel not that thy flock should have died, for misfortune ever waits upon wealth.'

I sought out the hermit St Ciarán who had built a dwelling deep in the forest out of light wood – whose fellow monks were a boar, a fox, a badger, a wolf and a stag. The woods of this country were full of hidden hermits, women and men who lived with the mad and rejected and found ways to talk to God and to hear God talk. They wrote their poems about birds and trees.

Under the protection of the chieftains, I wandered. Often I drank from the holy wells – from silver cups that hung on silver hooks pushed into the stones, marvelling that no one would dare to take the cups home.

When my father, King Osuniu, died in 671, I, Alfrid, returned to England to become King of Northumbria. I ruled, fluent in the Irish language, Latin theology, Greek grammar, poetry, sagas, histories. I composed my own poetry and spoke of the time when I wandered through my neighbour's land, a forest land of strange saints. And forever in my head I missed the sound of a tongueless bell calling me to the clarity of prayer.

Dymphna

The Burning of the Embassy
(1972)

Mickey stopped the van after a while, and I felt the basket open. I wanted to run off because I didn't want to suck him. I didn't even know what to be sucking.

He grabbed me arm and hissed in me ear, 'Yer a virgin, are ye? Or what kind of messing got you in with them nuns?' He was a big lad with a solid belly on him and a red face, I hadn't seen a man in so long I couldn't even tell if he was old. He put me down in the back of the van and after he shut the door he split open me legs and stuck himself in. He was sweating and panting. I put me hands up to me face and howled, and he told me to shut the fuck up and banged me head off the floor until I saw tiny white specks spin round in front of me like demon flies, and he stuck it in like Teresa said he shouldn't do. It was so sore I thought he was putting a knife in. So I had let her down already. After he finished, he growled at me: if I told anyone he'd track me down and murder me. He said no one would take me word, a dirty whore from the Laundry, against his. Then he threw me out and the van roared off.

I was left standing in a city laneway with no money, in the middle of winter, and no place to go. After when they called it Bloody Sunday, I always thought of meself there with the blood running down me leg under me Laundry uniform. Maybe I should just go back and get into me bed for the night. That them nuns mightn't have noticed me gone. But I thought I must be pregnant now and they'd know it, and I'd get such a beating and an I told you so. What was I like? *Barely out a few hours and already pregnant.* That's the first words I said out loud to myself. Rabbiting on to meself, so I was.

I walked out of the laneway, and them buildings were unlike any I'd seen before. They were lovely and grand, just like palaces in dreams. The houses had red bricks and steps up to painted doors. There was a park with railings, and I wandered until I found a gate and went inside. I was thinking to find the Dodder and get me bearings. I had missed that river. But I knew I couldn't show up to me ma and da, as they would see I was pregnant and not a virgin anymore and put me straight back to them nuns. It was always foretold I would let down the family, on account of the poetry writing.

For two days I hid under a bush in Merrion Square. I had nothing to eat and the pain between me legs was something else. I didn't know how long it took, but I was waiting for the baby to come so I could get rid of it and bury it and go back to them nuns and beg for forgiveness. If they didn't check me down there they mightn't know what I done. I was almost frozen to the ground. It was only the fear that kept me alive.

During the days I sat on a bench in the park. I hadn't been out of the Laundry since I was brought there by me uncle. And I'd never seen a city like this. This was a different part of town altogether. Women walked by in trousers that were wide at the bottom. They were laughing and talking loudly with men who had big hairy things coming down the sides of their faces and huge chunky ties.

All of a sudden, I heard a big commotion. Crowds started coming from all over the place and the Guards with them. Tons of people yelling poured into the park and beyond. They shouted and pumped their fists in the air. They were holding painted signs and chanting. There I was standing just outside the park, and men were running around with their faces covered in black masks and the Guards were pushing and shoving everyone, and one of the buildings was on fire. The Guards were running around bashing heads in and everyone had gone ballistic. I stood still as a statue and some young fella grabbed me and pulled me behind a lamppost as a swell of people galloped past. I pushed him away cos I thought he might stick it into me like Mickey, me knight in shining armour.

'Are you OK, love? Hey, hey ...'

I struggled away and made me way through the crowds. People were crying now, shocked and scared – running in every direction trying to get away from the burning building. I got as far as the canal and sat down to put me feet in the water by the lock. But the water was so far down, me legs just dangled blue from the cold. I closed me eyes. A couple of women came up behind me. They were dressed so nice. In short skirts and high heels, and all shiny and sparkling.

'What have we got here?'

'Jaysus, Mona, I think we've got a runaway Magdalene.'

'That's a Laundry smock, alright.'

'Is that what y'are, pet?'

I nodded. I closed my eyes again and tried to reach me feet down to the water to get the canal to make me strong.

'You'll freeze yer feet if they get to the water, pet. You'd better come with us. We'll get ya cleaned up and out of those clothes, so the Guards won't take yiz back to them nuns.'

'There won't be much business tonight,' the other agreed. 'The place is crawling with army and Guards. They just burnt down the fucking British Embassy.'

'Where?'

'Up dere, in fucking Merrion Square.'

'Yer codding me?'

'No, it's a fucking revolution, 19-bleedin'-16 all over again.'

They took me by the arms and pulled me up away from the canal. I wanted to slowly slip into it, to go down into the water and sink. One of them had a fur jacket and put it round me.

'Is there anyone we can take you to, love?'

I touched the fur.

'Don't run off with that now. It's only rabbit, but I like to think it's hare.'

The other one laughed.

'I have to get to Mary O Conaill in Kilbride in Meath,' I said. 'I have to tell her that her sister is in the Laundry and wants to come out.'

'We can take you up to the Coombe and back to our place and get ya sorted.'

'I have to get to Meath.'

'Meath? Ya poor frozen craytur. Yer a long way from Meath.'

Deirdre

All Extremists Should Be Shot
(1974)

Everyone called my mammy 'Baby'. Which was funny because she wasn't a bit like a baby. We were trying to rent a telly in a shop in Capel Street. The man told her, 'You can't rent one without your husband's permission.' Mammy shouted and told him she was earning money and he was a disgrace.

The man looked terrified. 'Those are the rules. I have to obey the rules. If you were a single woman, it would be no bother, but you put down "married" on the form. I have no choice.'

I felt sorry for him because, though her name was Baby, my mammy was fierce. She pulled me out of there in a fury. That's my first memory.

I was cursed with memory. I never forgot things that happened. In all the details.

A lot could be learnt behind the couch. I was the eldest child. Orla, my sister, was a year younger. Mammy was pregnant again. She let us touch her tummy and we could feel the baby kick.

All the grown-ups were in the living room as always, talking and smoking and singing, and my sister traversed the hairy green-and-orange swirly carpet, crawling from gin and tonic to gin and tonic, dipping her soother in each drink and sucking it. I guided her away from one of those big silver ashtrays that stood up from the ground. I brought her behind the couch with me and shushed her. We could listen in and not get sent to bed if they forgot about us.

Mammy and Daddy played badminton, and the badminton crowd were always over in our house smoking and drinking till the wee hours. Mammy's voice rose and fell. They laughed a lot. There were lots of letters – not ABCs, but IRA and UVF and RUC and SAS. My daddy had a soft voice and when he talked about stuff everyone hushed and listened. Mammy had to talk through people until they gave up and paid attention to her.

Uncle Iggy was over lots with his son Cormac, who was nearly my age, and Fionn his little brother, and their mammy was pregnant.

Mammy called him a 'permanent fixture'. But she said he was family, kind of. He was Mary's nephew or something. Mary was my grandma's housekeeper and we all loved her. She wasn't like a housekeeper; she was part of our family too. She was more important to us than our grandparents. She was the heart of the family.

From behind the couch, I heard that we joined the EEC. Uncle Iggy and Daddy claimed it was another loss of sovereignty, but Mammy said it would bring in equal pay for women, and that she could rent a telly without her husband's permission or take them to court. Daddy said Ireland was now even further away from a socialist republic and Mammy said the people don't want anything of the kind.

'And now women don't have to give up their jobs when they get married,' Mammy said. 'That's a great thing.'

Uncle Iggy said that if women work it takes away jobs from men and the men are the ones who have to support the families. And everyone agreed with that except Mammy, who got annoyed and asked Uncle Iggy who supported his family. That was after the third gin and tonic, and she could be mean.

Most of the mammies didn't work. They said that their job was their children, and Mammy told them that they were cossetted at the expense of power.

The other mammies didn't like that, I can tell you.

I learnt all this from behind the couch.

When they all left, Orla and I crept up to my bed, and in the morning I got up and played with the cigarette butts in the ashtrays. I took out the ones that were not smoked down to the end, and I put them in a box in the shed for me and Cormac. We smoked them a bit, but they were yucky, so we took out the yellow spongy bits from the ends and chewed them.

Cormac and I were going to *Joseph and the Amazing Technicolor Dreamcoat* with the daddies. The mammies were staying with the babies. The buses were on strike, and even worse for the daddies was that the Guinness Brewery was on strike too.

It was summer and I loved the smell of Dublin City.

'That's the hops from the Guinness factory,' Daddy told me. I held his hand and we walked through the city centre. We all stopped and took a sniff.

It was a great smell. Better than the Liffey, which was really stinky in summer. It was green and full of rubbish. Even the bin men were on strike, so there was stuff all over the place. The daddies were stopping in the pub, and Cormac and I raced around eating Taytos and peanuts and drinking cokes and I got sick from it all outside. Uncle Iggy was always singing songs and telling stories, and Daddy loved to listen to him. The whole pub listened to him. When he told a story, everyone was quiet. They were all having another beer because of the strike.

When we were heading up to the concert, the bombs went off and all the street was flying at us. The boom and the shake, I remember. We were running and screaming with the daddies taking us in their arms, and we got to a telephone in a pub and called home to say that we were OK but there were bombs going off in Dublin. Daddy and Uncle Iggy ordered two brandies at the bar. We never got to see *Joseph and the Amazing Technicolor Dreamcoat*. Cormac and I sat under the stools and played zoo monkeys. Everyone was talking about who did the bombs. We got out onto the street for a while and at first no one noticed we were gone, but then my daddy took the two of us home and Uncle Iggy stayed in the pub. Cormac didn't mind, since he liked our house. We had central heating and a soda stream, and everything was new and clean and warm.

A day later, behind the couch, I learnt that a family and their two baby daughters were killed instantly. One of the babies was discovered in the cellar of a pub close to the explosion. There were three bombs in Dublin and one in Monaghan that day, and thirty-three people were dead and loads injured and maimed.

'It was the UVF,' Daddy said.

They're all as bad as each other,' said Mammy. 'The IRA, the UVF, the Brits, all men, all thugs. All extremists should be shot.'

'Until we have a united Ireland there will never be peace. Colonization is still a factor here.'

'The Brits won't leave by themselves. They've been here eight hundred years,' Uncle Iggy added.

'It will have to be solved at a conference table,' Mammy said.

'But the Brits will have to be brought at gunpoint to the conference table.' Daddy's voice was shaking. 'This country is descending into anarchy. We're going to lose all chance of peace unless there's a united Ireland.'

'At what price? What price do you men put on life? Sure, we're all ruled by Brussels now, thank God. The Brits and London don't matter.' When Mammy said this a big row started. Mammy usually won since she could talk the longest.

She swiped Orla away from dipping her soother into the gin and tonic, and I reached out and pulled my little sister behind the couch.

Orla needed to learn that the secret to staying up late was to blend in.

Fionn

Monstre Sacré

There was a story I'd ask my father for, the story of Etáin. My mother loved to hear it too. For she knew how Etáin felt, not being in the right world, always restless, changing shape but never getting back to where she belonged. But in the end, she does. So, my mother, Esther, called her one daughter after her. Born prematurely in 1975 and weighing only four pounds, my lovely little sister, Etáin.

She told me all of this years later when I was a child, sitting watching her drink in a café in Leuven. My mother heard my father before she saw him. *Monstre sacré*, he was. And she in a corner of the party. Relieved to be out of the family home for the night. Paddy and Baby MacInespie, the hosts in their suburban home. She usually never ventured this far from Pembroke Road, but Paddy had been persistent. He was a PhD student and had interviewed Bubbe and her friends for a project he was doing on Jewish folktales. My grandmother, Bubbe, was always urging her daughter to get out more, she took a liking to Paddy immediately and enlisted his help. My mother was moping about the house after Paris with her heart, a mixed metaphor, in tatters at half mast, the love of her life staying with his wife after all. Her painting career stalled in Dublin where the arts was such a boys' club. My quiet mother had the talent required but none of the bluster, and besides she was a woman. So that was that.

I always imagined the other guests were bemused by my father. A young and feral Behanesque character, like an ancient bard, telling his tales in the other corner. His eyes kept finding hers. After his stories, people took up guitars and earnestly started strumming. She thought she'd scarper. Bubbe would be pleased she had at least made an effort. He blocked her as she went to slip out the front door.

He went to shake her hand. His hands like sculptures, twisted marble monstrosities. She could not help but take both his hands and study them. Were they hands? Each finger twisted away from the other. She thought she could paint them. It wasn't love at first sight. It probably wasn't even love. They were both just odd. She was ten years older than him, a loner, intense, given to bouts of depression. He was a man–child. Never fully coming into himself. Always avoiding his own centre, playing a part. She brought him home to our big rambling house, knowing her mother would be asleep. She stupidly got pregnant that first night. She was arranging to go to a Mother and Baby Home and put the child up for adoption, but Bubbe was aghast. Her grandchild wouldn't be raised properly as a good Jew. They wouldn't know they were Jewish. They married quickly in the synagogue. Only Paddy and Baby and Bubbe as guests, then lunch in the Shelbourne. Iggy and Paddy went off on a pub crawl and left the women behind. That's how Ireland worked.

My father told my mother some palaver about his family having land in Meath and getting an income from that. It was a year after Cormac was born when she realized Ignatius stood on Essex Bridge and told stories for money, and that was his only source of income. That half of the poor of Dublin knew him as Zoz. That he was really their bard. That he was shambling around in the dimness of their smoky pubs as their teacher. He was keeping the world alive with his telling of it. Strangely, he was as loved by the poor of Dublin as one of their own, just as he was tolerated at the university parties. But she wasn't welcome in that rough world. And then I was born, and she realized with resentment that she would never be able to get back to Paris. The Irish art world would never think a woman could do anything more than dabble as a hobby. She was stuck on the rock of doom. She would never paint his hands.

435

Walking Without a Sound
(1975)

I grew up all me life here and never been out once. They put me in as a babbie because me mother was a harlot. And I killed a wee three-year-old girl putting her in the scalding water, even though I said to them nuns that it was too hot and it was, so it was. Me and another girl had to push her in that bath screaming. Me own hands were burnt and red. She just went all limp so quick. I was eight and they didn't put me in prison, but I thought of that wee girl every day and reckoned that's why they never let me out. I didn't mean it but I did it, so I did. I wondered would I meet her when I died and I could say sorry sorry so so sorry to the little scrawny snot face with the thin hair. I'm so sorry. I didn't tell the other Magdalenes about my murder and they didn't tell me about any of their shameful stuff. We were not allowed talk to each other, but on Sundays we whispered after dinner.

I followed Teresa around because she named me Bright, and she used to look out for me until I ratted her out. After, she sighed when she saw me behind her, so she did.

'What's a hare?' I asked when she told us a story of the hare. I couldn't imagine what most animals were like. The nuns allowed her to tell her stories to us and they sometimes listened too. She answered sometimes, if I spoke my question to everyone and not to her.

'A hare has three traits: a lively ear, a bright eye and a quick run up the hill.' She didn't look directly at me when she said this.

'But is it like a cat?' I asked everyone. The nuns had cats at the back door on account of mice. I saw Teresa make a fuss of them when she could. She loved them cats, I watched her hold them like I wished she'd hold me.

'It's like a fecking rabbit but bigger,' one of the other women snapped. She'd also been given the name Big Bridget, but no one called her Bright. That's mine alone, the name Teresa gave me when I first came.

'And longer ears,' Mary said.

'Is a rabbit like them cats?' I asked.

They all laughed at me. The nuns didn't like to see us convene like this so Sister Paul clapped her hands as she always did, as if to squash us in the sound. I could see Teresa stare at me, her forehead creased in a line down between her eyes.

'The cat has three fortunes: the housewife's forgetfulness, walking without a sound and keen sight in darkness.'

Even the nuns liked when she told us harmless things of a Sunday. They didn't pay her mind. She wouldn't escape now, though she was so thin she could slip through a crack under the door like a mouse. We were shuffled off to bed at seven in silence. I tried to walk behind her like a soundless cat. Some of the others snickered.

'Look at Bright,' Big Bridget whispered to another one. 'There's a want in her.'

'Jesus tonight, she doesn't know what a bloody rabbit is.'

My hands were sore, raw from the ironing and carrying the hampers. I clenched and unclenched them. I lay in bed and tried to start with a cat and imagine what the animals have that are different from the cat. In me head I made the cat's ears long and straight. There were some animals in the church. The Virgin Mary statue was standing on a lizard. There were sheep in the stained glass. The Lamb of God. And there was a twisty picture of an eagle and a lion and maybe a calf on the Bibles. But I know they weren't really what the animals could look like. I'd seen birds come by the windows. What I'd seen I didn't forget, so I didn't. One night a bird bashed itself off the window and I got to see it dead close up. Another time a rat ran across the yard by the kitchen. I imagined a hare like a bigger rat.

I kept track of me age in my head. I was twenty-five, so I was, and I could see pretty well in the dark, so I could. I was seeing rats become hares until I was sure I got it.

I dreamt we were all sleeping, and a thing comes and dies against the window. The outside coming in like a bulky shadow. When I awoke, I looked to the top window to see if there was a smudge. A mark.

Caitríona

Thus Was the End of Their Feast
(1574)

Once the cattle were driven into our fort away from the wolves, we sat in lime-washed rooms as the stories of the great feats of the legendary Fianna were told. At night we would all gather as a clan, and I would be close to the centre as it was my duty to pour the ale into their golden cups and horns. The noble men and women would lie down as the harp played, their cloaks drawn around them, and the poet would tell the long, long stories that reached right into the past until we were not just ourselves but everyone who had gone before. The wolfhounds settled down with their long shaggy legs stretched out as the reed-and-butter candles lit the back of the hall. The fire burned in the middle of the great room, the roof open to the sky. We lay on beds of straw. The bards were as powerful as the kings in those old days, and they had been trained for years in the bardic schools. I had no schooling, but I knew the words to the stories and would whisper them, learning them from the old blind poet that the king always kept by his side. One story that hushed us all was the terrible tale of the great warrior–hero Cúchulainn's warp spasm. The poet would boom out:

'When the great Cúchulainn entered the warp spasm, he became a strange and terrible beast unlike anything ever seen. His whole being shook in a mighty fit and inside every organ and muscle twisted and pushed against his rippling skin and his elbows and knees and feet spun and twisted to the other side of his body until he was a spiral of angry brutishness. A killing machine.'

I was born to a family of churls. When you are on the bottom, you can see right up through the arsehole of the world, through the shit tunnels, the soggy intestines and past the tangles of guts, until the heart suddenly appears as a pulsating slippery mass of veiny pulp, then here are shuddering lungs – nothing is too special, it's all grotesque but functional. You know the thoughts of the kings and nobles because they speak out loud and you have to listen. Servants throughout time have always known everything before it happened. The nobles do not hide anything from us because they think we exist only for their convenience. They can't imagine that we have thoughts inside our heads. They never see us, but we see them. Strangely, the view is more revealing from the bottom than the top. The worms have no majesty, but they know the land better than the great elks. And we survived underground when they were hunted to their last end. For a churl, the world is revealed as it is, and we as we are – ravenous and calamitous.

From time to time, when a guest was at the feast, I was called on to tell a story. Because I had some fame as a servant who had met Henry VIII of England when I was a wee girl. That was many years ago. Truth was I had told it so many times I wondered if I had made half of it all up in my head, but I kept telling it.

I was an old crone, with nigh on three score years of serving and scrubbing and tending, and a few extra to atone for any of my shortcomings. My hair was long and grey, but I was still strong from all the work and had muscles as firm as many of the young whelps I had to train in. And the chief, Brian, trusted me to stand beside him and brim his cups at the feast.

We had lived our lives barely affected by Henry the King of England. He had concentrated on the south of the island, and we had little truck with that part, though we heard things were bad for other tribes. The English had their garrisons in Dublin, and they controlled some of the towns, but we had the countryside and that's where we preferred. The towns were full of plague and consumption, so we stuck to the forests and the glens and the mountainsides. Our nobility told us it was up to us to uphold the last bastion of Gaelic life and the old ways, just as it was up to the churls to empty the piss pots of the chieftains. I had worked for three different clans in my long life because of marriage and other circumstances and had been loyal and humble to those that kept me alive. I had two sons who worked as valets to our current chief. We at the bottom thought we hadn't much to lose – we were very wrong about that.

King Henry had a daughter who was even more rapacious than he, and she had an eye on us. The south was convulsing in rebellions against her, and she had laid parts of it to waste. There were so many ordinary peasants killed in the Desmond Rebellions that the land was turning back in on itself as if we'd never been. We heard they showed no mercy and would surround towns and move in to decimate all. We were told they had a habit of burning crops and ruining harvests, and starvation was one of their war methods.

They were collecting heads among the southern tribes, putting them in bags and bringing them up to Dublin to stick on spikes. We were wary of the English, but we could see our nobles were strong and the clans powerful. We had no choice but to put our trust in our betters. We got word, after their first failure to conquer us, that a second expedition had set off from Liverpool led by Walter Devereux, the bastard Earl of Essex. He came with a thousand men ready to fight us for our land. The English had a silly system whereby the first son got all, this produced an overabundance of highly educated but impoverished nobles who had to go out from England to the beyonds of the Earth and grab their wealth. So, we were plagued by the illegitimate sires of the English as well the second or third sons who stood to inherit nothing.

The foreign queen, Elizabeth, had told them to come to take what had been ours since the beginning of human time. As if we were only insects living in the grasses, she granted Devereaux the vast lands of Clandeboye, all the glens of Antrim, the Route and the island of Rathlin, and everything from the sea west to the River Bann and Lough Neagh. They said he mortgaged his estates in England and that got him ten thousand pounds; the queen then paid half the cost of his thousand soldiers.

Brian, our chief, was the first who saw the invading force. He felt it was wise to see what this Earl of Essex was up to. To fight him outright would have meant defeat, we all knew that. So instead he invited him to a meeting. I was serving them food when Essex slapped him on the shoulder and promised they could work together. My sons and I listened as Brian told his foster son that he was pleased he had solved the English problem.

'They're easily mollified. Essex will move on and bother another clan.'

Aengus, the foster son, bit his lip. 'I hear nothing but disaster from the south. They have destroyed so much. I don't know if submission works.'

'We can't fight them,' Brian said. 'We don't have their cannons; we don't have their guns or their numbers.'

'We're too busy fighting each other clan to clan.' Aengus pulled his cloak around his shoulders as if suddenly feeling a chill. 'They're ruled by one queen for the whole land.'

'That can never happen here. We are not like the English.' Brian shook his head. 'They know we are strong. This is the Gaelic heart of Ireland. We are warriors. They won't dare molest us.'

Then Essex quickly showed his hand and stole ten thousand of our tribe's cattle, using his soldiers to herd them to Carrickfergus. Brian was furious but not daunted – it was our land, after all, our cattle – and so he bribed the Guards at Carrickfergus and easily got the cattle back.

Meanwhile, the English soldiers didn't like our wild Gaelic Ulster and wanted to go home to their pies and their ale. I watched them sit in their piteous misery in the damp glens, shaking at the thought of what was surrounding them in the impenetrable spirit-ruled forests. They were as poor as we were and had no skin in the game. Some of them muttered that they should have tried their luck in the new worlds that had been discovered. Some of them began sneaking off back to England, and Essex hanged those wretches he caught. They left us to cut them down and bury them in this alien soil; without any fanfare they fertilized our land. His Queen Elizabeth announced that he was now Governor of Ulster, and we scoffed at this, as we could see he governed nothing. Essex came back and approached Brian once more. They came to another agreement.

'I am Governor of Ulster,' he told Brian. 'The Queen has told me.'

'You can't just declare that and believe it is now true,' Brian said. 'This is not England. You have no rights here except as a guest.'

Brian was worried enough. He had seen the chiefs down south conned out of their land and legacy but thought he could keep him contained, and so they put the business of the stolen cattle behind them and declared a truce. Aengus said he couldn't be trusted after stealing the cattle, but Brian surmised that he could continue being chief of his own tribe and pay some tithes to the man declaring himself governor.

To celebrate the agreement, Brian invited Essex and his thousand men to a grand feast. We worked hard to get the food and wine ready. Cattle and pigs were slaughtered and roasted on big fires; we cooked carrots, onions, turnips and parsnips seasoned with wild garlic. There were ample salmon, mackerel and trout on silver plates, and fresh bread and honey.

Three days and nights in Belfast Castle they toasted the English Earl and the Irish King. There was harp music and dances and a grand show of all we had. In between pouring mead and serving up the cuts of beef, I listened to the poets recite the feats of Cúchulainn. These stories I had heard since I was a wee gersha, and I knew them off by heart. As usual, I was called on to tell the tale of the time I went on a great pilgrimage to Rome and stopped at Henry's Court on our return. My father was a servant and brought me with him, when I was only about ten years old, to attend the noble women in the group.

Essex was amused that I was allowed to speak. 'You have strange ways, Brian. To allow a servant to speak to nobles at a feast. I thought you had trained poets for that.'

'Oh, the poets aren't trained,' Brian laughed. 'It is they who train us.'

'You don't clear the forests, and you don't sow crops,' Essex said. 'We could teach you our English ways of tillage. And all this constant cattle raiding from clan to clan. Don't you want to be civilized under one crown?'

'Tillage is backbreaking work for those who have to do it.'

'It wouldn't be you. You have your peasants for that. You could build towns and become civilized.'

'We have ample food and milk from our cattle,' Brian said, watching Aengus turn red and quicken to anger. 'We don't want to live in your towns. We have our own ways.'

'Tillage is torture,' Aengus snapped.

He gestured for me to tell my story and I stood in the crowd. We had a man who was a translator to put it all into English for our guests. They became silent as I spoke, and I told it well. I, a churl, who had met Henry VIII at a feast much greater than this.

When I said the last sentence there was a hush at the feast.

'Our king entered the festivities a king and left as a knight.'

'That knight knew what was good for him and his people, I'll wager.' Essex stroked his beard and drained his goblet.

Brian thanked me for the story and waved me away to make room for his fine poet. The English earl dozed through the long reciting of lineage, and it was all lost on him. Our chiefs sat in their cloaks and scoffed at the strange aspect of the English. They were uncomfortable among us. They had no stories to tell us. But at the end of the three days, exhausted with feasting, Essex and Brian lay down like brothers together. Essex whispering to Brian, and I sitting close could not hear what he said but was happy we were all to be civil.

During the night, however, there was a low whistle and the English men jumped up fully armed and killed men, women and children, all that were present and sleeping amongst them. They killed Aengus first. I only survived as I lay on the ground still and pretended to be dead. My king Brian was caught unawares, and he too witnessed the horror. Brian howled like a wolf in the woods watching the moon disintegrate and fall like brittle ash through the sky. All his people butchered before him. They held him tight to make him watch and bundled him off to their castle down in Dublin with his brother and his wife.

In Dublin they cut the three of them into quarters publicly. That's twelve pieces of them scattered on the stones. They stuck the heads of Brian, his wife and his half-brother on spikes around their English castle.

As the monks later wrote: 'Thus was the end of their feast.'

Deirdre

The First Colour Telly on the Road
(1975)

Every weekend we went to visit my grandparents in Trim and Mary, their housekeeper, took care of us. She was grey haired, fat and very comfortable to cuddle, while my grandmother was thin, elegant and friendly but distant. Mammy adored Mary and they would have long conversations about Mary's family. Mary's family had disappeared, and Mammy wanted to find out where they were. Mary was worried about this, but she knew Mammy was very determined. When Mammy wanted something, she usually got it. Mammy would sit and make lists of people to talk to and places to check out. Mary had a brother who got the farm, and no one could go near him even though he had the key to all the information.

'We have to get around that gobshite Seamus,' Mammy said, taking notes and drawing names and circling them and connecting them with arrows. And Mary would shake her head as if disapproving of Mammy's language, but she didn't correct her. This made me understand that Seamus was truly a gobshite.

'I will find Maeve and her child.' Mammy drew an arrow from Maeve's name and wrote 'child', then circled that. 'I know, Seamus and that sleeven of a priest, Father Gilligan, know where they all are. And there must be some way to track down Bridget in America.'

Mary had a little brother who died, but no one was allowed talk about him, or even say his name, or ask how he died. I found a creased photo in Mary's handbag once when I was rummaging through to steal some Silvermints for Orla and me. The photo was a brownish picture of a tall thin young man with blond hair dressed as a priest. His hands were in his pockets, his head was straight and he had a half-smile. I stared at that photo and wondered was it the brother we couldn't mention. I knew better than to ask, so I put it back and zipped up the inside pocket where I found it.

We roamed in gangs of kids up and down Monaloe Park Road. They were building more and more houses. We pushed the babies' big prams and roller skated and we all lived on our bikes. Every one of us was on wheels of some sort. It was brilliant.

'Be home before dark,' was all we were told. We had the run of the place. The world was ours, and the sun was shining, and we hopscotched, and skipped, and there was a gap in the hedge in our estate that led to Mackintosh, the council estate, and we ran through there and they had loads of kids on their side too who'd try to chase us off. Monaloe versus Mackintosh was our border war. There was a stream behind the houses that we paddled in and raced leaves and sticks along, and it was full of upside-down shopping trollies from Dunnes, and then it turned all white from the run-off from a factory.

Dunnes Stores was the big shopping centre across the main road, and we were not allowed to cross over there without a grown-up. But we could walk to Nugent's garage and get sweets. We played football on the green, and we sat and made daisy chains. I pierced the stalks with my nail and carefully threaded each daisy through. I made the longest ones and draped them on Orla.

Cormac and Fionn were always over. Our dads were best friends. There was great singing in the house at night. My daddy played a tin whistle and my mammy couldn't sing, but she tried some Patsy Cline songs sometimes at the very end of the night.

Mammy and Daddy were very tired and cranky. We had a woman who came in to help us when my twin brothers were born. They were called Nevan and Phelan. Which everyone said were pure Cavan names, but my parents liked them anyway.

They were identical, and they were boys. Such a big fuss. My sister and I climbed over the fence and sulked behind the house in Old MacDonald's farm. We had our gangs of kids to run with so we stayed out as much as we could. As much as everyone else. We played British Bulldog, tag, marbles. We got a colour telly. The first colour telly on the road.

Us four kids would stand by my parents in Mass every Sunday in Cabinteely. I was always struck by people getting up to recite the Act of Faith. It was after the homily. The priest would give a boring homily usually and everyone would drift off in his or her own thoughts. The priests never inspired.

We would recite together in dull tones, '*We believe in the one God and life everlasting ...*' There was no passion; there was just acceptance. But I knew early on that life everlasting was a fool's game. I knew it instinctively. Nothing lasted. The fields behind us got buried by the motorway. The lane I walked to school was gone. It was the outskirts of Dublin, and we spent our childhood among trenches and pipes and new half-built housing estates. All our drinking and smoking and kissing started in huge pipes that ran for miles. We shouted and laughed and insulted each other in the intestines of progress. The EEC were funding the roads and we were going for it. We watched the countryside behind our house swallowed and changed utterly, utterly changed. A new suburb being born.

Dymphna

Meetin' Tommo

Tommo was me first boyfriend. Or so I thought. I had met him in 1972 as soon as the girls brought me away from the canal where I was trying to stick me feet in. Used to think I got strength from rivers. I know now that was a load of codswallop. In anyways, Tommo was nice at first. He put his arm around me. I never had anyone who seemed to care, so I worshipped him. Thought his piss was port wine. Sure, I would have done anything for him.

And I did.

He said I just had to go out by the canals and pick up fellas until we got enough money to hightail it to England. He said he loved me. Of course he said that. When I got sick of it he battered me, and still I clung to him. But sure he had a whole stable of brassers like me, young ones, and lots of girls just out of the Industrial Schools too. Over time me nose got squashed and me cheeks crooked and off-kilter. Ah here, I said to meself. It cost me me face to get away from him, he beat me that bad.

He beat me for getting fatter and fatter, but I was having a baby for him, I knew it was his because he gave me condoms for work and I always used them. I didn't even cop on I was pregnant until I was screaming at the flat in Cork Street and one of the girls was dragging me down to the Coombe to have it out of me.

I held her in me arms. Jaysus but I was in bits that night. I cried and cried. All that them nuns, and me family, said I would be, I was. I swear I was still crying when the nurses told me I had to go home with the baby. One came to me and said I could put her up for adoption, that plenty of good families would want her. I knew she'd be better off without me. I agreed at first but then I thought of Teresa in the Laundry, and all the other women. And them lot pining away for their lost babies. I swear ta God, that's all they did. And the look in their faces when they thought no one was looking at them. It was all for their babies. So it was on account of them I kept her.

The nurses weren't too pleased with me. The matron, a nun, came and told me I was taking away opportunities and advantages for this poor baby. After three years in a Laundry, I hated them bitches. I told the nun to fuck off and I walked home with the baby in me arms. Tommo was shocked and told me I was a slapper and what would I be doing with a baby, and who would take care of it when I was down by the canals. He beat the head off me before he even looked at the child. I thought that now I was the mother of his baby he wouldn't put me back out working. That he would change and be nice to me.

Tommo was tall and slim and always took great care with his looks and dressed real snazzy, so he did. Shined his shoes every morning, shaved with a long blade and shaving cream real slow like, all the time staring into his own flinty blue eyes in the mirror. His face was narrow, but he had high cheekbones and a long nose like a king. His hair was short, as he hated those hippies. He dressed like a mod – with shiny suits and skinny ties – and he listened to The Who and bought a Vespa and a parka coat. He was fierce proud of his looks and I still loved the set of him.

Ten years before there was nothing to rob in Ireland, as no one had anything. Now everyone had tellies to take and stereos, but Tommo got sick of robbing houses with his mates. He worshipped the local gangsters and said he was sick looking out for all his women. He had ambitions, he said, and sometimes he'd run with the gangs and rob post offices and banks and stuff. Everyone was doing that those days. The poor culchie Guards couldn't do nothing about it because we had the guns and they didn't.

He arrived in one day with his friend Marlo and they threw a bunch of postal bags on the table.

'These are the special registered post bags,' Marlo said.

'What's in them?'

Marlo shrugged, 'They'll be full of cash and cheques.'

They went through them and found a bunch of cash and then fecked a whole bunch of brown envelopes under the canal bridge, saying there was nothing in them but shite.

A couple of days later, the papers said that 150,000 pounds worth of industrial diamonds had been found discarded by the canal. They had been from the postal van robbery, where two postal workers were held at gunpoint. The police were milling about the place.

Tommo was bulling, so he was. He hadn't thought them yokes worth anything. He kept looking round the canal after that when he came down to check up on all of us brassers. Still hoping to find one of his brown envelopes and the lost diamonds that could have changed his life. We thought it was kind of funny. But we didn't let on. He was fit to be tied. I got a kicking just for being the nearest one to him. The other girls told me to run off to England with me baby, but I was up the pole again and this time it showed, and I couldn't work for a while, so I needed him more than ever. And he hated me needing him.

It was on me mind every so often that I had to get to Meath to Kilbride to ask about Teresa's sister and get Teresa out. Though now I was up to me neck in the outside world, I didn't know if Teresa would be able to do what I was doing. She had to be a bit of a dirt bird to get herself into the Laundry and have the two childer, but she didn't seem like one. In anyways, I never went. But it weighed on me. I knew I had to go. I owed her that. I would go to sleep at night remembering the story she told about the children that were turned into swans. I would tell them stories word by word, just as Teresa told them to us in the Laundry. It was to get the childer to sleep, like:

'*Long ago when the Tuatha De Danann lived in Ireland there was a great king called Lir. He had four children – Fionnuala, Aodh, Fiacra and Conn. Fionnuala was the eldest and she was as beautiful as sunshine in blossomed branches; Aodh was like a young eagle in the blue of the sky; and his two brothers, Fiacra and Conn, were as beautiful as running water.*'

I would pet me own childer and say, you Regina are as beautiful as sunshine in blossomed branches. And to Conn, who came less than a year later, I'd tell him, you are as beautiful as running water. And they'd look at me, only delighted, as if they really were.

Deirdre

Protestant Chickens

Almost every child on that South Dublin housing estate had parents from down the country. The Dublin people said, 'Youse lot are not real Dublin. Youse are a pack of culchies.' 'Cabinteely is not Dublin, it's fucking Wicklow.' The estates were deserted on weekends, cos we all disappeared to our grandparents down the country. Didn't matter if the places were north or south or west, it was all 'down' from Dublin. Once we were down the country our culchie cousins would tell us, 'Ye think ye are so great because ye are from Dublin.' They would call us jackeens. In a way we knew they were all correct. We were neither city nor country. Ours was a threshold world of brand-new housing estates.

Every weekend we'd get in the car and go to Grandma and Granddad and Mary in Trim. We loved it there. Best thing, besides Mary spoiling us, was the Echo Gate. We'd run down the road and stand at the gate and shout to the ruins over the Boyne River and the ruins would shout back.

But once a month we'd go up on the longer journey to Tyrone, where Daddy grew up, to Bella and Jemmy, my other granny and granddad. They were outside Stewartstown on a small farm they didn't own; they lived in the gate lodge for the Protestants' big house. This was a different kettle of fish altogether. We called them by their first names, and I never knew why.

Daddy had eight brothers and sisters. Three of them were in America, one was in Australia and one lived near my grandparents with his family. But two brothers, Malachy and Jimmy, and his sister, Ita, lived in the small gate lodge with Bella and Jemmy. It was becoming harder and harder to visit them, on account of the Troubles. At the border there were soldiers all over the place; Daddy would get more and more upset each time. When we arrived, the conversations were all about shootings and paramilitary groups.

Mammy stopped coming. She said they were pulling innocent people out of cars and killing them out of spite. She said they were a bunch of savages, that men were eejits and loved to fight and kill and make themselves important and this was an excuse to vent their viciousness. Mammy said the planet was at the mercy of the male ego. Daddy said freedom must be fought for and won. Though he did say that the IRA should not be killing civilians but should just target British soldiers.

Mammy argued that the British soldiers were just a bunch of poor kids who joined the army to avoid unemployment. Mammy said they were spotty and underfed and were not the children of the men in the Parliament who came from Oxford and Cambridge and were making the decisions.

'Those kids are the victims of British imperialism as much as anybody,' Mammy said. 'And they all have mothers. If you were really a good Marxist, like you fancy yourself, then you'd show those men some working-class solidarity.'

Daddy called them legitimate targets.

Mammy said, 'Would you kill someone's son?' And pointed to the babies.

Daddy hesitated for half a second and then said, 'The Brits wouldn't be getting killed if they'd just fuck off home.'

Mammy declared as usual, 'All extremists should be shot.'

That always made Daddy laugh.

Mammy said the gate lodge had no room in it, what with Bella and Jemmy and Uncle Malachy and Uncle Jimmy and Auntie Ita in all three rooms. Since Mammy wouldn't come with us, Daddy would take Uncle Iggy and his two sons. When we arrived without the baby boys, Bella and Jemmy sighed and stared over our shoulders, as if the boys would appear at any minute.

We girls were invisible to them.

One time, when we were packing up the car in Dublin, I saw that Daddy put guns under all our stuff in the back before we drove up. There were probably twenty of them. He covered them with blankets and our suitcases. He had long fuzzy sideburns and his hair was down to his shoulders. Daddy saw that I had seen. He crouched down beside me, 'I'm bringing a few old shotguns up for Malachy and Jimmy to go shooting rabbits.'

I said nothing. Daddy looked back at our house, sucking in his lips, 'It's a surprise, so don't say anything to anyone.'

'Does Mammy not like it?' I asked.

'What? Don't let on to Mammy,' Daddy looked stricken.

'She likes rabbits,' I said. 'She probably wouldn't like you killing them, Daddy.'

'No, she wouldn't,' he agreed. He packed more and more stuff over them.

'I don't want you killing rabbits, Daddy.'

'You're a Dublin girl, born and bred. Things are different in the country. They'll take over the farm if you let them. You have to cull them, they're pests.'

'Mary said her family could turn into hares,' I blurted out. He looked startled. He almost smiled. I loved him, and was suddenly afraid.

'We don't talk any more about it. Say nothing and I promise you I won't kill any rabbits.'

'Does Uncle Iggy know?'

'Just say nothing. It's not a secret if it's known by three people.' Daddy seemed angry and he usually was always nice. When Mammy came out with Orla, I got into the car without a fuss. Happy that he and I had a secret. Uncle Iggy arrived with Cormac and Fionn, his wee lads, and he drank a bottle of whiskey all the way up and Daddy couldn't shut him up with the singing.

'How did the priest find the little boy in the long grass?' he asked us kids squashed in the back.

We shrugged.

'Eminently satisfying,' he said. We looked at each other puzzled as Daddy shushed him.

When we sat in the back of the car it was like being behind the couch at parties. This was how I learned about the adult world – by eavesdropping, not instruction. Auntie Ita was in the Charismatics and had gone all religious and was speaking in tongues. Malachy was the only Catholic in the birdwatching society, as birdwatching was a very Protestant activity. Jimmy would finally build a big enough house so he could bring a wife in and start his own family, and Malachy wouldn't have to sleep in the chair beside the fire. He wanted to make butter and cheese and have a small factory for it. Bella had been a beauty and a lovely singer but marrying Jemmy, and having the eight children, had never a chance to play or sing, but her son Jimmy promised her a piano in the new house.

At the border, the British soldiers pulled us over. Daddy's hands clenched the wheel. As the soldier came to the car, I whacked Orla, then I pinched her. She let out a wail, so I hit her a wallop. I had her in such a state that the soldier looked at the ruckus in the back and scratched his head.

'World War III,' my father said and shrugged. 'Want them?'

The soldier flickered a smile and shook his head. He waved us on. Daddy pointed to the big listening towers and put his fingers on his lips as he glanced at Uncle Iggy.

'They can hear us in our cars,' he whispered.

Iggy was sweating bullets, and he kept turning to look at me. Orla was still crying in outrage. Cormac cowered away from me and my sudden unexplainable ferocity. Uncle Iggy winked at me, and Daddy reached back and squeezed my leg.

Caitríona

Blinked Out of History Like a Sick Bull
(1574)

I was sore tired and felt the years gather on me. I made it out of there with another story to tell, one that drained me with each telling. A story that infected my sleep and had me awake, heart hammering and gulping, in the nights. I could see what was happening to be sure. The Gaelic feast was soon to be over, it had played out for thousands of years in the green glens, as we were driving our herds of cattle under the spittle of rain, while the hermits crouched in prayer in oak and hazel forests.

And where were we churls to go? We lesser beings, that stood at the foot of the world, we who had grown old in the shadows of others' greatness? Inside us were the stories of our people as the only sustenance left to us. Where would we hide in the wound of the world when the old times were sputtering to an end? Our world tottered and swayed like a great bull in his death throes, stumbling through the field to crumple to his knees and die out of sight. Our entire past was to be blinked out of history like a sick bull. This fire of ours was going to go out. Our once-potent world that had seemed so solid – the feasts and the music, the hunts, the raids, the stories – had spasmed to obliteration.

And this part I almost can't bear to say. I walked away from there with only a tale to tell. My two surviving sons had been murdered at the feast. Without companion or kin, without youth, without beast beside me – I straggled through the forest where the hermits once lived. We had gathered by wells that had silver cups hanging that no one would dare remove. I was too old to meet more strangers, to adjust to the minds of other clans. I walked through Ulster without any fear, only a deep grief. The beggar is no danger to the beggar, so what did I care. Shame is ever a part of poverty, but I was too broken on that walk to feel it. The ugly humiliation of losing. But I had to exist and survive; the nobles of another tribe heard my account of the feast and the treachery of Essex and sent me to work for the MacDonnells after that. They were a Scottish clan in the northern glens of Antrim, and I told them my bitter tale. In my head I kept coming back to the warp spasm.

His face became red and one eye went so far into his head that a bird could not pluck it out. The other eye plopped out and hung from his cheek. His mouth turned inside out, his gums and teeth were exposed as the skin curled back, his lungs squeezed out of his mouth and his liver came after. He was a monster.

Of course, it didn't stop there. The same bastard Earl of Essex launched a new campaign of slaughter and chaos. After the massacre at the feast, he set his sights on the glens. I quaked when we were told that three large frigates and several smaller boats had set out. The commander was Francis Drake, the famous pirate who had robbed Spanish treasure in Panama only a year before. Captain John Norris was another commander; his father had been executed for adultery with Anne Boleyn. All men with more to prove. The MacDonnells moved their families to Rathlin Island for safety as the men prepared their arms to fight the English in the glens. The women, the old, the sick, the children were to take shelter on this island. The very tip of the world. Their arrival there is one of the beginnings.

And I remained, as an old servant not even worth hiding, to feed the warriors as they got ready for the fight of their lives. I told them the tale of Cúchulainn's warp spasm to get them riled up. We would need a Cúchulainn warrior now.

His heart banged in his chest like a barking lion dog; fire and mist spewed from every hole in his body, so beastlike was his rage.

Deirdre

When Did You Last Hear a Corncrake?
(1975)

'Ach, did ye not bring the wee boys?' Bella and Jemmy said when we got out of the car. When Daddy saw his brother Malachy, he slipped back into a stronger accent than he had down in Dublin.

'Bout ye, big lad?'

'I'm stickin' out, big lad,' Uncle Malachy said, 'and yerself?'

Uncle Malachy was a bit odd. He always wore an old suit with the jacket buttoned over his round tummy. His bottom lip stuck out and you could see the veins in it. They sometimes called him Pastie Lip because of this. He helped about the farm, but it was Daddy's older brother, Jimmy, who seemed to do most of the work with Granddad Jemmy. Daddy always said Malachy was harmless. Malachy went to help with the suitcases, but Daddy stood in front of the boot quickly and said, 'Leave that for later. Put the kettle on and we'll have a cup of tae and Veda.'

Uncle Iggy took Bella in his arms and said, 'Where's Jemmy? Or have you got another man? You know it's no harm having plenty of old men in your life as long as there's plenty of life in your old men.'

'You've an awful tongue on you, Ignatius O Conaill,' Bella scolded, but she was as charmed by Uncle Iggy as everyone else. Daddy came in for a cup of tea, and Uncle Iggy was singing a song and Bella was pretending to be cross. Whenever we'd arrive Bella would have her special bread she called Veda with butter and cheese. Daddy threw his tea into the sink and slipped out. We could hear his car on the gravel as it pulled off. Malachy walked to the window, puzzled.

'Where's he off to?'

'How's them yellowhammers?' Iggy asked. He knew if there was one thing to get Malachy going it was to talk about birds. He perpetually had binoculars around his neck and his dad, Jemmy, said he cared more for the birds than the farm. Malachy seemed just as afraid of Granddad Jemmy as the rest of us. He fidgeted with his binoculars, 'Ach, I'm scared they're all disappearing. There's new houses and estates been built on the auld farms, and the seed-eating birds like the yellowhammers are not good with that. I haven't seen a lapwing down by the lake in a year.'

'The lapwings are waders, right?' Iggy said. I could tell he liked Malachy, even though Mammy would say there was a want in him. I too had a soft spot for him. We kids could just wander around the farm and Uncle Malachy would take us to look for birds. He didn't bother asking us stupid questions about school or what we wanted to be when we grew up. He talked only of redshanks, curlews, lapwings and snipes and how he couldn't find them anymore. If we met anyone out, he would say, 'Alright, big lad? When did you last hear a corncrake?' And people would look a little bemused at the grown man in an old suit and stained shirt surrounded by us children talking of birds. We didn't mind since he had boiled sweets in a paper bag in his pocket, and he let us look through the big heavy binoculars. In the corner of a field by the woods he'd made a little den of branches with a light roof and walls that could easily be seen through. We'd lie in the den and he'd bid us to watch the birds.

Malachy kept a wee notebook and would lick the lead on the pencil and write down the birds he saw.

Malachy told us the stories of the mad mystic monks who lived on jagged rocky islands at the tip of Ireland. They lived a life of birds. He would read to us from his notes in his little book on old hermits who wrote poems about birds. Of Donnchadh Mór Ó Dálaigh, who died in 1244.

Wrens of the lake, I love them all,
They come to matins at my call,
The wren whose nest lets through the rain,
He is my goose, my cock, my crane.

'Haul them,' he would say handing the binoculars to me, as I was the oldest. Since the accents were so strong up here, there was always a slight gap between when Daddy's family spoke and when I understood. I was quick to pick it up, though. Cormac, who was just a bit younger than me, pretended he didn't understand anything. He was itching to get a hold of the binoculars, but I deliberately took my time. I preferred looking through the wrong end and making everything small. Cormac was thumbing through the notebook and stopped on a long poem.

Malachy eyed him warily; I could see his eyes kept keen on his book. Cormac was a wild one and liable to do anything. He pretended he could read, but we could all see he couldn't. Malachy took the book off him and read it.

Sand ousel, well I know that tone
Of sorrow for they nestlings gone!

'Ach, that's a sad one about a bird whose nest is robbed, and her wee ones taken. It's a poem written in the thirteenth century.'

Cormac scoffed. 'I'm not sad about a fecking bird in the thirteenth century.' All the same, he took the book off Malachy to try to read the poem, a crease in his forehead.

We came back to the cottage as Jemmy arrived in from milking. He scowled at Uncle Iggy who had stayed to talk to Bella. Jemmy was not under his spell, at all, at all. Granddad Jemmy never even looked at Orla and me. Though Cormac and Fionn were boys they belonged to Uncle Iggy, who was not really family, so he paid them no mind either.

Uncle Iggy nodded and said, 'It's the man of the house. I wouldn't be leaving this lovely woman of yours alone for too long. It's a risk, considering her beauty.'

But Bella wasn't smiling any more.

'Where was yon Paddy off to in such a rush?' Jemmy asked.

Uncle Iggy shrugged.

'There's not much that goes on around here that I don't know.' Jemmy stared him down. Malachy scratched his head and started flipping through his pencil-scrawled notebook as if to look for lost birds.

Iggy muttered. 'People up here have a right to protect themselves.'

With utter contempt, Jemmy turned away and waved dismissively. He washed his hands in the sink. 'If you dig a grave for others you might fall into it yourself,' Jemmy said. He looked out the window towards the gate.

Uncle Iggy was restless. 'Let's go for a dander,' he said to us. We had just traipsed the fields with Uncle Malachy, but no one liked being around Jemmy. Orla and I and Cormac and Fionn followed him like a row of wee ducks. There was a tiny house at the end of the lane, and I told them all the story Bella had told me the last time we had come. I pointed to the small cottage with the slate roof. A thin exhausted trail of smoke was stringing from the chimney as if trying to write something faint and unhappy in the sky.

'Bella said that old man who lived there once married a fairy.'

Iggy brightened up. 'Go on, tell us more.'

'He was very lonely and had no company. But one day when he went to the well to get his water, a woman rose out of it.'

'A woman can't come out of the well.' Cormac seemed annoyed that his dad, Uncle Iggy, was very attentive to me.

'Whisht, would ye, let her go on.' Iggy waved his hand over Cormac's face.

'He knew she was a fairy since she came out of the well. They sat on the side of the well and they got on great, so he asked her to marry him. But she said she couldn't as he used salt for his food, and if there was salt in the house she'd be dragged back to the well. So he said he would prefer her than a bit of flavour for his food. He scrubbed his floors every day for the week and got rid of all the salt in the house.'

'Why did he scrub the floors?' Cormac fumed.

'In case any salt had fallen,' Iggy said as if this should be obvious.

'So she married him and they were very happy.'

'That's a bad ending,' Cormac moved closer to his father and tried to go in under his coat.

'I didn't say it ended yet.'

We were all standing at the small gate looking up the path to the cottage door. There was a cat sleeping on an upturned bucket.

'There's a fairy in the house, so,' Iggy said in hushed tones. The four of us wee ones stared into the house. The door was ajar but it seemed dark inside. There were weeds in the yard and a sad feeling with torn curtains on the windows.

'No,' I said in a low voice, and they all leaned in to hear me, 'Bella said a neighbour didn't know and came visiting with a bag of salt as a gift. The man's wife was sucked out of the house and down the well, and he has been fierce lonely ever since.'

Uncle Iggy looked at me as if for the first time seeing me.

'It's you who will be the storyteller,' he said placing his hand on my shoulder. 'You have the gift for remembering and telling them.'

And just like that, I was no longer invisible.

Suddenly, we all got excited to see Daddy's car. He pulled up beside us. Uncle Iggy handed him a flask and Daddy took a long swig.

'Your firstborn has been telling us all a yarn. We've found the next storyteller!'

'Want a ride back?' Daddy asked.

'I'm in no rush, truth be told. We're taking in the air.'

'You could cut the air up here with a knife.' Daddy had his hand out the car window and tapped the roof.

'There's hatred in it all right,' Iggy said. 'Your lovely Da just said to me – Put an Irishman on the spit and you'll find two others to turn him.'

'That's one of his favourites. Hop in. Let's go for a swall. We'll grab poor auld Pastie Lip and Jimmy if he's back in off the farm and get out from under Da's glowering.'

'You become incomprehensible as soon as you cross the fecking border. I'm not sure what you just said but I got the gist of it, we'll bring your brothers out for a pint, so?'

'Spot on.'

When the men went into the house to get my Uncle Malachy and my Uncle Jimmy who had been out in the fields, I got the keys to the car and snuck outside. Cormac followed me, as he always did, and I opened the boot and looked in. The guns were gone. I never saw him give them to my uncles or heard them mention it. There was no talk about rabbits.

We went back inside, and I put the keys back on the counter by the kettle where I'd found them. The family were gathered around a table looking at a big sheet of paper. Uncle Jimmy, the eldest son, was going to build a bigger house and milk shed. Jemmy wouldn't look at the plans, but all the others were excited.

'Arra, Jemmy we need more room,' Bella looked at Daddy. 'Maybe Baby would come up if there was more room and bring the boys?'

Daddy nodded a bit embarrassed. 'Ach, she would. You've rented and worked the land long enough. You should buy an acre and build.'

'We don't want to be drawing attention to ourselves,' Jemmy said quietly. Bella shook her head, 'We need the room. Jimmy needs to do this.' Uncle Jimmy was the only one who could ignore Jemmy and was the only one who Jemmy seemed to listen to.

'A new building and barns will be cracker,' Jimmy declared. He knocked on the big sheet of paper with his knuckles as if that would bang the plans into existence. Jemmy shook his head but seemed secretly impressed at his son.

When the men left for the pub, my Auntie Ita came home and took us for a spin in her Mini to the lake. She was a schoolteacher and always quizzed us about her stories after she had told them. 'You remember the last time you were here I told you all about the hole in Crosswiggy?'

'The hole in Crosswiggy. The hole in Crosswiggy,' Cormac started chanting nonsensically. She shot him daggers, so he shut up.

'A man fell into it?' I ventured.

'A piper fell into it,' she said. 'And no one who fell into that hole ever came back out. But if you went by it you could hear him play the tune, and we all knew it.' She sang to us:

'I doubt I doubt I'll never get out,
The further in the deeper Oh.

Come along, you sing now,' she instructed us in her schoolteacher voice.

We all sang the song for her,

'I doubt I doubt I'll never get out,
The further in the deeper Oh.'

She pointed to houses of people she knew as she drove.

'That woman there. She married a Pakistani dentist and has two wee dark children, black as coal. But he died and now she has a new husband who's from Omagh, and two more children who aren't dark at all. Isn't that something?'

'Why did they come out so different?' I asked.

'I don't know. I thought the second lot would be even a little dark, but they're redheads. I thought something might linger. Look we're passing by the hole in Crosswiggy. Let's listen for the piper.'

'I doubt I doubt I'll never get out,
The further in the deeper Oh,' Cormac belted out.

The shores of Lough Neagh were muddy, and Auntie Ita kept telling us not to get muck all over our guddies. But she found us flat stones to skim and got excited when she heard an ice cream van come around. 'Ach, I'll buy youse all a poke each if ye go to bed as soon as we get back.'

We stood wrapped in our scarves and coats by the long lake licking our ice creams.

'There used to be a ghost ship on the lough,' Auntie Ita said as we slurped away, our mouths full of sprinkles. 'It would pass by close to the shore and people could see it but never could see anyone on board.'

'Have you seen it, Auntie Ita?' I asked.

'Indeedn't I haven't. No one has seen it in two hundred years,' she said solemnly, and took out little packets of tissues from her handbag to wipe her face. So we stood. Auntie Ita with her coat buttoned up licking her ice cream. Orla, Cormac, wee Fionn and I all staring hard in case we were lucky enough to see a ghost ship on the wide lake. I knew I'd be able to tell that story now every time we'd come to the lake. I knew I would have to tell it. Iggy had knighted me the storyteller, and I'd found something to make me special.

In the morning before we left, Bella made us boiled eggs and toast and rashers and sausages and black and white pudding. There was a magpie on the windowsill and Bella chased it off. Jemmy who never spoke much, or really looked at us, watched Bella clap the bird away.

'You know, magpies came with Cromwell. They came through Wexford with him,' Bella told us. 'We won't be rid of the Brits till we're rid of the magpies.'

Jemmy slammed his plate down and hissed, 'Catch yerself on, woman, you'll have them as full of daft notions as you are.'

'It's like being married to a Presbyterian,' Bella sighed. 'He's been round them so long that he's more Presbyterian than the Presbyterians themselves.'

Jemmy shrugged. 'At least they taught us to raise our standards. If I ever go down south I see the state of the houses and gardens as soon as ye get to Meath. There's a lot more pride in Ulster than there is down there.'

Uncle Iggy patted his belly and said, 'By God, but Bella you make a fine breakfast.'

'I reckon, a lot of people in Meath came from the West of Ireland,' Jemmy growled, 'and they've no standards.' He glared at Uncle Iggy and Uncle Iggy winked at Daddy.

Everyone ate in silence, and even Orla knew not to squawk or mess. When my Granddad Jemmy had finished his food, he stood up and put on his cap. He never left the house with his head uncovered. I was so frightened of this thin man with hollow cheeks and bleary eyes.

He looked back at my Daddy as he opened the door and said quietly, 'Is yer head cut? I don't want ye ever coming back here, son.'

Bella cleared our plates, biting her lip, and went to the kitchen window to clap away another magpie. Cormac rolled out of his chair and onto the ground, but since he was always doing this no one paid him any attention.

'Mammy?' Paddy implored, but she turned and rubbed her hands dry on her housecoat.

'Ach, you know, I'll help youse get the wee ones into the car. It's an awful pity you didn't bring the boys. I made a ginger cake to take back to Baby. Tell her we were asking for her.'

Paddy rolled his eyes and Uncle Iggy shrugged; his piercing blue eyes washed over with last night's drink. The men got up to pack the car.

My sister and I had stopped eating.

'Eat up them wee eggs,' Bella said, squeezing my shoulder hard. 'Thems are good clean Protestant eggs. They come from good clean Protestant chickens.'

'Even the chickens have religion up here,' Uncle Iggy said.

On the way back home, Cormac told them all about the ghost ship and the hole in Crosswiggy, and I was unhappy it was not me. Now he wanted to be the storyteller too. He kept singing in the car.

I doubt I doubt I'll never get out,
The further in the deeper Oh.

Dymphna

In Those Days Sorrow Was Not Known in Ireland

My Tommo could have a soft side to him too. At night he would hold me tightly. He had nightmares and he would wake up shaking sometimes, and I would hold him and he would nestle into me like I was his mammy and he would tell me he loved me. When I held him as he shook, I got him to breathe deeply until his whimpering stopped. I felt something in him and in me. It wasn't love; I don't think it was, anyway. It was something big and empty and sad. Something with dark air like the grey pictures of the moon surface. As if we were down in a dry crater and the spaceship had left without us.

Tommo wanted to call our son, Conn, Antony, but I got me way with that. He said Conn sounded like he was going to be a swindler. Chip off the auld block so, says I. He and all his mates were from Artane Industrial School. They said that things were bad in there.

Only in the dark of the night did he admit he liked them stories too, so I told them to him and all, '*In those days sorrow was not known in Ireland: the mountains were crowned with light, and the lakes and rivers had strange starlike flowers that shook a rain of jewelled dust on the white horses of the De Danaans when they came down to drink. The horses were swifter than any horses that are living now and they could go over the waves of the sea and under deep lake-water without hurt to themselves. Lir's four children had each one a white horse and two hounds that were whiter than snow.'*

When I was telling them it was as if Teresa was in me, and whoever told her was in me too, and back and back until the story happened itself in the old ago before history, when dogs and horses and trees could talk. The stories were a link to the first of the people, and no one could steal them or beat them out of us. They survived the steam in the Laundries and the icy nights by the canal. They were medicine for our shame. As I told them to Tommo, his eyes would flutter and shut, and I'd have me mouth so close to his ear and look at the side of his fine long nose and his handsome cruel face, smooth as a stone. That made me feel good, that he needed me. But then the morning would always come and he wouldn't be able to catch me eye. There were nights when he even wet himself. Those were the nights I dreaded. I'd feel the wet and think, Jaysus, then I'd get him up and have to rip the sheets off and I'd put a towel on the patch and he would hate me for seeing that and I'd be in for it.

Cormac

Every Cripple Finds His Own Way of Dancing

Daddy put me and my brother Fionn up on the bar stools and ordered us cokes and himself the usual pint and a chaser.

'Why can't we sit in the other part?' I pointed to the lounge.

'We only sit there if there are women with us. And having women with you isn't always a good thing, son. Here a pint costs me 26p and in the lounge 28p. We're men now and you're a big boy. And do you know what day tomorrow is?'

His horrible hands frightened me. The fingers were crooked and bent the wrong way. I wanted to go back to my granny, Bubbe.

'I want to go back to Bubbe,' Fionn said. He could always hear me thinking.

'Yer a man, Cormac. Stop yer whinging.'

'Daddy why are your hands like that?' Fionn asked.

Daddy looked at his hands and raised them up before his eyes as if it was the first time he was seeing them. Afternoon sun came in and set all the dust dancing in the shafts of light. The barman shuffling cardboard coasters smiled at him.

'They're like this, son, because of the Holy Roman Apostolic Catholic Church.'

'Christian Brothers?' the barman asked.

'There was nothing Christian about them,' Daddy said, and the barman smiled and nodded. 'Or brotherly.'

'The Holy Roman Alcoholic Catholic Church.'

'It's a wonder ye can find work at all with hands like that,' the old man at the end of the bar said, without looking up from his pint. He drained his chaser. The barman poured more whiskey into the glass without needing to be asked. Daddy drained his own small drink.

'Sure, Iggy has never done a day's work in his life,' the barman said softly, but with affection. 'He's got himself a sugar mama.'

Daddy's face went hard and he stared straight at the barman who quickly poured him a very large whiskey without being asked. Daddy picked up the whiskey and held it to the light. He contemplated the colour and then drank it as fast as water.

'Every cripple finds his own way of dancing, Seamus,' he said to the barman. As he put down his glass, Seamus filled it up again.

'The Brothers taught me a trade, to be a cobbler. Then they beat it out of me. All in the space of a few years.'

'Hasn't stopped you lifting pints or lighting cigarettes,' the old man snorted.

'Yer a poet, Ignatius. That's a trade,' Seamus the barman said quickly. 'Yer a storyteller. You should see him in here some nights in full flow. The whole pub goes quiet to listen to him.'

'The day that was foretold has come. This is the day where no one wants the stories.'

'A sad day indeed. It's all telly and radio now,' the old man acknowledged. 'The young have no time for their heritage. They're ashamed of anything Irish. It's England and America they're looking to now. Their eyes are turned outwards. While inside grows empty with neglect.'

Seamus folded his arms as if to appraise the two men in front of him. 'That's cos everything is shite here.'

'True for you,' Daddy sighed, with both hands on the bar as if to steady himself. 'We've done nothing but beat the culture into the children since we got independence. It's no wonder they're running away from it.'

'You have a suitcase there. Are youse on the run?' Seamus asked.

'My birthday always brings back bad memories. I found my uncle hanged on my thirteenth birthday. However, my esteemed colleague Dr Patrick MacInespie has just got his doctorate from UCD, in history with a focus on Brehon Law – the ancient law of Ireland, before we were subjected to the colonial forces of the Brits and their adherence to Roman law. Dr Patrick MacInespie is taking me for a birthday jaunt up to the occupied territories of this Emerald Isle. We are to see the Miami Showband tonight.'

'That's an awful thing about yer uncle. Ah sure, it's music that keeps us all together no matter what the divides.' Seamus folded his arms.

'How right you are,' Daddy said, and he began to sing softly. *'Clap your hands, stomp your feet, and I'll come running.'*

'So Paddy is a doctor?' Seamus asked.

'He just finished his PhD this year. A doctor, not of the curing kind, but of the lecturing kind. No good in an emergency. But damn handy in a debate.'

'Those are two fine boys you have there.' The old man looked at us.

Daddy had forgotten us. He turned to me, 'Cormac, I named you Cormac, do you know who Cormac was?' ·

I shook my head. Fionn shook his head too and kept shaking it cos he must have liked how the world looked shaken.

'When we were snappers,' Daddy said. 'We got the name of the saint whose day we were born on. Tomorrow is 31 July, the feast day of St Ignatius. Now in Ireland, we can at least name our children

72

what we like. Now we can reclaim our heritage. Everyone's going back to the old names. You carry that name with pride, son.'

'What does Etáin's name mean, Daddy?' Fionn asked. He was daft over the baby sister. I wasn't.

Daddy's voice rose and he started the story of Etáin. '*Etáin was a God and lived in the world of the Gods but she was bored and tired and she said to the God Aengus, "I am weary of everything that I see; let me go into the other worlds with you." Aengus warned her: "When I go into the other worlds I wander from place to place and people do not know that I am a God. On earth they think I am a juggler or a wandering minstrel or a beggar-man. If you come with me, you will seem a poor singing woman or a strolling player."* '

'Maybe you are Aengus in disguise,' the old man smiled, as he waited for my daddy to continue the story.

I glanced at the door. As he talked more, I slipped outside. I sat down on the ground and picked a scab on my knee. I put my nails in under it and then loosened all the edges in a circle, then I pulled it and up it came up. 'Ya beauty,' I whispered. The middle part of my knee had a little yellow pus and the blood was lovely shiny red. I held the scab up to the light like Daddy with the whiskey. Fionn found me and sat so close to me I had to nudge him away or he'd topple me over.

'You tell me the story,' Fionn said.

I put my scab into my mouth and found a dip in a back tooth to squash it into with my tongue. Then I closed my eyes: '*Etáin swore, "I will ask the God Midyir to make a world for myself – all the worlds are full of weariness."* '

'Would you like a world to yourself?' Fionn asked and he touched my arm.

'Do you want to hear the story or not?' I flicked his hand off me.

'Is this the part where the God turns her into a fly?'

'Nearly.'

Deirdre

The Pooka Was a Horse Spirit Deformed by Solitude

Tyrone was always too packed in the wee house, and Jemmy's anger and the Protestant chickens meant it was tense. In contrast, Trim, with my mother's family, was gentle and easy and we were spoiled by Mary. There was no border to cross. We'd drive from Dublin and stop in Clonee in Kenny's shop for 99s. My grandma and granddad had a new bungalow beside the town, and we had the run of the place. We bought sweets all weekend, went to the ruins of the old cathedrals and the Norman castle, the Tower of Leprosy, and took the dogs down to the Boyne to swim, but best of all was Mary.

Mary called mammy her Luck Child, after one of the old stories. Though Grandma and Granddad were good to us and liked having us, it was in the kitchen with Mary where Orla and I wanted to be. Mary always wore a floral housecoat over her clothes. She had a dense solidity when I hugged her, as if she could anchor me to the Earth and I'd never drift and get lost.

To our delight, Mary didn't pay the boys as much mind as everyone else. Nor did she seem to notice, like everyone else did, that Orla, my little sister, was sweeter and prettier than me. For Mary, I was her beloved Baby's eldest child, and I got to sleep with her in the bed. She'd put her warm hand on my tummy at night and tell me to laugh.

'At what?' I'd ask.

'Just laugh and I'll feel the laugh in your tummy.'

And that would make me laugh and my tummy would go up and down and she'd laugh with me.

I'd climb on Mary's lap and rest my head against her, and she'd tell me stories and cuddle me. Ferocious hugs, hugs the like I would not get from another soul. She ate her white bread and potatoes and sucked her Silvermints, and she lit up when my mother came into the room. She would take all the skin off the chicken and fry it on the pan. Mammy wouldn't do that as she said it was bad for me, but Mary had me ruined.

'Mary, you should watch your diet. Potatoes with butter and salt and white bread are not good for your heart,' Mammy scolded her.

She would shrug. 'Arra, Baby, I've lost my taste for everything else.'

Mammy said that after Mary's little brother Seán died, she had stopped keeping pigs and goats and making butter and never ate another animal after that. No one knows why, it was just the way things were. She had lost her appetite and yet got fat.

She never talked to us about her brother's death.

'Cherish company that does not carry woe on its sleeve,' Mary would tell us if we came mewling and complaining to her about each other.

We could not feel the sorrow in her; she was always there to listen to us. She never raised her voice to us, and she showed us great affection when our mammy and daddy were busy with the twins or taking advantage of the babysitting and running off to the pub.

And no other grown-up ever listened to us but Mary. She would ask me things, and about what I thought of things, and had I ever seen a ghost? And best of all, when she settled the boys to sleep in their cots, she would sit Orla and I by the range and tell us her stories. Fairy stories, ghost stories, banshee stories, stories about all the invaders that came to Ireland and the Tuatha Dé Danann going underground, and how they come up now and then to mingle among us. And personal stories about her family and how she had lived in a village called Cill Rialaig on a mountain above the sea on the last road in Ireland. Until a man from the Land Commission came on a bicycle up that mountain and told them there was land to be had in Co. Meath to make up for Cromwell pushing them all off it in 1649. They were to move from the West to bring the Irish language back to the East. Her Mammy had stayed to have her sixth child. And how, after a few months, her daddy went back to get her mammy and was got by a hag. They never saw their mammy and daddy ever again. Mary had to pretend to be eighteen to keep the family together. They had to send the wee ones out to the fields to stand on the fairy mound, which was the only spot of high elevation, and watch out for the Cruelty Men in case they'd be taken away. We ran about the house taking turns to be the Cruelty Man.

Like Tyrone, the land was storied. She brought us out to the fairy rings and told us about the pooka in the ruins. The pooka was a horse spirit deformed by solitude. If he got you, he would throw you up there on his back and take you for a wild ride, maybe even up to the moon. And he would leave you back in the exact same place unharmed, but you'd never be the same again. I liked the sound of this and went looking for the pooka. Every place the old people brought us was not only what you could see, but its roots was the story that brought it alive. Just as the lakes of Ulster had ghost ships, the castles of Meath had horse spirits. Those stories bonded us to the land.

'Did the Cruelty Man ever get you?' I asked her.

'Not me. But he got my little brother Padraig who died in the Big House in Mullingar, and then he got my sister Maeve who disappeared. And then he got my nephew Iggy when he was a wee lad.'

'How come he never got my mammy or daddy?'

'Your mammy was the daughter of the schoolteacher. Your grandma and grandad were respectable people. They didn't have to be worrying. They only came looking for the likes of us.'

'Daddy grew up in a wee gate lodge with eight brothers and sisters.'

'That was Tyrone. Sure, that's another country altogether.'

'There's a hole up there in Crosswiggy that a piper fell down and you can still hear his song.'

Mary was very interested. She stopped her jam making and sat down in her chair and pulled me on her knee to finish the story. Only the stories could stop her working.

Mary told me that when she stopped keeping bees and gave her hives away, the old bees kept coming back. The new ones learnt but the old ones just couldn't get used to it.

Trim was my paradise. We spent time there in the fields and up the town buying boiled sweets from jars, and Beano and Dandy comics. Uncle Iggy often came with us and brought Cormac and Fionn. Uncle Iggy was Mary's nephew, but Mary never favoured them over us on account of blood. Cormac and I got up to all sorts of mischief. Mary said he was a bad influence, though it was usually me who decided what we would do, and poor Cormac did what I told him to. There were so many flies in Grandma's house. Mary was making the soup on the range, and I talked Cormac into scooping them off the windowsill and putting them into the pot.

When Mary served the soup that evening there were a hundred flies drowned in it.

I could have got in a lot of trouble for messing with her soup and making a show of her in front of the family. But she blamed Cormac simply because she liked him less.

'You're a bad article,' she'd tell him.

'What does that mean?' he'd ask.

'Go ask your father,' she'd say. 'He was one too.'

Dymphna

The Torcs

These days Tommo was always coming home from robbing in the West of Ireland. Easy pickings, he'd say. Them culchies don't even lock their doors. All them auld farmers with their money stashed under their mattresses cos they didn't trust banks. He said down the bog everyone left the keys in their doors; it was an open invitation, like. Though even the boggers were beginning to cop on, so they were. Tommo and his mates used to joke about how they'd tie up some old bachelor farmer and rough him up just cos they hated culchies. That's where all the priests and Guards are bred, they said. In the bog.

He'd pulled a few strokes around Connemara and on the way back to Dublin they were driving through some small town, and didn't they see a chemist shop with no metal guard on its door or windows. They pulled the van over after looking at each other, didn't even have to say a thing, and kicked the door down. There were no Guards at all in that town. There were two auld ones who were in their eighties sleeping upstairs, and they didn't even have a phone to call anyone. They just sat in their beds like mad hags, in their white nighties, with their long grey hair loose, and sobbed in fear. Didn't even bother tying them up. Tommo said it was real old-fashioned wooden counters and everything in little drawers, and his lads emptied the drawers into bags and hightailed it back to the van. The old sisters didn't even have an alarm on the place.

Tommo's gang were only delighted to see that they had got a rake of Palfium.

'See these little white pills,' he told me. 'I can sell them for three quid a pop.'

The others in his gang had divvied up the proceeds and Tommo asked for the Palfium for himself, and the others didn't really know what it was. There was some auld shite in brown envelopes and they fecked them into the rubbish chute outside.

Next thing the Guards were ringing at the flat.

'Where's Tommo?' the guard said gruffly, with his culchie accent. He brushed past me as I was holding the baby. Regina was sitting on the floor of the kitchen eating her cornflakes. I went into them. Them Guards hated all us Dubliners. They thought anybody living around there were criminals anyway. In anyways, we hated them back.

'We know you did the robbery in the chemist last night, Tommo,' the guard said. 'We're not going to get you for it because no one will testify against you, but we need something you took.'

Tommo lit a fag and stared at them. To him the Guards were the same as the priests that bet the shite out of him in Artane.

'Oh yeah?' Tommo said. 'What's in it for me?'

'We'll leave you alone to do your business. We could make it very hard for you down by the canals. Your lot of brassers could run into a lot of hassle.'

'Sound,' Tommo said shrugging. 'Just providing a service, as you know. You avail of it yerself. But go on ... I'm listening to ya. I don't want youse lot breathing down me neck.'

'There were envelopes with some gold torcs.'

'Ya wha?'

'Torcs.'

'What are them things when they're at home?'

'Flat gold necklaces. The old ladies who own the chemist had them from their grandfather who had been given them in payment. Some farmer had been digging for turf and he found them in the bog. Apparently, even the old ladies didn't know what they were, but they had them listed anyway. We have reason to believe that they are ancient Celtic artefacts. Gold necklaces, thousands of years old. The National Museum wants them. This is serious stuff. You couldn't sell them. They're only of use to a museum, but they're important.'

'Them yokes?' Tommo began to laugh. 'Sure we thought they were a load of shite. Threw them in the skip outside.'

'You think you'd have learned from those diamonds you fecked away, Tommo.' The Guard leaned against the wall and rubbed his eyes. 'You're not very bright.'

'Sounds like I couldn't have sold them anyways,' Tommo shrugged. 'I've given you the info, now fuck off out of me gaff.'

The Guard sighed and walked out to his partner outside, Tommo showed them where he put the rubbish down the chute in the flats. The door downstairs was bolted and the rubbish was due to be collected the next day. They were lucky. Word got round that there was gold in the rubbish and the Guards put a fella standing outside. We couldn't believe it. Them Guards were so psyched that they didn't have to rummage through a whole dump. Dublin Corporation came around and they took the skip full of rubbish off to the Garda headquarters where no doubt some poor eejits were sent to find the brown envelopes with our nation's heritage in it. They found them and all, and the old ladies from the chemist said that the museum could have them for free. Bleedin' eejits. I'd have charged through the nose if I were them. But when you have stuff it's easy to give stuff away.

Deirdre

A Difficult Woman

I was sitting on my daddy's lap when Mammy and Mary came through our hall door. Daddy always jumped up when she came home. The way he looked at her as if she was magic. Mammy was always trying to fix things. She had driven to Mullingar on Saturday with Mary and came back that night. It was always odd having Mary with us in our house anyway. She didn't really seem to fit. As if she was from a different world. She belonged to the world of her kitchen and her iron stove, and dandelion medicine and oddly shaped potatoes on the windowsill with plastic bead eyes and matchstick limbs. In Dublin, Mary stood in our hall with her buttoned coat slightly bulging and her head scarf tied over her short grey hair. Strangely, she went straight to bed without saying goodnight to us. Daddy made himself and Mammy a gin and tonic.

'We searched for her sister in the Big House in Mullingar, but they didn't have any records of a Maeve O Conaill.' Mammy sipped the gin and tonic Daddy had made for her.

'You're very good trying to help her,' Daddy said. I crawled onto his lap again, but he was not paying attention to me.

'I'm not sure she really wants me to,' Mammy took the lemon off the side of the glass and let it fall in. 'The nuns often changed their names, so who knows if we'll ever find her by asking around.'

'What if she's dead?' Daddy asked. 'Would it only upset Mary more?'

'There's graves there,' Mammy said, squeezing her lemon into the gin. Looking into her drink as if everything was in there. 'So many graves.'

'Did you look for her name on them?' Daddy asked. I leaned back into him, smelling his aftershave.

'They only had numbers. That's all they were to them in life. Numbers. Did you know her brother Padraig died there?'

'I didn't,' Daddy said. He took my hand absently in his and rubbed my fingers, as if to measure them against his.

'But they buried him at home in Rathcairn, thankfully. So he has a name on his stone.'

'You know her brother signed her in, so he could sign her out.' Daddy put me on one leg and leaned over to Mammy and brushed her hair out of her eyes. 'Can we not go talk to him?'

'We can try, but he's a piece of work, Seamus,' Mammy said. She absently held his hand and squeezed it. 'One of those mean farmers who shouldn't have ever gone into farming. But he was the eldest son.'

'Sure, don't I know it,' Daddy said. 'My father is a mean farmer.'

'Your dad is just tired. Eight children in that gate lodge, and always working someone else's land, and Catholic in a Protestant area. Sure, why wouldn't he be tired? Seamus was different altogether. Sure, remember his wife put Mary in the hospital last time they were there, at Padraig's funeral. Went at her with a shovel? No one's gone near them since.'

'Ask Father Lavin. He's a family friend and they would never touch a priest.'

'Father Lavin would only tell me to mind my own business like everyone else.'

'You do have a reputation of being a difficult woman.' My dad smiled and took her empty glass to make another. He gently tilted me off his knee. She gave him a lovely smile. When Mammy smiled the air softened and everything became brighter. That's why me and Orla would scoop up chunks from her big jar of Ponds cold cream when she wasn't looking and slather it on us, so we could shine like her.

Cormac

You Married a Right Dilsy

Uncle Paddy said he'd bring Daddy and us up to the North for his birthday. We hadn't gone in ages since Jemmy told him never to come back. My daddy didn't have a car, so they came to collect us and I was so happy to see Deirdre and Orla in the car. Deirdre was a year older than me so she was the boss, but she was also a girl, so I told her I would be the boss one day. She pushed me to the ground when I said that.

The four of us kids squashed into the back of the car and up we went all the way to the North. That's what we always called the six counties that weren't free of the Brits, the North. And I would look at the map and see that Donegal was the most northerly but was in the South. We stopped along the way in lots of pubs. It took us so long to drive up the length of Ireland, I thought it was a fecking continent.

At the border the British army stopped us. They looked in the back and saw us lot.

'Where are you going?' the soldier asked in his London accent. It was the first time I had ever seen a Black man, and I couldn't stop staring at his hands on the gun.

'I'm from Tyrone. I'm going to see my parents.'

'Who's he?' the soldier asked.

'It's his birthday,' Uncle Paddy pointed to my father. 'We're going to see a band.'

'What band?'

'The Miami Showband.'

'How long will you be staying?' the soldier asked. Deirdre said you could turn black from eating too much chocolate. I wondered if that's what had happened to him.

'I'm from here.' Uncle Paddy gritted his teeth. 'Look, we're leaving the kids with my parents and off to see the Miami Showband in Banbridge, Co. Down.'

Daddy had a record album in his hand. He showed it to the soldier. The picture was of a gang of men with flared trousers and wide collars, long wavy hair and massive sideburns. They looked like our dads.

'Open the boot please,' the soldier barked, waving the album away with his gun. 'Out of the car.'

He kept waving his gun as we clambered out. We stood at the side of the road. Other British soldiers lay flat by the ditch with their guns all pointing at us.

'They're just kids,' Daddy muttered. Paddy put a hand on his arm. And one soldier swung the gun right up to his face.

'No funny stuff, Paddy,' he barked. I was amazed he knew his name.

The soldiers searched our car. They tore everything out of the boot. They went through our suitcases, throwing our clothes over the road. The palms of the Black soldier were white. Daddy and Uncle Paddy put it all back in again when the soldier said they could. I nudged Deirdre when I saw her knickers on the road.

We drove on in absolute silence.

'I thought Granddad Jemmy said we weren't to come back here,' Deirdre said. Her arms were folded, and her forehead creased.

'Bella said it would be OK. He's in bed now and sick. We have to see him. He's not going to be around forever.'

When we got to their wee house, I always wondered how they had fit eight children in there, all growing up. Granddad Jemmy was in bed, and when we went into see him he ignored the girls and stared at us with close attention.

'I told ye never to darken the door,' he rasped. He was lying in bed but still was fully dressed in a shirt and a jacket.

'Mammy sent for us,' Uncle Paddy said. Sitting on a chair beside his bed. 'She said you were in a bad way.'

'You'd better not be up to any shenanigans. No guns in the car this time?'

'How are you feeling?' Uncle Paddy reached out as if to pat his father's arm but didn't.

'Are those your wee boys?' Jemmy glared at us.

'No, Daddy. That's Cormac and Fionn, Daddy,' Uncle Paddy said. 'They're Iggy's boys.'

'Ach, I had no mind to see them yortlins. Why didn't ye bring my grandsons?'

'There's not room in the car, Daddy. Baby has brought them down to Trim. They're still too much of a handful to take on a long journey.'

Orla had left the room, but Deirdre was at the end of the bed touching the bedposts as if they were something interesting. I went to stand beside her. Fionn followed Orla out.

'You married a right dilsy. She never comes near us. Are we not good enough for her? There'd be plenty room in the car if you didn't take yer man along, and his brood.'

'If Baby were a dilsy she wouldn't have married me, and Iggy is a good friend of mine, Daddy.' Uncle Paddy gestured to me and I came to him. He took me on his knee. Deirdre glared at me. 'His children are like cousins to my children.'

'You always were a wee gulpin,' Jemmy sniffed, and he waved Deirdre away from his bed and she went to the other side of her dad. 'He's no blood of yours. They're no cousins of ours. Aren't they Jews?'

'I see Jimmy has started work on the house and a new barn, that's great he got the planning permission.' Deirdre began to play with the little statues on the dressing table, the Marys and the St Martins, as if they were chess pieces. I wanted to join her, but I liked sitting on Uncle Paddy's knee. My father would never have me on his knee like that.

'The price of thon is a terra,' the old man snarled. 'We were fine as we were. He's only drawing attention on us.'

'Ach, sure who's looking at us?' Uncle Paddy said.

'There's plenty around here that don't like to see Catholics do well. Better to keep the head down.'

Uncle Paddy sighed and Deirdre left the room without him saying anything to her.

'I have my doctorate now, Daddy.' Uncle Paddy tried to smile. 'I'm a doctor.'

'Arra, you're not a real doctor, don't be putting on airs with me,' Jemmy said, as I backed out and went after the girls. Uncle Paddy was close on my heels.

Bella was the opposite of Jemmy; she was delighted to see her son Paddy. 'How's your father? Not like him to take to the bed like that.'

'Ach, he's just sulking because of the new house and barn,' Jimmy said. 'He hates to spend money.'

'He's just gurning, as usual,' Uncle Paddy agreed. 'The bile will keep him alive.'

Bella had made lots of food for us. We ate her Veda bread with larrops of butter and cheese, and the daddies were shaving and slapping on Brut aftershave and slipping into their corduroy jackets, brushing their long shiny hair. I showed Bella the album and asked if she could put it on, but they didn't have anything to play it.

'There's never been music in this house,' she said sadly.

'I told you, they are more Presbyterian than the Presbyterians,' Uncle Paddy laughed, as he came into the kitchen and rubbed his hands through my hair.

'Jimmy is starting the building on the new house, and he said he'd get me a piano,' Bella said happily.

'Ye lot be good now for Bella,' Uncle Paddy said. 'Or I'll rip the arms off ye and beat ye with them.'

We knew he was joking. Uncle Paddy never even raised his voice at us. Unlike Daddy, who could fly into rages.

Daddy was singing a song to Bella, and though she tried to look cross I could see she wasn't.

'Ach, it's so good to have a bit of life in this house,' she said. 'I missed ye coming up. It's been awful hard.'

Uncle Paddy looked at Daddy and said, 'He was hoping your sons were mine and he was wondering why I'm always with you.'

Daddy looked at his watch. 'Tell him even the scabby sheep likes to have company.'

Uncle Paddy laughed and slapped him on the back, and they waved at us all. They couldn't get away fast enough.

Bella stood in front of her son and said, 'Be careful. There's lots of checkpoints, and don't be drinking. It's not like down South. You can't be doing that up here. And don't be doing anything that would bring trouble to us. We have to live in this place. We're surrounded.'

Uncle Paddy put his hands together like he was praying, and he gave a little bow. 'You have my word. It was a once off. No more of that.'

435

A Blue Ribbon

We worked hard in the Laundry, under a glass roof. I would be sweating in the heat all the time. Me hands were red and peeling from the soap. The raw bleach poured in splashed back and sometimes these carboys of bleach would split and I'd be mopping it all up and me eyes stinging. We all nearly fainted with the stink of it. We were trained to stay at our stations until a bell went. I'd be waiting for that bell. Longing for it. At 8 pm it rang and we shuffled off to eat some empty-tasting soup with strips of cabbage floating in it. I longed for Easter morning when we got a boiled egg. One egg a year.

We were not allowed to talk. I would try to get beside Teresa and she would be avoiding me like. In the dormitory the nuns prowled to make sure we didn't talk, but me bed was beside hers.

Teresa sat like a stone on the edge of her bed. I whispered to her that I asked a nun if I was ever going to leave. Teresa suddenly looked up at me. She was seeing me. I felt I had become flesh and blood suddenly and not a ghost.

'They promised to make me a Child of Mary if I stayed, so they did.'

'Why do you want that?'

'They'll give me a blue ribbon.'

'Why would you want that?'

'They told me that there was no one on the outside who wanted me, so I'd have nowhere to go.'

'Is that true?'

'I'd have a blue cape and when I get married the other Children of Mary will come to the church steps and take it off, and underneath I'll have a wedding gown.'

'Bright, who are you going to marry if you're stuck in here? Who will ever see you?'

I didn't know what to say. I loved that she had said my name once more. The name she gave me. She kept still, and it was like she was in a trance and her soul had left her body. Her eyes were open, but no one was inside. She'd moved away from herself. Her hands were clutching the side of the bed. I waited for her to come back, and she did after a bit but sighed deeply and lay down.

'Where do you go?' I whispered.

But she had stopped talking to me again.

At night I could hear the other women whimper and cry as if no one could hear them. Outside I felt the shadows fly so close. Something at the window. Close by. Something coming for us. Something without a name.

Cormac

I Had a Bad Dream

We dug through his pockets for boiled sweets, bulls' eyes and pear drops usually. He bade us be quiet and listen, holding up one rough red finger as if to conduct the songs of the birds.

'Ach, that's a Siberian lesser whitethroat,' he said. 'The nest must be near.' Taking out his wee notebook. Licking his stubby pencil. Writing everything down. We picked daisies and put them in his hair and he didn't mind. I'd never known a grown-up like him. Something gentle. Forever when anyone in my life would say 'away with the birds' I would think of this big fella lying up against the ditch, distinguishing between the strings of bird sounds.

'That yon Siberian lesser whitethroat, you see it? Grey back and white breast, yellow eye. Listen! Its song is like a rattle of machine guns, tet tet tet tet tet tet tet. Its nest must be near. There'll be about seven eggs in it in the brambles. In a few months she'll be off to Africa. A wee bird like that will make it all the way over there.'

I looked at the wee bird and wondered were there Jews in Africa. Something had rearranged itself inside me with that word and the way their Granddad Jemmy said it. We were different up here because we were from Dublin. We weren't really family and were barely tolerated. But now there was something else different. A further distance from the trees above and the bushes and the ground beneath me. That wee bird though. That wee bird didn't belong entirely to here, for it also lived somewhere else. Far from here. Continents and oceans away. It belonged to the world. And maybe Fionn and I did too. I listened very closely and heard it plainly now and different from everything else, like a sound in an egg, inside the air: tet tet tet tet tet tet.

'Right, away home for tea, before we get a tonging,' Malachy said. 'Ita will be home from school and getting it ready.'

Auntie Ita was there waiting for us with cream cakes and eclairs when we came home. Sometimes it was OK up there.

We were all in one bed, us kids. I heard the daddies come in late, and they were shushing each other and talking in low voices and laughing. Malachy was sleeping in the big chair by the fire with a crocheted blanket over him. He was rubbing his eyes and making low sounds in his chest, but he didn't seem awake. I crept into the tiny kitchen where they were smoking and pouring whiskey. Uncle Paddy took me on his lap and put his arms around me.

'This is a great lad. A credit to you. Aren't you a credit to your reprobate of a father?'

I lay back against him. Daddy had never hugged me or even held my hand. I loved Uncle Paddy until my heart burst, and I turned around and threw my arms around him and said something I'd never said before or heard said to anyone around me. Except my Granny Bubbe, who always said it to me and Fionn.

'I love you, Uncle Paddy.'

It took us both by surprise.

'I love you too, Cormac. You're a fine man.' Uncle Paddy squeezed me tight, as my father watched. I could see clouds move over his face, but I knew I was safe with Uncle Paddy.

'Get back to bed,' my father slurred.

'I had a bad dream,' I said.

'Not half as bad as the reality I can make for ye if ye don't clear off. It's two in the morning, for fuck's sake.'

'Ah let him stay up, poor wee gossin. He needs a bit of company.' Uncle Paddy kept me firmly in his hug, even kissing the back of my neck and let me put my finger into the whiskey.

Daddy stared at us both as if we'd taken something from him.

Deirdre

It's a Bad Dream Alright

We heard it the next day as we drove back South. Daddy shushed us
and turned up the radio. The news said that the band was stopped
along the road. There were five men in the band's van, and they had
to step onto the road while the soldiers searched. They thought it
was a British checkpoint. But the soldiers were from the UVF and
as they tried to plant a bomb in the van it went off by mistake,
killing both soldiers. The saxophone player, Des, was blown over the
ditch by the explosion. As he was only slightly wounded, he was able
to escape and look for help.

The trumpet player Brian was the first to die; they shot nine
rounds in his back with a machine gun. Then they shot Fran, the
lead singer, twenty-two times in the face. Tony begged for his life,
but they shot him four times in the back. The bassist, Stephan, was
shot with a dum dum bullet but survived.

The drummer, Ray, had decided to go stay with his parents in
Co. Antrim that night.

As we listened to the radio, all the way down to the South, I held the album in my hand. I noticed something I hadn't observed the first time. All the men had their hands outstretched.

The radio reported bits of bodies and van wreckage all over the road. They had found an arm with a UVF tattoo.

'What's the UVF?' Cormac asked. Fionn and Orla were asleep over our knees.

'They're an illegal paramilitary group,' Daddy said. 'They want the Union with England. They're descendants of the Protestant settlers who stole our land.'

'What's that?'

'Black Protestant bastards,' Uncle Iggy growled.

'Was it that Black fella, who threw Deirdre's knickers on the road?' Cormac piped up.

'Not that kind of black,' Iggy said. 'But he shouldn't be here either. Bringing disgrace on his people.'

I dug my nails into Cormac's arm.

'This is not just the UVF,' Daddy said. 'This has the mark of the Brits all over it.'

'Two thirty in the morning. That's when Cormac came out to us and said he had a bad dream,' Uncle Iggy said.

'It's a bad dream alright,' Uncle Paddy said. His hands banging the steering wheel. 'It's all a bad dream.'

'What was your bad dream?' I asked Cormac.

'I dreamt I had been turned into a fly,' Cormac said. 'The dream had a stickiness that stuck to me even when I woke up.'

'Like Etáin,' Fionn said. He sat up rubbing his eyes.

The daddies stopped in a Dundalk bar as soon as we crossed the border, but Daddy was not singing his usual songs. The two men sat with their backs to us at the bar in stone silence. Their ponytails were almost the same length. We sat at the table and had toasted sandwiches and crisps. Daddy suddenly said he had to go and do a message. Uncle Iggy looked at him in surprise, but shrugged and ordered another pint. He never came to sit with us.

96

When Daddy came back he had sweets for us all, and he had got his hair cut short.

Uncle Iggy shook his head and snorted in disapproval. 'Ya buck eejit!' was all he said. Daddy put his hands self-consciously to the back of his head as if to feel for the phantom ponytail.

Caitríona

He Entered the Feast a King and Left a Knight
(1575)

When the wind blew from the west, we could not disembark. The dark-haired daughters took everyone to Rathlin Island for safety. I had been with the warriors but then it was decided I should help with the old poet, so they sent me to the boats. I watched as they waited for an east wind and the women steered small boats to the basalt shore. The cliffs loomed high. Hair tied back, the women patiently, anxiously guided the old, the sick, the children, those of wandering minds. These cloaked women herded their apprehensive clan. They scattered to be safer and hid behind rocks.

An old poet, Tadhg Ó Cléirigh, fumbled on the shore. I always had a soft spot for the poets. They sing us to life; they bind us to the world. Once he had eaten with his king off the same plate, but now he did not recognize his own daughters. They lifted him from the boat and lay him on the shore. They looked with pity as his eyes darted to their faces; he had grown weaker and weaker. The week before he could not tie the brooch to fasten his mantle. The day before he forgot how to swallow for half the day, and his daughters fed him water in dribbles so he didn't dry up like seaweed on the beach. But all this movement and sea air meant he rallied and gained some strength. His grandchildren were grown, and the boys stayed on the mainland to fight Essex's approaching army.

The poet Tadhg was agitated, so his daughter stroked his long hair, wiped the sand from his beard and whispered, 'The English are coming. Queen Elizabeth of England has sent the Earl of Essex. The same earl that ambushed Brian and all his people when they hosted him at the Belfast feast. We can't take chances. We will be safe here on the island. The men are poised to fight on the mainland. The English have near to a thousand men. But our sons and husbands will have their own land and kin to fight for so they will beat them.'

'King Henry?' the poet seemed to rally as the boats unloaded. They lay him on the beach, but he sat up straight.

'He's dead, Father. His daughter is Elizabeth. She's Queen of England now. And she's got her eye on all that's here.'

'Henry has a son. We are going to his celebration,' the old man snapped. 'Wee Prince Henry.'

'Though wisdom is good at the beginning it is better at the end,' her pragmatic sister said. As old as I was, I helped to carry the old poet over the beach. 'We could take shelter in the castle or the caves.'

'We'll bring him to the castle, but we can go to the caves,' the daughter said.

'No, we can't let him out of our sight. His mind is wandering,' I replied.

'Caitríona?' he said, lighting up, looking at me.

'I'm not she, I'm your daughter Deirdre, and this is your other daughter Madhbh.'

'I'm Caitríona,' I said, as I helped shoulder him towards the caves. They were shocked. I had been a new servant in this tribe. Taken in out of pity, an old woman.

'I knew your father when I was a child,' I told them. 'He was one of the great poets.'

The great poet swung his head around looking at all the birds.

'He once taught me the names of all the birds,' his daughter said, 'and how to recognize their call: guillemots, kittiwakes, crows, puffins, razorbills and choughs.'

I could see they were nothing to him: the birds were just flecks of ash in the sky, their calls no longer distinguishable; his own daughters were shadows cast from an unknown source. He thought he was still the young poet. He thought Henry VIII was still the King of England. He remembered he had a servant, and his servant had a young daughter called Caitríona. He thought I was that child again.

His daughters laid him down by the dunes to wave their arms at others of their clan disembarking. He clutched the wet sand of Rathlin Island, and only I knew he was remembering a night sixty-two years ago that no one who was present ever forgot. In his chewed-up mind he was the young poet to the king, the chief of the Ó Donnels. His family, the Ó Cléirighs, were the chief poets of the Ó Donnel chieftains of Tír Connell. In his mind he was not on the rocks of Rathlin Island being dragged by harried women into to the caves. He was young, a graduate of seven years at bardic school and sitting beside his king. They were eating off the same big plate. And he was waited on by me, wee Caitríona, I was a small redheaded servant girl who came with them on the great journey. He had taken a liking to me, and I sat at his feet and listened to the stories, and he could see that the stories became part of me. Sure, wasn't it only a pity I was not a noble or a boy, he used to say. I could have been sent to the bardic schools.

The two daughters in their bright cloaks now carried their father on either side of him like great wings. I hoisted their bundles of food and walked behind them. A trail of excited children followed us, thinking this was all a grand adventure.

'We are returning from a pilgrimage to Rome with my king, King Ó Donnel,' he shouted back at me.

'We're on Rathlin Island, Father,' his frustrated daughter told him. I wondered if I should tell them I was with him on that pilgrimage or would they have thought I was as mad as he. 'You must be calm, and we will be safe here. Once St Columba lived here. You had many stories of him.'

'Let him be where he wants,' her sister scolded her. 'There's no use. He's lost in his dream. And it has to be better than this.'

The daughters opted for a cave at the side of the cliffs. They huddled with their own daughters and sons who were too young to be warriors. I poured them water in small cups and handed it out to everyone. There were others there and in the mouth of the cave, silently bearing the old man's ramblings while keeping a wary eye out for ships.

'All of London is immersed in a wild party to celebrate the King of England's son Henry, named Duke of Cornwall. Crowds, such as we have never seen, dancing to music. Our small Irish procession passes through, and we weave through fine ladies wearing silks from China. Such a fuss for a new baby. Wee Henry is security, succession and stability. We are a small procession of weary Gaelic travellers walking wide-eyed through the festivities.'

I sat down clumsily, my knees hurting from age, and humoured him as he slid down the spiral of time – the present dissolving.

'We sailed from France, and our last stop was strategic.'

'To meet an English king,' I said. 'I remember it well.' His daughters were not listening anymore, they were relieved I'd taken him in hand.

'We too need our own security. We are barely noticed, despite our strange dress, our mantels tied at our necks.' He grasped his neck, scrawny, saggy and bumpy now as a goose.

'An Irish king with his poet, his bard, his Brehon, his physician, his wives and one of his poet's servants has a servant child, a churl – Caitríona. You are there.'

'So I was.'

All in the cave listened to his story, for he still had the gift of the poet to hold them in thrall. He took my withered hand, his hand even older.

'Child, your hand is calloused from work. There is nowhere for us to separate so we all go as one. Servant and king. We are ushered through an antechamber to wait for the king. Remember? The music lilts and we smile at each other to be warm out of the winter air, the short snap of January day leading into the dance of night. We are tired and glad to be finishing up our long journey. We miss our home. We miss our tribe. We know who we are but now we are not sure. This is insurance. We can see the power here. The scale of it. Even you, Caitríona, a servant's child, see this. Don't you?'

The other people in the cave peered out on the horizon. We spied the ships. Fear crept through the small group. Deirdre and Madhbh became wings for their old father again and led him back deeper into the darkness.

'Why are they coming to the island?' a wee boy said. 'They know there aren't soldiers here? What do they want with us?'

'They're meant to face our soldiers on the mainland.' Panic creeps through our small crowd like an ugly wind.

'They will gain nothing here. It must be a mistake.' Deirdre reassured the children. Her own daughter had a wee baby who started to wail.

I sat with her father who made a gesture with his hand, he was clawing the air by his face. He tried to swallow but coughed.

'Caitríona?' he asked. 'I'm a poet to the king.'

'Tell us what's happening at King Henry's feast,' I said.

'After hours waiting – a hush, the air crackles with power. A young red-faced man walks in. A king who can hold the entire long island of England together just by belief. Unthinkable. There are no tribes here, no smaller chieftains, and no sub-chieftains and territories. All the island is willing to coalesce into one great tribe. There are no lesser kings, but nobles who swear all their authority to him, and they fawningly surround him. There must be poets like me in this vast kingdom, but they are not in his company. He abides by laws passed down from the Roman Empire. The only mortal in the world he would have to kneel to is the Pope in Rome.'

'What does he look like?' someone asked. People were still listening to him, despite the ships, or maybe because of them.

'A great king in silk and velvet and a flat cap. Caitríona, you gasp, you are shocked as your own king kneels before him. A gasp, a moment of discomfort. A king kneeling before a king. Both kings are almost giddy, the ceremony takes minutes. Henry, the King of England, wants to sweep out to the festival. Bloated with pride for a new son who he's named after himself.'

'What was the son's name again?' I asked. My eyes were closed. I remembered all of this. I was there. No one else in the cave knew that. To them I was just an old servant, my own sons dead.

'Tiny baby Henry. King Henry's dreams lie there with the tiny child sleeping through this huge fuss. A city drunk and dancing for him as he sleeps in sweet oblivion. Unfocused eyes and only thoughts for milk. But our little group and the Irish chiefs aren't thinking of the tiny boy, we are eager to get home. So close now. The last leg of the long journey. We will sleep in London and hear talk of a new world found by Spain, and gold, and mentions of the silver trade with China. Oh, the great world that is stretching out before us under the heavens. We will not be concerned with that but will ride on our horses to the coast and sail on a ship to cross the slender channel into another world of tribes and forests and wolves and poets and harps and kings who sleep outside in the summer and listen to my stories. I have to tell the stories. Caitríona, you listen to them all. You are not a poet, but, be gobs, you remember them. I know that, because I hear you tell them to the other servants, and indeed they like to listen. You live for the stories, don't you?'

'I do,' I said sadly. We heard cannon fire from the English ships, and we huddled together in fear.

'You must silence the old fool,' the others in the cave said. 'Can't you hear? We are being attacked.'

I was shocked at their insolence. The old ways must be changing, to speak to a poet like this.

Startlingly, Tadhg stood up, wavering, his scrawny arms wide out of his cloak, 'A great feast in an internecine convolution of a city on a wide River Thames. River gods forgotten and commerce flowing. A new world found by powerful neighbours and a strong jealous desire for their gold and silver found, for having something that the great empire of the world might want. China shrugging Europe off, too poor, who wants wool when you can have silk? But China wants silver for its money to keep the trade flowing without the cumbersome barter. They ask for forts to be built. Security for commerce. They are land hungry, and we Irish aren't fools but our armies are smaller: we don't have cannons, we don't have guns, we don't have silver to buy them. The world is on the boil – we can feel it. And we only want to go home. Henry is happy that night. And our chief thinks he has got something he needed –'

'Hush, Father, hush,' his daughters urged.

The poet swung and pointed at me. Two mad auld ones bringing even more terror to the cave, but I couldn't stop listening to him. He always could command. 'Caitríona, you the servant child, know he entered that feast a king and left a knight. For I hear you say that many times, though not to the king's face. You saw two kings, your own king and a foreign king of a vaster realm. You saw a king kneel before a king. All Henry saw was a wild Irish chieftain to be secured and subdued. Submission. Sacrifice.'

His own daughter leapt up and gagged him with a sash to silence him as the cannons fired from the boats.

Deirdre

Enough Is as Good as Plenty
(1976)

When I had bronchitis, and my mammy and daddy were working, I got to go down to Trim for weeks and had Mary all to myself. No Orla, no boys. Like my mother before me, I learned more from Mary than I ever learned in school. Mary and I went to feed the donkeys by the castle and inspected the traces of black tar poured down by the Normans onto the Irish. We wandered into the Yellow Steeple where once the statue of the Idol of Trim was, before the English had her burnt during the Reformation. For Mary, history was spiralling around always into the present. Nothing was ever over. No one was ever gone.

Mammy gave me medicine to take and it tasted horrible. Mary poured it down the sink. She would be picking up stuff in the fields and telling me, 'This is *dwareen* and what you have to do with this is to boil it then put it down, with other herbs and a biteen of sugar, and drink it if you have pains in your bones. And we'll get the *fearaban* that grows by the river, *a stór*. And that's wild buttercup, pick some of that, and we'll have you drink that. You'll be as good as new.'

'Mary did you hear, Mammy and Daddy are going to go to New York to visit Daddy's brothers? And we're going to get to stay with you.'

'That will be lovely, *a stór*.' We walked hand in hand in the field by the ruins as I imagined she had done with Mammy too. Jess, the dog, jumped into the Boyne and swam, her wet shape rising in the shining water.

'The rains made the current strong today.' Mary's eyes followed her. 'She's not as young as she used to be.'

'Have you ever been out of Ireland?' I asked when Jess came yelping out of the Boyne, shaking herself all over us.

'I've never even been out of Meath since I left Kerry all those years ago, except for a few times in Dublin. Wait, I did go to Mullingar to visit my brother in the Big House when he was sick, God rest his soul. And again back down to the Big House to try and find Maeve with your mammy. I've never been out foreign. Ireland's good enough for me. I have a mind to go to Bray for a holiday, though. I'd like to see the sea again.'

'Mammy is still looking for your sister Maeve.'

'If anyone can find her it's your mammy, Baby.'

'My uncles come home from America and they bring us brilliant stuff. We had Pop Rocks the last time. Sweets that explode in your mouth. It was deadly.' I spun by the river, babbling away as she gathered all sorts of flowers and weeds, and put them in her basket. Jess dived into the Boyne again. 'Mammy and Daddy say America has it all, everything is bigger. They went to the moon. Everyone is rich and happy and there are trains that go underground. I wish I was going, but I want to be here with you too. You should come to America. We could all go together. Please, Mary, please!'

'I've sisters, Bridget and maybe Maeve, in America, and if I could get a hold of them I'd like to see them again. But they never write to me, and I won't go near my brother to get their whereabouts. Maybe they're angry with me for not taking good care of them all when I promised Mammy.' Mary sighed and she picked more and more buttercups.

'Mammy could find Maeve in America.'

Jess slithered out of the Boyne and ran up to us.

'She might.' Mary put me behind her, and we laughed as the dog shook water over us again. 'That's something I go to confession with each time, and Father Lavin, poor craytur, is sick of listening to me. He has to forgive me every month, and then I feel fine for a day or two until I can't sleep at night and it all comes back to me. I'd go to Bridget and Maeve to make up with them; it's their forgiveness I want. I'm sure America has been good to them.'

'Do you want to go to America?' We followed Jess along the river, Mary's basket full of flowers for my medicine.

'But I'm happy here, *musha*. Sure, what would I be doing with all of that over there? Do you know that the Irish word for "enough" is the same as the Irish word for "plenty"? *Go leor!* It's what they used to tell us growing up. Enough is as good as plenty.'

'I love Ireland, Mary,' I nodded vigorously. 'We have no dangerous wild animals, no poisonous snakes or spiders, no hurricanes, no tornadoes, no earthquakes, no forest fires, and no floods. It's the safest and bestest place in the world.'

'It is that,' she agreed. 'As long as you don't run into the black pig.'

'Or step on a stray sod,' I added earnestly, and she threw her head back and laughed out loud.

'I'd die for Ireland,' I said suddenly, and I didn't know why. But it was something about being beside the Yellow Steeple where the Idol was long gone, the soldiers and the border and Daddy's rage with them.

'And then where would you be?' Mary had a tea towel full of buttercups. She tied it up and placed it in the basket to separate them from the other plants, and I felt a bit hurt. I was serious.

'Everyone loves his native land,' she said.

'But Ireland is the best.' I was stunned. How could anyone think otherwise? 'And Daddy said it will be free. Don't you want that?'

'When the apple's ripe, it will fall.' She sniffed and we walked home with our basket full, followed by our wet dog.

'Why do you always talk in pictures?' I asked her, and that made Mary laughed out loud, and the dog barked in surprise to hear it.

Dymphna

The Stolen Golden Torc

Tommo was happy the Guards left him alone after robbing the chemist down the bog, but he couldn't figure out how they knew it was him so quick. He began to think there was a rat in his gang, and they set on one of the men, Shavo. They cut the tops of his ears off with a knife so the world would know he was a rat. Then Tommo confided to me that he reckoned Shavo probably wasn't a rat but the Guards had made a good guess. Though he had to be strict and make sure everyone was afraid of him.

It worked; we were all afraid of him.

Finally, he went to the top of the press one day and showed me that he had kept one of them flat paper-thin moon-shaped pieces of gold yokes in a brown envelope. The gouger had good enough instincts. He had thought they might be something but was so keen on getting his stash of pills that he had let the others throw them away without a fuss.

'Here,' he threw it at me. I picked it up off the floor and looked at it. 'And if I ever catch you wearing it, I'll cut yer flaps off and you'll never work again, cos God knows that's all you're good for, though yer passing yer sell-by date.'

I picked the envelope off the floor and looked inside. It was the only thing he ever gave to me. I think he copped on he couldn't sell it without bringing the Guards back.

'It's called a torc, ya gobshite,' I whispered under me breath so he wouldn't hear me.

When he was out, and the childer were asleep, I'd go get it in the bottom of me sock drawer and take it out of the brown envelope and hold it to me neck, without actually wearing it like, and sit looking at meself in the mirror as if I was Queen Maeve herself. And that would make me think of Teresa back in the Laundry. She had told me her name was really Maeve and the nuns had changed it to a proper Christian name. They had let me keep mine, Dymphna. The Patron Saint of the Mad. Wasn't I the buck eejit, sitting in front of the mirror holding up a gold necklace that had been hidden for thousands of years in the bog? I couldn't put it on for some reason, something held me back, maybe cos I didn't deserve it. In anyways, I wasn't going to give it up. I had the right to some part of this country, where my people were probably always poor, even if it was stolen.

Fionn

Etáin, Etáin – A '70s Childhood

We were raised with drunken adults talking politics and playing music and singing rebel songs, and endless parties that allowed Iggy and Esther to keep drinking so they wouldn't kill each other. They let us weave in and out of the mayhem, the stories, the singing, the arguments. The Kolitz family now became the O Conaills through her marriage. With the O Conaills came the MacInespies, entwined largely due to the friendship of my dad, Iggy, and Paddy MacInespie, and the fact that Baby MacInespie had been raised with Iggy's Aunt Mary as her housekeeper. She was our great aunt, though she belonged to the MacInespies more than us. Paddy and Baby's daughter Deirdre was loud and bossy; Orla, her pretty and less scary little sister, trotted after her. My big brother Cormac O Conaill, Deirdre's partner in crime, was up for anything. I was Orla's age. We stuck together, a bit in awe of our bold dominant older siblings.

Cormac got his life-size teddy and dressed it in children's clothes. When all the grown-ups were downstairs, drinking and carousing in the living room, he threw the teddy out the third-floor window. The grown-ups saw it fall and thought it was one of the kids. It became his party trick. Another favourite was hurling himself down the stairs like a stuntman. That made them come running.

He badly needed attention.

My mother, Esther, couldn't get out of the bed during the day, but she'd rouse herself for the party in the evening. Put some blue eyeshadow on and a streak of orange-red lipstick and come down the stairs. Once Deirdre nicked the keys from the cars of the guests. Cormac placed a stack of phone books on the driver's seat and drove us up and down Pembroke Road, Raglan Road and Haddington Road. He was nine years old. All of us were squashed in beside him only thrilled with ourselves.

A Guard stopped us and asked, 'What are your Christian names?' And went to write them down in a notebook.

'We're Jews!' Cormac answered and floored the car so by the time the Guard ran after us we had screeched into our driveway and hidden from him.

One evening the party was winding down about 4 am. It was a winter night and suddenly my grandmother, Bubbe, noticed Etáin was missing. She would have been three years old. We all went on a hunt for her through the big house. Room to shambling disordered room. Drunken adults out on the street and in the garden calling, 'Etáin, Etáin!'

We joined in, called in plaintive tones, as if looking for the shape-shifting goddess of old Ireland herself. Etáin who was turned into a pool of water, Etáin who was turned into a fly.

'Etáin! Etáin!'

We kids looked in the bushes and in the shed, under the beds and in wardrobes. Where had my baby sister gone?

I was frantic, beside myself. Even Paddy and Iggy were getting worried. 'Etáin! Etáin!'

Baby and Bubbe and all the guests were about to call the Guards. Esther stood frozen by the window and drained the last of everyone's drinks left on the table by the record player.

Finally, all the freaked-out adults began to take their coats off Bubbe's bed, where they had been thrown on arrival. We noticed a little hand. Someone called out. Everyone drifted into the room. We peeled off the layers of thick black winter coats, and there was Etáin, fast asleep under a mountain of coats.

Iggy, who had a soft spot for Etáin that he never had for us boys, stroked her head and mumbled, 'Etáin! Etáin! My fairy child.'

My grandmother Bubbe brushed his big strange hand off her grandchild.

'This little one with the strange name is my little Jewess,' Bubbe cooed. She never liked the fact that Esther had let Iggy name us. 'She's the one whose children will definitely be Jews here in Dublin.'

Cormac looked on in amusement. 'It's fairies versus Jews then, is it?' he snorted.

The MacInespies bundled their kids into the car, still laughing in relief. Paddy dropped the keys and picked them up again. Shivering, Baby pulled her big coat around her. Tottering slightly in her high heels. Her eyeliner running down beneath her eyes. She waved at me, and I put both my hands in the air, not a wave, a surrender.

I sometimes came back to that moment. It was emblematic of a '70s childhood. The drunken older generation running up and down the road, calling out for the fairy child they had buried when the party was over.

Deirdre

The Golden Eagle
(1978)

Uncle Malachy walked in crooked lines, looking down, and spoke to himself sometimes. He slept in his suit on the chair beside the fire and didn't have a room to himself. The adults just said he was odd, but we kids loved him as he was kind of one of us. And would remain one of us long after we had to become something else. An eternal child.

The dads had gone off to the pub as usual when Uncle Malachy stumbled into the wee house with a dead bird in his hands and tears rolling down out of his pale eyes onto his red veiny cheeks.

'Murdered, murdered,' he was muttering. 'This is some ogeous handlin'.'

'Ach, would ye get that out of the house, ya buck eejit!' Granny Bella screamed at him.

He sunk in the chair beside the fire in a right state. We stared at the huge bird, and him holding it like some lost baby he had found.

'I'm going to the police,' he said.

'Ach, you'll do no such thing,' Bella protested.

'I've a duty to report the suspicious death of an endangered bird,' he blubbered.

Uncle Jimmy, who took everything in his stride was shaking his head, as tender with his older brother as Bella and Jemmy were hard on him. He was sitting at the table going over the final plans for his new house and cheese factory. It was almost built.

'I'll run ye over, big lad,' Uncle Jimmy said. He grabbed his car keys and gestured to all of us. 'Sure, I'll take the weans for a spin too. It'll get them out of your hair, Mammy. We'll be back for dinner.'

'You're going to the Peelers?' Bella gasped. 'We've never had any dealings with them.'

'They told us in the bird society that if we find a dead bird in suspicious circumstances to report it to the local police.' Malachy was standing with the eagle looking hopefully at his brother.

'Ach, boys a dear! Go and give it to one of your Protestant friends.' Bella had her hands on her hips, talking to her sons like children. 'How can the likes of us show up at the police station?'

'They're meant to be our police too.' Uncle Jimmy shrugged. 'And he's up to high doh. Can't you see?'

Malachy was cradling the enormous brown bird and stroking it and rocking back and forth on his two feet. He kept saying, 'This is some ogeous handlin', this is some ogeous handlin'.'

Uncle Jimmy went to his brother and put his hand on his shoulder, 'What kind of bird is that?'

Malachy looked up through his tears, he seemed to come to himself all of a sudden.

'It's a golden eagle,' he whispered. 'They're nearly gone. Nearly all gone.'

'Aye. Aye. How do you know it's been poisoned?'

'There's no gunshot. There's no marks. And it's young and healthy. It had years to go. Years to go. Years to go.'

At the local police station, they weren't too interested. A daft old Catholic with a dead bird sitting in their station caused some amusement. Cormac, Orla, Fionn and I hovered around Uncle Jimmy for protection. But Malachy persisted, and Jimmy was adamant they listen to him. There was a man painting the walls of the station white. He stopped his work to watch the shenanigans. All four of us kids stood close to our two uncles and strained to understand what anyone was saying.

'Sure, there must be more of them then,' the RUC man said. He had a silver ring with a purple stone in it. I stared at it, as I never saw a man wear a ring before in my life.

'Aye, they're only introducing them back. They took them from Scotland. This bird probably came from Glenveagh, Donegal, and travelled across Lough Foyle until it arrived in Co. Tyrone only to be poisoned by a farmer,' Malachy said with authority. He wasn't crying any more. He seemed still and serious.

'It's illegal to bait by leaving poison outside,' Jimmy told them.

'They were probably just trying to kill crows or foxes,' the RUC man shrugged. 'I think you'd better go on off home.'

The policeman looked hard at the brothers. Fionn sat down on the floor in front of the counter. The man who wasn't behind the counter nudged him with his boot. I leaned down and picked Fionn up by his armpits. There was a dab of white paint on one of the toes of the policeman's boots. It must have been wet because it left a small mark on Fionn's polyester trousers. Fionn wiped it and it only streaked down. The RUC man wasn't paying us any mind.

'We've a lot more to be worried about than dead birds in these parts.'

'My brother is part of the Royal Society for the Protection of Birds,' Jimmy said. 'He keeps track of these things.'

'The Royal Society for the Protection of Birds?' The RUC man with the purple ring looked baffled. Even the painter guffawed at that.

'But ...' the other one said.

'Senseless and heedless,' Malachy said. And sat down on a chair with the dead bird on his knee, refusing to budge. His leg jiggling.

'Did you know it is a protected species?' Jimmy said. He wouldn't move from the counter.

The police did not.

'It might have just died of old age,' the RUC man said.

'It's too young.' Jimmy persisted.

'Ach, how do you know?' He was sounding angry, 'We can't be faffin' about with dead birds.'

Jimmy looked at Malachy, his leg stopped jiggling.

'Malachy, how do you know how old thon wee bird is?'

I thought to myself, there's nothing wee about that enormous bird. Malachy stood up and put the eagle on the counter. He lovingly fanned out the wings. They were huge. Even Cormac came to look closely.

'Look at this light patch on the upper wing, and the barring on her tail. She has a golden head. She still has her white patches on the wings and a large white rump, and her tail is dark. These white patches would have moulted off when she would have been about five.'

'See!' Jimmy was triumphant. 'He knows his stuff, does our Malachy.'

The RUC men looked at each other absolutely stunned. We kids were enjoying every minute and we didn't know why.

'You should take it in and test it and we'll see if the farmer is putting out poison he's not meant to be,' Malachy said. 'To make sure no more golden eagles die.'

'Where did you find it?'

'On Adams' farm.'

'That's your neighbour?' the man with the ring asked.

'Do you own your land?' the other with the paint on his boot said, moving beside Jimmy, almost too close to him. They were face to face.

'We own the half-acre with our house on it now.' Jimmy stiffened.

'Aye, so I've heard,' the one with the ring said. 'You're building that new house, and a barn.'

'I am.' Uncle Jimmy stood stiffly, and I could see his hands clench into fists hanging by his side. 'It's a wee factory. For cheese.'

'And the Adams are your neighbours?'

'They are.' Jimmy never budged, though the man with the paint on his boot was almost nose to nose with him.

'I wouldn't be causing trouble.' The police with the ring folded his arms and glowered.

'We're not,' Jimmy said, putting his fists in his jacket pocket. 'This is a protected species.'

'They were thought to be nearly extinct in Ireland,' Malachy explained.

'Didn't you buy the land through one of the Adams brothers?'

'He sold it to us fair and square,' Jimmy bristled. 'We've worked that land for generations. And Malachy is in the bird society with his brother-in-law.'

Both RUC men scrutinized Jimmy as if he was a crime suspect.

'They're fierce rare now,' Malachy said, rubbing the side of his head with his hand. 'We need to watch our farming because they have to have somewhere to be.'

'I wouldn't be giving anyone lectures on farming. Do you do any farming?'

'I do the farming.' Jimmy said. 'My brother is an encyclopedia on birds. He's actually respected by the Royal Society for the Protection of Birds. He keeps reports for them.'

Malachy looked at Jimmy. He looked at the two RUC men and stammered. 'This, this, this is some ogeous handlin', some ogeous handlin'.'

Jimmy didn't move. Malachy stroked the eagle's head. Its wings were spread over the counter. 'Like Jesus on the cross, dying for us all,' Cormac said out loud, reaching out to touch a feather. All the adults stared at him, as if they'd forgotten us kids were there.

Jimmy laughed, his shoulders relaxed, and he finally stood away from the policeman, 'Ach, I thought you and your brother were Jews,' he said, ruffling Cormac's hair.

The RUC man looked at us closely. 'Jews?' He was genuinely flabbergasted. 'As the fella says, are they Catholic Jews or Protestant Jews?'

And all the grown-ups laughed dutifully except Malachy who was still stroking the feathers. The RUC man shifted away from Jimmy and nodded over to his colleague behind the counter.

'We'll take the bird; I suppose we could have it tested. The Royal Bird Society, huh?'

Jimmy seemed to be satisfied. He left and we all traipsed after him. Malachy looked back reluctantly at the big brown eagle with the golden head.

'Ach, ya melter, farming brings us money, not birds,' Jimmy scoffed, as we crossed the road to the car, but in a friendly way. 'What are birds for? If you can't eat them?' Jimmy was serious but not mean, more like my dad, Paddy, and not like his dad, Jemmy.

Jimmy looked at us, 'Don't tell the da where we went, he's fierce careful about drawing attention. But they're our police force too. They can do something for us. We're landowners here now after three hundred odd years of them taking everything. And no one should be poisoning birds.'

'Protestants are my only friends,' Malachy said. 'The Protestants love their birds. They're the ones that really love them.'

Jimmy flipped the front seats so we could clamber inside the mucky battered car. 'Aye, I suppose you're right, they can afford to. The rest of us are trying to survive. We'd never have got that land sold to us if it wasn't for you and your friends in the bird society, Malachy. That's the only reason they trust us. Trust you, anyway.'

Malachy turned in the front passenger seat as if to say something, but instead he looked at Jimmy with an open mouth. His big bottom lip hung trembling and he began to cry again.

'Ach, go on. Whisht, would you,' Jimmy gestured back at us all. 'The wanes are scundered for you.'

'Thank you, Jimmy, thank you.' Malachy said, wiping his nose in his sleeve.

When we came back, Granddad Jemmy was up out of the bed and at the gate. Fit to be tied.

Jimmy hardened his face when he saw him and let him rant and shout.

'Let me spake,' he said to his father. 'They are our police too. They should know that. And the feckers can do something else besides harassing us.'

'Ach, catch yerselves on. You with your new house and Paddy coming up here like Moses with the Jews. We've enough trouble with yon Protestants without that lot. And now you take your Pastie Lip brother right into a police station with a feckin' dead bird found on Adams' farm.'

Malachy was used to the banter and them all calling him Pastie Lip and a buck eejit. But that hurt me somehow. I looked at Cormac and then at Fionn who was too small to know anything. But I had never thought of all of this before. Them being Jews. This was the first time someone had said it out loud.

'Are you a Jew?' I whispered. Though I didn't know what that was.

'My Da isn't but my mother is,' Cormac said, 'and Bubbe and mother take us to the synagogue. So that's a yes.'

'Ach, let's go,' Malachy signalled to us kids, and we left Granddad Jemmy shouting at Uncle Jimmy and Jimmy shouting back at Jemmy. We followed him quickly through the fields with his binoculars. We lay by the ditch, in his little den of branches, to listen and watch for birds. He was breathing heavily but soon settled.

'Alright, big lad? Haul them,' he said and handed Cormac the binoculars. I snatched them right off him. And this made Malachy laugh.

'Aye. Ladies first, so.'

Malachy nudged me, '*Iolar Fíréan*. I almost told them Peelers that that was the name of the bird.'

'What bird?' I was holding the binoculars to my eyes.

'In English it's golden eagle but in Irish *Iolar Fíréan*. Just as well I didn't.' He chuckled to himself. I handed him back the binoculars and figured I didn't understand anything and never would.

Hag

Like to Run Mad From Sorrow

A razor tide cut the silk soles of your bare feet. Salt blood-pink in the foam mingled like a spell, right where water met land. Your firefly lives shine and blink out, yet you eat into time and leave so much behind. Your legacy is pain and wonder, always striving to alter yourselves and manipulate me. You can see so much, but you will never understand how you are blind. Even pigs can see the wind.

The animals in the forest have more wisdom. They live each breath with the time allotted to them. They don't tell stories. They don't leave such residue. They recognize me when I come to them. They call me bone mother. I am the hag. In winter I scour the woods and collect the bones of their dead.

Turlough

The Lord of the Glens Was Like to Run Mad for Sorrow
(1575)

My mother, Caitríona, had always walked last behind them all. Emptied their noble piss pots into the hedges. I tracked her down to the glens, where I heard that she was now a servant to Sorley Boy MacDonnell's clan. She thought I had been killed at the great slaughter at Brian's feast. But my older brother Brendan was dead, and I was alive. Truth is I had hidden wounded in the woods with the wood kern for a bit and gathered my strength to search for her. I found out finally that the Lord of the Glens had taken her in.

I am the servant's son, a servant myself all my life, my grandfather was servant to the great poet Tadhg Ó Cléirigh whose mind unravelled, and he too was brought to Rathlin Island in his ramblings and forgettings.

They told me my mother was evacuated to Rathlin Island, safe from the English warships. They offered me a place on the boats to find her, but I deliberately decided to stay with her lord. For I had been asked to fight and grabbed the chance to be a warrior not a servant. That had always been my dream, and at forty years old I was not a young man; it was time to serve no more. It was time to fight. I crouched, with my spear, behind the Lord of the Glens. We had come to the very top of the island of Ireland and were looking out to Rathlin Island. We saw it all, even that which we didn't see. We could hear the cannons firing from Essex's ship and pounding the island. We heard the castle crack and buckle; the lead balls flew like angry beasts.

Birds circled like bad thoughts come loose. We heard the screaming. Essex's English soldiers put them all to death. And even those who fled, flailing, to hide in caves in huddled packs, women shielding their children begging for mercy, were all murdered with their eyes open. The Lord of the Glens shouting and howling and jumping, twisting about. His children and grandchildren were over there. The old were there. The sick were there. Essex knew there were no warriors to fight; this was a deliberate tactic, to be sure.

Sorley Boy MacDonnell, the Lord of the Glens, saw all he had ever had, all he loved, ripped through with iron swords. Tadhg's son, also a trained poet, stood beside him. The Lord of the Glens choked on his own words, eyes swirling. All the warriors knew their fathers, mothers, grandfathers, sisters and nieces and children were on the island. Gone gone gone, all of them gone. And Essex and his men cheering, for they had taken it with permission from the flame-haired daughter of Henry VIII, Elizabeth the Virgin Queen.

How did she think it was hers to give?

We warriors stood ready for a battle that wasn't going to happen. My mother would never know I had survived.

All the fit young men poised to fight instead ended up sailing to the island when it was all too late. We ran and shouted through the slaughtered bodies. Not one of them was left alive. Like chess pieces returning to their wooden box, queens, princes, priests, poets and churls were placed in the same big grave. In all the confusion I never found my mother's body to give her a blessing before she was buried. We knew there was a spy among us because we later heard that Essex told Queen Elizabeth that the Lord of the Glens, Sorley Boy MacDonnell, 'had stood on the mainland of the Glynnes and saw the taking of the island, and was like to run mad for sorrow, turning and tormenting himself and saying that he had then lost all that he ever had'.

Elizabeth was delighted at the progress.

They had laid the land to waste, the people were dead or starving, wood kern cowering in the old oak forests, the crops burned to ensure the famine persisted.

In a warp spasm of anger, I left the Lord of the Glens to go to the powerful O'Neills in Tyrone and offer to fight for them, because by the time these English had finished with us there would be nothing left to be alive for.

Deirdre

World of the Dark Shadow
(1979)

I had a black hound and a white.
The Day is long, and long the Night.

Uncle Iggy sang and Bella played the piano. I sulked cos Uncle Iggy had not brought Cormac and Fionn with him. He couldn't drive and had to squash into the back of the car to give my mother the front. We had him on the edge and the twins on our knees. We were glad to finally get through the border and to the house. My father and mother were upstairs putting the twins to bed. This was a night to celebrate Jimmy's housewarming and his new girlfriend. Uncle Malachy drank his 7up like us kids, the spiral of the birding notebook sticking out of his chest pocket. At long last, he would have his own room. He would not have to sleep on a chair by the fire. Though he protested that he liked to sleep by the fire. To watch the embers settle, fade, and their orange glow go red from weariness and soften to grey ash. He knew how to smoor a fire so it could be stirred up again in the morning with a few pokes. They all happily assured him he would get used to being upstairs in a bed.

We got him to recite the poem about the bird who'd lost her wee ones, and he read it from his notebook. Everyone was singing around the piano, glasses of whiskey in the hands of the men, and gin and tonics for the women. Iggy told the story of Etáin, and all was silent and solemn and full of respect. Poor Uncle Iggy, he was my father's shadow, and my father loved him with such tenderness and a small bit of horror. But when Uncle Iggy told a story, he could hold the room in his hand.

Etáin went to find Midyir, and as she went she saw below her the World of the Bright Shadow that is called Ildathach, and the World of the Dark Shadow that is called Earth.

Even Granddad Jemmy had not scoffed, for he was in his best Sunday suit and proudly showing us guests about his house as if it had all been his idea in the first place – he who protested every brick laid and bemoaned every pipe veined through the walls.

Midyir was looking down at the Earth, and a brightness grew on it as he looked.

Bella and Jemmy were happy that my mammy had finally come with the boys because there would be room to sleep. There were four bedrooms. Jemmy and Bella would stay on in the two-bedroom gate lodge beside it. Jimmy owned half an acre beside them. And you would think that he owned Ireland itself at long last.

Etáin was angry because Midyir cared to make a brightness on the Earth, and she turned away from him and said: 'I wish the worlds would clash together and disappear! I am weary of everything I can see.'

Once I realized that Mammy and Daddy were putting the boys to bed, I grabbed Orla and we crawled behind the couch for our blending strategy. I closed my eyes to put pictures in my head when Uncle Iggy told the stories. This way I could remember them word for word, and I could mouth the words along with him. Then I could tell them back to Mary and she would see that it was I who was special. For she had told them to her wee brother Seán and he had told them all to Iggy.

Then the Gods said to Etáin: 'You have the heart of a fly, that is never contented; take the body of a fly, and wander till your heart is changed and you get back your own shape again.'

I loved these gatherings, where the songs and the music would flow and the adults would let it all go and seem like the gods before time, knowing the world was beneath and waiting only for them to brighten it up with their attention.

A great wave swallowed up the sea,
And still the hounds were following me.

And Orla whispered to me as Iggy sang, 'Good job Bella got her piano cos Uncle Iggy can sing with her.'

The white hound had a crown of gold,
But no one saw it, young or old.
The black hound's feet were swift as fire –
'Tis he that was my heart's desire.

Uncle Malachy was standing drumming his fingers, more nervous than rhythm, like rain on the barn roof. Sometimes he would utter the rhythm of the birds under his breath and only we children knew which one, as only we had lain with him up against the ditch – tet tet tet tet tet tet.

There was a ringing and urgent knocking at the door, and everyone looked at each other. Because, as crowded as it seemed, it was only us. Really only family. Daddy and Mammy upstairs with the twins, Bella at the piano, Malachy by the fire, Auntie Ita in the armchair by the window, Jimmy with his arm around his fiancée in front of the fireplace, Uncle Iggy with one hand on the upright piano as if to hold himself up, a whiskey in his hand. Granddad Jemmy went to the door and opened it. Two men, wearing black balaclavas on their heads, barged in.

Balor's Eye, cranked open, exploding crack rip screaming time-stopping choke – the hag stretches her arm out from the inside of the Earth and places her spider hand on my head and squeezes hope out, and a stillness that devours comes in, wipes out erased thoughts, memories – I was there but do I remember do I remember? – I forget when I was born – I forget speaking for the first time – I forget my first tears – I forget the first time I was scared – I forget that I thought it was over before it began and I thought I was dead before I knew that I too would have to die – that all the adults in the room would be dead one day and some right there and then – and that the sun would swell and swallow the Earth – and all would then be locked away in a time – and the gaze would stop because there would be no eyes out there to perceive Balor's stink Eye – I will become a fly – I will wander will wander will wander – will overeat – will overdrink – will fail all my exams – will take every pill – will fuck it all up – every offer, every chance – will not post the letter – will not pay the bill – will cut my arms with razors to make me feel real – will not change the oil – will get within shouting distance of my dreams and flee from them – buzz buzz buzz – until my heart is changed – only then I can get my own shape back again – but what if there is no shape – because I was invisible when it occurred – the transformation left residue behind that couch, essence that would no longer be mine – become a survivor – a child, a number, statistic – an excuse.

Time gets stuck on this – a break in the spiral – stuck – will have to keep coming back to it. The great wave will swallow up the sea, I will turn into a fly, and I will wander the Earth – and Malachy would yelp like a dog and throw himself on top of Orla and me and tuck us in under him – but not before I saw it all kick off from behind the couch. He stood right by my head, from the side of my eye he would swallow us whole – I saw the shoes of the man shooting, there was paint on the toe – I saw the other man holding his gun and swinging it, he had a purple ring. *Iolar Fíréan*. What had they done with the golden eagle spread like Christ on the counter? – its golden-feathered head poisoned in the field – poison poison – which world had it slipped into? What had it to become? *Iolar Fírean. Iolar Fírean.* I wish the worlds would clash together and disappear! Oh, Etáin, that was a terrible wish – Malachy's body shuddered and shook transforming into something else – his legs going backwards. When the noise stopped, I squirmed out and grabbed Orla by the hand, pulled her from under him, and ran through the kitchen and out the back door – flinging it open and on out the gate past the wee lodge and up the dark lane, running and running –

You have the heart of a fly, that is never contented; take the body of a fly, and wander till your heart is changed and you get back your own shape again.

The day is long and long the night. We ran like two hounds – I thought the golden-headed eagle would swoop down out of the night sky and carry us away – and we didn't stop till we got to the old man's cottage down the lane. There was a light on behind the tattered curtains, and I hammered on the door with my fists.

The Sun and Moon leaned from the sky
When I and my two hounds went by.

He opened the door, and I expected him to be with his fairy wife, but he gasped at us – blood-drenched children – as if we had just been born aged ten and eight, in our matching pajamas with the wee pigs on them. I couldn't look behind me in case Balor's Eye was still wide open. I thought we might both be dead, there was so much blood on us. But it was not our blood.

Caitríona

A Web of Hate
(1575)

The tidal blood that would come would wash like a wave over the world to crash down on us, scatter us, smash us.

There are beginnings that feel like endings, and this was one.

It was over when it began. I survived as an old hag as the ancient feeble-minded poet lay on top of me like a golden eagle, and the English soldiers slaughtered everyone in the cave with their swords, babes and all. I escaped on a boat that I rowed myself alone, and I crawled into the forest to join the wood kern.

The generations who were to come were dead on arrival. Marked and doomed. The great bull loped among the roaming cattle, breaking out into a quick trot. Its horns glinting in the catches of sun through curdled clouds. The Lord of the Glens knew it was over, but it would have to be played out for centuries and centuries to come. A web of hate spun with bloody sinews of nerves.

Two lands side by side that were chasms apart. One of the new world and one of the old. One pulled together by commerce and central power. One tribal and held by stories in the dreamtime. One was England of the rolling gardens, tillage and hallowed halls. The imposition of the rational on the wild. The other with people who stubbornly would not go to towns but wanted to live through the land and didn't have time for the back-breaking planting but grazed great herds and sung their songs and told their poems and lived in the spiral of time, not year by year, measured out by accumulations.

This wonderful England had bards and Shakespeare and theatres, but it had a shadow.

Ireland would always be the shadow, the untamed world. Queen Elizabeth of England had told one of her nobles, Essex, 'If you can conquer it, you can have it.' She wanted Ireland settled and tamed, and Protestant, and loyal to her, not a door that could swing open and let in her nemesis, Spain. After all, her mother, the witch Anne Boleyn, had usurped Catherine of Aragon, daughter of the two great monarchs of Spain, Isabella and Ferdinand. Elizabeth's hate ran deep and practical.

So Essex came. And more after him.

Deirdre

A Sammidge
(1979)

We were two small children, covered in blood at the table of the man who had married a fairy. The black kettle of tea boiled on the range. He poured two cups for us and we sat in front of him. He said nothing. His hands on the table were like the roots of trees trying to dig into the ground. A grandfather clock tick-tocked. There was a crucifix on the smoke-stained wall. There was no salt on the table. A chair beside the fire. One chair. No others. His eyes were yellow, red triangles in the corner. His lines were like roads on the mountains winding up his face. His eyebrows were briar bushes, his ears were red at the tip and hair sprouted out. His head was a long egg and his hair was sparse.

He pointed to the yellow package of sliced white bread on the table. 'Would youse like a sammidge?'

I shook my head slowly from side to side. Orla's breath was small and shallow. I put my hand in hers.

I studied him and he studied us. His breath was raspy and phlegmy. I thought the fairy woman probably left well before the neighbour brought the salt.

'Don't call the police please.'

'Ach, I've no telephone here,' he said. 'I might have to step out. Are youse from the MacInespies' house?'

'They did it,' I said. 'Because of the golden eagle. I saw the paint.'

He drummed his fingers on the table. We were probably the first people to have sat in his house in a long time. The air was stacked with invisible bricks of solitary silence, laid night after night, year after year. Century after century of losing, until he was reduced to a small grimy kitchen and a bare light bulb hanging over the wooden table.

'Did you marry a fairy?' I asked him.

He nodded his head slowly. His eyes were watery and sunken as if there was a lake over them. He was looking at us from very far away, from the bottom of the lake. I thought we were on a ghost ship now. We'd never get back. The skinny-necked ghosts were thirsty, but the water was too salty to drink. My head hurt where Uncle Malachy had fallen on top of us, yelling out.

Orla had become a statue, compressed by the stillness of the cottage. Her whole body was rigid; robotically she put her small hand on the bare table, and it made a blood print.

Dymphna

D'yaknowhatimeanlike?

'I will in me fuck,' Tommo said.

We had a telephone now. He was pacing up and down with the curly wire getting twisted around his body as if he was bound by it.

'The border? I've never crossed the border.

'D'yaknowhatimeanlike?

'Stay well away from it. It's crawling with squaddies and machine guns. Sound. Sound. How much? OK. Why didn't you start with that. That's good. That's good. Ya spanner, why didn't ya say? Wha? The aul lady? An' the snappers? A normal family, like? Some chance? Nah. OK OK OK OK. Right right right. Sound. Bye bye bye.'

He hung up and looked at me. 'We're going on a holiday to Belfast with a stop in Tyrone.'

'Wha?' I was shocked. 'They're all mental up there.'

'You're mental,' he said.

'But they're all killing each other up there.'

'I could kill ya here.'

'Yer not joining the bleedin' IRA?'

'Nah. I don't give a fuck about Ireland. What has Ireland ever done for me?'

'It's not a holiday, is it?'

'Get the snappers ready and dress for a funeral.'

'Wha?'

'Who said I never bring yiz anywhere?'

'A funeral? Why not a wedding?'

'A funeral is better than a wedding. Ya don't have to bring a present.'

'What are ya like?'

'Here's some money, don't go looking like a brasser, go down to Dunnes Stores and get a funeral dress. Dark colours, wha?'

But I was excited all the same. I'd never been out of Dublin in me life. Tommo drove all over the country robbing houses, but he himself said he'd never been up North.

And I wasn't going to buy an ugly dress, funeral or no funeral. I headed straight to Henry Street with the wad of cash.

We drove up with baby Micko, and Conn and Regina between us. Tommo was in great form. He was singing songs and telling us of his plans.

'I'm going to get us a house off the council with a garden and get out of da flats. They're building all over the place in fields around Dublin and it would be brillo. D'yaknowhatimeanlike?'

'D'yaknowhatimeanlike?' shouted Conn – he adored his da. For a minute I thought he'd box the ears off him because Tommo didn't have much of a sense of humour. But he burst out laughing and put Conn in a headlock, which was as close to a hug as the wee fella would get.

'Ya big baluba,' he said. Conn was eating his crisps, happy out.

There was a line at the border, and he started sweating it then. He was clenching the wheel.

'What's in the back of the van?' I asked quietly.

'Sherrup, ya stupid cow,' he said. He pointed out the car at big piles of metal pylons covered in all sorts of discs and stuff. I didn't know what they were, but I didn't like the look of them. British soldiers with painted green faces, armed to the hilt, paced up and down the line of cars and trucks. I was shitting bricks. I fiddled with the wide black collar on me dress, Tommo looked mad.

'I told ya to buy something normal, ya slag.'

The kids were very quiet.

'Da, who died?' Regina asked.

Tommo kept looking ahead. He never had much to do with the kids. He had been taken away so young and put into Artane, so he didn't even know how to pretend to be part of a family.

'A whole family,' he said through his teeth. 'They fucking killed them all. The mammy, and the kids.'

We all began to shake and Conn's lip quivered.

'Are ya going to cry?' Tommo said. 'I'll bust yer dial.'

'Don't get all hepped up,' I said quietly.

The border guard came up to us and Tommo rolled down the window.

'Where you headed, mate?' he said in a British accent.

'To a funeral. A friend's funeral.'

'What's their names?'

'Eh, de ones in de news. It was on de telly.'

'The MacInespie funeral?' The soldier was wide eyed. He looked about twelve years old with a face full of spots. 'Are you related?'

'Yeah.'

'I'm sorry to hear that, mate.' The soldier waved us through.

Tommo handed me a fag and we lit up and smoked our heads off and began singing again.

'Tell one of yer stories,' Conn pleaded.

'The one where she is turned into a fly, Mammy, that one,' Regina said.

I didn't want to tell the story because I was looking at Ireland for the first time. The small roads, the hedges exploding with flowers. I'd never seen cows or sheep before, and there they were all in the fields as if it was the most natural thing in the world to have four legs and spend your time eating the grass. I thought that it was an easy life, until you got slaughtered. To have your food under you and have no one really bothering you except to shave your wool or milk you. I could have done with a life like that.

'Story, story,' Conn nagged. I looked at Tommo.

'Nah, fuck off. They put me to sleep them stories.' He shook his head. 'Make yerself useful and look at the map.'

We arrived at a country church. I got out and wished I had got an uglier dress. Tommo looked the part in a black suit with a white shirt and slim black tie. But I had got a bit carried away and wanted to look like a modette to suit his mod. I had a black-and-white chequered mini dress with a wide black collar. Me brown hair was a beehive stacked on top of me head. I wore white laced-up boots up over my knees. I was getting a few odd looks from these culchies, but we slipped into the large crowd in the church.

I was so used to Tommo lying to us that I didn't believe him about the family. But at the top of the church there were three wooden coffins in a row and the crowd in the church was numb and silent. We could only hear the shuffling of feet and coughs. There were three priests on the altar. I'd never taken the kids into a church before. Regina pointed at Jesus on the cross in astonishment.

'Who's that Mammy?' she asked. 'What happened to him?'

'Shut yer gob,' Tommo hissed, and she did. Conn was looking around at the candles.

'Is it a birthday?' he whispered, and I shook my head. I took him on my knee. As we were waiting for it to begin, I whispered the story to them to keep them quiet. Tommo's eyes closed. He was nodding off in the pew.

'Etáin became a little golden fly, and she was afraid to leave the World of the Gods and wished she could get back her shape again. She flew to Midyir and buzzed round him, but he was busy making a brightness on the Earth and did not hear her; when she lit on his hand he brushed her away.'

That was as far as I got. Everyone stood when the family came in and made their way up the aisle of the church. I couldn't take my eyes off them. They walked tall but you could see they were broken. I couldn't even imagine that kind of pain. I only loved me kids, and once I'd loved Tommo. There were lots of kids with them, in beautiful black dresses and suits.

'The story?' Conn urged. So I whispered it into his ear to keep him settled.

'*She went to Aengus, and he was making music on the strings of his tiompán; when she buzzed about him, he said: "You have a sweet song, little fly." She lit on his hand, and he said: "You are very beautiful, little golden fly, and because you are beautiful I will give you a gift. Now speak and ask for the gift that will please you best." Then Etáin was able to speak, and she said: "O Aengus, give me back my shape again. I am Etáin, and Fuamnach has changed me into a fly and bidden me wander till I get back my shape."*'

'What's a *tiompán*?'
'Sshhh!'

The priests moved on the altar slowly and methodically as if in a trance. For the first time in me life, I could see there might be some use for them. The first priest motioned and the whole church stood to their feet.

'May the Father of mercies, the God of all consolation, be with you.'

'And with your spirit,' the people answered back. They were a people used to funerals.

It struck me that I hadn't been to Mass since the Laundry. And as soon as I thought of the Laundry, I thought of Teresa. I closed me eyes. She had told me the story of Etáin turning into a fly and it had been my favourite of hers. She had teased me about it.

'If we could turn into flies we could buzz on out of here,' Teresa had told me.

'I don't want to be a fly.'

'After a while you'll dream of anything to get out of here.'

Back at the Laundry there was the little streel of a creature, Bright, who followed us around. Teresa had tolerated her but said she wouldn't talk to her or around her, as she was a spy for them nuns. We did anything we could to avoid Bright, but she was like an unwanted shadow who could not be cut loose from our heels. Were they all still there? Surely not.

The kids nudged me, I was standing up in the church and everyone was kneeling down. For a moment I thought the priest looked directly at me and me insides turned into liquid. A buzzing in me ears. Tommo yanked me down onto the seat.

'Just copy what everyone else is doing, ya spanner,' he snarled.

The priest raised his arms: 'For those who have fallen asleep in the hope of rising again, that they may see God face to face. We pray to the Lord.'

And the people answered in their trance: 'Lord, hear our prayer.'

435

Always in the River

The floor was a river – always we waded in this river of soapy dirty water. We breathed in the steam and they made us stand on either side of the ironing board – the colander, they called it – and we worked silently, from eight in the morning to noon, and from three in the afternoon to eight in the evening. Everywhere there were big buckets of boiling water for starching and steaming. In winter the night would press against the glass like a stern hand. In the dim light I would look at Teresa and she would look through me and then to the windows with iron bars up high. The smell from the dirty stuff that came in made me want to vomit. When the bell would sound, we could stop. Watery soup and prayers, then back for another shift.

Since last year they said we could have a time called 'recreation' and we could talk then from eight till nine in the evening. Sometimes Teresa would tell her stories, but other times she would sit in the corner and stare away from us all, through the walls. The nuns said she was devoted to St Teresa on account of the name they gave her, and she was seeing visions. The nuns had belts around their waists, but they were only a warning. They didn't use them on us. No one had been beaten, except Teresa for always trying to escape. I had even forgotten what the Little Poet looked like. Her name was Dymphna and she had a fierceness about her that you could only get if you were raised on the outside. She used to strut around and laugh out loud – that would make the nuns look. They didn't beat her, but Mother Michael would go up and give her a thump in the back on account of that laugh. I was never beaten in the Laundry, so I preferred it here to the Industrial School I was raised in beside us, but then I never laughed here neither. I saw the wee childer from the school look at us as if we were even lower than them when we were all in Mass together, but I didn't want to go back there and get the strap like I used to. In anyways, I never did anything to get beaten for over here. I did me work and there was nothing else. Just the work.

Teresa used to tell the story of the children turned into swans. Once the Little Poet went away, she told the story of Etáin, as that was Dymphna's favourite. The stories brought us all closer. They were the thread that sewed us all together, so they were. Teresa's stories kept me alive and that's why she could never leave. I wouldn't let her. I'd watch her every move. I said the stories in my head and let them come into me while I did the washing. I whispered them into the steam and they rose like mist to stick in little drops on the glass ceiling. I felt so much for poor Etáin when she was turned into a fly and could only be human when locked up in the Rainbow Palace.

Aengus looked sadly at the little golden fly, and said:

' "It is only in Ildathach that I am a Shape-Changer. Come with me to that land and I will make a palace for you and while you are in it you will have the shape of Etáin."

' "I will go with you," said Etáin, "and live in your palace."

'Etáin was happy for a long time in the Rainbow Palace, and Aengus came and played to her and told her tales of all the worlds; but at last the old longing came to her and she grew weary of everything she could see.

'"I wish the walls of the palace would fall and the trees wither," she said, "for they are always the same!"'

When Teresa said these words, she said them louder than the others. *'I wish the walls of the palace would fall and the trees wither.'*

I was a baby when I was taken to the Industrial School beside the Laundry. I never touched money. I never saw a man who wasn't a priest or the old caretaker and gardener. I had never seen a field or a car or a hare. But I couldn't wish for these dull green walls to disappear because even if there was no one in here for me, there was definitely no one out there for me either. Only the nuns and the other women knew I was alive.

No one ever touched me.

Cormac

The further in the deeper Oh

I was raging that the one time we didn't get brung up to the MacInespies all the stuff happened. That wasn't fair. The stupid girls got to be in a massive shootout and so here we were in the funeral and they were sitting right up front and everyone gawking at them. They'd even got to go inside the cottage of the man who married a fairy. That's where they had been found.

Da held my hand. He never did that. He needed me and Fionn for something. To show something. Something he really wasn't. And deep down I wasn't either. But even my mother, Esther, came up this time, with my grandmother Bubbe, and the funeral was huge. But no one was looking at me.

We'd gone into churches a few times. They mostly looked the same. Statues in the corners. A stage up front with a big table. Stained glass in the windows with pictures of stories that I didn't know chopped up into little coloured pieces. The cross that was in almost everyone's house with a man being executed on it. What could you do with him? Why pray to him and his problems? Me Da once said, 'The Jews killed him.' And when Fionn and I were puzzled, he added: 'He was a Jew though. They conveniently forget that part.' Bubbe took us to the synagogue on holidays, but we didn't have to go all the time like our other friends had to go to their churches.

I was wondering if this funeral was ever going to get interesting, when I saw a man swagger in with a beautiful woman. They looked like film stars or more like rock stars. They were different from everyone. He had tattoos on his neck and his hands and was wearing a white shirt and skinny black tie. His hair was cut short and spiky on top in contrast to the longish hair all the men in the church had. The skinny woman with him had high white boots and a mini dress like a chessboard. They had three children with them who looked as ordinary as everyone else. I thought they should have better children. I made my mind up there and then to never have children. Fionn and I held onto Da's hands. We were proud of him. Da had been in the shootout and all. Everyone got to be in it except me and Fionn. No one seemed to be talking much. The church was quiet for such a big crowd. The priest was fuming.

'This community is being torn apart. These are good people. They were not involved in any paramilitary activity. Their crime was to build a house. To buy land.'

I didn't understand why they'd been killed for a new house, but it seemed to fit into everything once you crossed the border. The world became inside out, and the air was tight. I couldn't understand half of what they said. My mother and Bubbe were nervous and awkward; they kept looking over their shoulders as if there would be another shooting. I was wishing there was so I'd have my own story. As usual Da wanted to wriggle away from us and be beside Uncle Paddy and Auntie Baby. Uncle Paddy signalled to him, and he got up out of the seat and helped to carry one of the coffins.

They brought the coffins out one by one. I counted, one, two, three. Fionn said very loudly in the silence, 'Who's in there, Bubbe?'

Bubbe shushed him.

'Are they in there?'

'Who do you expect to be in there?' I hissed at him.

But a line appeared between his eyes, and he shifted on his feet. That wasn't really the question he was asking.

We were getting out of our seats and following the coffins. I was now beside the cool tattooed man and his wife with the boots and her hair all piled up on her head. I puffed out my chest and tried to look important. I really wanted people to know I was part of this. My Da had been there. All the bullets had flown around him, and he had been singing a song when all the bullets were fired around him. Like Superman, he never got so much as a graze off a bullet. He told us his whiskey was still in his hand at the end of it all and he drank it in one gulp. The woman in the mini dress nudged her fella when Da went by, shouldering the coffin as if he would carry death itself without flinching.

'That's yer man Zoz,' she said pointing. 'What's he doing here? That's gas.'

I stared at her, how would she know my Da? Why did she call him Zoz? I couldn't put my finger on it, but she seemed very outside of us. Not like Auntie Baby or my mammy, or all the women at the synagogue. Though whenever we were in Dublin all sorts of people were always stopping Da to talk. It took us hours to get down a street.

There were a bunch of black cars outside covered in flowers. They were shovelling the coffins into them. Men in black were slithering around like invisible ghosts, closing doors and starting cars. Bubbe was discussing whether to go to the graves and onto the house.

'We'll go to the graves but maybe not the afters,' Mammy said.

My grand-auntie Mary was here with Deirdre's grandparents. I usually avoided her as she seemed to have it in for me. She was always telling me, 'I've got your number.'

And she never told me what it was. I didn't even have my own number. So how could she have it?

But Mary was very nice to me that day, and she took Fionn and me by the hand.

'I'll go to the house and help with the food. There's such a big crowd,' Auntie Mary said. 'I'll get Baby to take the boys. We'll take Etáin and the twins.'

It was brilliant. I got to sit with Deirdre in the black car with a coffin in the back; everyone watched us get in and I could see the seriousness in their faces. That sombre importance filled me up and I looked out the window with great dignity. Deirdre was quieter than usual. To cheer her up I leaned in and sang in her ear:

'I doubt I doubt I'll never get out
The further in the deeper Oh.'

Dymphna

Ask Me Bollox

It was hard to clamber through that crowded graveyard in me high spiked boots with all the stones and bumps and graves. Tommo had left me alone with the snappers and had gone off with the van to talk to someone. I had meant to check what was in the van, but he had guarded it well and kept us away from it. Not to protect me, I'm sure, but because he never trusted me and me big blabbermouth.

I felt like a bit of a weirdo at some funeral where I didn't know anyone. Like looking at something on the telly that you couldn't just turn off. I'd never been to any funeral before. The culchies were shooting me weird looks and I didn't know what to talk to them about. There wasn't much I knew about cows and sheep and grass or whatever they thought about all day long. So I squirmed through the crowd trying to get to yer man Zoz, relieved to see a headcase from Dublin to talk to. There was a wide grave dug and they put the three coffins in beside each other. I'd figured it out though I still didn't know the story. Two brothers called Malachy and Jimmy and their ma, Bella, all gunned down when they were at a party in a new house. Their dad, their sister and one of the fella's fiancée were hit but survived. The women were still in the hospital; the da was part of the funeral.

I couldn't figure out why but that's how they were up there. Mad as coots. Always killing each other even though they all looked the same, but Dublin was heading that way too with the gangs and all. Yer man Zoz was a right character who stood himself on Essex Bridge and told stories and poems and bits of history to locals and tourists. He was a bit of a fixture. He usually had some kind of walking stick and wore a big long coat with the neck of the bottle of whiskey sticking out the pocket. A right character around all the pubs. Everyone knew Zoz. People listened to him because he knew his stuff, history and stories like. He had a big beard and seemed to be the genuine article. When the coffins were in the grave and the priest was done talking, I came up beside him with Micko the baby on me hip, and I saw he had two wee boys by the hand who were looking at me very closely. Me other two kids were running around, lepping over graves and acting the maggot.

'Zoz!' I said when I got close to him. Zoz swung around and stared at me as if I had two heads. 'I know you. Yer always on the bridge telling stories. What are ya doing here?'

'Go ask me bollox,' he snapped. I was taken aback, as he was usually very friendly to everyone. And I knew some of the same stories told in the same way. Almost word for word. I'd had many a chats with him on the bridge, as we were both creatures of the night.

Once he told me his uncle was a priest and it was he who had told him the stories first. I told him I had got them from a Magdalene in the Laundries. He had been one of the few men who would chat to me without ever needing anything off me.

'Was just lookin' for some Dub solidarity up here,' I said.

He took me by the elbow and whispered,

'Hold yer whisht. No one knows me as Zoz here. Understand?'

People were lookin' at us both as if we were suddenly the main attraction.

I was mortified and glad to see Tommo come back through the crowd. I hightailed it over to him.

'Can we actually go see something?' I pleaded, putting the baby on me other hip. 'This is fecking miserable. A whole family slaughtered.'

'Don't worry,' he said. 'We'll get ours. Our day will come.'

'Our wha?'

'Revenge.' He put a cigarette in his mouth but didn't light it.

'I didn't think ya cared for all that?'

'Ya think this is OK?' he said. 'Slaughtering us like this?'

'I couldn't care less about a free Ireland,' I whispered to him. 'Didn't I live in the free part, and hadn't they put me in as a child to them Laundries to work like a dog for three years without seeing a penny for it?'

'Yer right. I fucking don't either.' Tommo almost smiled. The cigarette bobbed up and down as he talked. Conn had come up to us and he caught him by the collar. 'But I just got paid. Let's go to Belfast for the craic.'

'Now yer talkin',' I said. 'But is it dangerous?'

'Not if ya stick to the right parts,' he said. 'I got some tips. We just haveta stay out of East Belfast. Or was it West? Shite. Wanna go back to Dublin?'

I didn't and I did. The priest was beginning to say the prayers around the grave and I knew I wanted to get out of there.

'I have to go back to the fuckin' house for a sec but we won't go in,' he promised. But then Tommo was never one to keep a promise.

Deirdre

The Bird Watchers

The last words my gentle misfit, mad mystic monk Uncle Malachy wrote were *confirmed breeding corncrake, corner of Adams' field, left of oak*. Without thinking, these words rise and move like LED lights through my head, *confirmed breeding corncrake*. I don't even know what a corncrake looks like. I don't know what it sounds like as a bird. Only how humans say it because he wrote that in his column for bird sounds. Crex crex. *Confirmed breeding corncrake*: it runs around my head in dots of red lights, feeding itself from a hidden source, always renewing itself, always disappearing and reappearing. Meaning nothing.

Granddad Jemmy wouldn't go back to the house Jimmy built where they were all killed stone dead. So we were back to the gate-lodge cottage for the funeral reception. The wee house was black with people. So many men stood outside in the cold air with their hands in their pockets. Rocking back and forth on their feet like muted crows. The women clucking around with sandwiches and scones. 'Scones? Scones?' they squawked.

The thin gangly old man who had married a fairy came with his lopsided walk through the gate; his face broke out in a big smile when he saw me. He put his tree root hand on my head.

'Yer a great wee girl,' he said.

'We have sammidges,' I told him, and said it like he had said it.

Daddy came up to him and shook his hand.

'I never got to say thank you for minding them,' Daddy said. Patting him on the arm. 'There was so much going on.'

'Ach, Bella was a great woman in her day,' the old man said.

Daddy's shoulders sank. 'She was, she was that.'

'And Jimmy a great man for the work ... And Malachy ...' his voice trailed off in bewilderment. Daddy was just staring now. There were too many names. Three of them full of bullets and gone. Granddad Jemmy took a bullet, too, but it didn't kill him. Auntie Ita, behind the piano, had not been hit directly but had ended up in the hospital with some shrapnel.

Did Malachy fall on us when he was hit or did he lie on top of us to protect us? I would think of that all my life and not be able to get to an answer.

'Ach, a terrible business, altogether,' the old man who married a fairy said.

'I know you didn't have a phone to call the police,' Daddy said softly.

'She cured my shingles. Your mammy, Bella. Twenty year ago. I had an awful dose. Thought the devil had poured tar on me.'

'So many people today told me the same,' Daddy said. 'Seems like the whole parish had shingles one time or another.'

'Ach aye. She had the cure. Bella had the cure.'

Daddy nodded and took my hand. 'Did wee Orla speak when she came to you?'

'Is this one Orla? She spoke alright.'

'No, this is Deirdre.'

'This wee lassie told me not to call the police,' the old man whispered, pointing at me. 'She said that it was the Peelers who did it.'

152

Daddy frowned. His hair greyer after all this trouble. I stared up at him, watching him. I wonder had he loved me less because I had seen the guns in the car that time. I always wondered that.

But then everyone loved Orla more than me. She was prettier, smarter, kinder and no trouble. When Mary tied her hair in bows, they stayed perfect all day.

'Ach, she was in shock. It was a miracle they didn't get hurt. Malachy had been on top of them. Orla, the little one, hasn't spoken since the shooting.'

'He was a great man for them birds,' the old man said.

A woman came up with a plate of scones oozing with jam and cream.

'Scone? Scone?'

'Ach, I don't mind if I do. The old man took two and put one in his pocket, jam, cream and all.

I looked up at Daddy who was watching the man pocket the scone.

'When we took the golden eagle to them with Uncle Jimmy,' I said, 'the policeman had paint on his shoe and it was the same one who came shooting. And the other one had a ring.'

Daddy leaned down to me, 'Whisht now. I want you to put it all out of your head. You're getting all mixed up with that eagle and poor Malachy. No more. We won't talk about it anymore. This nice man brought you back – there are good people in the world. He took good care of you. Most of the people in the world are decent.'

'He's going to have a very sticky pocket,' I said.

'He is.' Daddy stroked my cheek. I thought maybe he didn't mind about the guns in the car. That all this could fix it. That he could love me as much as Orla.

The old man ploughed on with a mouth full of scone, 'The wee one slept, but this one stayed awake and told me about thon eagle.'

'She's confused. In shock. Terrible shock,' Daddy said sternly and finally as if to put an end to it. He was relieved when some other men came up to shake his hand. We were seeing our American uncles for the first time. They had a look about them. Different hairstyles and straight white teeth. Their clothes were strange and brighter. Long fly-away collars and flowers on their ties. Their voices twanged softly. Their faces were more open wide than the faces of Irish men. I walked away from them all; the stark sun was bright but not warm, and the air was chilly. Mary was always taking us to wakes, but they were wakes of old people. They weren't like this. This crowd was solemn and dazed.

I found Cormac over at the hedge using a stone to scrape the gatepost and asked him, 'Do you remember the Peeler with the purple ring?'

'Peeler?'

'Police.'

'When we went with Uncle Malachy and Uncle Jimmy with the dead bird?'

'Yes.'

'A purple ring and the other one had paint on his shoes. It got on Fionn's trousers.'

'Yes.'

'So you remember.'

'I do. But Fionn made it worse by rubbing it and Bubbe was cross with him.'

'They were the ones who came shooting.'

'You couldn't have seen that.'

'I did. I saw both things.'

'No you didn't,' Cormac said, scraping deep lines into the gate and then making criss-crosses. 'You're only pretending.'

'I was under Malachy but that man's shoe was by my face.'

Cormac picked up a piece of gravel from the driveway and made motions as if to throw it at me.

'I watched the gun in the other man's hand. And he had the ring.'

'You didn't see that. You only think that.' He fired the pebble, but it didn't hit me.

'No.' I ducked, staring after the pebble as if it was alive and ready to jump at me again.

154

Cormac put his big round face close to my face. 'Don't think you're important now. You're only a girl.'

I didn't know what to say to that. There was no argument to it.

Mary came over to us. She was holding Orla's hand. Orla wouldn't speak anymore.

Mammy walked beside them.

'Deirdre, pet,' Mary said. 'You're going to come stay with me for a while, yourself and Orla. Your Mammy has to be at work, but you don't have to go back to school just yet, *a stór*. You'll stay with me.'

'I'm not drinking cod liver oil,' I said. And Mammy laughed.

Cormac was raging, 'What, no school? Ya jammy bastards.'

Mary was cross with him as usual: 'You've your father's tongue in that wee head of yours.'

Mammy put her arm gently on Mary, 'He's grand. We're all in shock.'

'I'll shock you,' Mary said to Cormac, 'if I see you throwing stones at the girls.'

Suddenly, there was a commotion as a car pulled up and four men got out. They were wearing suits and ties. Not black suits like the other men but tweed ones. Fear spread through the mourners like an electrical current. Mammy started to shake and breathe deeply. Mary tried to grab me and Cormac to drag us inside, but we wriggled away from her.

Granddad Jemmy broke the stillness and limped forward. He had his hand in a sling where the bullet had hit him in the arm.

The four men were scanning the still crowd and they hesitated by their car. Their foreheads all had the same crease.

Jemmy shook each of their hands awkwardly with his left hand.

'We're sorry for your troubles,' one man finally stuttered.

'Malachy was a great man. He kept such meticulous records. He'll be hugely missed at the society.'

'I was going to come over yestreen,' one of them with a moustache said. 'But we thought we'd come together, as a society.'

Daddy sighed and said out loud to everyone, 'They're from the Royal Society for the Protection of Birds. Friends of Malachy's.'

'Yestreen,' I hopped up and down. 'Yestreen. Yestreen.'

Cormac took a notebook out of his pocket. It was Malachy's. It was covered in blood. He spoke out loud and pretended to write down.

'Spotted, four Protestants. Not normally seen so far south.'

Turlough

Devil's Bridge
(1608)

On the sacred hill in Tullahogue, Tyrone, where our nobles sat to be inaugurated as kings, Lord Mountjoy smashed the great stone chair of the O'Neills, to hold up a mirror to our broken power. I rode with The O'Neill to the bottom of the country. In three hours we were obliterated on the field by the English army at Kinsale and lost everything. We should have never met them out in the open, for they had the stirrups on their horses and could ride down at us from the hills, brandishing their lances, without losing balance. That a world could end on account of stirrups. On account of stirrups, the rest of our lives would be on the run until we took some ships off the coast and fled with all the earls and nobles. The last of their kind. Hugh O'Neill waited and waited for his son Conn who was meant to join us, but Conn never came and we sailed off with much consternation.

We landed in France. After months of journeying through great cities, and being arrested by some and feted by others, we set off for Italy. It was the feast of St Patrick, and while crossing Switzerland into Italy our fugitive party came to Devil's Bridge. The glen below was snowbound and deep; our packhorse slipped and plunged into nowhere. It was I who led the climb down the snowy ravine. The horse had 120 pounds, most of our money. After hours I managed to pull the poor frightened creature up, but we had lost the bag. When you lose as much as we had lost, when you lose a whole civilization – a way of life, a way to be free and be who you are in your own native place – it is as if a hole is slashed in the world and all your luck runs through and is gone. There's no going back. We trudged on to Andermatt, through St Gotthard Pass, Bellinzona and Lugano. We came onto Lake Como late in March and made our way to Milan. We were starved and poor and weary. Governor Pedro Enriquez de Acevedo gave a feast in our honour, but we could not stay because the English ambassador, some buck eejit, Sir Cornwallis, protested at our presence. Since they could not keep us, we went on to Rome itself.

But who were we really? A curious sight from a vanished world. A world gone into memory and closed off to us. It was over. We heard the land being cleared of our kin, the great forests felled and the plantations begun with funding from England. We were caught up in the forlorn fevers that would wrack our party, the poisonings, the futile attempts to enlist help to return and take our country back. Our people would wait at home in vain. Some would come straggling from finding work fighting in other armies, from Sweden and then down to us in Spain to see if there was a glimmer of something left of our power. But there was not. Even the King of Spain lost interest in our cause. For we could do nothing. Refugees under suspicion, we bitterly felt our uselessness the rest of our days.

Cormac

Crex Crex
(1979)

Mother grabbed the notebook off me. 'Where did you steal this? This is not yours.'

'I found it inside the house,' I protested. I had meant to keep it. Because of the blood on it. To show people back in Dublin. I wanted something to prove it all to my friends. My daddy had been there and no bullet hit him. If he was dead, it might have been something. Bubbe and Mammy wouldn't have minded at all.

Mary walked over and handed the notebook to Uncle Paddy, and he stared down at it.

'What's this?'

'I don't know.'

'It's the birding book,' Deirdre chirped. 'He wrote everything down. It has old poems from monks and stuff. All about birds.'

Paddy walked slowly to the four men who were shaking their heads. They didn't want to come inside. Only wanted to offer respects. Jemmy was insisting they come into the house, and they were looking at each other in panic. Uncle Paddy went up to them.

'Daddy, if they don't want to come in that's understandable. It's enough that they came. Here.' He offered them the notebook and they looked at it, their eyes widening. 'It's his birding log.'

That changed things: one of the men in the tweed jacket took it as if it was the most precious object in the world. He turned to the last page that was written in.

'*Confirmed breeding corncrake*. Oh my!' he said, and the others seemed to have forgotten their fear and murmured among themselves. I had never been so close to a Presbyterian, and I noted their cufflinks, waistcoats and thick ties. 'That's very rare,' he told Paddy. 'We had caught wind that he had found a corncrake. They haven't really come to these parts since we started to use machines in the fields to cut the hay.'

'The hay is cut before they can have their young,' one of them explained blusteringly.

'I see,' Paddy was almost smiling but not. I loved Uncle Paddy more than I loved my own father. I trusted Uncle Paddy way more than I trusted him. He saw me in ways that I was never seen by Iggy, who always seemed to want to get away from us all unless he was with Uncle Paddy.

'Look here,' one of the men said, leafing through the notebook. 'Breeding corncrake. Extraordinary. Extraordinary. He's even written the name of the field and the exact location. Adams' farm. He was a great record keeper. This is enormously helpful.'

'Crex crex,' one of the men said.

'I beg your pardon?' Paddy said.

'That's the call, they're terrible singers,' one said. 'The worst.'

The men nodded in assent.

My dad Iggy had walked over to not miss out on the craic.

'Crex crex,' one of the others made a grating noise.

'Might we have this? We can give it back.'

'Please take it,' Uncle Paddy said. 'Keep it. He'd have wanted that.' He almost touched his arm, but his hand hovered in the air. The men looked at the hovering hand, the almost touch. They shifted on their feet.

'Ach, we'll be off now. We're very sorry for your troubles and we wanted to pay our respects. Malachy is a tragic loss for all of us at the Bird Society. His singular dedication will be dearly missed.'

Jemmy had stood still for the whole conversation, almost in awe of these formal men. One of the men twisted his cufflinks.

The scone woman returned.

'Scone? Scone?'

They all shook their head, staring as if they it was the first time they had seen a plate of scones. I wondered did Protestants eat scones. I thought that they must.

'It was an honour, thank you for coming,' Jemmy said quietly, as they awkwardly got into the car before shutting the doors, visibly relieved to drive off.

'Decent men,' Jemmy said to the air. 'To come here on a day like this. That took courage.'

And so the world started up again. The crowd went back to quietly talking, the women came out of the house and the children resumed their running around.

'Crex crex,' I called. 'Crex crex.'

'Yestreen,' Deirdre called back. 'Yestreen yestreen.'

'That's one for the books,' Jemmy said. 'Fine men. Good men. He was a Catholic and still they let him among them. And they came here out of respect.'

'The nerve,' someone beside him scowled. He was standing with a group of men to the side. Jemmy looked sharply at them.

'They're welcome here,' Jemmy barked, moving his arm in the cast. 'They're good men. All of them. Decent men. Decent men.' He said it like a hammer to the side of their heads. The adults all seemed to be glaring at each other. Not sad like they were supposed to be, but angry.

'Crex crex crex,' I sang, skidding on the gravel until my heels scraped through the stones and scarred the driveway.

'Yestreen, yestreen,' Deirdre sang back to me. I jumped before her and grabbed my head with both my hands and sang loudly. 'Crex crex crex. Confirmed breeding corncrake.'

Jemmy turned away and went back inside the house. I picked up another stone and ran my fingers down the scratches on the gatepost I had made before the Protestant birdmen had shown up.

I saw two men exchange glances. Some signal. Some code. Everyone up North spoke without saying anything. The people I met up here were all busy saying this country was the same. The one country. But it didn't feel like that. I always felt foreign here. I saw the men leave. There was a white van parked at the gate. I hopped up to it on one foot and looked inside. There was the strange family who were at the funeral. The man glared at me as if to melt me. The woman in the chessboard dress was smoking. She had known my dad. This disturbed me. She wasn't like us. She painted her eyeshadow right up under the brow. Her lips were bright red. Her baby was asleep, curled into her. The two little kids were eating sweets and they looked out the window at me. I made a face at them and the little girl, who looked about four years old, gave me two fingers. Then her younger brother, barely more than a toddler, did the same.

Dymphna

Tapioca

Tommo always joked that an Irish beauty was a woman with two black eyes. I just did what he told me, even when he drove off from that funeral and parked the van and went crawling over the fields, armed to the teeth, with some other headcases. I sat in the van and didn't say a word when he came back, didn't ask him what those gunshots were. I knew he'd lay into me, even if the kids had to see it. Since we came back from that funeral he was away for days on end, either robbing or off in England doing God knows what. It gave me time to breathe, and the kids were better off too. The tension from the flat disappeared and we could have a laugh and watch the telly and tell stories. As Teresa back at the Laundry used to say, he was as bad as Barrington's Bloodhound to us. Regina, me oldest, liked to hear all the stories that I'd got off Teresa. Regina was a gas ticket; she'd be up in front of the telly doing dances and wiggling her bum and telling fibs. You couldn't believe a word that came from her mouth. I don't know where she got her notions from, but she was a tonic and I wouldn't have had her any other way.

One day she decided she wanted something and none of us knew what she was saying, she'd probably picked it up from something on the telly.

'I want tapioca,' she said.

'What's that when it's at home?'

Not satisfied, she marched into the local corner shop and didn't she ask for tapioca.

'Do youse have tapioca?' she said and held her money up to the counter. Well, no one had heard of it.

After that, the lads on the road started to call her Tapioca. She was bullin' but she couldn't shake the name. By the time she was five, it was only them teachers at school who called her Regina.

Tapioca. Even her brothers started to call her Tapioca. Until I took to it too and she put up with it because she had no choice. If ya got a nickname in Dublin you were stamped, it stuck, and it was usually after something that was wrong with you, so she was lucky it wasn't anything worse.

A Place to Be Buried

Mother Michael, who wasn't the worst of them, told me I could become a consecrate and remain in the Magdalene Laundry for life.

'You have been most exemplary with regard to your work, conduct and the observance of the rules of the institute; you might consider consecrating yourself to God in this Magdalene Home.'

I began to think of this. Becoming a consecrate.

Everyone would be crying in the nighttime. All our beds in a row. We could hear whimpers in the darkness. Misery of the nights matched by work of the days. Teresa whispered to me from her bed.

'Don't do it.'

I didn't know she had been listening to Mother Michael tell me about it.

'I would get a new name.' I stared up at the ceiling. 'A name in penance.'

'A man's name?' She snorted. 'Like them all them nuns have men's names to go along with their moustaches and hairy chins.'

'It means I would have a place to be buried here.' I wanted to keep her talking. She hadn't talked to me in years. So this was brillo.

'Why don't you ask them to leave, Bright? Why are they keeping you?'

'Why do they keep you?' I rolled over in my bed and saw she was looking at me.

'My brother Seamus put me in here and he'll keep me here forever.'

'Maybe the Little Poet will come back for you?' I was trying not to cry. I was so happy she had broken the spell of silence.

'I told Dymphna to go to my sister Mary in Kilbride. I told her to tell her I'm here. That's my only hope. Mary will get me out. I laughed at a priest once. By mistake. I wish I hadn't. I wish I had run when they were taking me from Trim. I could have got the boat to England and had my babies and put them up for adoption and got on with my life.'

'You had two?'

'Twins. That meant they treated me like a repeat offender.' Teresa sighed and ran her hand over her short light-blonde hair. 'Why on earth don't you ask to get out? No court has put you in here. You've been here since you were a baby. Why would you want to be a consecrate? That's not even a real nun.'

'Otherwise where will they bury me?'

'That's what you care about?' She flopped over on her side, facing away from me. I lay for a long time, happy that she had talked to me finally.

The shadows gathered, winging their way, breathing into us. I saw a dark scrawny hand reach in through the window, bony fingers growing longer as they stretched in almost touching, and I sat up sweating, my heart thumping. Teresa was lying in the bed beside mine with her eyes open. Her face was sunken but her eyes were blue and shining. We looked at each other.

'You saw it too, didn't you?'

Deirdre

Mary Scooped Us Up and Stitched Us Back Together

When Mary was a little girl in Kerry, she watched her mother pick a chick off the floor with a split stomach and stitch it back together. In the time it took to stitch up a chick, she had us cry out at the Echo Gate, hear our voices coming back at us from the ruins, clamber through the ruins of the old Tower of Leprosy, leave our pins at the Jealous Man and Woman, visit St Brigid's Well at Iskaroon, another St Brigid's Well in Kilbride and finally St Dymphna's Well in Kildalkey, where she dipped the cloth in and tied it around Orla's head.

In the time it took to stitch up a chick, we sat behind the trees and watched the hares gather and dance in a circle, we tied our ribbons on fairy trees, drank our cod liver oil, winced as we swallowed our dandelion juice.

Mary's stories were the real medicine. Not just the old-ago ones, she also told us so many stories of my mother, Baby, as a child that

I felt she was there with us from a different time. My mother was my friend if I closed my eyes and spun away down that spiral, back through a door in a far-off star.

'Your mother was my Luck Child,' Mary said, and told us the story of the Luck Child.

The fields too were all named and storied. Mary knew who lived in each house, who had seen the pooka, who had met the devil on the road. We ate blackberries off hedges down the lanes. Father Lavin brought us walking sticks made of hazel branches. Mary fed us the wee nuts, which she called *cno*, and she told us the word for wisdom was *cnocach* like the nut.

'There was a sacred well surrounded by nine hazel trees. Their nuts dropped into the well and the salmon ate them and became wise. Each bright spot on the salmon showed how many nuts he ate.'

Father Lavin, the old parish priest, loved to hear her stories and add his own into the bargain. Father Lavin, with his liver-flecked hands like the salmon itself and his gentle manner, would often pick us up in the car. We could feel the reverence he had for Mary and she for him.

'It's great to see her back with the bees.' Father Lavin leaned against a tree. We watched from a distance as she worked with her beehives. 'You know she never kept animals after her poor brother Seán died up in Dublin.'

'Did you know him?' I swung my hazel stick like a scythe, cutting off the tops of the grass.

'Indeed I did.'

Orla watched me and started to do the same with her stick. 'Copycat,' I jeered.

'She has one of the old minds,' he said, as Orla stopped swiping and went over to him.

'What's that?' I asked.

'Everything is sacred,' he said. Orla leaned against him and he patted her head.

'Mary told us about the hag,' I tested him.

'Sure, Mary is a pagan,' he laughed. 'Christianity is just a thin veneer over paganism for most of my parishioners. Meath is just about in the mediaeval world. But the old ways are on their way out. We are making great strides but there's much to be lost, no doubt. Your parents are into science, right? They are the future.' It seemed as if he didn't really want the future.

'My grandmother Bella had the cure for shingles.' I skipped over to them. This made him pat my head too. We stared at the bees that rose above Mary's head and she walked back to us.

Mary brought us to his Masses. He never talked about God or Jesus or saints but rambled on about the meadow grass and wildflowers, and how the rye grass was taking over the pastures. As his congregation sat patiently, he explained that the hares are pollinators just like the bees. When we read the bits about Jesus from the Mass, that all seemed very far away. He would bring in blue flowers and put them on the altar and tell his people that these were spring squill, *sciolla earraigh* in Irish. He said they were found mostly in spring and their pale blue was the promise of the sky with the clouds gone, warming the ground after winter. I told him about my Uncle Malachy and his birds, and he listened in a way that adults rarely did. Neither Mary nor Father Lavin ever asked Orla to speak to them like all the other people did.

We walked proudly with our new hazel sticks down the lanes and listened and absorbed as we munched on the hazelnuts and picked juicy blackberries. We lingered in the ruins of the Yellow Steeple where the Idol of Trim had performed many miracles. In the time it took to stitch up a chick, the land healed us, gentle Meath, the fallen-down past; we stood where the statue had once been. But Orla never said a word.

Mary told us again how the man from the Land Commission came up their Kerry hill on a bicycle, and how they all were settled in Meath in order to speak the Irish. Their mother was too pregnant to come in the horse and trap. But her father was a mountain man and could not live in the flat plains, so he went back to find their mother to see if she had her child. That was the last they heard of their parents except when someone said they were both dead.

She told us that her youngest brother, Seán, could talk to the fairies and died trying to take care of his nephew Iggy in an Industrial School. She never told us how he died. Her little brother Padraig was beautiful and innocent of the mind, and he died when he was taken to the Big House in Mullingar, where they broke his back giving him electric shocks. She told us of her sister Brigid, left to be a maid at twelve years old, who went to America but never wrote again. How her other sister Maeve walked away from the farm and how it started to rain, and she had to walk the miles to Trim town from Rathcairn with no shoes on her feet to be a servant for shopkeepers. How she might now be in America, but she too never wrote again. How her brother Seamus, Uncle Iggy's father, married a wife with a briar tongue and had lost both his leg and his arm in separate farming accidents.

She wove her own stories with the old stories of Ireland until we learned that life is like this, and love is a big risk, but what we have here for now was safe and warm. The fire would be lit and the ashes taken out each morning, and the sun trembling over the low hills would keep coming back and back. For now, the sun was the great star of the Earth and the land fed us and cured us and we spoke it into existence by our stories, and the hag walked in winter with her own hazel staff, until the Goddess Brigid brought the summer with her warm cloak. And through it all Orla never spoke, and Mary never asked her to. Mary kept us all winter just as the old hag, *an Cailleach*, the bone mother, gathered the bones of the dead animals in the winter forests and fields and stored them, and kept them safe, and sang them back to life for spring.

What would that song sound like?

Then on the eve of St Brigid's Day, the last night in January, Mary had us put out some clothes on the bushes.

'Now is Brigid's time, the hag will sleep: Brigid will bring the summer and she'll bless the clothes we put out as she comes through the land.'

Orla put out her gloves and scarf and I put out a wool hat. Mary spread her housecoat.

That night by the stove, as we toasted white bread on iron toasting forks, Mary explained to us that this was not the only world. After this one was the fairy world, and beyond that one, if you crossed the water, lay the Many-Coloured Land.

'Then beyond that one you cross through fire and reach the Land of Wonder.'

'And after that?' Orla asked. And I held my breath and Mary acted as if it was the most natural thing in the world to hear my little sister's voice again.

'Well, *mo mhuirnín bán*, no one knows what you have to cross through to reach the last place we know of, the Land of Promise.'

'Can we visit these worlds with you Mary?' Orla plucked her hot bread off the toasting fork and turned it the other way, placing it back close to the embers.

'In a way it's enough to know they're there. Everything we see has long roots that reach into the other worlds, and all that we see here is not all there is. We would be so vain to think that.'

And we lay in the scullery bed with Mary that night, she held Orla in her arms and kissed her head. In the time it took to stitch up a chick, Orla had begun to talk again. And it was Mary's stories that had stitched her back together.

We were safe sleeping with Mary in her bed beside the kitchen. She was a great rock, a mountain with a beating heart. She told us pigs could see the wind and the Earth wouldn't end till we saw the

Black Pig. Though we were spoiled by my gentle Grandma Patricia and Granddad, it was Mary who minded us, until Orla was chattering through the lane with blackberry juice stains and her hazel stick held high and pointing to the crows, the hungry tears of the hag dropping through the sky.

Hag

Bone Mother

In the winter fields I found your bones as I picked through cloaks of rotting leaves. Badger, deer, hare, calf, bull, hedgehog, crow. All your bones mixed in my hands.

Bone mother, my hawthorn hair crackling, I cradled them through winter and sang to their scatter crackle crank as they clattered in my sinewy arms. The skull bones that housed dreams, the small bones that were a spine tunnel, the tired bones that sheltered hearts and caged lungs.

I sang so you could come again in spring. Song notes appeared suddenly as water drops emerged on the purple foxgloves in the cold morning. My song squeezed through from another world. And yet another world before that.

I gave you your voices back when you had been muted by savagery. And you children were not new. You had been here all along. You were just something else.

Caitríona

Queen of Everything
(1609)

I had outlived myself. So many of us hiding in the woods. We built light shelters that could be abandoned quickly. We kept moving. I sat by the fire at night and the wee ones gathered around me. I told them the stories and they listened now more than ever, as if it was the last meaning left, as the forest disappeared under the axe and the English cleared the land for the foreign settlers. We still had something to lose, but that would be gone soon, and we felt it in our livers, our lungs, our guts. We who were born at the bottom of the world with nothing. We had just the stories and songs as the last thing they could not tear from our heads. So I told them and sang them as I poked the meagre fire, shuffling the flames, afraid of it becoming too big and giving us away:

In the storytime, Ulster had no rightful heir. Two brothers had to get on their boats and race for her. They were told, "Whosoever's hand is the first to touch the shores of Ireland, he shall be declared the king." One of the brother's boats fell behind: he could see he was losing, so he cut off his own hand and threw the bloody thing to the shore. Thus, the red hand of Ulster became a symbol to all who claimed her.'

But they always asked me about Henry VIII. It was my own story. And now I rose like a golden eagle above the tale and told it knowing the ending. Knowing that it was a beginning and an ending all in one. Yestreen, when the king became a knight. And the children wanted to know what happened to everyone there. The feast for wee Henry, named after his powerful father. So I told them:

'The tiny prince – so well feted, so anticipated, so welcomed – gave a windy smile. He was the New Year's boy, the beloved. Destined to be king. All England smiled back. A week after the wonderful celebration some poor nursemaid found him dead as a stone in his royal crib. Aye, her scream would unsettle a continent for centuries, no doubt.

'The king had a daughter he didn't want, he killed her mother for witchcraft, and he would never know this, but his unwanted daughter Elizabeth became the queen of everything. But she died childless and now James I, son of Mary Queen of Scots, was king of everything. We hid in the woods from his men as they shred our world apart as easily as a half-made cloak on the loom.'

'And the treacherous Essex?' they ask. The man who mortgaged his estates and came to Ireland to make his name and fortune. The man who, instead of fighting warriors, went to the island to exterminate the innocents. The Lord of the Glens went after him, but Essex fled to Dublin where he started shitting all his sins out of his red arse. In the end, what profit did his slaughter bring him? What did Ireland bring him? We never got to avenge those innocents on Rathlin Island. Essex died of diarrhoea. His own unfaithful wife poisoned him. He was thirty-five years old.

Oh, to be sure, we celebrated to hear of this, but we knew this would not be the end. In fact, we heard that it was through this very series of disastrous events that our neighbours realized one subject alone could not colonize our Gaelic Ulster. They would need the Crown's money and the Crown's army to do so. But the Crown didn't have all that money to spare, so the rich merchants would all chip in and expect returns. Not only for us, but for our kindred in the vast lands of the Americas, for all of the world's people who had something that they could put up for sale. We tribal peoples who lived woven into our land, listening to its pulse, arra, we were helpless in the face of the new order of men from vast cities. We were fools in the woods, but we knew what it was to lose a world, to be the last of our kind.

'But whisht, this sorry tale is so sordid,' I told the barefoot, tattered children who had nothing to inherit and no more place in the world. 'You wrecked me head with all the talk of dead babies and diarrhoea, and submissive nobles, and bags full of heads, and treacherous spies. My sons are dead, killed at the feast. So, I, the churl, the servant, the emptier of piss pots, it is the grand old stories that I go back to. When Ulster was a place of warriors and giants.'

'And now?'

'Now there are only thirsty ghosts.'

And the children's faces faded as the suppressed fire went out with a snivel. But I could feel them listening intently in the disappearing wood of their vanquished world.

In the dark woods, I raise my hands beside my head, the wee ones lean in to listen. Somewhere in the dreamtime the greatest warrior who ever lived in Ireland, Cúchulainn, is coming out of his writhing warp spasm in full ugly bloody strength.

Now a giant, an implacable beast,
Tall as the tallest ship's mast, and a smoking streak of blood,
Jet black, spurted from the centre of his crown,
And he was ready to go fight his enemies.
And he hunted them down. And killed a hundred. Then two hundred.
Then three hundred. Then four hundred. Then five hundred ...

Deirdre

A Lost Puzzle Piece
(1979)

Granddad Jemmy, like a cardboard cut-out, sat in the corner of the room. The newspaper rattling in his hand. His eyes yellowed over. He wore a three-piece suit, cufflinks and a tie every day. He had a watch on a chain. There was an inscription on the watch. *To my darling Jemmy on our 20th anniversary – Your Bella.*

We kids in the house grew up around him. He was distant, but present – a long-dead star. His yellow face turned red. Like all the displaced people of the Earth, he was a plant taken far from its soil. His leaves browned from their shrivelled edges.

He slept in our chilly playroom, which was a converted garage. He lived among his own ghosts, muttering to himself. Ghosts reflecting their slight yellow, like the shadow of the buttercups we held to each other's chins.

And the walls still had our drawings and some posters out of magazines. The Bay City Rollers, the Miami Showband, Starsky and Hutch. A poster of the ABCs. We didn't play there anymore, but the cupboards were scratched and crayoned and still full of jigsaws with pieces missing, board games with lost figures and no dice.

The adults in the house kept him fed and took him on errands. They invited him in to watch the news at night. He didn't like my mother, Baby, to use the new dryer and prowled around the washing machine so he could hang up the clothes even in the rain. Baby gritted her teeth. My dad Paddy rolled his eyes. Granddad scowled when we got a dishwasher. He tried to wash the dishes himself. Baby sometimes went out to weed the garden even when it was raining. Paddy watched her from the window and sighed. The old man Jemmy sat by the radio with his watch in his hand and ran a calloused farmer's finger over the inscription on the back. He was in our family photographs. Communions, confirmations. Not touching anyone.

Only I could hear him. I was the last one listening. Crex crex crex. Since I felt the weight of my Uncle Malachy gunned down on top of me, I had tuned into Ireland. *Confirmed breeding corncrake.* I had heard the bog bodies whisper as they were laid down in the bog. *Confirmed breeding corncrake.* I heard the senile old man on Rathlin Island hiding in caves. *Confirmed breeding corncrake.* I heard them slaughtered as they slept on the last day of the feast. I heard the conversations of the decapitated heads in the bags carried up to put on spikes in Dublin. I heard the abandoned servants tell their stories hiding in the woods with the wolves as if they never existed. *Confirmed breeding corncrake.* And I could hear Jemmy too. The cardboard old man. Finally driven from his Ulster. A lost puzzle piece in the damp South Dublin playroom, whose window opened to the small driveway where his son Paddy and his daughter-in-law Baby parked their car in the newly built suburbs. No view. Just the cars and their grills and nothing much beyond them. Doors slamming, groceries brought in, the lawn mowed, the hedge cut. He took on duties. The washing on the line. Wouldn't let them use their new dryer even in the winter. Waste of electricity. Shrinks the clothes. But really it took away the work. And there's salvation there in the work.

My Granddad Jemmy slept under the ABC poster, his bed the bottom of a bed that was once a bunk for the twins. The posts of it with the wooden carved cylinders to fit the top.

The top not there. The mattress thin. The Winnie the Pooh pillowcase he put his quiet head on each night. Not for him. Faded. Only I dared to enter the old playroom. Sometimes to search for a game. A lost toy. He never noticed me – I was still only a girl.

He said, over and over again, 'Four decent men. Four decent men. Murdered.'

He ran his finger over the watch's inscription.

'Four innocent good Protestant men looking for a corncrake shot dead at the corner of Adams' field.'

He cleared his throat the way my mother hated him to do. 'Malachy's only friends.'

Only I heard him.

'Ach, Bella,' he said in almost a soft low hymn. 'You wouldn't have wanted that.'

Hag

The Affection of a Hag Is a Cold Thing

I have more bones to collect. Milesian, Celt, Egyptian, trader, stolen slaves, Scottish soldiers and settlers, Norsemen, Protestant, Catholic, Spanish from the Armada, failed French on doomed ships and fallen English, and the poisoned man Essex, sent to conquer. A horse with the money falling into a deep snowy ravine. All the skulls on spikes outside the castle. All mine. All part of the story. And I have to sing to them all. And my songs are droplets on their parched ghostly lips. You can't even imagine that song.

PART II

The sight of 'the heddes of their dedd
fathers, brothers, children, kinsfolk and
friendes' brought 'great terrour to the
people'.
   – Sir Humphrey Gilbert, Colonel of Munster
   (1569–71)

Bubbe

We Were More Wolf Than Human
(1980)

I was not yet ten when my father and I stood among an utterly silent crowd along South Circular Road and watched as the Brits left the barracks and marched to the docks. First came tanks, then armoured cars and then men carrying heavy equipment. Nobody shouted or jeered, there was a palpable sense of disbelief. When my father asked an Irishman did he remember when they arrived, the man touched his hat and said, 'Well that would be eight hundred years ago, it started with the Anglo-Normans. They said we needed to be civilized, sir. We were more wolf than human. I remember it as if it was yesterday.'

It was almost a curiosity to our Jewish community, as we were only one generation here, after all. Though we knew what it was like to live under a hostile gaze, so we could appreciate the moment. The soldiers marched to the docks and boarded ships, and the English were finally gone, from this part of the country anyway.

We hoped we'd still be tolerated here. As immigrants, all we wanted was stability.

Our family had come from Lithuania around the end of the 1860s. We were swept in a pogrom out of the east and boarded a boat for New York. We were conned by a greedy captain who docked the boat in Cork harbour and announced that it was New York. The duplicitous captain was eager to stuff the boat with as many starving native Irish people as he could. He had already got the full passage from us hapless Jews, and so he sent us off looking for Ellis Island.

Cork – New York! We didn't speak English or know the Roman alphabet. It sounded the same. Ay-vey, what a mistake!! To think of what we could have been.

My grandfather was a skilled tailor, and he quickly moved from the starving West to Dirty Dublin. Our family had a tailor's and a haberdashery shop on Clanbrassil Street and consistently married into the Dublin Jewish community, that is, until my youngest daughter, Esther, met Ignatius O Conaill. She was a decade older than him. Remember, a single woman in her thirties was an old maid in 1969. I was the *schnook* who urged her to go to that particular gathering, as I knew Paddy MacInespie. There was a wild party bristling with intellectuals like Paddy and beauties like his wife, Baby, and poor Esther wanted to be a painter and had studied in Paris for it; the foolish woman got pregnant with the worst *shikker* there. She could have closed her eyes and picked better. Bohemianism, Dublin style, never really worked.

Of course, she didn't see him for another few months, but when she found out, to our horror, that she was with child, she had to go looking for him. He was staying with Paddy and Baby, and they were only too eager to get rid of him as they had a new baby girl, Deirdre, in the house themselves. When that lowlife *shegetz* heard he'd got her pregnant, he was about to bolt to England, as he swore he'd never set foot in a church again so how was he going to marry? Apparently, Baby laughed at him as she was whooshing him out the front door, and said, 'Sure, isn't she Jewish! Ye won't have to.' I insisted the children would have to be Jews otherwise I wouldn't have them live in the house. Well, he was only too glad of that, which was the only thing he had going for him in my view.

Ignatius O Conaill mustn't have believed his luck when he moved into a grand old four-storey house in the finest leafy part of Dublin 4, Pembroke Road, with his new old bride and me, her horrified mother.

There was no other way then, I suppose. No boat to England for an abortion. Or maybe poor Esther wanted to have a child and get married; he was a great charmer in his own right when he wanted to be. Could turn that charm on and off like a tap. She had always been a bit of a dreamer and a loner, Esther, never fully in this world at all, and though she could have been attractive, she mostly wore baggy heavy clothes and tied her hair back in a plain ponytail.

Cormac and then his brother, Fionn, were born and then my darling, Etáin, a few years later, so I had a house full of children that I loved and cared for and watched over and told stories to. Ignatius O Conaill had his own room and study upstairs, and when he wasn't yelling at us all he was gone to the pub so we could push him out of the story. I made sure the stories were of our family and not of that *yutzi*.

I was born in 1913 in 6 Greenville Terrace, delivered by Ada Shillman from Lithuania. I remember the smell of O'Keefes the knacker yard and the lamplighters with their strange flames on long poles going round in the evenings lighting each gas lamp on the street. The British Empire still held a quarter of the world and didn't want to let go. I remember the Black and Tans when I was a child, they were a savage lot sent from England. They had arrived in Dublin and the War of Independence was raging. We had stumbled into all this. In 1920, my family was just trying to survive and build up a life for ourselves. But we were irrevocably dragged into Irish history.

My uncle was a ragpicker and went around with his horse and cart to collect the wool clippings from all the clothes factories. Uncle Bethal must not have paid attention to the curfew that evening because the Black and Tans caught him leading his horse and cart home over a bridge on the Liffey and shot him in the face.

The burial society announced the death in the early-morning service in the synagogue, and we sat shivah in our little house, eating hard-boiled eggs and bagels. All the community joined us for this week and shook their heads over the fact that Bethal had escaped the pogroms in Lithuania to come to Dublin to be shot in cold blood by some *meshugge* soldier from England who had come to Ireland to keep fighting after World War I was over.

I was the youngest. My brothers' friends were always over at our house or outside on the street, Bimbo and Ucky, and Lubs and Jabella, oh, and Gluer and Saps. Everyone came to pay their respects, even the native Irish. So different from the Irish wakes, they told us. We were a different lot, but tolerated. All of the parents never took holidays; they never drank or went out to theatres or picture houses. They solidly worked all their lives so we would have opportunities. It wasn't even a sacrifice for them. It was the stuff of life. So Ignatius O Conaill was not going to impede our progress in this, our chosen land.

435

Sad Wee Shadow

We did everyone's washing but didn't wash ourselves. Once a month we were allowed to take a bath. Teresa always got in first and I think everyone let her because it was she telling us the stories and we'd have been lost without her. I was last in and so the water was dirty and cold and there were black dots floating on the top. I scooped one up in the palm of my hand and saw tiny legs. I jumped out of the bath as fast as shite from a goose. There was drowned lice floating on the water.

I told the other girls when we were allowed our hour talk at 7 pm. They all went quiet and looked away in shame.

'Lucky lice,' Teresa said. 'They could escape and I can't.'

'Arra will ye stop banging on about escaping. Either do it or don't,' another one called Bridget said. Teresa bristled, and I thought there'd be a fight, but she just held her hands up and we saw the scars on her palms. She'd tried to get out a while back – dragged a chair to the wall and scrambled up to the top. There was glass stuck in the top and her hands were shredded before she fell.

'Do ye think yer Jesus with them holes in yer hands?' Bridget snapped at her. She had a fierce temper on her, and she and Teresa seemed to be vying for who was our secret boss. Bridget once growled at me when I got near her. Her own hands were red and burned because it was her job to put the steaming hot sheets in the mangle.

It's that feeling I got when I slept. Something outside. A bird making frozen circles in the sky. Watching us. We slept in rows and there were windows way up at the top of the walls. So high we couldn't look out and still they had bars on them. At nights I'd sense a dark feathered something gathering, pressing against the glass in a stifled noise. Then the glass shuddered, and it was gone. Back up till it was a watching speck.

I followed Teresa around. One day she'd forgive me. She needed to get up to use the toilet at night. There was always a nun on guard. They took it in turns to sleep on a big chair by the door. Like a crow crouched.

The sister scoffed, 'There you go, Teresa, with your sad wee shadow.'

I looked on the floor to see it but then realized it was me.

Deirdre

Black Armbands
(1981)

We never talked about what happened to the family in Tyrone. Quickly, I had learned that people got especially agitated when I said the shooters had paint on their shoes and a purple ring like the policeman at the station. So I shut up and let it be. Mary got Orla talking again, but she said she didn't remember anything. My granddad pottered about the house doing jobs and chores and not speaking much. We were far away in Dublin from the Troubles of Northern Ireland. But my dad was a still a Tyrone man – he made us wear black armbands when the hunger strikers died.

Orla and I were walking through the housing estate to school and our friends were laughing at our armbands.

'What's that for?' one said.

'Bobby Sands died last night.'

'The hunger striker?'

'Yes.'

'What's that to do with you? Is your dad in the 'Ra?'

'No.'

'My dad said he was.'

'He's not!'

'My dad said they're just as bad as the Brits.'

'They're not.'

Orla silently slipped off her armband and put it in her pocket as we got to school. I made it through to lunchtime but ripped it off before I went into the yard and was pestered. When I came back in my teacher looked immediately at my arm.

'Why did you take your armband off?' she asked in her strong Kerry accent. I squirmed around and the class started giggling, relishing my interrogation.

'My Dad ...'

'It would do you well in life to have the courage of your convictions.' She looked at me over her glasses. 'An empty sack does not stand.'

435

Under Thy Protection

O Mary, conceived without sin, wishing this day to place myself under Thy protection, I choose Thee for my patroness, my advocate, my mistress and my Mother.

I became a Child of Mary and the nuns gave me a blue ribbon with a miraculous medal on it to wear. It made me feel special.

'So this poor wee craytur's a Child of Mary now,' Teresa said, as I prayed loudly and proudly.

'It's deadly,' I said. 'I feel I have a mother.'

'You never met your mother, did you?' Big Bridget asked. I knew she only talked to me to annoy Teresa.

'No, I was here since I was a baby. My name was 435. Until Teresa called me Bright.' As I fingered the medal, I continued the prayer I was taught to start every morning with.

My Queen and my Mother, I offer myself entirely to Thee. And to show my devotion to Thee, I offer Thee this day, my eyes, my ears, my mouth, my heart, my whole being, without reserve. Wherefore, good Mother, keep me and guard me as Thy property and possession. Amen.

I felt different or something.

'Child of Grace,' Teresa scoffed. 'A real mother wouldn't want you as property and possession.'

'Leave her alone, will ya? Yer only fecking jealous,' sneered Big Bridget as we made our beds, ready for the day's work. 'Let her have her blue ribbon. The eejit has never even been outside these walls.'

'A real mother would have come and got her.'

'Like you went and got yer babies?' Big Bridget snapped. Teresa sucked her lips in and I thought she was going to hit her a wallop, but Big Bridget was a tough one and she stood her ground. Word was that Big Bridget was meant to go to jail but the Guards gave her to the nuns instead. She had been furious because jail would have an end and this place didn't. We would all die here.

'Did you ever read the Bible?' Teresa wound her grey-blonde hair up in a bun. 'There's not much about mercy there. Read Exodus 21:7, *And if a man sells his daughter as a servant, she is not to go free as the menservants do.*'

'Are you not a Catholic?' I asked, watching warily as she approached Bridget.

'Being a Catholic is a condition not a religion.' Teresa stood face to face with Big Bridget.

'Wind yer neck in,' Big Bridget curled her upper lip at the corner.

I was smiling, this was all about me. I stroked the blue ribbon and said a wee extra prayer to Mother Mary.

Fionn

Sing Your Rann Now, Little Man
(1983)

Ignatius, my father, could not walk by a Catholic Church without his face contorting and his shoulders folding in. Ashamed of his schooling, he avoided any subject about either his family life or his time in St Joseph's Industrial School. He never told me anything personal about himself, but spouted old stories and songs as if he could skip history and live in legend. My mother, Esther, had been widely travelled, but her cosmopolitan life abruptly stopped when she had us children. Cormac, my big brother, was bulling when Esther and I left the country. She was invited to show her paintings in Belgium. It was me who she decided to bring along. Not my father, not Bubbe, not Cormac and not little Etáin. It was her only exhibition since she left Paris, and it was set up by an old Parisian contact at the Irish College in Leuven.

While she set up the show, I plunged into the history of the place, as there was nothing I could do but read a history book on the town one of the Franciscan priests gave me. On the streets of Leuven I conjured the ghosts of the Irish nobility, some of the fleeing O'Neills and O'Donnells who had stayed on there, the poets who had no place under colonization, the exiled scholars. Refugees sick for home.

Not many came, but I was happy enough to see all her paintings displayed in a room. She could not bear being looked at, but she always longed for others to be moved by what she painted. This event let her feel that she was a true artist, belonging to the great family of artists of the world. In truth, she was trapped in an unhappy marriage with three young children whom she felt detached from, and she furtively poured her first gin after she brushed her teeth every morning. I knew she kept the rectangular green bottle in the bathroom medicine cabinet. She told me that no one took her seriously as a lady artist anyway; women were strictly relegated to being either beautiful muses or practical supportive artist's wives. Every family has their tragic myths, the families that were never made, the families we became because of their non-happenings. She should have never returned to Ireland after her heartbreak. She should have stuck it out in Paris. I agreed with her absolutely, though not without reservations, because then Cormac, Etáin and I would not exist.

Once free from Ireland, she and I grew extra close for the few late summer weeks.

'I found out that this town was a refuge for the scattering of the Irish people,' I said, as we sat at an outside table in a café on a lovely square. Me drinking a coke and she a gin and tonic. 'Leuven had been one of the many Irish colleges set up after the Penal Laws were imposed on Ireland and it was impossible for Irish natives to get an education in their own land. You know they had a head tax? They'd pay for bags of heads to be delivered to put on spikes around Dublin as warnings.'

'I'm glad you're reading that book,' Esther smiled, lightly pushing my hair out of my eyes.

'I really like history,' I glanced around at the old square. 'Maybe I could become a historian like Uncle Paddy.'

'He's not your real uncle.' She took the lemon from my coke and squeezed a little into her drink.

'I know that,' I said, flicking my hair back. 'Though really he is.'

'Your real uncle Daniel lives in Israel. Maybe you should go over there to school. You talk of the sixteenth century. But your other people, my people, were eternally scattered when the Babylonians destroyed our temple in 586 BCE.'

'So this city was our Babylon.' She looked puzzled, so I added, 'For the Irish side of me.'

Esther lit a cigarette. I felt she almost offered me one, but I was a child. One day I'd smoke with her, I decided. 'We could move here, Esther. Let's get off the rock of doom. Bring Bubbe and Cormac and Etáin. This would be so much better for us.'

'You're Jewish, Fionn.'

'Even better to be on the continent then.'

'I'm not so sure. The Catholics and Protestants in Ireland are so busy hating each other they leave us alone. Remember what happened on this continent a few decades ago?'

'Bubbe is attached to Ireland.' I drained my coke; my feet were tapping on the ground and my fingers fiddling with the paper coasters. 'And so is Iggy.'

I was practising being a sophisticated continental by calling my parents by their first names. If I went back and did it in front of Cormac, he would be mad jealous I somehow got there before him. I didn't want to ruin the rare moment of connection by pointing out that my father would have to find a bridge here to tell his stories for pennies. 'Honestly, I don't know why, but she's born and bred there, I suppose. She's found her place.'

'Unlike us.' She stroked my hand. 'Bubbe used to tell a story of the only Irish-Jewish person to be killed in the Holocaust. She married a man from here and he took her away from Ireland. They went to Antwerp and France and were finally sent to Auschwitz. She should have stayed at home in Dublin.'

She ordered another drink and drained it quickly, and we walked back to our hotel. Esther told me that not one of her paintings had sold. She linked her arm in mine. The child holding up the wavering mother. In a small supermarket, she bought a little bottle of gin for the room.

'Why do you and Iggy stay married?' We were sitting up reading in our twin beds. I could see her profile in the dim light, her face was lovely and worn out. If I had money I would have sneaked out and bought all her paintings.

'I never loved him, and he never loved me.' She rose from her bed and placed the empty gin bottle by the window. There was a small gathering of them there. Then she returned and pulled the thin blankets over herself. 'I certainly never should have been so impulsive to get pregnant with his child and been obliged to marry him. I suppose I fell for his mystic schtick! I thought he was one of the old bards of Ireland.'

'You know there was a family of poets called the MacBrodins in Co. Clare. They had been poets for centuries.' I closed my book and had to get out of my bed to turn off the light, reaching my arms out to not bump into anything on the way back to bed. 'And when Cromwell's men came, they took the poet MacBrodin and the British soldiers threw him off the great cliffs of Clare to his death saying, "Sing your rann now, little man!"'

I don't know why I told her the story of the poet's murder. But in the years that followed I always pictured MacBrodin flying into the endless marbled Atlantic. The last outpost in Europe. An ending to be sure. Annihilation was built into the plan. That the English paid for bags of Irish heads was as grotesque as it was strategic. Could we convince Bubbe to move to Belgium, to this town, just like the Irish scholars, and nobles, and priests, away from our histories, and start again? What held us to Ireland?

I blinked anxiously awake as Esther snored. Even from my own bed I could smell the alcohol oozing out of her onto the starchy sheets. Her vaguely cubist paintings would remain on exhibition, unreviewed, with a smattering of curious people walking through rooms mostly unmoved by her efforts. She painted the old Jewish quarter of Dublin, which had disappeared by the time Cormac, Etáin and I had been born. The Prussian blue people were shadow strokes on the fractured street, as if a stone had been thrown into the mirror of the world and splintered the buildings. Though I was meant to be starting secondary school at Wesley College, my mother kept me another few weeks till the exhibition ended, and I revelled in knowing how Cormac would be beside himself. He'd make me pay one way or the other. Esther's efforts would then be folded up neatly and stored away, shipped back home to lie against her damp studio wall, and the larger culture would wipe its hands of her. The gin bottles collected by the hotel room window and, finally, the morning light pierced through them to cast a pale green shadow on the windowsill. Only then did I fall asleep.

And after that it was all that was left for her to paint. Empty bottles. A thousand still lifes, trying to capture the light moving through glass and the shadow cast, the nothingness of it, the everything of it. The slight green vibration of filtered summer dawn light. She told me that this was the last moment of hope for her painting career. And I knew that she meant for her life, this was all she was to get, nothing more given, the green glass as frozen liquid, as amorphous as herself.

The morning we left, when she was paying up downstairs, I cranked open the stiff old window and fecked the lot of them out the window into the small courtyard. I whispered to them as they fell.

'Sing your rann now, little man!'

Satisfyingly, they shattered far below.

435

The Little Golden Fly

'*I wish the walls of the palace would fall and the trees wither, for they are always the same!*' Teresa kept saying that over and over when she was ironing the sheets. '*I wish the walls of the palace would fall and the trees wither, for they are always the same!*'

'Shut yer gob,' Big Bridget hissed. But the rest of us glared at her because we knew Teresa might tell us the rest of the story soon.

Big Bridget pretended not to listen when we sat in the long dormitory in the evening. She lay on her bed staring at the high ceiling and the far up and away. Teresa pointed up at the windows and said,

'*Etáin went to the window in the East and unbarred it. She saw the sea outside it, wind-driven and white with foam, and a great wind blew the window open and caught Etáin and whirled her out of the palace, and she became again a little golden fly.*'

'I've seen flies,' Big Bridget said. 'They're never golden.'

Teresa ignored her as she walked between the beds. I hadn't realized she had got so rail thin. We all hated the food, and it was never enough, but Teresa was the only one who wouldn't eat everything put in front of her. Though when she was in full flight telling us a story even the old nun guarding us couldn't take her eyes off her. This old nun wasn't the worst of them.

'*She wandered and wandered through the World of the Bright Shadow till she came to the World of the Dark Shadow that is Earth, and she wandered there for a long time, scorched by the sun and beaten by the rain, till she came to a beautiful house where a king and queen were standing together. The king had a golden cup full of mead and he was giving it to the queen.*'

Teresa picked up the nun's cup of tea and the nun didn't even say anything. She wanted to hear the story too. Teresa looked sharply at the rim of the cup as if she could see the golden fly. '*Etáin lit on the edge of the cup, but the queen never saw the little golden fly, and she did not know that it slipped into the mead, and she drank it with the mead.*'

Then Teresa drank the nun's tea and even the old nun laughed. I was happy, thinking maybe we were all happy here. Perhaps Teresa wouldn't run away again. Teresa placed the cup back on the saucer and walked back towards Big Bridget.

'*Afterwards there was a child born to the queen – a strange beautiful child, and the queen called her Etáin. Everyone in the palace loved the child and tried to please her but nothing pleased her for long, and as she grew older and more beautiful they tried harder to please her but she was never contented.*' Teresa stood at the foot of Big Bridget's bed. A few of us giggled nervously. Big Bridget was never content. But then Teresa wasn't either. Teresa stopped talking. Big Bridget never took her eyes off her. We could hear the rattle of the wind on the tiny windows so high up. They stared at each other like that and I felt a shiver down my neck and arms. I put my fingers on my medal.

The old nun coughed loudly. Teresa turned and glided back to her own bed continuing the story: '*The queen was sad at heart because of this, and the sadness grew on her day by day and she began to think her child was of the Deathless Ones that bring with them too much joy or too much sorrow for mortals.*'

Dymphna

Tommo Gets Life

We'd be sitting down in the Jetfoil pub, talking about the hunger strikers, out of our trollies. Tommo and his gang scoffed at the paramilitaries, but the mystery of the dying hunger strikers had their respect. That they gave everything by taking nothing. That they did it for Ireland and who was Ireland but us, even though we knew we were nobodies. Tommo began to boast that he too had done his bit for Ireland, drove a van over the border to a funeral and got justice for a massacre. Made some bastards pay. But that was all swagger, really Tommo, that tosser, was robbin' and doing tie-ups all over the place, and one night I called him 'a souped-up Granny basher'. That was it for me teeth. I could never afford to get them done. I looked like an aul one from then.

He dedicated the last robbery to his brother Jo who got stabbed in Ballymun, and he said before he went out, 'Jo, I do this in your memory. Hand on gun, finger on trigger.'

All the others had looked at him like the bleedin' mentler he was. That's what everyone was doing – kidnappings. The paramilitaries and the ordinary criminals breaking into people's houses, bank managers, jewellers and the like, and taking their families hostage while the husband had to go out and get the money. Tommo said the banks were the real criminals and the jewellers were all Jews who ripped the Christians off for years anyway.

'Tha's why they bleedin' call it Jew-elerrie,' he'd say.

He had a way of making himself the big man, Robin fucking Hood. But he had us starved at home.

They took a jeweller hostage in Dalkey and tied his wife and kids up the Wicklow Mountains. The jeweller brought him to the shop and tried to talk Tommo out of taking all the stuff that was in for pawn. 'That belongs to the poor people of Dublin,' the jeweller said. 'Don't take that.'

Who did he think he was talking to? Tommo pistol whipped him for having the nerve to talk of the poor and him living in a big house in Dalkey. Tommo took it and all. Of course he did.

Meanwhile the eleven-year-old girl had got untied up the Wicklow Mountains and freed her mother and brother. The wee fella was only about five. The petrified family ran for help and the Guards surrounded the jeweller's. Tommo shot at them with his handgun. He hit one Guard in the shoulder. There were armed detectives there and they shot back. Tommo shot again and this time hit a Guard in the chest and killed him. Tommo knew the game was up, he didn't want to die. He came out with his hands up.

When I heard word he'd killed a Guard, I knew that I was free. He was given life and so was I.

Deirdre

My Mother, Baby

When I was thirteen, for some reason I too began to call my mother Baby. Everyone else did. Besides, it absolutely suited her. Not because she was infantile but because there was something new and fresh about her always.

She was nearly forty but I thought she was still beautiful. She never cut her hair short like all the other mothers, as if she alone, among women, had the licence to go over thirty with long hair in this country. She was tall and elegant and wore scarves stylishly around her neck. My Dad adored her, and he brought her breakfast in bed every morning. My father had got his PhD and was teaching in the university, in the History department in UCD. We had a happy home there in Monaloe Park. Our parents played golf in Bray and we had the run of the amusements while they were on the course. The nineteenth hole, as they called it, took up much of their time. Anyone of their generation who didn't crawl out of the '70s a complete alcoholic was doing well. Drink was as central in their lives as it was in all their friends'. We didn't pay much mind; we ran around in the dark eating endless packets of crisps and peanuts and drinking coke. Trawling around the amusements in Bray with my little sister Orla and the twins, we were blissfully unsupervised and free.

The big arguments in our house were not personal but political. Baby was repulsed by IRA violence and all men who took up arms. Dad was still a quiet supporter, though he winced every morning when we got up and turned on the radio and heard the familiar sentence,

'A man was shot dead outside his house last night ...'

Baby and Dad brought us girls to the theatre and we saw most of the Abbey plays. They read *The Irish Times* and embraced a new identity as Europeans now that we were in the EEC. Even though all our culture was coming from England and America. What did it mean to be suddenly European? Apart from now eating yoghurt for breakfast and drinking wine at the dinner? Opening the first bottle my parents felt so French, but as they were reaching for the second it would go all Irish again.

Cormac

There's No Fireside Like Your Own Fireside

Níl aon tinteán mar do thinteán féin.

'There's no fireside like your own fireside,' Dorothy would have said if she was Irish, as she clicked her ruby slippers.

There is a photo of my father Iggy from that time, very young, louche, long dark hair over his eyes, head cocked to the side. He had attitude – I'll give him that. A young James Dean, if James Dean had crawled from an undisclosed location out of the bog and spent a nebulous amount of time in an obscure institution that he would never divulge the name of. Mother is standing beside him. Older, slim, ethereal, her dark eyes as complicated as his. Her narrow intelligent face, her small hands holding a paperback, *The Third Policeman*, a gift he no doubt stole for her. That strikes me because she was an avid reader, but it was mostly French and Russian literature. *Le Rouge et le Noir* was her favourite book. I had it on my shelf, with her comments in the margins. I was proud she could read and write in French. He spoke Irish fluently, but what use was that? An entirely useless language that the Christian Brothers bet into us since independence and then wondered why we all hated being forced to learn it.

Lucky for Dorothy she had a way out of the Emerald City, but did I? Did I fuck!

Níl aon tinteán mar do thinteán féin.

This was one of the phrases from a sheet of expressions in school that we were to shove into our Irish essays to make them look good. I was great at this. Sure, it wasn't from the stones I licked it. The man that's full of *nohawns* will never have an empty hearth, as my father would say. My useless eejit of a father. Him and his fucking stories and expressions. Hiding behind them all like some diddly-eiddly stage Irishman. Oh, the Yanks loved him. He'd the gift of the gab to be sure to be sure. Swallowed the Blarney Stone like the snake he was and it sticking in his craw. All of Uncle Paddy's brothers who came back from America on visits would trot him out and look wistfully at him. He was a queer one alright, the genuine article. But was he fuck?

I had worshipped my father as a child. And he took Fionn and me around with him quite a bit. His two sons. Made him look like he had something. But it wasn't until later that I realized he never saw us. Never looked at us. Never touched us. People would pat me on the head when I was a lad and tell me that my father was a great storyteller and a credit to the nation. I began to hate the fucker. He told me stories alright. Told us all stories, but that was all he did. He never left me to school, went to my rugby matches, never did anything.

He was a bollox.

My mother was way out of my father's league, of that I had no doubt. Strangely, at first everyone was relieved she was moving past the love of her life. They married quickly, and I arrived five months after their wedding. Iggy had happily married in a synagogue as he hated his own religion, and he wore a yarmulke at any chance. He was more insistent that we be raised Jewish than my mother, and for that alone my grandmother Bubbe put up with him and let him into the house. Iggy never introduced us to any family except his sister

Mary, a housekeeper for Baby's mother and father. This certainly didn't endear me to him, seeing as his family were all servants or culchies. He inserted me into my mother's uterus and moved into our house on leafy, exclusive Pembroke Road, Dublin 4. The jammy bastard had fallen on his feet alright.

My aunts would come from New York and my uncle from Israel, and they would look at my father as entertainment. They were horrified that he had no job, no income, but he would dance around them and use his expressions and *cúpla focal*: some kind of demented stage Paddy.

Poor fucking useless dowdy Esther, though I preferred her – as he was a monster, frankly – she was useless as a mother.

It was my granny Bubbe who did most of the caring for us when we were babies, and it was Bubbe we went to for hugs and kisses and love.

Bubbe had had three children, but only one of them stayed in Ireland. My mother, Esther, never really ventured out of the house or out of her studio from among her paints. Bubbe's real passion was for us, her grandchildren.

Níl aon tinteán mar do thinteán féin.

Bubbe sent me in one Saturday morning to talk to my mother. 'The Old Dear', as we called her, cos that's what our friends had taken to calling theirs, was in her studio painting. Trying to find the right blue. There were green bottles and clear bottles and jars on a table. She had a green gin bottle hidden behind her sketchbooks. Who did she think she was hiding that from? She was way older than the Old Man.

Jesus, they were ill-suited. She, the youngest of a good Dublin 4 Jewish family, he, a bogger from the arse end of Meath who didn't even get a secondary education and ponced around the bars of Dublin like some kind of journeyman poet. This schtick that he carried on with couldn't be further from the truth: the only journey he made was from Dublin 4 to the Waterloo Bar on Baggot St.

Unless he ran out of money for drink. Then he'd stand on Essex Bridge and recite stories and poems for change. We were mortified when we found this out. He'd called himself Zozimus, after some wanker a hundred years ago who used to do the same. He didn't even come up with the idea himself.

The Old Dear wasn't really of this world. She was away, far away, on Planet Gin. Nearly fifty, and her hair grey and long, tied in a messy bun with bits sticking out of it. The studio was ice cold, so she wore woolly sweaters and two pairs of trousers tucked into her furry boots. She was not one for glamour, the Old Dear.

I stood in her studio making demands and trying not to look too hard at the state of her. I said to her, 'If I'm going to go through the charade of making my bar mitzvah, then you'll have to have a party where I make as much money as my mates make from their confirmations.'

'Bubbe and I will bring you to the temple. Sure what do you want a party for?' She lit a cigarette and inhaled sharply. 'These big bar mitzvah parties are a new American import.'

Rather than looking at the set of her, I strolled around the studio inspecting her paintings. They were gloomy, oil on canvas – still lifes of light moving through empty bottles with watery shadows. Very well executed, mind you. I'll give the daft old bat that.

'For fuck's sake, Mother, I don't even believe in God. I'm not doing it without the party, and the money,' I said, poking my finger into a blob of oil paint and smelling it. And she sighed, brushing her hand through her grey hair and streaking it with blue paint in the process.

'It would kill Bubbe if you didn't do it. OK. I suppose. Sure, what harm? Ask your father.'

'What does he have to do with it? He's not a Jew. And I don't want all his cronies hanging around my friends. He only knows drunks and terrorists.'

'Are you referring to the MacInespies?' She smiled a little. 'I actually like them.'

'Fine, he can ask Uncle Paddy and their brood. That's it. I control the guest list myself.'

'Talk to your father. You can fight it out with each other.' She stubbed her cigarette out half done in an overflowing ashtray. 'You're more like him than you know.'

'And just remember I'm doing this for the money. I'm not listening to a load of codswallop from that demented old rabbi either.' I took her half-smoked cigarette and stuck it in my pocket.

'You do sound like your father.' She put her sleeves over her hands in the cold studio.

'Is that all you can say to me?'

The Old Dear narrowed her eyes as if to focus on me but lost interest and turned back towards her 12,345th painting of empty bottles. She had emptied most of them herself, no doubt.

'Bubbe knows the rabbi,' she said as I left. 'She'll tell you what you have to learn for temple. Cormac, you are clever, but don't think you know everything. You don't care about this now, but you will see its value in years to come. *Gay ga zinta hate.*'

She and Bubbe sometimes spoke in sad old dead Yiddish. Just like Irish, it was dying noiselessly as a drowning child, the odd phrase popping up like the last frantic hand stuck out of the water before the long silence.

I walked through the narrow, overgrown garden from her studio back to the house. We had a great big kitchen, and since the fire was there it was usually the warmest room where everyone gathered. We even had the TV in there.

The Old Man sat in his big overcoat, glued to the news of all the sit-ins in the factories. All over the country the factories were closing and people were taking them over and going on hunger strike to try and get the government to nationalize them and run them.

'Pathetic,' I said, as I stood behind him. 'Why would you try so hard to keep a shitty job as the lowest pawn in the capitalist system?'

'What would you know about work?' the Old Man glowered. 'You've been raised in privilege and mollycoddled by yer granny. Raised as a little tin god. These people were dragged from farms into factories and now they're a class no longer needed. They know they've been thrown away. It's a last stand. The last gasp of trade unionism. It's happening all over Europe. This is the end of the Industrial Revolution, son. And as shite as that was, who knows what's to come? Your generation will wake up to that soon. Humanity has overshot itself on this planet and is self-destructing. And what are they going to do with this whole class who are no longer any use? Do they have gas chambers in the Phoenix Park for them? Maybe they can con them into a new pope's visit and just round them up and exterminate them?'

'Save it for your mates at the Waterloo,' I yawned. 'Where's Fionn?'

'How the fuck should I know?' he growled, and stayed watching the news.

'I don't see why you are in such solidarity with the working classes,' I said to him. 'You never worked a day in your life.'

He raised both his hands to show me. The bent and twisted fingers were always his excuse for everything. The priests had destroyed his hands. Convenient, that – allowed him to mullock around the high ground all his life.

'As far as I can tell it was the solid useful work of Bubbe's family that got us this house. And you've seen to it that that's all we have now.' I took the half cigarette out of my pocket and used his matches to light it. 'By the way, I'm going to have a bar mitzvah party in the house here in a month. Before my thirteenth birthday. You can invite Uncle Paddy and the MacInespies. But none of the other tossers you know. Bubbe will pay for it.'

The feckless old cruster brightened up at the notion of all the free booze supplied by Bubbe and a chance to drag in all the reprobates he called friends.

'Don't you be so cheeky. You're lucky I didn't beat you like my father beat me. I left ye alone. Never forget that, you posh little twat. And I'm the man of the fucking house now and not that auld hag in there singeing her shins off the Superser. As it happens, it's my thirtieth birthday so we'll have a double celebration.'

'Way to make it all about you,' I took a long drag on my cigarette. 'Anyone who comes has to give me money like a confirmation. Remind them.'

I found Fionn and said, 'They are the most mismatched couple on this cold, third-world island of mismatches and dispatches and muck wretches and fag packets.'

'So are you having a party?' Fionn asked.

'Fuck it, I suppose so.'

The worst of it, as I said before, was that our house was a beautiful Georgian in Dublin 4 and we had no money. Oh yes indeed there's no *tinteán* like our own *tinteáns*, and the fireplaces were all the heat we got. Except for the Superser Bubbe hogged. But who could begrudge her that bit of heat?

Dymphna

Thirsty Ghosts

St Teresa's Gardens. It had a lovely ring to it – St Teresa's Gardens. I can't describe the brilliant feeling when the keys turned in the door for the first time. It was February, the very night that the IRA stole the horse Shergar. When the corporation gave me that flat, I thought me troubles were over. It meant that much. It was a good omen cos of the name of the place, like. St Teresa's Gardens. In me own demented head I thought it was Teresa back at the Laundry being me guardian angel. As if she had the power. But sure, me head was addled anyway. After a few years on them streets, I'd lost all me good looks and me nose was battered in that many times it was crooked on me face, and some of me teeth were knocked out at the side so there was no more smiling for me. There was nothing to do but look at me face as a map of how far I'd come.

With the two older ones behind me, and taking wee Micko by the hand, we walked into the flat and found it spotless and empty. There was a spider in the corner of one of the bedrooms and Conn wanted to kill it, but I wouldn't let him.

'We won't kill her,' I insisted. 'Teresa, me friend, said to never kill a spider.'

I was feeling that queenly, didn't I scoop her up in me palms and feck her out the window as if I was doing her a favour? Instead, I was throwing her out into the cold away from her web that she had worked hard for. Me eight-year-old daughter, Tapioca, was hanging outside over the balcony shouting.

'There's a ship down there, Mammy.'

'That's not a ship,' I told her. 'That's the pram shed.'

'But it has windows like a ship, Mammy.'

There was no heating or immersion, and we had to light a fire to get any hot water. I didn't have much in the way of furniture, but the good people down at the St Vincent de Paul gave me mattresses and a table. Me flat in St Teresa's Gardens – it was the first place in me life that was me own. I was that determined to make a go of it and raise me kids decent. First night in, I prayed a thank-you prayer to the big white statue of St Teresa in the yard. Her beautiful face lost in concentration.

The only man who had ever been alright to me was me friend Zoz. After I had seen him at the funeral up North, I went to find him on the bridge out of curiosity. He was much friendlier to me away from all his family. I told him I had some stories too. Some told to me in the Laundry by Teresa. He never wanted anything from me except stories and listening. I was a good listener. I kept the radio on in the kitchen the whole time, day and night. For company, like. And the posh voices coming out of it like the fancy voices of me customers, but kinder men than that shower of wankers. Bodiless radio men who were only words, who couldn't touch me.

It was Zoz who told me about them heads in a bag. He was a great man for the history. He had an uncle who had told him everything, and Zoz never forgot anything he was told. The way he told history would still a whole pub, so it would. The Brits would demand a bag full of heads to put on the spikes around Dublin to show us Irish who's boss. Head money, it was called. They'd pay people to collect them heads. One English colonel fella named Gilbert would spike the heads of whole villages he took over and make the people walk up the path to bow to him with the heads of their family and friends on all sides. Zoz called it ugly theatre.

I sometimes dreamed of them all talking to each other, chatting from spike to spike. As if they didn't understand they were only heads, like. In anyways, the Brits had been chased out but there was still plenty willing to collect heads as far as I could see. And if you listened close like, just after rain, somewhere inside the grimy guts of the gloom of nights, you could hear the heads still whispering. Am I rabbiting on too much?

Thirsty ghosts, Zoz said they were.

Thirsty ghosts.

'Dymphna, me auld flower,' Zoz would say. 'You are the genuine article.'

But I couldn't pretend to be anything. I was a headcase meself. A warning.

Zoz convinced me to get a telly for the sitting room. At first I didn't want to, as there was only one electrical socket in the whole flat and that was used for the heater when I couldn't be bothered with the fire. But Zoz brought me a cube plug with a few sockets. I didn't know there was such a thing. I traipsed down to the canal again for a few nights so I could get a colour telly. With Tommo in jail, I could keep all the money and no one would touch me on account of him. He was still feared, even locked up. I'm glad I did, an' all. Sure it was only brilliant having a telly of me own. There were only two channels, RTÉ 1 and RTÉ 2, but fuck it, I got to choose what to watch.

Not all of it was good though. These days they were banging on all the time on the telly and the radio about either Shergar, the missing horse, or the rights of the unborn child. It made me want to puke me ring up.

The rights of the unborn child. What were they like?

And what about when they are born? They stop giving a fuck then. Was that it? I just couldn't make sense out of them holy rollers.

The peace didn't last. I wasn't a month moved in here when yer man Madser showed up. I only opened the door because I thought it was me friend Zoz. Madser had met Tommo inside and Tommo said I was to be looked after. Me heart sank like a shopping trolley in the canal.

I suppose I put up with Madser as I was dossing about all day with my three babies, but they drove me up the walls too. I didn't really know what I was supposed to do with them. Them nuns didn't teach me much.

'But Dymphna, you ungrateful slag,' Sharon, me auld comrade in arms, would say when she saw me down by the canal, 'you did get a flat off the Corpo on account of them little bastards, didn't you?'

'True dat,' I agreed.

'An' you don't have to work anymore really. Only when you want something extra. You can pick and choose your nights these days.'

Could I fuck?

In anyways, I wasn't long in the door of me brand-new flat when that mad yoke Madser came knocking. He came with his cough mixtures, asthma powders, bricks of hash and half his face and all his neck swamped in a blister from a fight in the chipper where an Italian fucker threw a pan of hot oil at him to stop him dealing on the premises. I let him kip for a bit on the sofa until he became a permanent fixture.

'I'm not allowed have ye here all the time.' I told him. 'I got the flat for me and the snappers.'

'Yer wreckin' me head,' Madser said. And didn't budge.

Madser came and went without warning so I got used to it, and there wasn't much I could do about him if he was a friend of Tommo's. In me dreams the heads on spikes would start their chatter. The poor crayturs never knew they were beyond help. Thirsty ghosts gagging for a drink.

The radio and telly were me only company – a break from the screaming kids – but the nights got long and lonely. Zoz had a family by the canal so I didn't see him but once a week, unless I went all the way to the Liffey to the bridge where he plied his trade. That's why I let Madser in. He was a bit of a laugh, so he was. He'd be telling me all his stories with his eyes swirling around in his head. Both eyes goin' in different directions at the same time. And I thought he'd keep all the other headbangers away. Like I say, Madser was his name.

He gave me some smack one night.

'Ah here!' I says to meself. 'This is the business.'

I'd never felt that good before. I felt pure. It was lovely. I was lovely. Took me back to them innocent days when I was a young one down by the River Dodder with me feet stuck in it and making up poems. To a time where I was the Little Poet, as the Laundry girls called me. But I couldn't hear the heads on the spikes anymore. Everything just dissolved. I could feel the whole pulse of Dublin throb through me as if the streets were veins and I was its blood.

I became the sea. Me breath the waves.

That kind of feeling of everything being in its proper place.

Pure holy heaven of nothingness.

435

Five Other Fucking Bridgets!

Big Bridget was a tall strapping girl with broad shoulders. Her hair was always messy and she had a giant birthmark on the side of her face like a map of somewhere I would never visit. She let it be known she wasn't in here because she had a baby or been with a man. The courts had put her in for beating up her brother-in-law who had hit her sister a wallop in the kitchen in front of her. I had never had a chance to have a family, but I had seen two sisters put in the Industrial School as small children. They'd looked after each other until the nuns separated them. The nuns steered clear of Big Bridget, and it was interesting to see them a little afraid. I'd never imagined nuns felt fear like humans. We were sitting in rows eating our cabbage soup with a bit of stale bread when Mother Michael walked by and made some remark to Big Bridget. They were always giving out to her.

'My name is not Bridget,' she yelled in a rage at Mother Michael. She was holding a blunt butter knife in her red fists. 'My fucking name is Nessa. Youse have no right to take me name as well as me whole life. If I kill one of youse, they'll send me to prison. At least I'll get a release date. The court had no business to shove me in here.'

'Bridget,' Mother Michael said. 'Put down that knife. This was in your best interests.'

'There are five other fucking Bridgets in here. I'm Nessa. That's what you will call me.'

And just like that one of us got her real name back. At night the old nun on guard had dozed off and Teresa went to Nessa's bed. I heard her whisper.

'My name is Maeve not Teresa,' Teresa said. 'You know Nessa was once called Assa, which meant the gentle one. She was beautiful and intelligent and loved to learn. She was always surrounded by twelve teachers who taught and protected her.'

'Fuck off, you stupid cow.' Nessa kicked her leg under the covers at her. 'Go tell your stupid stories to the rest of them eejits.'

Teresa giggled, as if delighted by her belligerence. Nothing could stop Teresa from a story, so she went on. I hadn't heard this one, so I was all ears.

'This creepy druid Cathbad wanted to have her and so he murdered her twelve teachers. She was so horrified that she assembled a troop of warriors and set out to get vengeance. She never had a sword in her hand before but now she was angry and called herself Nessa. That name means ungentle.'

'The ungentle?' Nessa sounded like she was smiling. The old nun stirred, uncrossing her legs on the chair. She groaned. Her head lolling to the side and her mouth open as if she was dead. I hoped she wouldn't wake up. It was completely forbidden to get into anyone else's bed. 'You're not the only fecking storyteller here. Your dozy little shadow can tell them too.'

'What?' Teresa sounded surprised. I cringed.

'She tells them to herself. Like a loony. I have ta work beside her and it's all she does, mutter away. Same stories that you tell. She knows them all.'

In the dark my eyes adjusted. Pretending to be asleep, I saw Teresa kiss Nessa on the mouth and Nessa hold her head in her hands and kiss back. That was it. I jumped out of me bed and the nun woke up like a shot. She didn't see Teresa was out of the bed. I stood in front of her.

'What's the matter, musha?' The old nun's veil was a bit off. It was strange to see she had some grey hair under there. I'd never once thought the nuns had hair. I didn't know what to say so I closed my eyes and began to say the story. As the nun stood up and guided me back to bed as if I was asleep I chanted the story:

'One day Etáin said the Queen's singer had no songs worth listening to and she began to sing one of her own songs; as she sang, the Queen looked into her eyes and knew that Etáin was no child of hers, and when she knew it she bowed herself in her seat and died.'

Teresa had slipped out of Nessa's bed and crawled under my bed. I kept saying the story to give her time.

'The king said Etáin brought ill luck and he sent her away to live in a little hut of woven branches in a forest where only shepherds and simple people came to her and brought her food.'

'This is your doing! The poor craytur is addled with all your stories,' the nun hissed at Teresa now back in her bed.

Teresa was staring at me in the dim light. Her mouth had fallen open in shock to hear me tell one of her stories.

'Do you know what happened to her in the forest?' Her forehead creased and her eyes narrowed.

I raised my voice a little and hoped I'd remembered it word for word.

'She grew every day more beautiful and walked under the great trees in the forest and sang her own songs. One day the King of all Ireland came riding by. His name was Eochy, and he was young and beautiful and strong. When he saw Etáin he said:

' "No woman in the world is beautiful after this one!" And he got down from his horse and came to Etáin. She was sitting outside the little

hut and combing her hair in the sunshine, and her hair was like fine gold and very long.

' "What is your name?" said the king, "and what man is your father?"
' "Etáin is my name," said she, "and a king is my father." '

The nun tut-tutted and glared at Teresa, 'You've filled this poor child's head with your nonsense. She's like a little parrot.'

'My name is Maeve, not Teresa. And she's not a parrot. That's how the stories are passed down.'

'Wait, that's stupid, how come she was sent by a king and another king came to her?' Nessa was sitting up in her bed as others began to stir with the commotion. 'How many feckin' kings were running about the place in the olden days?'

'Ireland was split up into lots of clans. Like Scotland,' Teresa said, over me to Nessa. 'Everyone got to rule their own part.'

'Now you're all at it. You think yer giving lectures. This place is infested with *splaincíns*.' The old nun shook her head and went back to her chair. 'Don't be getting ideas above yer station. Just be grateful that we give ye all a home. No one else would have ye. Ye are the rubbish of Ireland.'

I lay down triumphant. Teresa was staring at me from her own bed. Her pale face glowing in the dark like a light on a lighthouse. I couldn't have her love Nessa in case they'd run off together. Nessa seemed like a runner. And I wasn't sure the nuns would run after her.

'See, I told you,' Nessa said loudly from her bed. The nun shushed her. The women were all shifting and groaning to be woken up.

'Shut up,' someone shouted. I raised my voice.

' "It is wrong," said Eochy, "that your beauty should be shut in this forest, come with me and you shall be the High Queen of Ireland."

'Then Etáin looked at Eochy, and it seemed to her that she had known him always. She said, "I have waited here for you and no other. Take me into your house, High King." '

The old nun went and growled at me, 'You are a Child of Mary! Behave! This is very unlike you.' The thought of losing my blue ribbon put an end to my outburst.

Nessa swung her hairy legs out and sat on the side of her bed. She looked straight at me.

'What was yer name before you came in here?'

'When I came in here I was called Bridget, but Teresa called me Bright for short and it stuck.'

'Before, ya eejit,' Nessa scoffed, 'ya weren't born here.'

'They told me I came from a harlot. I was in the Industrial School beside here since I was a baby.'

'So them fucking nuns reared you like a farm animal to work for them. And what was your name at the school?'

'435.'

Nessa snorted, 'Jaysus, nuff said. OK, we'll stick with Bright then.'

And that was how Maeve and Nessa got their names back and I stayed as Bright. Though in me own head I was always 435.

Deirdre

A Crap in the Bidet

Nobody but the very rich went out foreign on holidays. Though some of our friends were starting to go on packages to Spain, it was rare to leave Ireland for leisure. Our holidays were in a cottage in Wexford that Dad bought from money they got when they sold the farm and house in Tyrone. Dad spent a lot of downtime there fixing it up. He suddenly showed an aptitude for DIY and completely refurbished the place, putting in an indoor toilet and shower. It even had a bidet, or an arse-washer, as dad called it. That was the new trend in bathrooms. First it was indoor toilets, now it was bidets. We had to pronounce it 'bee-day', not 'bid-et'. That's because we were European now. Though I suspect the Irish never started washing their arses. Frequently, I'd go to parties where there was one installed and invariably someone would crap in it by mistake.

The Sunny Southeast, they called it. In truth, we sat many an Easter with a fire on and the rain streaking the windows, our only escape the Courtown Amusements, where I would stand obsessed in front of the penny falls machine and its broken promises.

This particular August was boiling, though. The twins were ten years old and brown as berries, on the beaches till all hours of the morning. It was light to almost 11 pm. My sister and I hung out in the local chipper playing Space Invaders. We still had to get dressed up for Mass each Sunday, and I protested all the way.

'Why do we go to Mass? It's boring.'

My brothers were on my side for once.

'We just do,' Dad said. And Baby, always in the passenger seat, nodded in agreement.

'I'm a schoolteacher, Deirdre. And last time I checked UCD was a Catholic university. Your father and I have a reputation in the parish. We have to go to Mass.'

'But we're not in Dublin now!'

'Nobody would know,' Orla echoed.

'Pleeeeaase!' the boys implored.

'We just do. That's who we are,' Dad said.

'Or what you are,' I said sulkily.

Baby turned to me with eyes of fire.

We were on a long Sunday drive through the countryside. But we still had to go to Mass. We pulled into the church in Fethard and reluctantly dragged ourselves into the boredom of the ritual. Baby had been inspired by the women's movement in the 1970s. But at the time she was working and had kids, so she didn't have time to get personally involved. Now we were getting older she vowed to do something meaningful. First, she tried to get us to write to the bishop and demand that we be allowed to be altar girls. Only boys were allowed on the altar. She even drafted the letter for us, but my sister and I were aghast. We didn't want to go through the whole rigmarole and be dragged into the church for every shenanigan, christenings and all. Her generation wanted women to be allowed to participate in the Church; our generation didn't want the Church at all.

The boys craned to see what was on the altar. We couldn't see it properly until we went up to get communion. There was a woven cradle with a wee baby doll inside it. Her plastic arms were sticking up and a sign on the cradle read: *Thou Shalt Not Kill.*

Baby shifted in her seat as Father Fortune ranted and raved at us all about the amendment that the Catholic Church was trying to put into the constitution, placing the life of a foetus on the same legal scale as the life of the mother. Father Fortune said that Ireland had gone to the dogs and the young people were turning from the Church in droves and sinning. Next there would be legal contraceptives and, shock—horror, divorce.

Baby and Dad kept looking at each other. I could see Baby clutch the wooden pew in front of her as if she was about to get physically sick. I felt smug. As we left the church the altar boys blocked every exit and handed us leaflets instructing us to vote for the amendment.

Baby refused to take a leaflet, though my father did, more out of politeness.

In the car she put her head in her hands and said, 'OK, for your sake, girls. We've got to fight this bloody amendment. What they really don't like with all their talk of liberalism is the few tiny steps women have taken towards equality in this country. And I mean tiny.'

'Why does Daddy always drive?' Nevan piped up.

My father put his hand on his neck and stroked it. He started the car and drove back to the cottage for the Sunday roast.

I announced that I was becoming a vegetarian. Baby nearly threw a whole pot of spuds at me. She poured herself and Dad a gin and tonic. Dad raised his eyebrows and said to her, 'That's her prerogative. You're not the only one allowed to make proclamations around here. Sure, she's her mother's daughter.'

'Her daddy's girl more like,' Baby said. But she served me a plate with only spuds and cabbage.

Dymphna

Shergar, the Wonder Horse

Madser would ride me sometimes, but I'd only do it if I got paid for it, even if it was in smack. That was me rule. Get paid for it. I don't know why we were designed this way. Why men crave sex but it's mostly awful for women. Sandra said she enjoyed it from time to time, but I didn't. If most of the time it's boring and hurts like that and makes me feel like puking me guts up, then at least I had to get something for it, right? I didn't have any friends in the flats. They weren't the worst, but I was. Me kids were around the other women's houses most of the time when I'd forget to get them dinner. They never let their lot come over to me. I was fine with that, so I was. They were always fighting over the washing lines in the yard, and I had a clothes horse on me balcony for me bits and pieces. Other women thought I was the lowest of the low, but they got compensation in other ways, their rent was paid for, or their clothes, their kids were supported. What's the difference if it's one man or many? It's still the currency, right? And it wasn't just the women in the flats. I'd be walking down

Grafton Street and seeing the posh women's lips curl up if they noticed me, but I kept me head as high as me heels. That lot were gliding around Switzers, with their silky shampooed hair and their giant shopping bags, like long-necked white swans on the canals and their husbands off working.

We're all whores at heart, ladies.

The smack seemed like a bargain. One bag cost the same as a few pints and felt better. At first, I was spending forty or fifty quid a week, but soon I was spending more than a hundred a day. So I had to go out when the kids were asleep. Even then I was sick half the time. But I couldn't even think of doing without it.

It was as if it happened overnight. As I walked up the stairs to me flat, I had to step over young ones, as young as twelve, with little ponytails, bows in their hair and sparkly pink leggings, sticking needles in their arms. The place was flooded with gear. Seems like everyone was on it. That changed everything. Women were afraid to hang their washing out as the junkies stole anything that wasn't nailed down.

On the telly they cared more about the fucking kidnapped horse Shergar than they did about what was happening to all of us.

Shergar, the wonder horse, won every fucking Derby! Of course they cared. Did Ireland proud, so he did. The Aga Khan could have given him to America but chose Ireland, and wasn't the horse given a parade in his honour when he arrived in Kildare? I saw his picture in the papers surrounded by the fine Switzers swan ladies in stupid feathery hats at the races. He had one blue eye and a white stripe down his face. Oh, the shock of it when the IRA took him by gunpoint in the middle of the night. They demanded a ransom but couldn't prove he was alive. Couldn't exactly send a hoof in the post, could they? And a horse like that is hard to take care of if you're not a horsey sort of person. Zoz and Madser both reckoned he got injured and they had to shoot him. So every guard was out scouring the lovely green country looking for a dead horse. I tell ya, the IRA lost more support over that fucking horse than any human they kidnapped or shot in the previous ten years.

While they were looking for a dead horse, we were here.

St Teresa's Gardens.

Thirsty ghosts.

Cormac

This Man's Father Is My Father's Son

I had to listen to my father's stories even though I couldn't care less about all that nonsense fantasy about fairies and pookas and bulls and hags. Bubbe was a storyteller in her own right, but her stories were real to me. They were my history, not some peasant folktales – they were what made me and, crucially, they were true.

They were Dublin, whereas he was just some culchie with a family he never brought us near to, except Mary, some fat old housekeeper down the bog who wore her housecoat pinnie like some superhero costume. Irritatingly, she littered her speech with ridiculous Irish sayings, just like my father. I didn't like going there because it would allow Deirdre and Orla and their cretinous twin brothers to look down on us. They only lived in a housing estate in Monaloe Park, Cabinteely, full of culchie blow-ins, whereas we had Dublin pedigree. Our family resided in a true Georgian house in Dublin 4. So fuck that for a game of soldiers.

As if I'd ever want to claim that Mary yoke as a relation.

Bubbe was a queen; she ruled our house from the armchair in the small room off the kitchen. She sat with her cardigans pulled round her in front of the Superser heater. Around her scrawny neck she wore Hermès scarves pinned with a cameo brooch. A mink stole with the head and feet still on it was draped around her shoulders like a strange trophy.

Bubbe smoked her cigarettes in long enamel holders and kept them in a silver monogrammed case. She was a glorious, stationary creature and showered us with gifts from her huge black purse. Wracked with acute arthritis, she only really moved to have afternoon tea once a week at the Shelbourne Hotel. There in those salubrious surroundings, she would hold court with her coterie of old Jewish ladies, lamenting the decimation of the Jews in Dublin. Once there were ten thousand, now there were only about two thousand. There was no pogrom here, they just drifted away. My aunt and uncle had gone to New York and Israel respectively. She'd kvetch to them constantly. Poor Esther, her youngest daughter, had got up the pole with some chancer bogman who had installed himself in her beautiful house like a big cuckoo and proceeded to drink and gamble all the money away. No wonder she hated him. He was the antithesis of everything her family had built up and struggled for in this country.

Bubbe told me all the stories and would sigh dramatically for emphasis. I kept an eye on her ever-growing ash from the slender cigarette in her cigarette holder. I moved the glass ashtray back and forth when she spoke to catch it, otherwise she would end up covered. Her mink already had round burns on its fur and one on its skull. It was already dead, but a war was still being waged against its remains. I lifted a paw and scraped the claw lightly off the back of my hand. She was ten watching the Brits leave, and then the rumbling and bombing of the civil war followed. Many of the Jews were unemployed, and the young men in her family left.

'That's the good thing about the Jews,' my father Iggy would say. For if he caught Bubbe telling stories he would hang in the doorway and listen. Always the doorway; he was a threshold beast. 'They didn't get mired down in this country. They had sense.'

'There used to be thousands of us all, Little Saul.' Bubbe ignored my father. 'Now there aren't so many.' Little Saul, she called me. That was my middle name.

'Aye, they had cop on,' my father would say. She let him listen, and when I was a small child I was under the mistaken impression that they liked each other. In reality she didn't pay any mind to his blathering. He never told me any facts from his life, just pishogues and, worst of all, daft puzzles.

My brain wasn't logical enough for those puzzles, it was little Fionn who would figure them out.

'Brothers and sisters I have none, but this man's father is my father's son,' he said challengingly to me.

'What?' My head spun.

'Who is this man?' he demanded.

I learnt to ignore him and turn back to Bubbe. I was definitely her favourite.

'I've blessed him by giving him the blood of the Hebrew,' my father used to say when he was sitting on his barstool in the Waterloo pontificating. He took me and my brother out with him, maybe because my mother told him to, but all we did was sit in pubs and play cards with each other and try to shut out his booming voice.

Brothers and sisters I have none, but this man's father is my father's son.

The barmen loved him. The clientele of the Waterloo loved him. He seemed to have endless acquaintances that enjoyed drinking with him.

'The blood of the Hebrew,' the barman said. 'And what had your priest to say about that, Iggy?'

'I don't have a priest,' Ignatius said. 'I set them all free a long time ago. Yes, indeed, I've blessed all my children by giving them the blood of the Hebrew. To dilute the Celtic despair. For we've had a bad time of it on this land. We must have done something, for we were cursed by it. We saw the hag but turned from her into the safer, warmer arms of the Roman boy St Patrick and his opposing Slane fire.'

'Sure, haven't the Jews been chased from land to land?' the barman shrugged. 'They must have their own fill of curses.'

'Jealousy and greed of the Gentile, sir. That's what that's about. The Jews educate themselves and put their heads down and work hard and earn themselves skills. Of course, they did well. And so the resentful Gentiles want what they have and create ructions until they can grab it off them. Tore even the gold out of their mouths before sending them to be gassed. Jealousy and greed.'

'We did nothing to them here,' the barman said.

'We didn't do anything for them either. No, we were too busy hating ourselves. The Hebrew is tough and resourceful, whereas the Celt is morose and dissipated. The Hebrews are intellectual, whereas the Celts are lost in imagination. They are people of the book; we are of the land that we can never quite have. When our ancestors came, after the Ice Age, there were a magical people living in it and they asked us to go back and try again. We went out and waited in our ships over nine waves away. Then we came again. What kind of conquerors do that? Come in and retreat quickly? A bunch of messers from the beginning, we were. We came back and all that was sacred fled underground, and we were left with ourselves in an emptied but haunted land. When you think of it, the Jews mostly came everywhere as humble immigrants, not as violent conquerors. That's why they can see clearly where they've arrived. But we are blind. Are we still trying to arrive upon this land?'

Men were mesmerized by him, or at least amused. There were no TVs in bars.

This man's father is my father's son.

As I sat, with my delicate girly little brown-eyed brother Fionn, my father pointed at me.

'Saul is his middle name. His granny won't call him anything else and maybe she's right, but I called him Cormac. A father gets to name his sons, after all. And I wasn't calling them after any old saint or martyr to the church, or anything biblical either. Do you know who Cormac was?'

The row of men with hats and coats leaned in to hear a story they'd heard before. If there was a new man in, he would get a nudge to listen in too.

'Art was king in Tara and was told he would be killed in a battle by a pretender to the throne. Art lay with Achtan, the druid's daughter, and though Art was killed the next day, nine months later she had a boy. She called him Cormac Mac Airt, and her father chanted five protective circles around him: against fire, against sorcery, against wounding, against drowning and lastly against wolves. Achtan had to run with the baby into the wilderness, and one night he was taken by a she-wolf and she raised him with her own cubs.'

'Wait a minute, wasn't that the story of those fellas in Rome?' a man said. 'Eh, Ronan and Raymond or something.'

'Romulus and Remus, ya tick,' another man said. All those men propping up the bar loved to throw their knowledge around.

'So the legend is mirrored. Our true kings should be part beast.' Ignatius was not about to stop with his story. I would nod to my brother, and we would sneak out onto Baggot Street and go wandering up to play on the locks of the canal among the malevolent swans.

Brothers and sisters I have none.
But this man's father is my father's son.

I told the puzzle to Fionn and he scrunched his face up, and, even with his eyes closed, I could see the wheels of his brains throwing around sparks. He would sort it out and I could go back to Daddy and tell him. Though why I felt the need to impress him was beyond me. However, I certainly didn't want him to get the better of me.

This man's father is my father's son.

I picked up a rock and fired it at the swans. I was trying to get them to take off so I could see how wide their wingspan was, but they were tough city swans and lugubriously moved away through the water after glancing at me with swan rage.

'It's you, Cormac,' Fionn said.

'What's me?'

'It's the son. That's who "this man" is.'

'You're his son too, Fionn.'

'But it says "brothers and sisters I have none", so you have to discount me and Etáin.'

'That wouldn't be hard.' I pretended to aim the rock at him, to punish him for figuring out the puzzle where I couldn't. He automatically ducked and I sneered.

Sometimes it was late when my father, Ignatius, would come weaving up Baggot Street and find us by the canal.

We would try to hide from him, but he always rooted us out of it. As we three walked home in the night, everyone on the street knew and greeted him. He must have looked like a lucky man. Swaggeringly tall, long hair flowing, mad sideburns like Roman columns, long black open coat and denim flares, sauntering home to his big house on Pembroke Road flanked by two fine sons.

I only ever pitied my mother. She was an ancient half-creature, with her postcards of Paris stuck to her mirror, so many she couldn't see her own face. But my father was once a giant to me. And once I did love him. Oh, I did. But Bubbe opened my eyes. Her father came to Ireland, just after the Famine, and struggled, and married, and never took a holiday or a day off, and worked for his children and saw them all leave except Bubbe, and in turn she saw all her children leave except my mother, Esther. They had built up an apparel business in Dublin City, moved from Clanbrassil Street to Pembroke Road, and then my father had come crawling out from the bogs of nowhere into the lamp-lit world and, like a big broken parasite, stole it all from under them.

He took Esther's jewellery to the pawn shop, shouted and mocked my mother, called her the old hag, and she retreated into her studio to sip icy gin and paint empty bottles pierced by light from a never-seen sun. Only friends of Bubbe's bought her paintings, out of kindness.

This man's father.
She had known.
My father's son.

The Jewish side of my heritage I wanted. Never too big in numbers, all of them around us were lawyers and doctors, and we had a Supreme Court judge, several members of parliament and, as Bubbe said, six mayors. And Herzog, the son of the Chief Rabbi of Dublin, was now the President of Israel.

In contrast, my father had spent all the money they had so carefully saved, and he was the reason we sat in the freezing-cold, giant house unable to light fires anywhere but the kitchen, unable to install central heating or hot water. He was the reason for the rectangular patches left on the wallpaper after he took any oil painting worth a few shillings and pawned it. Apparently, we had had quite a collection. My mother had bought them over the years, and they say she had a great eye.

Bubbe's arthritis was crippling her, and she had to take four hot water bottles with her to the damp bed and sleep with a woolly hat. She, who had been a close friend of the famous Lord Mayor of Dublin, Bob Briscoe, now had to rely on the Board of Guardians to give us help to buy food. The money going straight on the horses or behind the bar in the Waterloo. When they'd get sick of him there, he'd go next door to Searsons.

Bubbe got me to put on her records of Moshe Stern and John McCormack and told me how her parents and their generation told them not one jot about the place they had come from, as if they had started at zero in Ireland, for it was too painful to talk about. But they had built a life here and had been successful, and all her friends would come round once a week on Fridays and play Pisha Paysha, and their sons were doctors, lawyers. And they brought her *challah* and cinnamon rolls from the kosher bakery so we could eat on the Sabbath. She referred to my father as *Shabbos goy*, and that made them laugh. She would not let us turn on lights and use electricity but would say, 'Get that good-for-nothing *Shabbos goy* of a father of yours to do it.'

And he did. Damned that he did. Sometimes. When he wasn't out drinking and gambling what little was left of their entire legacy. *This man's father is my father's son.* Thank God Bubbe owned the house, or that would have been lost too. She saw right through him.

So I was this man. This man's mother. Who was she? Fucked if I knew. A missing person in her own life.

Bubbe would snort through her nose if he came near her. He would mutter, 'Like an old gelded bull ye are.' He'd already taken most of her rings and sold them for drink. The only thing they could agree on was the massacre of the Miami Showband.

Bubbe would be writing letters off to the British government on behalf of those poor slaughtered musicians. Since her Uncle Bethal was shot by the Black and Tans, she was staunchly Republican.

That was another embarrassment for Fionn and me in Dublin 4. That our father and grandmother were terrorists.

He'd come in and read her the newspaper to rile her up. They were both especially interested in the Miami Showband Massacre.

'The former serving MI6 agent, Captain Fred Holroyd, and others suggested that British army officer and member of 14

Intelligence Company, Captain Robert Nairac, organized the attack in co-operation with the UVF. Surviving band members echoed this allegation: Stephen Travers and Des McAlea testified in court that a British army officer with a crisp English accent oversaw the attack.'

Bubbe wrote letters to the Queen of England on their behalf. Fionn and I used to try to imagine the queen sitting there at breakfast with a corgi asleep and farting at her feet and her opening Bubbe's powdery-smelling letter demanding an investigation.

'Do you remember, Cormac,' the Old Man said, 'How Deirdre said the people who shot their family were the police, the RUC? She might have been right.'

I bristled at that. The idea of Deirdre having some secret knowledge, some key to history, really irked me and I didn't even know why.

'She made that up,' I scowled. 'She told me herself. She just needed attention.'

I petted Bubbe's stole and was relieved that the two of them were sitting in the same room without hissing at each other. Though, to be sure, my father's violent temper was always brooding beneath his hippy seán-nos beard and ponytail and his wide lapels and flairs. He put down the newspaper and eyed me stroking the mink's dead head.

'Shouldn't you be out playing football? Yer a real Granny's boy!'

'He's going on again?' Bubbe would say.

'When there's little in your head you say it,' I'd say to her.

I would lay my head on Bubbe's shoulder to spite him. Inhaling her musty old lady, Ponds cold cream smell. Dad would curl his lip in disgust and watch me pet her stole just to get up his nose.

'In spite of a fox's cunning, many a woman wears its skin,' he'd sneer.

Bubbe would laugh low deep inside her chest.

There are two sides to every story, and two stories make every child.

This man's father is my father's son.

Of course it was me.

435

Sister Liz Allowed Me to Pay the Breadman

The Laundry was me life, and at least the nuns here never hit us like at the Industrial School I was raised in. I had never even walked down a street or seen water that wasn't coming from a tap.

Nessa was not of here. Not at all. She seemed to be able to talk to people who delivered loads of sheets and blankets from prisons and hospitals at the back door. She even got her hands on a radio and convinced the nuns that we could keep it. In the old days we were not allowed to talk to each other and everything was whispers, but the world seemed to be changing outside and these changes leaked into us here. They had got a bit more lax, them nuns, and let us gather in the evening in the dorm and talk as long as we weren't too loud. There was a new nun, Sister Elizabeth, and she wore a skirt below the knee, not down to the ankle like the others. She said to us, 'Call me Sister Liz.'

She even made us sugar sandwiches on Sundays and gave them to us in the dormitory without the other nuns seeing. Most of them nuns would eat the head off ya for even thinking two thoughts together. Sister Liz wore her veil so that you could see the front bit of her brown wispy hair. One day Nessa asked to see her hair and she took off her veil, her brown hair was cropped short, and she went bright red when we all nearly fainted to see a nun's hair.

I was very happy, so I was, that Sister Liz allowed me to touch money when I telt her I'd never seen it. So I could pay the breadman. I told everyone who would listen.

'I'm to pay the breadman when he comes.'

Nessa asked me to tell her when I was paying him next.

The dorm had fourteen women. Some were stone mad and rocked away on their beds and weren't great at the work. They just fed sheets into the big rollers all day and talked to themselves. Many of the women had small suitcases they had brought with them. The nuns had emptied all the stuff out, but they clung on to their cases and sometimes carried them around, swinging and empty.

They let Teresa change her name back to Maeve, and we were getting used to calling her that. Now she wouldn't answer to anything else. I was hoping she would finally settle here and never leave me. She and Nessa would stand in the small grounds where all those of us who died were buried, unmarked. The two of them would stare at the high wall with the sun catching the sharp broken glass that was stuck on the top, embedded into the cement, like a beautiful necklace.

Now that Sister Liz allowed me pay the breadman, Nessa sat down and asked me a rake of questions.

'Does he come every week?' Her furry eyebrows joined together in the centre, over her block of a nose. 'When does he come? How come they let you do that?'

I shrugged. I didn't want to get into trouble and lose me ribbon.

'They let her do it because she wouldn't run off with him,' Maeve said.

'Why would I run off with him?' I was scared to even talk like that.

Dymphna

One Beetle Recognizes Another Beetle

I'd leave Madser to it and feck off out to find Zoz, me auld flower. We had a game we played together. We'd walk along the street and pretend to point to the heads affixed on spikes. Zoz explained that the families couldn't bury the body because the head was the most important part.

'The burial place is where the head is. So the taking of the heads in bags to Dublin to decorate the place was very disturbing to the people.'

'No shit, Sherlock,' I said.

'Hello? Hello?' interrupted the heads. They decorated our way like hideous lanterns all down Donore Avenue to Cork Street, and even along the Coombe. I'd turn onto Patrick Street and see they were still talking up a storm. I'd walk through the Liberties onto Christchurch Place, earwigging all the way on their decapitated conversations, onto Lord Edward Street, nearly there, then Eustace Street, left onto Wellington Quay. Thirsty ghost heads whispering their stories all the way and me talking back to them like a bleedin' spanner, out of me face.

I'd find Zoz on the bridge, with his long coat, blackthorn stick and stove pipe hat, telling his stories to tourists and barristers for money. He was a bit of a local character, and there was no harm in him so everyone put up with him; he was part of what made Dublin a little loony and special.

He even said he had a friend who was a university professor who he drank with and brought him and his chislers on holidays. Zoz could move between worlds like that. I don't know what they made of him in the posh part of town. Because I could tell in one second that he'd been through them Industrial Schools. So had Madser, so had Tommo, and I'd been in the Laundry. One beetle recognizes another beetle, and there's something about the way you move, and the way you look at people a little crooked, that we could recognize each other on the spot, as if there was a radar for those of us who'd been reared in them cabbage-smelling halls. We too were thirsty ghosts, full of holes never to be filled, unquenched needs.

Could the fancy people not see it? Could they not smell it off him? Zoz didn't seem to care as long as they were buying the drinks and paying for the holiday. But to me one Zoz was worth all of them posh eejits. To me he was more important than the mayor. He was the keeper of it all. A piece of Dublin that they tried to tear down. Just as they did the fine old tenements and houses when they built their grey boxes of flats to shove us into.

He waved to me, and we hung for a moment over Essex Bridge and looked at the green Liffey, breathing in the dense smell of hops from the brewery.

'Old Essex, he murdered the innocents on Rathlin Island while the Lord of the Glens watched all he loved destroyed. He died of diarrhoea. His wife poisoned him.'

'Was she disgusted with him for all the killing?'

'Not at all. Nothing to do with being a genocidal colonizer, she was having an affair.'

239

'Look down. The river has somewhere to go,' I told him. 'She's in a hurry.'

'Dymphna, have you ever seen the sea?' he asked.

'No, I've only been down towards Ringsend and the docks when the sailors are coming in off the ships. I never saw the sea.'

'The river goes to the sea, like we mortals go to God. James Joyce had it that it was the river daughter going to the father sea.'

'Then I pity the river,' I laughed. 'Do you want to go for a dander?'

'If you lend me ten quid, I'll buy you a pint.'

'That's an auld one.'

'Why would you pity the river?'

'I used to spend me days by the Dodder. Cos me father was a drunk and did nothing for us. He left me ma with the whole brood to raise, and she wasn't up to it.'

'My own father was not a drunk,' Zoz said as he linked my arm and we walked down the quays. 'But he was a mean old bollox, called me a walking hoor and beat the bejaysus out of me so that I was only too happy to go to St Joseph's with my uncle. I had it cushy at the start, but then he hanged himself. I was stuck there like all the other walking hoors before I knew what hit me.'

'And your ma?'

'Some used to say that my mother had the face of a pig licking piss off a nettle. Others said she had a heart full of briars.'

'Then we were both badly reared,' I said.

'Can't you tell?' he laughed.

Deirdre

SPUC Off

Baby put on her lipstick and her gold earrings and clacked off in her high heels to an anti-amendment meeting with Orla and me in tow. I hadn't wanted to go, but seeing all the girls turn up in school with wee gold foetus feet on their uniforms got me away from the telly and lacing up my Doc Martin boots to follow my mother.

Orla just came for the craic.

Baby told us that she could lose her job in the local school for taking part in the campaign. Even RTÉ wasn't allowed to have people on who condemned the amendment.

'This is McCarthyism Irish style!' she told us. As she clutched the steering wheel, I watched the movement of her long red nails like a school of fish flickering around in agitation.

I bit my own nails. My torn jeans had the zips sown into them. My hair was cut spiky and dyed blue. I was a punk rocker.

I had become a punk the weekend before last. I was the only punk on the estate. I was always alone. Baby let me be a punk even though she seethed about her reputation in the parish; she still let me sit in the car beside her with my spiky dog collar. Because beneath all the lovely cut trouser suits, scary high heels, weekly blow-dries and manicures, and the insistence on us all attending Sunday Mass, my mother, Baby, was a punk rocker too.

In a big hall we got to hear Senator Mary Robinson speak. Suddenly, during the speech she was interrupted by the pro-life crowd who called themselves SPUC – the Society for the Protection of Unborn Children.

Baby was furious. 'That's Mina Bean Uí Chribín, she's a holy terror,' she hissed at us. 'A right-wing nutjob.'

'Do you know her?' I whispered back.

'She's all over the papers and becoming famous.'

The woman yelled at Senator Mary, 'What would you know about morals anyway? You've the morals of a tomcat.'

My sister nudged me and I nudged her back. This was great craic altogether. Baby was distraught when Mina and the SPUC crowd wouldn't let anyone talk. A poor hapless Methodist clergyman got up to speak and up jumped the bauld Mina again.

'Who cares about Protestants anyway?' she screamed. 'The wording should read, "Get all the Protestants out."'

All hell broke loose. Baby jumped up and was wagging her finger at the protestors. Everyone was yelling at everyone else, pointing fingers, shaking fists.

When the meeting was over there were SPUC members handing leaflets to us outside. They held up a placard that read: 'Instead of women controlling their fertility men should control their virility.'

Baby turned to them and roared, 'SPUC off!'

Orla and I followed her, cringing in awe.

When the Archbishop of Dublin, Dr Ryan, wrote a letter to be read out at all Masses in Dublin on the Sunday before the amendment telling everyone to vote Yes, I told my mother that I was never going to Mass again.

'You will while you are under this roof.'

'But why? They're all men on the altar. Why should they decide what goes on inside me?'

'I have a reputation in the parish,' she said weakly, looking imploringly at my father for backup. 'Whatever the Church's flaws, we need some moral framework.'

'Don't forget next weekend we have Cormac's bar mitzvah,' Dad said, resting *The Irish Times* on his lap. 'Maybe Deirdre should convert to Judaism.'

'This is serious, Paddy.' Baby was standing behind the bar in the living room making two gin and tonics. She plucked the ice out of the silver bucket with a silver tongs. 'Why don't you ever support me? Would you look at the state of her! She's going to be expelled from school if she turns up like that.'

'I'm sick of the nuns. I don't want to go back to that school. I want to go to a school with no religion involved.'

Baby scoffed, almost spluttering out her drink. 'We all had to suffer through the nuns. But it does put a bit of polish on you.'

'I'm a punk.'

'As of last Friday. You'd better snap out of it by Monday.'

'You of all people should know what the nuns are like, you were always complaining how they tortured you.'

'You have no idea how spoilt you are. You have it easy. I was in boarding school. Your father had won a scholarship to board at St Columb's in Derry, miles from the comfort of home, and those priests weren't easy either. But he felt himself lucky and wouldn't have considered wasting it. Paddy, you talk to her.'

'She's a teenager,' Dad shrugged, and took his drink in the Waterford crystal glass. 'She'll put her hair back to normal when school starts. Won't you pet?'

'We didn't have an option to rebel!' Baby fumed. 'There was no such thing as a teenager in the '60s in Ireland. We did as we were told and had respect for our elders. I'd never have talked to Mammy and Daddy like she talks to us. I don't know where all this resentment comes from in your generation. Your rebellion is merely the product of rampant consumerism.'

'I don't have any money to rampantly consume,' I fumed, watching her skull her drink in one gulp. 'I'm rejecting all the teenybopper stuff Orla is into and all you do is give out to me.'

'You are the ones having it easy.' Baby was pacing and making a second drink.

'It's not just because I'm a teenager. Do you know that Bishop Cassidy declared that the most dangerous place in the world is in a woman's womb? They are not my spiritual leaders!' I yelled. 'They do not provide my moral framework.'

'Who does then?' Dad was mild but he did have a hidden temper.

Baby handed him a second drink, but he had barely sipped his first. He raised his eyebrows but wisely said nothing.

'Paul Weller of The Jam. Joe Strummer of The Clash. Edwyn Collins of Orange Juice. Ian Curtis of Joy Division. Sid Vicious of the Sex Pistols,' I declared, and marched out. I stopped. 'Oh, and Ian McCulloch of Echo & the Bunnymen.'

'Sure, they're all men too.' My father laughed out loud and retreated behind his newspaper. 'And a shower of Brits,' he muttered. I froze at the door. He had a point.

'I don't agree with what the bishops are saying, and I won't vote for their wretched amendment,' Baby yelled after me. 'But we still go to Mass. We can't throw the baby out with the bathwater.'

Throw the baby out. Throw the baby out.

Baby, Baby, Baby.

The second bottle of wine, the crap in the bee-day. Everyone sitting at Mass, dozing off, checking out who was there and what they were wearing. The constant talk among my teacher parents with other teacher parents about who got what grades in the Inter Cert and the Leaving Cert. Boring boring boring Ireland. Fifty per cent of the population under twenty-five, no work, no future, priest riddled. The nuns still telling us not to wear black patent-leather shoes because it would reflect our knickers. Home Rule is Rome Rule. The fucking Unionists were spot on! Who would want to join this kip?

Throw the baby out. Throw the baby out.

What if the baby is the Church and State? What if the baby is only empty plastic with arms outstretched pleading for a life it never had anyway?

Oh, they put the baby in the pot they boiled the cabbage in,
Then they took the baby out and they put the cabbage in again.

I sang and swung my arms. My nails painted black. My hair shaved into a mohawk. Opening my flagon of cider that I'd hidden in my coat, I took a long swig. I got a good buzz off it immediately. I rooted out my packet of ten Major, shook out a cigarette and lit it with an angry flourish. All the kids laughing at me. The truck drivers yelling at me as I marched to the bus stop. 'Woof! Woof!' they'd bark, presumably a witty reference to my new dog collar. The auld ones glaring at me. The horror, and her parents decent and respectable. I marched up the road in my Docs to take the 45 into town and go to Grafton Street, to Freebird record shop to try to find some other punks to hang out with. Fuck this place, I'd bide my time and get out of this dump of an island as soon as I finished with school. And I'd never come back. Never. Ever.

Dymphna

More Vikings!

Zoz sauntered along with me as if we were royalty. He was the only one who would be seen with the likes of me. And maybe I with him. We were a right pair. As we walked back up Thomas Street, we'd slip into The Clock for a few scoops. That could take a few hours, depending on who Zoz would meet, and we'd fall out into the ragged light of day to walk up Meath Street.

I could see their eyes swivel as he shuffled past in his big duster coat like a cowboy out of an old Western film. Zoz was the only one I'd discuss the thirsty ghost heads with. It was him who named them that.

'That's why, Dymphna,' Zoz says, 'you can still hear them chatter. They weren't buried. Thirsty ghosts. Dublin is full of them.'

'Head cases alright.' I said. 'Do you die the second your head is off the body?'

'Oh indeed. Without your blood circulating you don't get oxygen, so you lose consciousness within ten seconds.' He sliced a curly carrot finger along his neck and clicked his fingers.

'What ten seconds!' I shuddered.

'Death takes longer, three to six minutes, so the fella says. But you wouldn't be aware. People said they could see the face twitching after the head was removed but sure that was probably reflexive, not exactly deliberate.'

'Then why are they still chatting to us?'

'Everyone likes to be acknowledged.'

'Look,' he pointed to one. 'That redheaded fella with the beard. He's annoyed because it was a fellow tribal member who removed him of his crown. For money.'

'It wasn't just the Brits?'

'No. No. Not at all. The Brits paid, but others were willing. Look, we weren't a centralized power. There was no idea of Ireland then in the sense we have of it now. The Ireland that Madser wants to die for is a new enough creation. Then there were just Gaelic tribes and old English who were part of the Norman invasion ruling as lords. Eventually, the Brits brought us all together in equal misery.'

Zoz was all the schooling I got. I couldn't remember anything from the time before I went into the Laundry except a lot about monks monks monks and how it was St Brendan who discovered America but didn't do anything with it. Zoz told me the gory stuff.

'These were the finest of the heads. If you wanted the real head money you cut off a really important head, and you would make your way up to Dublin with a bag full of them. They paid for the heads of chieftains here. Not just any minor heads. That fella there,' Zoz pointed, 'he has a Norman nose, would you say?'

'Them Normans,' I asked him. 'They were French?'

'They were settled in France but they were originally from Norway.'

'More Vikings, then.'

'More Vikings.'

'Would you be up to them, Zoz?'

'I wouldn't, Dymphna. But they weren't the worst. When they were in France, they learned French and became French, and they learned the Irish here and took on many of the Gaelic customs. They wanted power and land, to be sure. But the English wanted to annihilate culture and turn the world into them. Their mission was to annihilate the wild Irish tribes. We didn't stand a chance.'

Another head was swivelling there on its pike, ghastly yellow skin, and mouthing silently – Zoz approached it.

'Shh, this one has something to say. Doesn't like the city life, so he doesn't. Not surprising. The people of Ireland never liked cities. The Vikings and then the Brits established the towns, but the Irish stayed in the forests and had big roaming herds of cattle. They didn't have to do the backbreaking farm work that the Brits wanted off them. Much of the conflict was agricultural versus pastoral. You can graze your cattle through the land and camp at night to tell your stories and sing your songs. And the women, Dymphna. Be the hokey! Sure, they were fine creatures. Let me tell you the story of Iníon Dubh, the dark daughter. Raised in the Stuart Courts of Scotland ...'

And as he told me the story I'd have walked anywhere with him, all the way through the Liberties and down by the Cathedral, the tailor shops on Clanbrassil Street. He told me he had a Jewish wife on Pembroke Road in Dublin 4 and three Jewish children in private schools, and I almost believed him.

The heads were chattering like excited children to finally get attention.

'We're lucky we can drink,' I said. 'They must be gagging for one.'

'We could hold a pint of the black stuff up to this fella's lips.'

'But it would only run out his neck,'

'He'd stay thirsty so,' Zoz said solemnly.

'Do you think we could find their bodies and sew them all on? Give them another chance to rest in peace, like,' I said.

'Or better yet, regeneration? We'd need St Féchín from Connemara. My schoolmaster taught us about him.'

'Have you been there, Zoz? To Connemara.'

248

'I grew up in Meath, surrounded by the good people of Connemara.'

'And who was he when he's at home? Yer man Féchín.'

'He was beheaded by Viking pirates.' Zoz stopped to act it all out. 'And he scooped up his head and managed to make it to the holy well on Omey Island. Then he dipped his head into the well and placed it back squarely on his shoulders.'

'Did it work?'

'It did Dymphna, me auld flower, it did.'

'Well, Zoz, me auld flower, that's our man then.'

'That's him.'

Deirdre

There Are Fish That Can't Swim

I belonged to these newly built housing estates mushrooming around Dublin. We thought everything Irish was crap, and consumed America and England raw from the telly. This disconnection meant I could just drift through my world like a fish on a reef that can't swim. I was that fish that just drifted about, swept by currents, its eyes mirrors. Perhaps we were all like that if only we could see inside ourselves instead of just reflecting back each other's suburban emptiness.

That's why I envied the brothers Cormac and Fionn. They lived in a big house in town. They had a little sister, Etáin. Their house was different from my ordinary house on a housing estate. Theirs was in leafy Dublin 4 and had oil paintings on the wall. Even the bathroom had stacks of books and magazines, a yellow carpet and oil paintings. There was no bidet in sight. Hardcover books of poetry and literature, and stacks of journals on art. I had no idea why they would read in the bathroom. That fact alone – reading on a toilet – made them the ultimate bohemian family in my eyes.

The walls were painted deep reds and peacock blues. They had a way with colour. The rest of us peasants just painted our houses cream and magnolia. I instinctively knew that colour was class. Poets and artists would come and sleep the night there. Their father, Iggy, was a storyteller and their mother, Esther, was a painter. Their mother was much older than their father. The exotic list went on. They had a mad old Jewish granny called Bubbe. She sat in full elegant attire, powdery make-up and elaborate hat, even inside the house. Though, actually, she had to wear a hat and coat because the place had no central heating, and the windows were either stuck or rotting, so it was freezing.

Mind you, Uncle Iggy had a bit of a rep for nicking stuff. Baby used to say to my dad that he should check Iggy's pockets when he left our house. He would often steal a newspaper while we all created some kind of diversion at the kiosk.

'You would nick the holes out of a flute,' my law-abiding father would say to him. But my father loved him.

'Easy for you coffee-and-crames, bread-and-tay boys,' Iggy would chide him. 'This society has served you well.' And up would go his twisted hands.

Uncle Iggy was the first real punk-rock adult man I knew. And he didn't need a mohawk to prove it. My straight dad could only live vicariously. He was always lending him money.

'Forgetting a debt doesn't pay it,' Bubbe would warn my dad, whom she liked better than all of Iggy's other friends. She was raised by merchants and businesspeople, and she hated to see her family owe money to professional men like my father.

But Dad was generous to a fault and never expected it to be paid back.

'Do ye have to pay him to be your friend?' I said when I was only eleven. My dad nearly had a conniption.

'None of your business, young lady,' he snapped. 'Uncle Iggy is the real McCoy, a national treasure.' And this was from a man who never lost his temper.

I was the child of country parents living on a housing estate in South Dublin. We had a soda stream, a colour TV, central heating. My parents played golf and badminton and saw new plays in The Abbey, The Peacock, The Gate. They read *The Irish Times* and believed in it. They took good care of us, went to all our school concerts and debates and matches.

The country people were now educated and up in the city. Here, in this new part of Ireland, in the vast, sprawling housing estates of South Dublin. We were the heirs of the second generation born in free and independent Ireland. Except the country was broke and in a recession, and the reality of it was that most of us would get our education, thank you very much, and hightail it over to one of the cities of the empires of the world – London, New York, Boston, San Francisco, Hamburg, Sydney, Toronto.

I tried to hang out with Cormac and Fionn as much as I could because they seemed so different. Though they never had as much money as those they associated with, they had breeding. They could ignore their culchie Irish background and concentrate on the Jewish part of themselves; it gave them a European allure. Cormac, though as good-looking as Fionn, had a hard edge like his father. Definitely, he was more of a lad's lad.

All three children were sallow skinned and had wide, brown, soulful eyes and fine features. All three were slim, dark and beautiful. They had something else I could never put my finger on, some *je ne sais quoi* – I didn't have that. I spent my days aching for something more real in my bright suburban bedroom, with posters from *Smash Hits* and *NME* surrounding me, listening to Joy Division and writing bad poetry. I felt sorry for myself for no apparent reason, which made me feel even sorrier for myself.

I trawled through George's Street Arcade on a Saturday looking for suede jackets and tried to emulate the girls that Cormac and Fionn hung out with. Thin, aristocratic girls with double-barrelled names. Actual Protestants! Girls whose parents were broadcasters, famous architects, renowned art teachers in the National College of Art and Design. But I could never look like those lithe, cool specimens. We were from stock that had survived history, pushed to the edge by Cromwell, then starved back out of the West, lured to the city so our parents could work in service industries like teaching. We were bred to pick potatoes on the land they stole from us. Only the hardy, sturdy ones survived, out of huge broods of fifteen. Just because we had won everything back didn't mean we could change genetically.

Even more humiliating was that I was in love with Cormac. He was a genius: mad, irrational, acerbic. He was the pooka. Though I was a year older than him and had once bossed him about, now I was terrified of him. He had his father's trait of reading you, sussing out your weaknesses and then letting you know he knew what they were. He skimmed the surface of the person and could find the fault line. With a sweep of paint, he would bring the crack to the fore. He tore the person apart publicly, yet his attention was so lyrical and intense that the victim basked in his attention and the ensuing laughter. People were drawn to him. If you were in the inner circle, then you were eviscerated but loved. And everyone in Dublin wanted to be forgiven for being themselves and loved in spite of it.

My sister, Orla, was in love with his younger brother, Fionn. He was gentle and funny and lazy and even more exotically beautiful. Fionn followed Cormac about but was as terrified of him as everyone else. Fionn was gentler and never went for the kill. Maybe I was in love with them both. When we were children, we played without self-consciousness. Then when I turned thirteen, I saw how beautiful Cormac was. How his face was carved out of ice and his eyes were always singing and brown and big and sad.

He was way out of my league, and I mooned around while he went out with a parade of very pretty, well-connected girls. I clunked from my childhood into reluctant adolescence, unlovely, big-chested and full of self-loathing.

Pay attention to me, Cormac. I tried to send signals to him. He seemed to still like me and accept me. I even think when I became

253

a punk rocker it was so he would notice me. But he would never go out with me. I used to pester my father to take me around there. My father was still his father's best friend, after all. He worked as a professor in UCD, and he considered Ignatius something of a Dublin icon. He seemed to love him as much as his own sons despised him.

Oh, Cormac! I could find him with his hands in his pockets all around Dublin city centre. Fionn was his beautiful shadow. As sweet as Cormac was vicious. They were Dublin. Over the years that followed, I met them in narrower and narrower streets. The alley up to Powerscourt from Grafton Street. The alley from Dame Street to the Stags Head. On their way to Grogan's. Down Merchants Arch, the entrance to Temple Bar from the Halfpenny Bridge, on their way to the dealer. The old walls of original Dublin. Cormac was a shapeshifter. Fionn was his familiar.

Sometimes Cormac was a wolf and Fionn a bird who hovered over the wolf's head. Sometimes Cormac was a lion. Often, he was a curly-haired twisted letter from the *Book of Kells*. The head of an animal, but human eyes. They were on land but I was underwater. A mirror-eyed fish. No one could ever see inside of me, just themselves reflected. I was so far from the surface, so far from their world. I knew my place but was unable to swim away.

435

Nessa the Ungentle

Maeve seemed to tell all her stories to Nessa now. I could just about catch the words.

'Nessa the Ungentle came to the rescue of the common people who were in trouble. One day she was bathing in the river and the old and bitter druid Cathbad, who had once killed her teachers and took her gentleness, saw that her sword was out of her hands by the riverbanks, and he lunged at her in the water and brutally raped her. He knocked her unconscious and kidnapped her; taking her back to his dwelling, he kept her captive and tethered and raped her every night. Nessa plotted her escape, and when he sent her to get him water from a holy well, she noticed two worms in the bucket. She quickly drank the contents of the bucket, holy water, worms and all. Soon she realized she was pregnant. Finally, she escaped the evil druid and named her son Conchobar Mac Nessa which meant Conchobar son of Nessa. She raised her son herself and told everyone that one day he would rule Ireland.'

'In your stories,' Nessa asked Maeve, as they lingered by a door to the big kitchen, 'how many women get pregnant by drinking flies or worms?'

'How do women get pregnant?' I asked, and they both turned around.

'You were earwigging again? This one is attached like a barnacle to you.' Nessa came behind Maeve and took her in her arms and whispered something I did not catch in her ear.

'What are you gawking at?' Maeve asked me.

'Should we take the poor craytur with us when we leave?' Nessa raised her bushy eyebrows.

Maeve grabbed Nessa's big arms and unclasped them from her and turned.

'She's a dose, she'd rat us out for the fun of it. She'd rather that blue ribbon they give her than freedom.'

Nessa winked at me, 'Go way outta that, she can't be stuck here forever! How is that fair?'

'No. Nessa. No. This is my last chance. Keep your gob shut.'

'I'm only codding ya! But she's the one that pays the breadman. And she gets to open the front door.'

I skulked away in shame. All my feelings seemed to be in a tangle in me tummy. The only outside was a small yard with a cross and a tiny patch of grass. That's where they buried us when we died. The world was small for me, but the stories made it big. Maybe I could let her go with her Nessa now that I had most of her stories. But more stories kept coming, and once Maeve left there would be another wall around the world, an ending to what I could know.

Then I'd be left solely to the nuns. They fed us watery soup with nothing much floating in it except a biteen of fat and a few greasy bubbles at the top, and it was hard to keep going with all the heat and the work. I lived for that one wee boiled egg at Easter. But I'd never eaten anything better, and I knew it wasn't the food keeping me going. It was that I could float off into the stories as if they were realer than the big dryers, the steaming iron, the water we slopped around in that kept my feet wrinkled and stinging. This other world, of druids and kings and women with swords and worms in holy wells and gods turned into flies who were hidden in the forest yet always found, was more real than our bottle-green uniforms and cropped heads and hairy-faced nuns. Maeve was the spring for the stories, she was the holy well. If she left, I couldn't go on. I'd have to rat her out again.

The stories were me only outside.

Deirdre

The Bar Mitzvah in Dublin 4

Cormac had his bar mitzvah in the synagogue in Adelaide Road. Afterwards, we shared a joint in his bedroom. Then we walked downstairs to survey his dominion. I was stoned out of my brains for the first time in my fourteen years of life and, as that fish on the alien reef, that fish that could not swim, I drifted through the strange crowd. This was definitely not Bray Golf Club. Cormac was now trying to shake me off, but I wouldn't take the hint.

All the Dublin Jewish elders were there. Bubbe was in her element, surrounded by faces from her childhood. Her son Daniel, home from Israel with his wife, and her daughter Ruth, home from New York. The elusive Esther, Cormac's mother, was sick and sitting on an armchair with all the springs collapsed. She wore a headscarf tightly wound around her head, and her grey face turned to look away from all the people and out the window. A gin and tonic trembled in her hand. Sometimes her gaze would wander past the people, into the fire in the grate. As Mary used to say, 'A woman who looks out the window is edgy; a woman who looks into the fire is worried.' Esther was both.

Cormac's loud, brash, rugby-playing, confident friends from Wesley College were here. He was surrounded by his adoring girlfriends, those pretty daughters of famous or powerful fathers. There were also many beautiful Jewish girls and aristocratic Protestants with posh accents from the neighbourhood.

Our family too were there in full force. My father's brother and sister had returned from New York, on holidays with their Irish-American spouses. Baby, my mother, was looking stylish and fresh in a low-cut September-coloured dress and black heels. Some of Iggy's friends from the Waterloo tried to chat her up. They were a mixed bag of hardcore alcoholics and regular story-listening drunks. Also present was the strange array of artists, actors, paramilitaries, writers, journalists and dodgy characters that gravitated towards him always. In the hall, with one eye on the door, lurked some awful creature called Madser with a burnt face and neck whom everyone seemed to avoid as if he had a plague.

Cormac

Bit of a Dead Weight

My family flew from all over the world for my bar mitzvah. Uncle Daniel was home from Israel; he was tall and tanned and spoke in a posh accent. Raised in Dublin 4, he had left when he was only twenty-two and had completed his law degree at Trinity. This was my party and my loser dad, Iggy, stood there with his Palestinian scarf on and his ponytail, like a right eejit.

'The Poles and Germans and French and all those chancers moved ye from your houses and moved right in, drinking tea from your china. Then youse went and did the same to the Arabs. Moved them from their houses and youse moved right in and sat on their chairs. Terrible suffering doesn't make humans better.'

'We were expelled from Israel with the fall of the temple,' Daniel said, pointing derisively at my Dad's scarf. 'There is no such thing as Palestinians. They were Syrian Arabs oppressed under the Ottomans. They could move on to Lebanon or Syria and be at home. Israel is the most successful return of indigenous displaced people ever. You should be celebrating us.'

'Why didn't you stay here in Dublin?' Iggy smiled sardonically. 'Your family came from Lithuania as humble immigrants and did well.'

'We were rather limited here.'

'So you decided to move and limit someone else?'

'Let me ask you a question. Why are you not haranguing the Americans here? What about my sister Ruth in New York? What about the Indians that inhabited that land? They made it into the most important and desirable country in the world. Should they too, as Europeans, all hand it back to the savages who never ploughed the land?'

'Ah, the auld plough,' Iggy said as he handed Daniel a Waterford whiskey glass and filled it. Daniel hesitated, but then shrugged and accepted it. 'The bastard plough was never the liberator it's made out to be. It was always there to break our backs, and the poor horses who had to pull it. The Brits too thought they could take the land here because we savages weren't using it as they saw fit.'

Daniel's Israeli wife, Hila, turned on her heels and walked over to Aunt Ruth. Hila was beautiful, with long blonde curly hair to her waist and green eyes. They had children that they never brought back with them, so she was trying to convince Bubbe to come to Israel and stay a while. Bubbe was cleverly keeping an eye on her errant son-in-law. She had called Paddy over – she liked Deirdre's father, she liked to introduce him in her imperious, half-addled way as Dr MacInespie, son of a bishop. Bubbe asked him to take Iggy away from Daniel before the Palestinian and Israeli issue divided the whole party.

Aunt Ruth was shaking her head and muttering. She came over to me and put her arm around my shoulder, even though I was now taller than her. Fionn, my forever sidekick, was on one side, and squat little Deirdre MacInespie on the other.

'This is your day, Cormac, don't mind him.'

'Every time some eejit in Dublin finds out we're Jewish, they bring this up and Fionn and I just tell them the same thing.'

'What do you tell them?'

'I tell them to blame it all on Cromwell,' I said.

'And I blame it all on the Famine,' Fionn added. We had the timing down perfectly.

'I've never left this Rock of Doom, as Deirdre calls it, why am I expected to have opinions on the Middle East when my family came from Lithuania over a hundred years ago on their way to New York and disembarked in Cork by mistake?'

Aunt Ruth went to speak but nothing came out; she went over to Bubbe protectively.

'Is this what you have to put up with? In our family home?'

'As I see it,' Iggy boomed out in that irritating declarative way of his, as if anyone wanted to listen to that shitehawk, still hovering around poor Uncle Daniel, 'The Jews were the people of the book. Their loyalty was to each other and to scholarship and philosophy and not to a patch of land. That's what I admired about them. What made them unique. But after the horror of the Holocaust, and in the face of absolute industrial evil and slaughter, they thought controlling the land would protect them. As the great Sufi Rumi would say, *"Why get involved with a hag like this world? You know what it will cost."* '

I looked around to gather my troops and make an exit away from all this fuckery. But everyone was quiet and listening to my mad father.

'I have great sympathy for them as migrants escaping eternal prejudice. They too were conned, told of a promised land where they would be safe forever. A land without a people for a people without a land. Wasn't that the lie they were sold? But at that stage of history there was no empty land left in the world. Was there? Was there ever empty land? Was Ireland ever empty, or was the hag sitting here waiting for us?'

'You talk a lot of rubbish,' Daniel snapped, and downed his whiskey trying to back away.

'And your argument about coming back to roost after a 2,000-year absence,' Iggy was pouring Uncle Daniel another whiskey, and gesturing at Uncle Paddy's American family who were standing around. 'Even after ten years away from this country, we don't want these Yanks back. They've become utterly gormless.'

Bubbe looked at Paddy imploringly. 'Dr MacInespie, please.'

Paddy grabbed my father by the shoulders and spun him around, 'Speaking of gormless Yanks, my brother-in-law is an American and he has a notebook where he's collecting Irish expressions. I said you were his man. The genuine article.'

Iggy made a murderous face at Paddy but allowed himself to be dragged away, as Bubbe was introducing my Uncle Daniel to her friends and saying, 'Daniel, this is Bob Briscoe's son. Can you believe it?'

The Irish-American looked at Iggy like he was some quaint folk leftover from a bygone era. My dad, Iggy, could be horrible and cruel, which was the only part of him I ever found interesting. I looked on to relish the carnage. Deirdre MacInsespie was still annoyingly shadowing me. Charitably, I'd given her a blast of a joint, but it had the unintended consequence of making her clingy. She was a bit of a dead weight that I had to dodge.

'What have you got in that fucking notebook?' Iggy asked him.

He was taken aback, but then with an American confidence he flipped open the notebook and said, 'Actually, sir, I had a question that Paddy said you could probably answer. These are two terms I've heard in the last week. Ignatius, what is the difference between a gobshite and a bollox?'

'I'll tell you the difference,' I said, as I swept past them and out of the living room, signalling to some of my friends to follow. 'My father is a bollox to the core. But you are a merely a gobshite.'

Everyone laughed, but my exit was blocked. We turned to see an old priest standing in the door. It was my Aunt Mary's friend Father Lavin.

Baby went over and hugged him. Father Lavin smiled at her stiffly. 'I'm so glad to see you, Baby. I need a word with Ignatius.'

There were two Guards with him. I could see the fella Madser slip out towards the front steps and hightail it away.

Iggy went into the hall with the Guards and all the adults shrugged at each other. A silence fell.

He came back into the room and said, 'I have to go. My father has been murdered on the farm.'

'Oh my God!' Baby said. 'I'll have to get down to Mary.'

'Who murdered him?' Uncle Paddy asked, always the historian.

'Considering anyone who crossed his path would have had a motive,' Iggy shrugged, but his voice was trembling, 'I don't know.'

'Get him out of here with his murdered father!' Bubbe shrieked, thumping her fist on the mantelpiece until all her Venetian glass shook.

Deirdre

Little Nurse Fartingale

My sister, Orla, came up to join us and I felt like shooing her away. But I was too stoned to move or speak. Paralysis had seeped into my every anxious, self-loathing cell. Fionn seemed to sense this and he touched my shoulder kindly. 'Fair play to your father and mother for going with my old man to sort all that mess out. The rest of his friends were just here for the drink.'

I looked hard at Fionn for the first time. He was no longer just a little child and seemed to carry something much older than his twelve years. Much more than I could carry. Cormac's friends were titillated by the sudden news of a murdered grandfather, and we gathered in the overgrown, neglected garden.

'I've never seen him in my life; I'm hardly going to grieve,' Cormac shrugged.

'Where is he from?' they asked.

'I'm afraid Fionn and I have sprung from the loins of a bogger but we hid in the womb of my Jewish mother, thank God!'

'That makes us Jewish,' Fionn was quick to add. Bubbe had trained them well.

I saw how well their outsider status served them. The tinge of exoticism was something I could only dream of in my middle-class housing estate.

There was a group of girls around Fionn, which I found shocking as he wasn't even a teenager yet. He was tall and quiet, and his brown eyes concentrated on his surroundings; he was always present for the people he was with. A born observer. I could see Cormac notice this too.

'Are you ok?' Fionn raised his eyebrows at me. I rocked back and forth on my feet but was mute.

'Little Nurse Fartingale,' Cormac said to Fionn, and everyone laughed though no one knew why. Fionn looked hurt. We were all out in the long grass smoking another joint. Orla had moved past all those exquisite girls around Fionn and stood right beside him.

Cormac pointed at Fionn, 'Did you know that he made a Valentine's card for his sick mammy?'

Fionn opened his mouth, but nothing came out. His forehead creased. 'Do you know, ladies,' Cormac continued, 'the remains of St Valentine, the Patron Saint of Love, are buried in Whitefriar Street Church in Dublin?'

While the adoring crowd of scary posh children digested this nugget of information, Cormac added, raising one eyebrow, 'and Santa Claus is buried in Kilkenny.'

I started thinking about Valentine and Santa Claus. All the bones collected in Ireland. A country of relics.

Fionn drifted away. Orla followed him. I wanted to but my feet weren't working.

'Goodbye, Little Nurse Fartingale,' Cormac called after him, waving.

After midnight, I remember drunkenly going up to Cormac's room and knocking. I could hear him in there holding court, but they would not open the door.

I stumbled to Fionn's room on the next floor to crash. My head was spinning, and I thought I might get sick. I assumed Fionn would be with Cormac but he wasn't.

He was on the bed with my thirteen-year-old little sister, Orla, who I suddenly realized was becoming the image of Baby, and they were kissing.

I ran to the bathroom with all those books and oil paintings and made it to the toilet just in time.

Fionn

The Story of Esther

Purim was the first festival we celebrated in the Adelaide Road shul every year. We dressed up in costumes for it. It was my favourite of all the festivals because it has a happy ending. Inside the synagogue, Cormac and I would listen to the Megillat, which is the story of Esther. I liked it because that was my mother's name. I was always my mother's pet.

The rabbi unrolled the scroll and started to read.

'Esther was a beautiful queen of Persia, and she was Jewish. The Prime Minister, Haman, had a plan to slaughter all the Jews in the Persian Empire. However, Esther persuaded King Ahasuerus to stop him. The Jews were saved, and the king executed the wicked Haman instead.'

At the mention of Haman, we children all shook rattles and banged our feet ferociously on the floor.

Bubbe would make *hamantashen*, cakes filled with poppy seeds and honey. The cakes were made with three corners, Bubbe told us that was because the diabolical Prime Minister Haman wore a three-cornered hat.

I used to come home in my costume to my mother in the studio and she would let me sit on a stool and tell her all about it. I felt proud of her name, Esther. To me it was the most beautiful name in the world. I was the only one allowed in her studio when she painted because I knew how to be quiet. Cormac called me a mammy's boy, but it was the one place I could go to be safe from him if he was in one of his moods. He had never forgiven me for my mother choosing me to escort her on her trip to Belgium when she had her last art exhibition. Neither he nor the Old Man would ever come here to her studio. And as for poor little Etáin, I don't think she ever even knew where her mother was.

Though now my mother was sick and never went to her studio.

It took three days to clear the house of stragglers from that epic bar mitzvah party. I helped Bubbe get Etáin to school on Monday. Even when I was making sandwiches for Etáin's lunch, there were still people sitting in the kitchen as if they didn't know how to go home. I took my mum up her breakfast in bed and sat beside her. She held my hand for a long time, and I told her bits and pieces of news and who was left downstairs. But I never told her any of the bad stuff. Like how Cormac was now getting hash from Dad's friend Madser and doing quite a business selling it to his friends in school.

Cormac seemed to like Madser, but just being near him made me feel as if creepy-crawlies were scurrying under my skin. Bubbe took one look at him and snobbily said, 'He's just not PLU.' People like us.

In the mornings I sat with Mum in her bedroom, and most of the time we were just silent. I knew she liked me there, and no one else came near her.

She told me that I must go see Paris one day and I promised her I would. I knew she had been happy there, studying art.

I came up and down the frayed stairs with trays of food and helped her to the toilet, which was two floors down. Sometimes she soiled her bed and I'd take her out and put her on the chair and change the sheets. I really didn't mind doing this. At least I knew what love was.

Nurse Fartingale, Cormac began to call me, and the bloody name stuck. I hated that name.

'Esther,' I whispered to her, 'Esther, everyone is finally gone. Dad has come back from Meath. His father is dead and we've all to go to the funeral. Do you want me to get you ready?'

She shook her head. 'I'm not up to it. He never introduced me to anyone from his family except his Aunt Mary.'

I squeezed her hand. 'I'm not sure why we even have to go. I'll be back after the funeral. Your hair is growing back, Esther.' I touched her tiny curls. 'Maybe you're on the mend. Bubbe is going to stay and mind you.'

'When you have your bar mitzvah, we'll have a party for you too.'

'No thanks,' I said, and she actually laughed. A crunching dry laugh that made her gasp a little. But still so good to hear her laugh.

I found my dad, Iggy, downstairs bustling about, washing his hair and getting Etáin to iron his suit. She was humming and wielding the big iron, which she could barely hold. Bubbe helped her. Etáin was the only one who threw her arms around Iggy when he had come back. Like Cormac, I found it hard to mourn a man that I had never even heard one story about. My father only told made-up stories. He never said a word about himself. I didn't even know what school he had gone to, if he had ever gone to a school. He barely noticed me most of the time, too busy going at loggerheads with Cormac.

We didn't have a car, so Paddy MacInespie offered to drive us there. They had two cars. They were that kind of family, organized like. I used to go to their house and bask in the order of it all. It was way out in the suburbs of Cabinteely, but they had central heating and things like showers and Tupperware containers with food stored in them and their parents liked each other. I could imagine them doing homework with their kids and going to parent–teacher meetings. Bubbe used to show up for our meetings smoking, with her beloved dead mink around her neck and a hat with black lace hanging over her face. I was always mortified.

'Ah, here's Nurse Fartingale. Did you know there's talk of demolishing the big chimney on the Shelbourne Road, you know the one with the giant swastika on it?' Cormac was burning a piece of hash and crumbling it into the tobacco on a rolling paper at the kitchen table as Etáin ironed. He was mad for the hash now.

Etáin stopped ironing for a minute and cocked her head. 'What was that place anyway?'

'The chimney was part of the Swastika Laundry that Bubbe used to take her sheets and tablecloths to,' Cormac said, licking the edge of the paper. 'Maybe it was one of the ones where unmarried women were put if they had babies. That's what might have happened to Mum, so she married Iggy and accepted that as her lot.'

Iggy took his shirt from Etáin and kissed her on the head. He shot a cold look at Cormac. For once he wasn't taking the bait.

'I used to think it was the Nazis and nuns together capturing the women,' I said.

'When I was a child, Cormac told me it was a concentration camp,' Etáin said. 'But Bubbe said that was just a name.'

'I don't like change,' I said. 'Even change for the better.'

'I wonder if this unknown grandfather dying on a farm means change.' Cormac lit the joint and looked over at Iggy.

'Change is all there is, boyo.' Iggy swiped the joint from Cormac and took a toke. 'Can't live in the past.'

Bubbe shuffled into the kitchen. I went to pull up a chair for her at the table. I glanced nervously at Dad and Cormac smoking that joint. I wouldn't smoke in front of Etáin or Bubbe out of respect.

'Are you coming to the funeral?' Cormac asked her. 'Not like you to miss a funeral, Bubbe.'

Bubbe shook her head and popped a cigarette from her silver case into her cigarette holder. If she was ever to get cancer like her daughter, at least she would do it in style. Cormac lit her cigarette with a flourish like an over-eager waiter. Bubbe was the only human that Cormac had absolute respect for and never messed with.

'Do you like change, Bubbe?' Etáin sat beside her granny and put her head on her shoulder. Bubbe squeezed her hand.

'My darling *shefele*, I've seen so much change in my long life. But I can still name every shop on Clanbrassil Street from when I was a young woman in the '30s.'

Cormac looked impressed, 'Go on, then.'

Bubbe closed her eyes as if praying, 'Woolf's was the drapery. Erlich's the butcher. Barron's the deli, Freedman's the grocer, Betty Fine had a drapery. Jackson another grocer, Fine's milk and grocer. Weinrock's a bakery, Samuel's a butcher, Wertzberger's were wine. And across the street leading back up there was Gross the watchmaker, Aronvitch the grocer, Isaac Goldwater the butcher, Janie Goldwater had poultry, and Leopold's another poultry beside her, Rubenstein a butcher, Ordman a grocer and Atkins the bootmaker. Oh, and on Upper Clanbrassil Street there were two chemists, Nightingale and across the road Misstear's Chemist.'

'Why so many butchers and grocers?' Etáin asked.

'But that's all gone,' Iggy spoke, sucking his breath in and handing the joint back to his eldest as he exhaled, 'Only words in your brain. An electrical trace.'

'Gone,' she agreed, and lifted Etáin's hand up and kissed it. 'But I have my little *zeeskeit* here.'

Etáin was the only person in our family that everyone loved without complication, so we all smiled as Bubbe kissed her head.

Paddy MacInespie came and collected us. Iggy got into the front of the car in his newly ironed black suit. Cormac, Etáin and I clambered into the back, and off we went to a world we'd never been told of.

PART III

Our children are our legends.
You are mine. You have my name.
My hair was once like yours.

And the world
is less bitter to me
because you will re-tell the story.
     – Eavan Boland, 'Legends'

Hag

Spiderlings, Spiderlings

Only I know what's underground. When I die my legs will curl up like a dead spider's. I am not restless like ye; forever shape-shifting from fish, to rodent, to ape, to human. You can find me in amber 130 million years ago. Before I was a hag, I was a spider. It was when you came to my shore that I took your shape. I can still sprout six arms when I need them above my spindly legs: I can't shake my spidery ways.

'Spiderlings, spiderlings,' I call on the abandoned mountainside on Bolus Head, in the Barony of Iveragh, Co. Kerry. They are not spiders, these little ones. That's just my pet name for them because they are mine. They are your detritus. Your leftovers. Your forced forgotten. They were only wee babas. I poke my withered arms into the earth of the limbo graveyard and retrieve those little ones who you wouldn't even take into the afterlife with you.

'It's time for a day out,' I coo to my limbo babies. 'A jaunt up to Dublin. I can only take six of ye this time. So I'll have one spider hand for each.'

I look human, apart from my six arms. The bus driver smiles slightly when he sees me wait by the road in Kerry. We bus it up to Dublin. The limbo babies open their mouths and make popping noises with their lips. Grateful to be out of the ground. I spit on a tissue and wipe some of the dirt from their faces. They are in varying states of decay, most still look like human babies. I took the presentable ones so we could move in public without too much furore.

'We will have fun, little ones,' I whisper into their putrefying ears. 'There will be storytelling at the Leprechaun Museum, then up and down the slippery steps in the Phoenix Park, hearing the roar of the lions at the zoo. We'll do all of that, but really I wouldn't go near Dublin only I have to see my bog bodies too. I haven't been able to talk to them since they were pulled out of me. I've heard they've created a fine exhibit in their honour.'

The babes coo and smile toothlessly, happy to be above ground and see the light they weren't allowed.

Fiona

It Must Have Been Her Ghost
(1622)

I got word that Turlough MacMahon was back from Spain and on
a horse, wearing a mantel, the great old cloaks of yesteryear. Riding
tall through the glens as if the old world was still in place. Turlough
had been one of the warriors who had fled with the O'Neills on
the ships to go supplicate the powers of Spain and Rome for help
in defeating the English and pushing them back to their own land.

I sought out this old man Turlough because I knew his mother
when I was a wee child. She was an ancient crone telling stories to
us wood kern. Those of us who fled into the forest to live and hide
from the settlers. Those of us who waited in vain for the nobility to
come back and save us.

To find him I had to creep carefully out from the woods. The
trees held the spirits of our dead. Now forests were disappearing,
even our lovely ghosts were being obliterated and the land given to
floods of settlers coming from England and Scotland. Men who had

once gone to Poland and Sweden as mercenaries, starved out of their own place, now found ample acres here among us barbarian natives.

I found Turlough in the glen washing his face in the stream. I had come up behind him quietly, but he heard me and turned, reaching for his sword. I had my own *claideamh*, and a *scian*, and a bow and javelins. I touched them in a way to show none were drawn.

'Turlough, we heard you are coming. Do you bring news for us?' Once I spoke the Irish he relaxed. His forehead softening. He was not too tall but held himself very erect and stately. His face and arms were tanned brown from his time on the continent. He got on his horse and pulled me on behind him. I put my arms around him and kept my head high. He whistled an old tune to release us from any awkwardness. I showed him the way. The night was settling in and when the forest was too dense to ride through, we dismounted and led his fine dun horse through the thickest parts. When we reached our tiny camp, Turlough bowed to us all as if we were remnants of the great old Gaelic courts instead of a dozen hungry, ragged forest creatures, some too ancient and some too young, half of us clothed in wolf skin.

We put him up for the night in this small dwelling in the woods, wood thrown up and calfskin. The wind blustered, as if a creaking fairy horde trampled on our roof. I explained the situation to him as we hunched around a small fire. A motley gathering of wood kern, we had some wolf pups that we had found when their pack was killed by the settlers. Their low deep chorus howls kept trouble away. As we huddled under our low roof, we bombarded him with questions.

'Will Hugh O'Neill raise an army and come back to throw these settlers out?' one of the men asked.

'The Earl of Tyrone is dead many's a year,' Turlough said, pulling his cloak around him. 'He died of a fever in Rome.'

'Ach, we heard that and were hoping it was a lie.' I gave him a cup of *bainne clabair* and we shared our oatmeal from the pot. 'And what of his children? He had five wives, after all. He must have a whole clatter of sons.'

'And how many husbands have you had, Fiona?' I saw his blue eyes in the firelight.

'Most Februarys I'd get rid of one and take another,' I said.

'Ah, the old ways,' he smiled. 'They are gone. You will be under the Roman law now. For the British adhere to that. No more throwing off your husbands if they don't please you in your beds. I can see with my own eyes what has become of Gaelic Ulster, but tell me for you have lived it.'

We were conquered people now and scrambled for life, even the land had forgotten who we are. The great cattle herds were gone. The new masters were swarming in and they were many, and backed by their powerful king. They were dour and industrious, deliberately deaf to the land's fog tongue. Their stories were all from the Bible – about control and punishment, a glowering growling God; they threatened even themselves with damnation. Many were younger sons who inherited nothing but violent hearts and the compulsion to be colonists. Everything sacred for them was in their book, their Bible; the land was there to be ploughed, that was all. Our ancestral trees were only timber to them, our sacred oaks were being felled to build their navy ships and wine barrels, and they saw us merely as toilers on their farms and estates. At first, we thought they would extinguish us, but they still needed us to work for them. Our kinship names gone, they told us to take names of the services we performed, to become Cook, Baker, Weaver, Potter, Tailor.

We told him all of this and he murmured that he had seen it all as he had moved through the glens. We had hoped he was doing reconnaissance and would bring news of great foreign armies. But he did not give us any indication of this.

'So there can be a new O'Neill,' another of us said. 'The clan can elect any of his kin.'

'The English will only acknowledge the first son.' Turlough shook his head. 'A clumsy inefficient system, to be sure. But anyway, they're all dead. Henry the Earl's son by Joan O'Donnell, his second wife, who fled with his father, is dead of the fever. Shane, his son by

Catherine Magenis, his fourth wife, died in the siege of Barcelona. He was named the Viscount of Montjuich by the King of Spain upon his death.'

'Lucky him to have such a grand title in his grave,' I snorted. I did not like any of this news. 'And Conn, his wee son who never made the ship?'

At this Turlough only shook his head and shuddered, as if remembering those terrible days when the defeated nobles all scurried like rats in desperation from their own land.

'Poor Conn, how we hunted for him before we fled. O'Neill's children had been fostered all over the land, in the old tradition. For days we searched for Conn – he was only six years old then. But he was out bringing in the great cattle herds of his foster family from their summer grazing. We sailed without him. He was immediately taken by the English and sent to Eton College to make him into a loyal subject. But they soon thought better of it and grabbed him from that school, the bastion of all privilege, and flung the poor lad into the cursed Tower of London. They took the Earl's brother too and imprisoned him there, and there they both died.'

'We heard there was another,' said one of the wood kern desperately. A man with matted hair and wild eyes. We were all half-wolf now. 'What about the child with six toes on one foot?'

'That wasn't his son, that was considered lucky, to have such a child on the journey. We sent for that one and took him off his foster family to bring him on the boat. He was with us on all our journeys, growing up among defeated men. A shambles of old nobles without their cattle, their warriors, their people, their land. Sure, they were as low as us churls in the end. The six-toed one, he's still alive; he'll melt into the great soup of Rome, no doubt, for he has no memory of this forsaken place. Another son, Brian, got out of Ireland under the dark nightfall and escaped to a school in Brussels. We thought he would be safe, but, for shame, he was found mysteriously hanged.'

'By his own hand?'

'No. That would be most unlikely. Both his hands were tied behind his back.'

'Ach, they obliterate us. No one is coming,' I said, as the little wolf cub chewed on my fingers.

'It's up to ye to keep the resistance going,' Turlough said. 'I hear you give them great consternation and they are afraid of ye.'

'They put their cattle in at night and, if they don't, we move and take them. We swoop in on smaller settlements and break their ploughs and snatch their chopped wood. But they keep coming. They feel entitled to a land they've never seen and where they have no kin buried.'

A gust of wind blew the roof, and one of the wood kern reached his hairy muscled arm up to hold it down for us all. We huddled together, knowing we had lost and wouldn't last like this for long. The wind spoke through the last standing trees. The breath of the land, momentum unspent. Telling the story we were not ready to hear, in a language we soon would not understand.

'Will you go back to Rome?' I asked quietly when the wind settled.

'You could come with me,' he said suddenly. 'I'd say you would make the journey. What's here for a beauty like you becoming half-wolf in these woods?'

The others watched me over the fire. I was the fiercest of them. The leader of this pack of wood kern. A small wolf on my knee. I would never leave this land, my fellow wood kern, my wolves, my woods.

'I won't leave, and I won't settle and work for them. I'll stay until the last woods are felled. And then I'll turn myself into a rock and wait them out.'

'That doesn't seem wise.' He took a branch from the wood pile and poked the fire.

'It's not a choice. Those who settle and work for them are punished with endless tithes; they break us in any way they can. Make sure we do not get close to security. We who are war-torn and poor and landless are crippled with payments for breathing itself. We who shit under trees, slip through the gaps in the seam to find the mystery, to speak the poetry. They look at us and want to charge us for living.'

'Tell us a story,' one of the other wood kern urged him. Their eyes all watching him, knowing we were left to ourselves, that no one was going to come to our defence.

Turlough told us the old tales he had got from his mother, Caitríona, a great storyteller. I told him that I had met her in the woods when she was old, and she had passed the stories down to the children who could remember them. Even the hunger couldn't erase the tales. He said, no, his mother died when Essex, sent by Queen Elizabeth of England, slaughtered all the innocents on Rathlin Island. I insisted I knew her, for there was none like her, and she had the story of how she had met the English King Henry and her only a churl. We agreed it must have been her ghost. He told us the story of Macha.

The farmer Crunden was in bad shape, as his wife left him his three small children. His house grew messier and messier, and they lived in squalor. One day he came home and found the house spick and span, and his children happily playing by the lit fire. He could smell cooking in the pot. A beautiful woman by the name of Macha told him she had decided to come live with them to be his wife. Soon enough he knew she was a fairy woman, as she ran so fast when going up the hill, and when she ran it seemed her feet didn't graze the ground, but who was he to question his good luck. Many a man would be happy to have such a wife from the Otherworld, and his children loved their new stepmother.

When Connor the King of Ulster was hosting a great feast for his new chariot horses, Crunden set off. Macha told him not to speak of her and he promised this. The king's grey horses galloped faster than any other horses Crunden had seen. He heard other men at the feast boast about their wives, but he stayed silent. However, when the king declared nothing in Ireland was faster than these fine horses, he told the king and all at the feast that his wife could outrun them.

The enraged king seized Crunden and told him to get his wife, and if he had told a lie to shame him at the feast he would be killed. And so the king's warriors set out to bring Macha to the feast.

I concentrated to get the story so it would be remembered. One of the men had a wooden whistle and played some tunes, and I had a pair of bones I held in one hand and let them clatter out a rhythm. Turlough joined in in the old songs, songs that had been passed down from the spiral of time. Songs from wood and bone, the voice of the forest and our dead flocks. Turlough told us not to be expecting the nobles back to save our skin anytime soon; he was the son of a churl, he missed the old ways and he had no real faith in his own authorities.

I laid with him that night, and though he was old he was tough and firm and undefeated. He was surprised by my advances but did not resist as I climbed on top of him like Macha herself and my hair falling about his grey beard. I watched him sleep that night, his breathing rapid at points, which made me worry. He might have a fine mantel and a story to tell like no other, but he would be considered a vagrant beggar around these parts, and people were now reluctant to take those in. Under the new laws, if you let a beggar into your house and gave them some assistance and momentary shelter, they demanded 2s 6d off you if they died under your roof.

Cormac

He Died of a Tuesday
(1983)

'May you be as well as you can bear to be.' A crumpled old farmer met my father, Iggy, at the gate of a tiny cottage in the middle of nowhere. I feigned a look of amusement and derision at the set of him. So these were my father's people? Meath to me had formally been some kind of green patch around the city. Dublin was the only place of interest to me on this rock of doom. Fionn and I glanced at each other. I was mortified already.

'Patsey!' Iggy shook the farmer's hand as this Patsey character hoisted his trousers up under his tits.

'These are the little heathens Mary was telling me about?' Patsey stared amicably at us.

Etáin danced out of the car as if she had always belonged there and went to pet a sheepdog by the little gate. The dog winced as if expecting a beating. The cottage was tiny and bare. Net curtains, yellow with age, hung in the windows. We walked into the smallest living space. There was one chair by the fire and a kitchen table with a few mismatched stools and chairs around it. Despite the size of the cottage, there were people milling everywhere. Fionn and I went into the bedroom off the side of the room to look into the open coffin and see what Iggy's father looked like dead. There was an old woman in there with a wooly tartan scarf around her head and a buttoned-up padded anorak. She never acknowledged us, so we just nodded at her. Her lips were thin and colorless, her cheeks were sunken and her eyes were swimming in their own yellow juices. She looked as if she wasn't long for this world herself.

'Oh my God!' Fionn whispered. 'He has one leg and one arm.'

'Did someone try to chop up the body?' I gasped.

Auntie Mary walked in and put her hands on my shoulders and whispered, 'Whisht, Child of Grace. He lost his arm in a thresher, and a few years on lost the leg making slurry. He never liked the land, and it didn't like him back. God help him. Sure, he was never the better for it.' She blessed herself. Auntie Mary touched her dead brother's hand. There were rosary beads entwined in his fingers. She took a packet of twenty Major out of her bag and put them in his jacket pocket. She never once looked at the old woman on the chair beside the coffin; I wondered if only we could see her.

'And don't be talking about murder,' Mary said softly, as she stroked his hair. 'That was just Patsey's panic. He was killed by a bull out in the field. The poor craytur. Never was cut out for farming.'

A man wearing the haggard angular look of my father, but ten times more savage, stomped in and glared at us over the body. Must be one of the brothers.

'He always hated that story I told about the bull. Thought it was way too long altogether,' Mary said to the man. 'Wasn't he a terrible man for the smoking? Though it didn't harm him in the end.' Mary patted his jacket over where she had put the cigarettes, she then extracted a box of matches but, changing her mind, put them back in her own voluminous handbag.

'Poor Seamus. He won't be needing a light where he's going.' She stroked his cheek and walked back out of the room.

'That's a bit of a letdown,' I whispered to Fionn. 'I told my mates it was murder most foul.' Fionn nudged me and nodded towards the gaunt old woman. She looked half-drunk. 'What did he die of?' I asked this creature, but she ignored me. I turned to Fionn and said louder, 'Ask me what did he die of?'

Fionn gave me a beseeching look.

'Ask me, Nurse Fartingale. What did he die of?'

'What did he die of?' Fionn whispered, blushing.

'He died of a Tuesday,' I boomed out loud to the strange woman. I winked at Fionn, who wasn't amused. I was storing up stories to tell the lads back at Wesley. That's if I had any use for letting on that these were my people. I was going to tell them that *she* said, 'He died of a Tuesday.' Everything that happened to me I had to formulate, condense, highlight and elaborate until they were tall tales for the lads at school. He died of a Tuesday, cheap I know, but they would get a laugh at how these boggers speak.

Mary returned with Patsey, and they looked at the body once more. Patsey turned to Mary and said, 'Doesn't he look wild like himself?'

I might not have to make things up, after all.

Mary ushered us away out of the room, brought us to the kitchen and gave us some sandwiches and tea. She told us the foul old woman with the tartan scarf who was in beside him was his wife and that made her our granny. I paled. It was hard to put that exhausted old mute peasant woman near the dynamic, imperious, wonderful Bubbe.

As I stood in the kitchen eating Mary's eternal scones of grief, I felt utterly detached from all of these people and this place; they were not mine, this land did not hold me. I was a Dubliner. And by Dublin I meant Dublin 4. The curved-necked swans gliding the canals, the leafy grandeur of Pembroke Road, the fallen cherry blossoms in Herbert Park like a delicate currency after the rains, the tall redbrick houses, their bright painted Georgian doors with the Child of Prague statues in the fanlights dreaming of losing their heads. Dublin 4 was the vessel into which I was poured. Nowhere else had any meaning.

Hag

The Bog Body Replies

After the trip to the zoo where we were gawked at more than the animals, I take them to the National Museum. I ignore the stares of the Guards. We are quite the sight, the old spider hag trailed by six mucky crawling limbo babies. I check my bag into the cloakroom, then march off to find the bog bodies. While they were underground, I had contact with them, gave them a bit of hag affection over two and a half millennia. I thought I had so much to say. But as soon as I enter their tombs, I can say nothing, only remember.

They lie on display. The Iron Age seems like yesterday. My rotten precious limbo babies press their tiny noses to the glass as I hold one in each arm. They gasp at their kin, the perfect fingernails, the emptied-out lives, the cut nipples. Sacrificed men. I remember the Iron Age nights you went down, boys. I remember the faces of those who killed you. I remember them cutting you under the nipples so you could never be kings. I remember your last meal. How you looked to the sky at the new gods coming like flashing streaks of light. You were pushed into the earth, into me, your old hag mother, a vanishing god.

'I told you that I would come, lads,' I whisper.

I'm worn out from all our excursions today. There is a bench beside the bodies and I sit, the babies utterly silent and solemn in my arms.

'Is it OK now?' I ask them. 'Is time the great healer that everyone keeps saying it is? For me, you see, time goes in spirals; everything keeps coming around again but at a different level. Whisht now. They are all gone, your murderers, but you are still here. Take some comfort.'

The bog body replies: 'Fame is poor revenge, indeed. Would I have not chosen another night? Just one more night under the stars before my sacrifice?'

I touch him, my fingers going smoothly through the exhibition glass. I am tender, he shivers but lets me. A man like what's left of him can't be fussy.

'What took you so long?' he asks.

'Arra, don't whinge. I'll never let you down. I'm not human.'

My limbo babies are getting fidgety and scuffle around the place. I have to keep an eye on them or they'll be up to all sorts of mischief in the museum. Two have disappeared already. Some French tourists are staring at me with their mouths hanging open. Here I am, Ireland herself.

'Every culture holds a sacrifice as its igniting force,' I whisper. I get ready to leave, looking around for my little spiderlings.

'Yes, I was their bog Jesus,' he says to me through his black skin. His perfect fingers twitch and clench. 'Aren't all sacrifices really acts of convenience? Isn't there always someone to get rid of?'

More tourists gather and everyone witnesses the moment the bog body moved to talk to the hag.

'Shh,' I say, 'wipe your tears, hush now.'

'Was it worthwhile?' the bog body asks. 'What is Ireland now?'

'Hush now,' I whisper, 'maybe some day you'll be back inside me. Maybe I'll gather ye up.'

'They sucked the fluid out of me like a spider.'

I let go of his hand; he did look like an empty school bag.

'Nothing to do with me. I gave you all the affection I could.'

'A hag's affection, you know what they say about that?' he snapped.

They've said all sorts of things, spiderlings. And what they've done is worse than what they said.

Fionn

Burial
(1983)

Patsey and my father were walking out to the sheds so I thought
I'd get away from Cormac and his haughty derision. Frankly, he
embarrassed me.

The two men walked purposefully out over the field beyond,
and I pursued them. Having been Cormac's shadow my whole life, I
found it easy to be there close to them and not be seen. They came
to a clearing surrounded by trees. Patsey poked the ground with a
stick. Neither of them noticed when I caught up with them.

'There's going on half a dozen buried here, I reckon.'

'Are ye sure?' Iggy said, scratching the back of his neck, as if his
collar was too tight.

'Aye. I'm sure. I didn't want to go to Mary about it. She'd enough
after wee Seán's tragedy. Took the light out of Mary, though she's a
great woman. She could never even keep an animal after that, you
know. Then I thought about the priest. Not Gilligan, but Father

Lavin. He's more of the understanding type. But he'd have just had to go to the Guards. And I knew no one would be the better for that.'

'The fucker,' Iggy said. He stomped the ground with one foot as if to rattle the earth.

'It'll stop now, I suppose,' Patsey said, he bent down and picked something up. 'I still find your uncle Padraig's whistles here in these woods. They've lasted a long time.'

'He was before my time,' Iggy said. 'Wasn't he gone in the head?'

'Oh, he was a bit innocent of the mind, to be sure,' Patsey fingered the whistle. A wooden carved tiny bird. 'Harmless, though.'

Then Patsey turned to me and gave me the muddy wooden whistle.

Iggy startled and looked at me as if noticing me for the first time. Maybe in his life. 'Fionn! Are you following us? What do ye want?'

'How many brothers and sisters do you have?' I asked him, glancing back at the packed house.

'I had five ahead of me.' Iggy spat on the ground.

'Sure, he was just the shakings of the bag!' Patsey said, and they both laughed.

'How do you know it will stop? What if it wasn't him?'

Patsey pulled his jacket around his ample tummy as a gust of wind pummelled us.

I wanted to ask what kind of animals were buried out here. But I didn't dare.

Patsey leaned forward to Iggy. 'The Guards were asking, and I don't know what to be telling them.'

'Was it your bull that killed him?'

'Aye. Seamus had no patience with animals,' Patsey scratched his chest. 'I remember a time you stared down an angry bull. You were a fierce little fucker. I'd wondered about you over the years. Heard you did alright. Dublin 4, wha?'

'Did the bull kill him on account of this?' Iggy was hunkered down and poked the leafy, muddy ground. The wind came through the trees in a pounding gust and we three faced for home.

'Maybe so.'

'Let it lie,' Iggy said, standing up stiffly and rubbing his palms together.

'Aye. I reckon I will,' Patsey said. And the two men began to walk back to the house. My father was strangely at home here.

'So what's this I hear about you getting married, Patsey?'

'Aye. It's the truth,' Patsey beamed. 'Aren't I entitled to a bit of company in me old age?'

'Did you need to?' Ignatius looked sharply at him. 'There's places in Dublin I could take you to. I still can. I could meet you off the bus.'

'I've never been to Dublin,' Patsey said. 'Trim is enough of a town for me.'

'What's she like?' Ignatius asked.

'Ah,' Patsey shrugged. 'She's not much to look at but she'll stand in a gap for ye.'

Ignatius laughed and clapped him on the back. 'I never had you down as such a romantic, at all, at all.'

Watching their backs, I noted that both walked kind of crooked, Patsey with his hat on and my father with his big long raggedy coat and his blackthorn stick. Both believed that a bull would know what was buried underground and exact justice. I now understood he had never left these fields somewhere in his tangled mad head.

As if in a dream, I couldn't follow them. A wave of shock came from deep underground, like the twisted roots of all the long-gone trees, yew and ash and hazel and oak. They tangled their way up through the soles of my feet, up inside my legs, grasping and intertwining with my veins and my muscles and gripping my organs until this sodden field, the roots from the patch of small surviving old woods, pierced my heart and held me immobile and trapped as the two men; my bad father and his lonely neighbour disappeared back into the cottage with its smoking chimney. And I stood locked into the land until the wispy figure of Etáin came skipping down the field like a fairy child.

'Etáin, Etáin,' I called her. She danced up to me and smiled and shivered at the same time, her hands deep in the pockets of her thin orange corduroy jacket that was way too small for her. No one ever thought to buy her clothes, especially now that our mother, Esther, had been sick for so long.

'Fionn, can we move here when Esther dies?' she asked me.

'Here? Are you mad? From Pembroke Road to the bog?' I laughed at her earnestness. 'Don't let Cormac hear you, he'd have a conniption.'

But she did a pirouette in the muddy field, and her brown hair flew around her head.

'I love it here. Did you see they have pigs and cows in the shed?' she said. 'Maybe when mammy dies Bubbe will feel sorry for us and let us have a dog.'

'Etáin, don't talk like that,' I scolded. 'Esther will get better. She's over the worst. Her hair is growing back.'

'It's kind of curly now,' Etáin said. 'Let's go pet the pigs. Maybe Bubbe would let us have a pig? Not for eating, of course.'

'I can't move,' I said and reached my hand out to her.

Only when she took me by the hand to lead me back was I able to dislodge myself. We walked hand in hand, her skipping beside me, back to the crowded sunken cottage.

Deirdre

The Bright Light of Tomorrow

When we arrived in Rathcairn, we all ran into Mary's arms. Even as teenagers we clung around her and she swallowed us up in her hugs and kisses and gave us Silvermints out of her pockets. It was unnerving to see her out of her housecoat. As if she was acting as someone else. I walked into that smoky packed lung of a house. Orla and I made a beeline for the dead man, as we did at most funerals. I could hear nothing much good being said about him. That this was the grandfather of the three beautiful O Conaill children blew our minds.

'He still had his confirmation money.'

'He'd skin a flea for a ha'penny and sell you the hide.'

'He was murdered.'

'No, no. He was over at Patsey's and hadn't closed a gate. Patsey's bull had crossed into his field and knocked him down, dragged him for a few hundred yards and stamped him to death.'

'The bull's hooves crushed his heart.'

'He raised his children speaking English when the land was meant to be for the Irish.'

'Sheila never loved the baby Ignatius and was only too glad to send him off to the Industrial School.'

I spent my childhood eavesdropping on adults who told us nothing but were too careless to shelter us; this talk around the corpse was the loosest.

'Mary's brother Seán was a Christian Brother, and him teaching in St Joseph's. Seán had meant it to only be for a few months but Seamus and Sheila wouldn't take yon Iggy back so Seán was stuck in the school to protect him.'

'Seán was a delicate sort; he could take no more so he hanged himself.'

'It was Iggy that found him.'

'Seamus never even showed up at the funeral, saying suicide was a mortal sin and the family was disgraced.'

'Seán had to go where the limbo babies were put.'

Eventually, we got tired of standing in the corner and drifted off to get some grub. Patsey, Mary's friend who often visited her in Trim, was talking to my father, Paddy, in the small living room.

'Paddy, they say a Tyrone woman will never buy a rabbit without a head, for fear it's a cat.'

'That would have been my mother alright, Patsey.' Dad sipped whiskey from a small scuffed glass. 'I hear you are going to get hitched after all this time. And we had you down for the quintessential bachelor farmer.'

Patsey touched his cap and said, 'Well, I'd proposed to Mary often enough over the years and she wouldn't have me.'

'You're too old for me, Patsey.' Mary was furiously washing glasses at the sink, 'I'd be looking for a young man now.'

'Better an old man's darling,' Patsey put his arms around her shoulder, 'than a young man's slave, Mary.'

Could all these old people be flirting with each other and talking about marriage at a funeral?

'Oh, Patsey. You're a tonic,' Mary said, taking the tinfoil off the trays of her egg salad and cress sandwiches, all with the crusts cut off and ready to go. 'I'm long enough on my own, and what would the Lyons do if I up and left them?'

'We wouldn't let you,' Baby said, taking a tray to pass around, and she meant it.

'I'm not hitched yet, Mary. Just remember, there's an old sock to fit every old boot.' Patsey elbowed his way through the crowd to pour some more whiskey for my parents, 'And what's more, old boots are likely to be without tongues.'

Mary set to making hot whiskeys, slicing lemons, putting spoons of honey and cloves in them. I glanced around and saw Cormac and Etáin sitting in a corner on the one chair. Etáin was on Cormac's lap, and he was whispering in her ear. Orla and I squashed through the crowd to them. Cormac smiled at me, and I blushed. Instantly, I loathed myself.

Orla had been terrified that Fionn would have said something about them getting off together. That would be such ammunition for Cormac. I promised her I'd say nothing and could only trust that Fionn was as afraid of his slagging as the rest of us.

'Ah, emissaries from civilization!' Cormac said. 'Most of the people here are either speaking in Irish or in an English I can't understand.'

He gently pushed Etáin off his lap and said, 'Want to see a dead body?'

'We've been in there with it for ages.'

'Where's Fionn?' Orla scanned the crowd. I shot her a look. But she knew I was into Cormac, and I couldn't claim both brothers.

When night fell outside, a wild wind was rising and whipping rain off the windows. Most of the neighbours had scarpered, leaving the strange unmarried brothers of Ignatius leaning drunk against the shabby walls. On a manky armchair sat his mother, the thinnest bitterest human I had ever encountered. Cormac, Fionn, Orla and I kept our own corner. We snuck out for cigarettes and watched the evening unfold. Like a bad stage-Irish play, as Cormac said. Only the washed-out haggard daughter of the deceased, yet another Bridget, kept vigil beside the dead man.

'Ask me what did he die of?' Cormac kept saying.

'What did he die of?' I said dutifully, though I was sick of it by now.

'He died of a Tuesday.'

My twin brothers and Etáin were in the barn, excited to see actual animals and be on a farm. We were about to follow them.

A car pulled up outside. Its light filling the side of the house. Father Lavin arrived into the gathering from Dublin Airport with a new Bridget, Mary's sister. Mary had not seen her since she went into service at ten years old. Mary and Bridget embraced and wept and walked together into the side room to their dead brother. We four kids sidled in beside them to listen. The American sister Bridget was well dressed and looked much younger than Mary. She wore big rings, lots of make-up, and had good teeth and gold earrings and a very warm fur coat.

They stood side by side over the coffin.

'I was hoping you'd bring Maeve,' Mary said.

'Maeve?' Bridget kept staring at her brother as if trying to associate him with the child he was when she had left.

'Isn't she over there with you in America?' Mary asked. 'Seamus said.'

Bridget shook her head. 'I'd asked news of her for years. And Seamus said you wouldn't talk to any of us.'

'I wouldn't talk?' Mary said. She walked around the other side and they were facing each other. 'And you believed him?'

'I was a child when I left, Mary. It was over forty years ago. I only remember bits and pieces. Sure World War II was just over. Remember they said the Germans had landed in Navan and we were all terrified?'

Mary smiled at her sister over the body of her brother, 'I remember that.'

My mother, Baby, came in and tried to usher us out. Her face was flushed. She was staring at Bridget. Mary introduced them. We four wouldn't budge.

'I'm Baby Lyons. Your sister Mary raised me. I'd heard a lot about you over the years, Bridget,' Baby gushed. 'I'm so glad to meet you. You were always the American sister.'

'I was a young girl of twenty, and the family I had been with for nine years took me to America to work for them,' Bridget sighed, her accent slipped in and out of that distinctive American twang that seemed so exotic to us. As if they were all actors. 'Sure, I was only delighted. It was around 1949.'

'You must be exhausted,' Baby said. 'Can I take your coat? Let's get you a drink.'

'It's good to see you, Bridget,' Mary said as Baby took the coat. They all walked out of the room.

Bridget took a hot whiskey from my dad, Paddy. 'I remember leaving Bolus Head on the pony and trap. I vaguely remember Daddy leaving us to go back and look for Mammy and you taking care of us all those years and all the work you did to feed us.'

'I was terrified of ye going to them schools,' Mary said.

'It was out in that field that we'd stand on the hill keeping an eye out for the Cruelty Men in case they'd come and get us.' Bridget turned to stare out of the window as if she could see it but instead the wake was mirrored back to her.

'He got Padraig,' Mary said. 'That was Seamus's doing.'

'Maeve and I were so close.' Bridget sipped her whiskey, wincing a little. Baby got her a rickety wooden chair so she could sit after her journey. 'I used to love combing her long hair. I remember how it looked when the light hit off it. Like pure gold.'

'So where is she then?' Mary asked, and she touched the younger Bridget on the shoulder. Bridget shrugged blankly.

'How has life treated you in America?' Baby was still holding Bridget's fur coat.

'I got married twice but I'm on my own now. I have two children. I always remember you telling your stories, Mary. I'd love my children to hear them. But they're grown up now, of course, and have kids of their own. Did you have children, Mary?' Bridget asked.

'I didn't but I felt as if I did.' And Mary looked over at us standing by the wall in the small house. 'All these years I was hoping Maeve was with you. Living a grand old life in New York.'

'Seamus wrote and said she had her troubles and went to the Big House after Padraig.' Bridget was cupping her hands around the whiskey glass to warm them. Her nails were nicely manicured and painted purple.

'There was nothing wrong with Maeve,' Mary frowned. 'She was the strongest of us all. But, aye, I heard that too. I went looking for her there, but she wasn't down on any records.'

'Did she get herself in trouble?' Bridget asked.

We all knew what that meant.

'Yes, she had a child. I've been trying to find her for Mary.'

'Baby has been the best,' Mary said. 'She found Iggy on Essex Bridge many years ago.'

'Maybe Father Gilligan would know,' Baby said, scanning the party. 'He seems to have a hand in everything.'

'Bridget, why didn't you write?' Mary said. She seemed suddenly very tired.

The younger Bridget looked up as if about to answer. Instead she took a sip of her drink.

'Seamus told me he was passing on all the letters and I thought you'd write if you cared. I had a new life, I suppose. Isn't that what happens?'

'Seamus passed on no letters. You'll stay with us in the Lyons' tonight,' Mary said.

'Is there room? You've a lot of kids and teenagers to put up.'

'Musha, we have room. Of course we have room.'

Bridget took her coat from Baby. Then the two sisters, without a word, went outside into the rain and the wind to walk the uninviting fields in the dark. When they came back, Bridget's make-up had run and her fur coat was wet and bedraggled. Mary looked exhausted.

Patsey jumped up and offered them a ride back to Trim. We were getting ready to go. The O Conaill kids were to sleep with us in my grandparents' house. Daddy and Iggy chose to stay with Iggy's father; they were already drinking whiskey and talking low. I could see Daddy would not leave Iggy on his own with his wretched family, and I loved him for that.

Patsey, who was three sheets to the wind, drove us, weaving all over the place on the small lanes back to Trim to avoid the Guards. We were squashed into his car, and when we got out a rattled Bridget said she was jet-lagged. Baby and Mary helped her with her case. Grandma and Granddad were asleep. Fionn stood outside the house and blew a whistle.

'Where did you get that?' Mary turned to him.

'Patsey gave it to me. He found it in the woods today.'

Bridget and Mary exchanged glances. Fionn gave Bridget the whistle and she held it in her hand.

'You keep it,' Fionn said. 'They said your brother Padraig made it.'

'You are all such sweeties, such dear children,' Bridget said, and stroked his hair. 'I'm so tired, Mary, honey.'

'She can have my bed,' Baby said. 'I'll sleep in with you, Mary.'

Patsey took his leave, no doubt heading back to the wake, stumbling slightly in the dark, slurring.

'May we see the bright light of tomorrow.'

Hag

A Happy Meal

Before I cause a riot in the museum, I run off to gather my bold
wee spiderlings as they crawl about the displays. They are begging
me to hold them up to look at the torcs, golden moons lightly
incised. Only I remember those who were noble enough to wear
them. Who could have their heads rise from a thin gleaming moon.
My limbo babies are satisfied. They were so young when they died,
most of them didn't crawl. I hold one in each arm and march out
of the museum to cross the road at St Stephen's Green where the
tour starts. We'll go in the shape-shifting boat past St Patrick's
Cathedral. The man in the Viking Splash Tour gives us a funny
look. An old hag and her six dead and decaying babies. There are so
many crows following us that he keeps glancing in consternation at
the sky above. But we have cash, so they give us our plastic Viking
helmets and off we go. He tells us about the grave of Dean Swift.
The inscription on his tombstone reads: 'Here lies Jonathan Swift,
where savage indignation can no longer lacerate the heart.'

I wish I could lie somewhere like that.

The Viking Splash Tour drives into the water by the canal, the babies all clap in delight.

One claps so hard her finger falls off. I pick it up and pocket it.

Last stop before we go home, I buy all my putrid limbo children a Happy Meal in the McDonald's on O'Connell Street. If they can never sit close to God, they can at least have a Happy Meal.

As they eat, I watch them for signs of happiness, and I think I see a glimmer. I sigh as they snuggle up to me. I hate to have to put them back inside the mountain on Bolus Head. But they wouldn't last long here. Not on this diet. I shake my head at the table as we finish: all the paper, and the cardboard, and the drinking straws, and the plastic toys that they have lost interest in already. It is a carpet of ruin. No, you will not survive yourselves if this is your residue from one feeding.

Deirdre

White Cow, White Cow at the Church Door
(1983)

The following morning, we all stood in the small graveyard and Bridget and Mary held onto each other as Seamus the unloved was lowered into the ground. Uncle Iggy stayed at the house. He didn't do funerals, and no one was in the mood for a fight. I peered into the hole. Their whistle-carving uncle Padraig's coffin was in the grave, and so was Michael who had died age three, run over by a car. Now Seamus would join them – fifty-six years old and killed by a bull. My family, the Lyons, were all present, my uncles Joseph and James and my Aunt Eileen, all with their own children. Except James, of course, who was a priest. The O Conaills and the Lyons felt like the one family now. So many open graves we had stood around together.

Bridget whispered, 'Where is Seán's grave?'

'The poor gossin couldn't be buried here,' Mary said, as everyone turned to walk away from the grave. The two sisters remained, and I stood behind to listen.

'Of course. That was such a selfish act,' Bridget tutted. 'After all you had done for him.'

'I loved him so much,' Mary said. 'There was nothing selfish about him. Who are we to know what terrible state his head was in?'

'It was his choice to teach there,' Bridget said with American pragmatism.

'Arra, he was only staying there for Iggy,' Mary said. 'Iggy shouldn't have been there in the first place. But he had a wild streak in him, and Seamus was always convinced by Father Gilligan to let the children go. Poor Padraig was sent to the Big House in Mullingar and poor Iggy to St Joseph's.'

As we left the graveyard to go back to the house, Bridget whispered to Baby. Baby, elegant in her high heels and belted red coat, went up to the three priests, Father Lavin and Father Gilligan and her brother Father Lyons. I was right behind her, as was Cormac. We both had nosiness in common, though I suspect for different ends.

'Sorry, Fathers, just a question,' Baby said in her poshest voice. 'Mary and Bridget are wondering where Maeve is? Perhaps now is the time to find out? This family has suffered enough.'

The alarmed priests exchanged glances. Father Gilligan immediately walked on, with a face on him like a boiled shite, nodding to Father Lavin but not even looking at Baby. Father Lavin put his arm around my mother. 'Let's go back to the house. We have to support Mary and Bridget in a time like this.'

'I'm asking for them,' Baby said. I could hear that edge in her voice. The hopeless edge when she met one of the many brick walls in her life. My mother, Baby, could have run the country, but in the end she was only a woman. Father Lavin looked kindly at her in a distracted way and went on to shake Patsey's hand and walk off with a group of men. My uncle James, the priest, took Baby's arm and walked with her. Baby wasn't happy, and Cormac and I trotted after her to keep up.

Back at the house, Baby had downed a few hot whiskeys and her voice grew shrill. She wasn't addressing the three priests directly, but they were all in the room in earshot. 'Maeve was last seen when Seamus had her sent to the Mother and Baby Home in Castlepollard. Then there was some talk of her spending time in the Big House in Mullingar. What exactly happened to her? Someone must know.'

Father Gilligan left abruptly without so much as a by your leave. Father Lavin, who was a friend of the Lyons' and Mary, seemed suddenly shifty. The strange cast of gaunt brothers looked on with a collective smirk. Dad put his hand on my mother's shoulder. Iggy who always looked at my mother with a helpless hungry passion was walking towards her.

'I'm going to track down Maeve for Mary and her family. They have a right to know what happened to her and her child,' Baby declared. 'There are people who know where they are.'

'This is not the time, pet,' Dad whispered to her, holding her elbow. 'We'll look into it.'

'When is the time, Paddy?' Ignatius knocked back a whiskey, glancing back to see if Baby was watching. He stood nose to nose with my father as if about to punch him. 'Things have always worked out well for you, Paddy. But for our wee family here maybe it's time some truths were told. I was packed off too, you know? What did my father do with my Aunt Maeve? I want to know too. We were dispensed of like a dog's litter by Church and state.'

'How could you say things worked out for my family?' my father said softly. 'Sure, weren't they gunned down in their own house?'

'And what did you do about that?' Iggy said pointing at me. 'Did that even get investigated? Was anyone brought to account for that atrocity? Your own child was trying to tell you who did it and you did nothing about it.'

Everyone looked over at me and I was mortified. I couldn't really remember much about that time, and I didn't even know what

I really remembered or thought I remembered. My instincts were to protect my dad here.

The gaunt brothers began to shuffle, and Shelia, the mother, growled. It was the first time she'd spoken: 'Shut up, Ignatius. Yer father is still warm in the grave.'

'That would be a shock, as he was never warm in life,' Iggy retorted.

'A walking hoor,' Iggy's mother Shelia said. 'That's what yer Da always called you. A walking hoor.'

'Ye can't just come up from Dublin after all these years and stir shit,' his brother Kevin said, curling his hand into a fist. Kevin was the oldest and would finally get the farm. Maybe he was the bull that killed him.

'White cow, white cow at the church door,' Patsey stood into the fray and asked suddenly. 'She'll eat life but spit out nothing. What is that?'

We stared at him.

'It's a puzzle,' he said. 'Go on, figure it out.'

Mary and Bridget were looking to Baby and Baby's lips sucked in as her brother, Father James, clapped his hands together. 'That's a good one, Patsey. Let me think, what was it again?'

'White cow, white cow at the church door,' Patsey said.

'Go on,' Father Lyons said, he was looking at Baby frowning and my father was whispering something in her ear.

'She'll eat life but spit out nothing,' Patsey said.

Things settled down and everyone went back talking. Mary and Bridget resumed their role of scone walking. 'Are those Mary's scones?' Father Lavin said. 'Nothing like them.'

'Scones, scones,' I muttered to Cormac. 'This entire country would have murdered each other if it wasn't for them scones.'

Cormac signalled to Fionn to follow him, so Orla and I, and my twin brothers and Etáin who were all suffocating in the little house, took our opportunity and trailed after the two lads. Cormac groaned when he saw the lot of us following. However, he and Fionn stayed out in front. The rest of us kids followed like ragged serfs after two strange young lords. Cormac had a shovel over his shoulder.

We came to a small wood at the end of the field. The house was just out of sight. Cormac threw the shovel to Fionn.

'Is this the place?' Cormac asked. Fionn nodded haplessly.

'Start digging!' he ordered.

Fionn looked terrified. 'You dig.'

'You know where they were talking about, Nurse Fartingale.'

'Is there treasure out here?' My brother Nevan grew excited.

'What's buried here is why he was killed by the bull,' Cormac declared to us. 'Fionn overheard them say that yesterday.'

'And they said the bull knew what was here,' Fionn said gripping the shovel, 'and killed him for it.'

Fionn struck the ground but barely made a dent.

'He's only twelve,' I said. Cormac was a much broader kid, even at thirteen. 'You dig.'

Fionn stopped digging. He looked up at the grey sky and the black tumbling clouds. 'White cow, white cow at the church door. She'll eat life and spit out nothing.' Fionn spun around to us, as if something dawned on him. 'I know what it is.'

'What?' I asked.

'It's a graveyard,' Fionn said to us.

'It's a limbo graveyard,' Etáin said. And since she hardly ever spoke, we all turned to her with attention.

Cormac shrugged and grabbed the shovel to start the dig. He didn't get much further, so we got on our hands and knees, enjoying the drama of it all. All of us children began to furiously scrape at the ground.

BANG

A shot sounded out. Two of Iggy's brothers were there. Kevin, the dour eldest, and Joseph, one of the scrawny jittery younger ones. Their shotguns were pointed at us. We froze, our hands covered in clay. The earth was in our fingernails. Suddenly, behind them there was Patsey, Iggy, Paddy my father, Baby, Mary, Bridget, Shelia the granny, and Father Lavin and Father James, all standing in the clearing.

They were not looking at us as if we were their beloved children.

I realized that the older generation had secrets numerous and sinister. I believed that they were capable of killing us all and burying us with whatever it was we were looking for. The gates of limbo are different to the gates of hell.

They marched us back to the house under the stern grey sky. I knew with certainty that we would never ever find out what was underground.

Dymphna

Beautiful Horse: Ireland Grieves You

Them nuns back in the Laundry had a big poster up in the dormitory saying, '*A God who became so small could only be mercy and love* – St Teresa.'

A God who was born so small.

I needed a bigger God to get me out of this mess.

I was itching for some more gear. But Zoz melted away when he saw who was guarding St Teresa's gardens.

'I'm not messing with those heavies.'

'Wha? Where are ya off to? Don't leave me alone with Madser.'

'I'm off to hunt for Shergar.' He raised his blackthorn stick in the air above him. 'I'll be the man who finds him. The hero of all Ireland. It will be my moment in the sun.'

He bowed and left.

I laughed and let him go. I was scared of them meself. Concerned Parents Against Drugs trying to keep out the hordes of junkies that made their way to the dealers here in St Teresa's Gardens. They stood on the stairs like guardians. Guarding what? Guarding who? Their own children, that's who. Their own children who had lost soul and spirit to this monster drug that came just in time to keep us all quiet. That's what they were guarding, the decapitated souls of their own children. Anytime they found Madser coming up the stairs they sent him packing. They glared at the state of me, but I didn't care. I wasn't dealing. I was just using. So they couldn't run me out.

The born aren't worth as much as the unborn.

Spiking ourselves.

Head money.

I went inside my flat and immediately turned on the box. I had started yelling at the telly. It was me only company unless Madser and his mates came round with a bit of gear and we had a laugh. The snappers were too young to talk any sense. Men in suits on the telly blathered on about marijuana leading to hard drugs. I swear ta fuck.

I never saw any bleedin' marijuana in me life. It was heroin all the way for us all here in the flats. There was a junkie behind most doors. And if there wasn't, there should have been.

Who wouldn't be?

What else had I got but those few moments when I spiked myself and rolled back onto the bed and all was drowned out – the kids mewling, Madser charging his friends to ride me, the women arguing over who used whose pegs on the washing lines, the hunt for the dead horse, the protection of the unborn child. I became the sea I never saw.

Get out of the radio! Come out of that telly! Come down here the lot of youse.

We made it through the Vikings, the Normans, the Brits, our own people sawing off our dear heads for silver and gold, the minefield of our mothers' fed-up wrung-out wombs. We made it through the schools that failed to beat the Irish back into us that the Brits had beaten out of us. Here we were. With knobs on! You whinged that we'd never work a day in our lives in anything proper. Cause you had nothing for us.

Jaysus, I'd have swapped any one of me little ones for a fix those days. Me habit had built up so fast and so powerful it's all I was. A machine to get the stuff into me. I didn't give a flying fuck.

St Teresa's Gardens me arse. I tell ya, it was like living in a plague. There was no stopping it.

Smack was the best thing that happened to me. The only good thing. If I was on smack, I could go out and fuck anyone and take the money and not feel a thing one way or the other.

The telly was me religion now. It was all I got. Now that we had started to get the English channels it was almost as good as talking to Zoz. I watched a programme on the Big Bang and outer space. That's what the fella says, we come from one enormous universe fart.

If I died and went to hell, it wouldn't feel any different than here. Except me few moments of heaven when the gear went in. To get to that peaceful central place, that place inside me with no past and no future, the Sea of Vast Emptiness, Holy Nothingness. That blessed state before the Big Bang banged us into never-ending misery, that before-place that was just empty, the place without thought, without violence, it took more and more and more.

Now I had to do it just to stop getting really fucking sick.

Madser emerged – he had been hiding in the bedroom of me flat. He was bulling.

'What are ya like? Shouting at the telly. Where were ya? The Concerned Parents are all over the gaff. I can't leave. An' the social took Micko.'

'Where's Conn and Tapioca?' I asked.

Madser shrugged. The older two were probably out with their friends. They never came home. Just as well, as the social might have taken them too.

And just like that, Micko was gone. Micko was only a baby, like. I'd let them take the others, who was I to say I could raise Conn and

Tapioca in me present state? But then I was afraid of losing the flat. If I was back on the streets, I'd have been dead in a week.

It's funny to still want to live, but I had instincts I suppose.

I was learning all that on the telly.

There was a brilliant programme about spiders. How they eat their men when they finish having sex.

I wouldn't want that though; I wouldn't want any more of them inside of me.

They slowed it all down so you could see her make her web. No one teaches them spiders to do that. They just know.

Tommo was the first fella I had when I got out of them Laundries, he pimped me and beat me. He was a spider. I couldn't get away from him for years. He drank and drank and drank. He was always langers. I hated the drink. I hated all them fellas drunk all the time. Give me a junkie any day. Spiders can't eat solid food, the telly said, spiders enmesh their prey and reduce them to liquid and drink them.

Tommo was that blue mouldy for the drink. All drinkers do that to the people they live with. He tried to do that to me, you know. Tried to reduce me to liquid so he could drink me.

Thank fuck he was gone for now. Madser I could handle, and he never raised a hand to me.

'Cook it up for us, would ya?' I asked him and he nodded and started preparing the gear. I lay on the floor waiting for him to give me a hit. The news came on.

Shergar, where are you, you poor creature, what did they do to you? Those murdering bastards, you who won the Derby for us.

Beautiful horse: Ireland grieves you.

The whole country was shook by it.

'It's a fecking horse!' I sat up and yelled at the telly.

Madser sniggered and, as he gave me the hit, we both broke our shites laughing.

Spiders hatch hundreds of little ones but only some make it.

That's what nature does. It gets rid of dead weight.

But it really fuckin' hurts when that's what you, and everyone around you, are.

Dublin was a headache in a bag, and we were only thirsty ghosts waiting for the spider.

And I thought I'd got rid of it, the first thing I moved in here, but this was a web if ever I seen one.

'Way I see it,' I drawled to a nodding Madser slumped against the wall, his narrow head hitting his chest and lifting up again and again, 'the telly and the heroin came just in time for all of us in St Teresa's Gardens. For me, for you, for Zoz. Otherwise, we'd be out burning down the house.'

Deirdre

Paralysis
(1985)

From the top of the bus on the quays, I saw Uncle Iggy walking on the street with a rough-looking woman. In her high heels, and cheap fake leather coat, she reminded me of someone, someone I'd seen before. But I couldn't think of where. They were pointing to things that didn't seem to be there. They were stopping and talking to something, but I couldn't see what it was. I was bunking off school as usual and had my uniform scrunched up in my yellow canvas bag. I didn't think Uncle Iggy would care about that.

Should I tell the lads what I saw? Cormac and Fionn had little time for their father but I had a good dad, so I was happy to have Iggy as a mad uncle. Upstairs on the bus I saw everyone's backs. I wondered if they had faces. Where did the world start? Where did it come from? Was I of any significance? Was I here? Was I as real as other people? Were other people real? I was paralyzed on this bus. I didn't feel inside myself but I wasn't anywhere else. My hand went up by itself to grip the rail over the seat, but that hand might not have been mine. It was like I had never seen it before. Everything felt foggy.

My legs took me off the bus and I walked not knowing where I was going, I found myself on Marlborough Street among a shivering gathering of gaunt junkies with foetal faces and hunched shoulders. I slithered down against a wall and took a razor out of my pocket that I always kept on me. Surreptitiously, I slipped it out of its paper and pulled up my sleeve. I made a quick slice on the inside of my arm. Two junkies were beside me, watching as if it wasn't happening. When the blood came out rushing red I gasped and slid back into myself. Then I heard a voice, as if from the end of a long tunnel.

'Deirdre.'

'Uncle Iggy,' I said. He was framed by the grey buildings. He hunkered down beside me.

'This is not a place for you to be.'

'Is it a place for you?' I put my razor into the little bag I had for it.

'What are you doing to yourself?' Uncle Iggy took my arm tenderly, like a nurse. He saw the crisscross of scars. 'This is all you're doing, child? You're not scoring?'

'Are you?'

He rolled his own sleeve up and showed his arms, tracks screeching from every red puncture. 'And they said you and I survived without a scratch, huh?' He offered his enormous, malformed paw to pull me up.

We walked for a while up the shabby quays, Uncle Iggy and I. There were bushes growing out of dreary derelict buildings. I had never been alone with him in my life.

'What were you and that woman looking at?'

'Dymphna? What do you mean?' Then he smiled. 'Oh, you saw us talking to the ghosts. Here on Essex Street where the old walls were, they excavated and found so many heads, you know, all the skulls showed the evidence of how they had been skewered and on display. Power and authority and fear are always a combination. They're just heads, these ghosts. Severed heads are the detritus of all civilizations. But still, heads have power. And these ones have a fierce thirst on them.' He stopped suddenly on Essex Street. 'This was the northern limits of the old walls. Walls and heads, boundaries, sacrifices, warnings. Anyway, let me get you a pint. What age are you anyway?'

'I'm sixteen,' I said. 'But Bruxelles and Pygmalion always let me in.'

'We can do better than those kiddie-corner bars. It's time you grew up.'

Two pints of Guinness on the table in Grogan's later, I squirmed awkwardly.

'What did you mean we survived without a scratch?'

'Tyrone.'

'Oh, yeah, that.'

'I believed you. You were spot on.'

'What?'

'The purple ring, the paint on the shoes.'

'Did you see them too?'

'No.'

'Oh.' The blood was still caked under my sleeve. It hurt, which was good, so I focused on the pain. It was like an anchor that tethered me to the world.

'I remember you as a storyteller. So tell me about what happened.'

So I told him the whole story, the golden eagle. The RUC men who came to kill us all. Me taking Orla up the lane to the man who married the fairy. Orla putting her hand on the table and leaving a bloody handprint.

He sat up straight when I told him this part. 'The red hand of Ulster,' he said.

I told him how Orla was mute and how Mary stitched us both back together. And when I came to the end, he stared at me intently.

'Give me what you have.'

'I didn't score.'

'But you did.'

'Why do you care?'

'I do care,' he said, sipping the pint. 'When your mother, Baby, came and found me all those years ago on Essex Bridge, she was pregnant with you.'

'I don't do it to fill a hole, I just want to discover something,' I said. 'I've only tried it once or twice. I'm not as thirsty as all your ghostly friends. Not for that anyway. It just numbs me even more. I'm not looking for more of that. Please don't tell Baby and Paddy. They'd have my guts for garters.'

I took a little folded packet out of my pocket and put it on the table with my hand over it. He slipped his fingers under my palm and put it in the breast pocket of his enormous coat. His blackthorn walking stick was strapped to his arm, and it clattered off the table when he lifted his pint. He had a long beard now that was turning yellow grey.

'One question.' I put my finger into the Guinness and drew a line in the foam. 'At that strange funeral of your father, Cormac and Fionn's granddad in Rathcairn. What were we all digging for? What was underground?'

Iggy shook his head, there was the foam of the pint on his upper lip and shrugged.

'There's no use in boiling your cabbage twice.'

'Said no historian ever.' I raised my eyebrows and he laughed. 'Was it babies?' I said suddenly. 'Isn't it always babies?'

'Only the hag knows what's underground. Get off the rock of doom, isn't that what Cormac told me you call it?' He leaned in with his blue eyes flecked with brown and green. 'Go flourish. Forget it all.'

'Do you tell that to Cormac and Fionn?'

'Take them with you, just go. But sure you know them better than I. Only Etáin talks to me. She's ten now so that could change. I'm their father but I'm not their dad. Didn't know how. I'm a cat flap on a submarine in that department.'

'Why didn't you leave?'

'Arra musha, where would I go? I'd be lying on the streets of London with all the other tramps with my gums bleeding, and who would the poor auld ghosts talk to?'

'Thank you for believing my story. It was the police that killed our family. It was so long ago I'm not even sure I believe it myself.'

Then he rose up as if to go and said, 'You have the truth but it doesn't set you free, does it? No one wanted it.'

'So you're not like my dad? You don't want a united Ireland?' I knew by this question he would sit down again, and I'd nothing else to be doing in Dublin that day and no one to meet.

'You know the English don't really want Northern Ireland.' Uncle Iggy indeed sat back down, lowered his voice, and looked from side-to-side whispering. 'They don't like the Unionists very much, they're embarrassed by them, when they think of them, which is not very much.'

'It's not about what they want though is it? The English?'

'And we Southern Irish don't really want a united Ireland because we'd be stuck with the Unionists, bellowing from their pulpits.'

'You're not wrong.'

'There is no United Kingdom: the English, Scottish and Welsh see themselves as English, Scottish and Welsh, so ironically the only people really invested in being Brits are the Unionists in Ireland, but really they've been here four hundred years living off the food of this land, breathing in the oxygen the Irish trees give them, they're as Irish as we are. Unlovable fuckers that we all are.'

'They certainly make a big fuss every year on the 12th of July,' I said, 'the Battle of the Boyne and all of that.' It occurred to me that very few people ever discussed this with me. My family didn't want to dredge up the tragedy, and people in Dublin thought little about it as if the North was truly another country.

'Sure, their big triumph over us is that they sided with a Dutch king over an English king, whom we Irish called Séamus an Chaca,

James the Shit, in a battle where the Irish had little skin in the game, two foreign powers fighting by the Boyne River.'

'Ah, the Boyne,' I brightened up. I loved that river where Mary would take us as kids. 'The Salmon of Knowledge swims in its depths.'

'It's the salmon we wanted,' Iggy said, slapping his enormous hand on the table, making people glance over at us. 'The trees, the places to graze our herds and sing our songs and tell our tales. We Irish were left to be slaughtered by a foreign shitehawk English king who really was an enemy, and the Orangemen go beating their drums every year to remind us of something we don't care about at all. Would ye be up to it all?'

I had nothing to say. My pint was gone, and I was hoping I could give him money and he'd buy us another. I sat and watched him banter with the barman, who called him Zoz, not Iggy, as I made my sixteen-year-old self as unobtrusive as possible in the little booth. Finally, he sat back down with two more pints.

'I'll be back,' he said. 'I have to go shed a tear for Ireland.'

'Did you get that one from my dad?' I smiled.

'What? Your dad got everything from me.' And he whooshed off, stick and all, to the bog. When he plonked himself back down again, I knew how to keep him with me. Uncle Iggy slid up and down the spiral of time like no other I'd ever met. My academic father talked a lot about history, but Uncle Iggy seemed to be in it.

'No one ever told me all of that history like that. I guess we just learn a simplified version.'

'Every country is built on myths and lies and propaganda. Fuck it all. And there's nothing for a wee girleen like yourself here. A deep thinker, a witness to history's horror. You felt the full weight of history when yer poor auld Pastie Lip uncle fell like a slaughtered tree on top of ye and covered yourself and your sister in blood.'

'I hated when people called him Pastie Lip.' I marked my pint with my finger again, and then took a good swig. 'Uncle Malachy was a smart man. He knew what mattered.'

'Aye, them birds. They do matter. But even they get out every winter and wing off to Africa. Scoop up my sons, take a boat, take a plane, build a raft, learn to swim, grow your own wings but get on the fuck out of here to somewhere where they have shorter memories, and don't let me see you in Marlborough Street ever again.'

And then he drained his pint in one go and off he went without a by your leave. I sat alone with half a pint left thinking, Uncle Iggy just stole my fucking drugs.

I might have been the only person on the entire planet to ever take advice from Uncle Iggy but, buoyed with the drink, I went to the phone box and called Cormac. It was time to go to London and find real punks. I would ask him to get all his Bar Mitzvah money and take him with me to London and we'd get off this rock of doom and leave Ireland forever. I'd finally have him to myself.

Dymphna

The Bang Bangs, the Forty Coats, the Dicemans

Zoz was pure Dublin to me. He was the last of the characters. The Bang Bangs, the Forty Coats, the Dicemans, the mad auld wan all in black doing her pirouettes, dancing her heart out with her big crucifix on O'Connell Street. Sure, the life and craic had gone from the city centre. Used be docklands and Guinness and all the factories, but now there were machines to do all the stuff and we'd been left with one arm as long as the other to pump all the gear into us, cos what was left? Dublin had always been rough and dirty, but in the blink of an eye the smack sucked the life force out of us. We'd been moved from the teeming tenements, stacked up in the flats like yesterday's bread, and then they wiped their hands of us.

And we were so out of our mouldy heads we didn't know what hit us.

Working class. Sure, there was no work left. So what were we? What class of eejits were we, at all, at all?

Heads on spikes we were, a warning. Talkin' away, not looking down. Not knowing everything is gone from us except our bad thoughts. A right shower.

And as Zoz and I walked, talking to our long-dead severed heads, the barely living slumped into the shadows of doorways scratching and nodding. An unquenched insatiable surplus. Thirsty ghosts, all of us, the dead and those trying to live before death, and those bringing death.

'Oh, Zoz,' I said, as we walked among them. Future ghosts ourselves. 'What do they think of us? Do they think of us at all?'

'Dymphna, me auld flower,' Zoz said. 'When have the dead ever understood the living?'

435

Fingers in the Cathedral
(1987)

The nuns had a telly but we weren't allowed to watch. Instead, we huddled around Nessa's transistor radio and listened to the ructions that were going on outside with the IRA and the INLA and the RUC and the MI6 and the SAS and the UVF and the UFF.

'Who is the IRA?' I asked, and Nessa snorted.

'Jaysus tonight. What rock have you been hiding under?' Nessa shook her head and stood up and stretched. 'They're trying to get the whole island of Ireland free from the Brits.'

'Are we in the free part?' I asked.

'Can't you tell?' Maeve laughed and slapped her thigh, and she and Nessa seemed to think this was very funny.

There was a story about a fox called Dessie O'Hare that I was trying to make head and tails of.

'Is he really a fox?' I was trying to fit my picture of the outside world together, but I never had all the pieces.

'I can't talk to this one, shush,' Nessa waved her big shovel hand in front of my face as if I was an annoying fly. That was the trouble with the radio. Maeve rarely told her stories anymore because of it.

'I missed that bit cause she was rabbiting on,' Maeve said, putting her hand on Nessa's arm. 'What did they say?'

'They said the Border Fox kidnapped a dentist in Dublin and took a chisel to him and chopped off two of his fingers.' Nessa took Maeve's hand in hers.

'Is he in the IRA?' I asked.

'No, he's in the INLA. They're like the gouger version of the IRA.'

'But do they want us to be free too?' I asked.

'A dentist with missing fingers.' Maeve ignored me mostly. 'Not good for business.'

'Have you ever been to a dentist?' Nessa asked her.

'I wouldn't let them near me,' Maeve said, and she showed her lovely white straight teeth. I put me hand to me mouth, mine were overcrowded and crooked.

'The victim instructed the gang members to cauterize his wounds with a scalding kitchen knife so he wouldn't bleed to death. The man on the radio said.'

'Why are they doing that?' I looked at the light in the high windows above and was happy to be safe in the Laundry. I didn't like the sound of the outside and these mad foxes.

'They were asking for 1.5 million pounds,' Nessa told Maeve.

'I've handled money. Sister Liz let me pay the breadman,' I said, but they weren't listening to me. I didn't like the stories that were coming from the radio, they made me feel like my tummy was full of stones. 'Remember the part where Etáin has heard the fool singing and she goes to him?'

Maeve had started talking to me since she knew I had memorized all her stories. Though this made Nessa meaner.

'Whisht!' Nessa said.

I stopped as Nessa turned up the radio to drown me out:

'O'Hare, otherwise known as the Border Fox, claimed that the refusal to pay the dentist's ransom "just cost John his two fingers".'

Nessa stood up against the wall and held up her hand, bending two fingers back as if they were missing. A few of the girls thought that was a hoot and fell about the place laughing.

No one wanted to hear my story. The radio continued, the ads came on, trying to sell us things we couldn't buy. Nessa stood by the wall looking serious, and she did a thing with her right thumb and left hand that made it seem as if her thumb could come off. One of the old women made noises that were almost like laughter.

I took a deep breath and tried to drown out the awful radio. I began to walk up and down the centre of the dorm and raised my voice.

Etáin turned from the door and went into the room where the Fool was. Her dress swept the young green leaves, but she had no thought of them or of the little flowers the Fool had put with the rushes.

'"Go on singing!" she said. "I wish my heart were as lightsome as yours."

'"How could your heart be lightsome, Queen," said the Fool, "when you will not give the flower a chance to blossom, or the hound a chance to catch his prey, or the bird a clear sky to sing in? If you were of the Deathless Ones you would burn the world to warm your hands!"'

'And would you?' Maeve said.

'What?' I said.

'Not you, ya eejit,' Maeve took her hand out of Nessa's. 'I'm talking to Nessa. Would you burn the world to warm your hands?'

'I would,' Nessa said, so sure of herself. 'Jaysus, you're doing me head in. We have the radio now. We don't need those fecking stories.'

Maeve stood to face her. 'Someone has to remember those stories. Otherwise, there'll be nothing left in the country but nuns and head-the-balls running amok with all their messing and finger chopping, and ads for Des Kelly the Carpet Man.'

'They're fighting for our freedom,' Nessa said, pounding her fist on her own thigh.

'Are they going to break down these walls for us?' Maeve asked. 'How do they treat their women, do you think? Any different?'

Mother Michael had had enough of us all.

'I need to take that radio away. I'd rather you just told those stories. They're innocent enough. The radio is driving you all mad. There's too much about the outside world and you won't ever be fit for it, so why occupy yourselves with it.'

Nessa threw her eyes up to heaven and then we all stopped in our tracks, including Mother Michael, as the ads ended and the radio finished the story.

'The photos and the note demanding the money were found in an envelope in Carlow Cathedral behind the statue of the Blessed Virgin. The fingers were also in the envelope.'

'Jesus, Mary and sweet St Joseph.' Mother Michael blessed herself with her own hairy and very much intact pudgy fingers.

'Janey Mack,' Maeve said.

Nessa put her hand on my shoulder and said, 'See what it's like out there? Ya dum daw. Full of feckers like the Border Fox. Stay dog wide of the world. Leave it to the experts.'

Mother Michael shook her head, 'I never thought I'd agree with Nessa about anything, Child of Grace, but she's spot on. Stick to your fairy tales. The world is not for the likes of you.'

Fiona

Tithes Tithes Tithes
(1623)

Tithes tithes tithes. Sure, we always made a payment to our priests for the usual funerals, marriages and christenings. But now the new Briton pastors appeared, they didn't speak our language but they imposed a double charge on us. This new church which none of us were part of still demanded a payment even though we wouldn't let them near us. They fined us for not going to their services and tore the very roofs off our own places of worship. Why would we convert to their religion when they despised us?

I was pregnant on account of the night I had with Turlough, and I moved to my sister's house where she and her family were labouring on the settlers' farm in Tyrone. We could own nothing anymore, and most of the pay went to the rent. The local priest was none too happy to see me with child and no man around, but I paid him little mind and helped my sister and her family with all the work, taking care of her cows and bringing the milk over the fields to sell. I never gave much mind to the priests at the best of times. When my sister died suddenly of a fever in her house, the settlers' parson, may the devil swallow him sideways, came with the English soldiers and they demanded a tithe to take her and bury her. We didn't have the sum they asked, and they took our three cows and the rolls of cloth in the house we had to make our clothes.

My poor wee baby boy was born dead, choked by his own cord, and the priest said I had no right to bury him, unbaptized and illegitimate, in the Catholic church's graveyard. The settlers had torn the roof off the church anyhow, and I scoffed at him, who was he anyway, a priest with a roofless church. To hell with him. I had to carry the poor boy myself to the limbo graveyard, which was up a hill by a stone circle. I dug the grave myself. I said my own prayers and lay him in the ground. I beseeched the hag to take care of him. She was the one who gathered the bones in winter. The one who had to take us all in whatever state we came.

That night I sat by the fire as if all the world had closed in on me, still mighty sore from the birth and longing for the woods and my wolf cubs, two of whom I had tied up in my brother-in-law's shed. There was a gruff knock on the door. The settler's parson had caught wind of the stillbirth. This same parson who had taken the cows and cloth when my sister died only a few months past. This living dread stood, with the English soldiers, in the house. I was still limping from the birth and could barely get off the wooden stool by the fire. But let me tell you, I didn't shy away but looked right at him. He must have looked bland when he was young, but now he had a big bushy white beard foaming around his face. The years had allowed him to fake wisdom, depth, belonging; he had the soldiers around him, an assurance of authority. But he was still just a settler.

Flanked by the English soldiers, he demanded a tithe of 7s 8d for my dead child. I didn't know much of the English, so my brother-in-law translated what he could for me.

'Tell him *Go n-ithe an cat thú is go n-ithe an diabhal an cat.*'

My brother-in-law mumbled a few words in a pleading tone to the parson and the soldiers, but I could see he wasn't translating for me.

'Ask him why we have to pay a tithe for a dead child.'

'He said it was the law,' my brother-in-law said to me. He went about the house and looked under the straw beds and in a wooden box and scraped what little he had to pay my fine. When I saw him give the money to them, I was livid. I rose up and faced the beardy dryshite, '*Imeacht gan teacht ort.* When you charge me a tax for burying my dead child,' I said to them. 'You won't last. We will wait you out. Even if it takes a thousand years.'

They got their money and turned on their heels, out into the wretched night, not interested in my brother-in-law translating this. 'Curse of the seven snotty orphans on you.' I howled, and my wolves in the shed set up in chorus.

'We might outlast them,' my brother-in-law told me when they left. 'But the trick is to not forget who we are.'

'I'll take my wolves and go in the morning. I'll not burden your family. And I'll not work for them settlers.'

'You don't have to go anywhere. You can help me with the weans.'

We had little food that night and no cow's milk anymore. My nieces and nephews sat listlessly by the fire, their bellies sticking out with hunger. Some neighbours heard what happened and dropped in the scrapings of their pot. They asked me for a story. So, I told him the one Turlough had told me the night I had sought him out. When I lived in a little place deep in the woods. Woods that were now gone and fields of flax in their place. The baby was dead, Turlough had sailed back to Rome, but I still had the story of Macha.

> '*King Connor sent his warriors to Crunden's house and were shocked to see Macha was heavily pregnant. They urged her to come, or her husband would be killed for shaming the king. She agreed reluctantly, leaving Crunden's children alone standing by the door in consternation.*

'Macha stood before the king and implored him to see that she was pregnant. She told him she would return after she had given birth and recovered. The king coldly refused; with all the people assembled watching him, he didn't want to back down. Macha then stood before all the Red Branch warriors of Ulster, the Craobh Rua, and insisted that they should protect her and change the king's mind. She told them that they were all born from a woman and to remember that. Not one was brave enough to stand up to the mighty Connor. After all, they were drunk and wanted to witness the race and see their beloved king kill the boastful Crunden.

'Connor took the reins of the chariot himself, and Macha stood beside him on the grassy field by the fort. All those servants, churls and warriors who were at the feast gathered to watch.

'The king's chariot was fast as the wind, but Macha ran faster. She seemed to glide and leave the wind behind. A terrible sound screeched from her throat. She screamed as she ran from the pains of birth. Those gathered felt a terrible shame when they heard those awful screams. Macha crossed the agreed finishing line just in front of Connor's grey horses, but she lay in the grasses and her twins were born dead. She gathered them into her arms, weeping, and that was when she turned to the warriors and put her curse on all warriors of Ulster. She declared that their strength and training would be useless to them. That when they needed to fight this famed strength would abandon them, and for nine days and nine nights they would feel the pain of a woman in labour. She declared this curse would last for nine generations, and as soon as a man became of fighting age and started to grow his beard he would be under the curse. Macha never even glanced at poor Crunden, who had broken his promise to her. Holding her dead babies, she gave a big leap over all their heads and ran off up the hills into the woods, and no one saw her again. From that day forth, the fort of the King of Ulster was known as Emain Macha: the Twins of Macha.'

The next morning, with the smell of fire smoke in my hair, I went to my brother-in-law's shed and took my wolves who were mighty glad to see me. I opened the shed door, and they came into the light, their bushy straight tails, so still. With a blanket wrapped around me and fastened with my dead sister's old silver broach, one that was handed down through many generations, I walked away from the farm and went to find if any of my brethren were still in the woods. I felt recognized by the forest when I went back into it. And I knew when the forest was gone I'd never be known again. The three young wolves followed me closely in that fluid straight way they have of walking. Their heads low to the ground, following the scent of a lost wild world that once had room for our kind.

435

Scapegoat
(1987)

Nessa was finishing her lunch of watery soup and stale bread, and I proudly told her that I was off to the front of the nun's house to pay the breadman. Sister Liz told me the door to the convent was open, and I knew the way down the stairs and around the corner and through the parlour. I was a Child of Mary and they trusted me, so they did.

'When she lets you through the door, wait a bit and open it for me,' Nessa whispered.

'I can do it on me own,' I said. 'Why do you want to do it? You've seen money. Sister Liz said I should have a chance to use it sometime. It's training.'

'For what? They'll never let you out of here. You work too hard.'

'Is that why you don't work hard?'

'You poor eejit. If a thought entered your head it'd die of loneliness.'

This time Sister Liz shut the big door from the Laundry to the convent. I stood in the dark corridor with me eyes blinking. Then I opened the door a bit and Nessa snuck in.

'Let me give it a lash, I can pay him this time.' She grabbed the money out of my hand.

I was entrusted to open the big front door and wanted her to see that I could work a bolt and a handle, which, after all, was the threshold to the outside world. Nessa pushed me aside and dashed out into the street. She ran like the wind, the money for the bread in her hand. The breadman in his brown coat was as gobsmacked as I was. His eyes opened wide and he stuttered. We watched her leg it down the road. He didn't even stay for his money but got back into his van and drove off quickly. I started screaming and the nuns ran to the door. They had a phone in the hall, and they called the Guards to go find her. They were yelling at me as if I had done it.

Maeve made me tell her what happened again and again.

'She just legged it? She never said a word to you?'

'They'll find her,' I said. 'They always bring the runners back. You still have me. I'm the one who knows your stories.'

'She grabbed the money? She just pushed you and ran?'

'She told me to tell her the next time the nuns gave me money for the breadman.'

'And why didn't you tell me? Why didn't she come get me?'

'I didn't know why she was asking.'

'It's always you. It's always you. Yer the bane of my life.' Maeve lay back down on her bed and rolled around pushing the pillow into her face and her crying like a banshee.

Mother Michael came to Maeve's bed.

'Teresa, did you put her up to this? Was this your plan? Like you let Dymphna escape all those years ago?'

Maeve just screamed into the thin yellow pillow. Mother Michael turned to Sister Liz her eyes blazing like a demon.

Mother Michael did a scan of the room and grabbed the little radio off the end of Nessa's bed. 'You let them have too much,' she snarled at Sister Liz who hung her head low as if being beaten. 'Allowing this gobaloon pay the breadman and having them listen to the radio. What next? Outings to see blessed Oliver Plunkett's head?'

At Mass the next morning, we Laundry women sat on the scratched-up, scuffed wooden pews assigned to us. The Laundry had a side door that opened into the church. From another side door the wee bedraggled scabby-legged children filed in from the Industrial School. Maeve stuck her tongue out at them sometimes for the craic, but not today. Today her eyes were red and raw, and dimming. The light inside of her was fizzling out.

I loved Mass cos of the stories they told. There was a story the priest was telling us about two kid goats. God was telling Moses how to do things, and he wanted to live with the people and give them rules to get rid of all the sins they are born with and even all the ones we commit just by thinking of them. I tried to imagine what a goat looked like, and Maeve said it was like a sheep. They would sacrifice a goat to God, and they would lay their hands on the head of the living goat and tell it all the sins, putting them onto the goat's head. Then they'd send this other one out into the wilderness. This goat that they let escape was called the scapegoat, and it would take all the sins of the tribe into the desert. That way the people could be pure and with God because all their sins left with the goat.

Maeve was listening to the priest's story and she turned to Sister Liz beside her and said, 'At least they let the goat free. Here you've taken our babies and trapped us all inside.'

I thought they'd bring Nessa back and Maeve would be happy again for a bit. But Nessa was never caught, and worse I was never allowed hold money and pay the breadman ever again either. Even the older women who never seemed to pay attention to anything now asked Maeve to tell her stories cos the radio was gone.

'Teresa, pet, tell us a story would ya?' one said. They still called her Teresa.

'I'm done with them stories,' Maeve said, stretched out on her bed, staring at the ceiling. She pointed her finger to me without even looking over. 'She can tell them to ya now. She's taken them as well.'

I found Nessa's empty brown leather handbag under the bed. She had come in with it. I offered it to Maeve cos she didn't have a bag or a case either. She shook her head and told me to keep it, so I did. Every night I sat on the bed and opened it and looked through all the little pockets. It was like a little empty building full of secret rooms. There were zips and buttons, and the lining was torn, but I was happy out, even if there was nothing in it. I would find the deepest hidden pocket, a zipped one with another tiny pouch inside, I would keep my wee blue ribbon in there, so I would.

Hag

A Hag's Handbag

With all my wee rotting babies scooped up, we make our way to Busáras to catch the Tralee bus. I don't know Dublin all that well, so we get lost in Marlborough Street. The lost junkie tribe on Marlborough Street gather in shivering clusters. The light has gone out of their eyes worse than even in all the famine times. What really shocks me is that everyone else is moving about obliviously, while their own people stand soul destructed as they wait for the dealer. Are they just zombie ghosts? Can no one else see them? I know what that feels like, to be sure. All of them are the most wounded, the ones who could feel the hurt and couldn't get through it unless they were numb. The brick-by-brick fort walls built always against them. Now they have been rendered as automatons where meaning has slithered out of their brittle shells. The detritus of history where no justice is ever served. There was more life in the bog bodies. This is beyond my powers, all is forgotten or not learned, unremembered, the corners are too well lit, the food is processed and the approaching night is uncommitted to its own dark nature.

I stand up shudderingly straight – an old old woman with six arms and two legs, carrying my limbo babies in various stages of decomposition – though some of the junkies look right through me, a few seem to register my presence.

What I see here shocks even me. I who have been witness to all since the Devonian, since the Cambrian, since all the world was one big country of Pangaea. Since I, Ireland, was two halves that collided. I, who had once been moored by Australia. I, who have witnessed years in the millions. I see it has come to this. Was it for this you crawled out of the water? Was it for this you came down from the trees? Was it for this you walked the land bridge from Africa? Was it for this you set out on small boats from the foggy coast of northern Iberia and made the first landing on Bolus Head?

Suddenly, as I spin around looking for the way out of this miserable street, one of them swoops by me, my handbag that was dangling off one of my six arms gets snatched.

'Lousy fucking junkies,' I howl. 'No one cares about ye. Where will ye pawn a hag's handbag?'

My limbo babies begin to cry in chorus, like a tiny baldy pack of wolves, and it almost takes the good out of the Happy Meal. A stinking man, stinking worse than my desiccated babies, rises from the doorstep where he sleeps on cardboard. He sees me clearly. He has the gift, he's one of the ones who can see the fairies, the ghosts, who has stood before me as a child.

'It's the hag herself,' Iggy smiles with derelict teeth. He gives a quarter bow and doffs his hat. 'And all her weans. I do believe we met before when I was a lad. In the ruins of the old cathedral in Trim.'

'Aye, we have.'

He puts two wee babies into his great pockets of his long coat, and they peep out like marsupials. With his blackthorn stick sweeping before us he grandly escorts us to the station. We stand at the entrance, and it begins to rain.

'I'd hate to importune you at a moment like this. I see you have a lot on your plate. But have you anything to tell me?' he asks, as he gently takes the babies in his enormous messed-up hands and places them carefully into my arms.

'The stories mean that the pain won't always kill you,' I tell him. I'm a little distracted.

'Sure, I could have told you that.' Iggy winks.

I'm looking over my shoulder.

'Take shelter,' I shrug. 'A storm is coming.'

'But I don't think I can go inside anymore.' He swings his stick around with a flourish.

We stand outside the door of the station. He touches his hat and slips off into this old garrison town. A shadow of a shadow of an unquenched ghost.

Since we have no bus fare, we mount onto the roof of the Tralee bus. Their little human bodies are so flimsy; one loses an ear to the whipping wind. I gather them closer to me, wrapping my hairy old arms around each of them.

At the end of the journey some of them pretend to be asleep, just like real live children do. Just so I carry them. It is a way from the bus, through all the evening quiet of towns Castlemaine, Killorglin, Glenbeigh, Kells, Cahersiveen, Ballinskelligs, a few miles more along the narrow dark winding road to Bolus Head in the far west of the Iveragh Peninsula. We trudge past the hungry ruins of Cill Rialaig village, where once the tattered children chased the fairy horses, begging them for the cure for whooping cough.

My babies smile toothless when they see the dark shapes of the islands, as old as the Rings of Saturn, lying like unacknowledged but expectant gods in the great torn-up Atlantic Ocean. A flock of sheep is huddled together in their standing sleep on the hill in the limbo graveyard. We don't startle them at all. I sing one more song to them all, to the sleeping sheep, to the rotting babies, to the density of the mountain. A prehistoric song in the old language before the land broke apart and drifted over this tiny watery sphere. Out there in the water, the eels are making their way back through the veiny rivers to the mouths of the ocean, and on to the Sargasso Sea, where they will perform their mysteries. They cross paths with the salmon who are returning, leaping exposed in the dangerous moment of air. The birds are quiet in the night, holding their crex crex crex – razor-ugly cries to shred the day. The Skellig stone huts are empty and dark where once the monks let me visit and they sang this eerie song with me until the wind took it through the spiral of time. And back it came again and again. But enough, enough, the song is only for myself, for the sheep are lost in the bleat of dreams, the mountain is locked in a granite trance and the wee babies are all done after their big day out. They long for their limbo sleep.

Exhausted, I tuck them back into the dark deconsecrated mountain on Bolus Head, my wee spiderlings. Rest now far from God, no grace granted to you, only me here to take care of you.

Is fuar cumann cailleach.

The affection of a hag is a cold thing.

Acknowledgments

Initially I wrote this book with the terrible title of *The Affection of a Hag* in a studio on Eleanor and Paddy O'Sullivan's farm in Co. Meath. Eleanor's dad, the wonderful Barney O'Dowd, lived below the studio and was kind enough to remove mice for me when needed. I will always be grateful to their family for the space and atmosphere needed to write. *Thirsty Ghosts* was born out of *The Cruelty Men* but both can be read independently.

Big shout out to Jacqueline Grohs, David C. Perez, Cory Massaro, Ruben Zamora, and Mighty Mike McGee – my San Jose writing squad who were the ones who helped shape this book. Without them, I would not have had the discipline to manage a full-time job, teenagers and, worst of all, my own easily distracted brain. They are all wonderful and accomplished writers who take their craft seriously, and they became my community of artists here in California.

Seán Farrell, my patient and diligent editor at Lilliput, who has that rare gift of allowing my voice to remain while shaping the text so that it has coherence.

I thank my wonderful family and my parents, Eamonn and Marguerite. Their past and roots are reflected in the book and give it resonance. Marguerite's family were Tyrone and Ulster, and that provided the setting for the first part. In 2021 we lost my lovely dad, Eamonn, but the setting of Kilbride is his family house, where the character of Mary was based on his housekeeper Patti Dalton who took me to see hares dance and to make offerings at fairy trees. My Uncle Val has been a teacher in how to live a life of service and connectedness.

I always need to acknowledge the strength and support my family give me in my work. My inspiring sister, Ciara Martin, and her husband, Kieran Fulcher, who always open their doors for us and provide the feast around which we can gather! My nieces Aisling, Roisin and Clodagh, who take such pride in the Irish language which was lost on my resentful generation. If the language survives, and it must, it will be because their generation reclaimed it. My brother, Daragh, who is a fellow lover of ruins and gives the best tour of Tara, otherwise it could be mistaken as just bumps in the ground.

Alison Crosbie, Linda Quinn, June Caldwell and Maria Behan were first readers and had to read this book when it was the original massive beast. I thank them for their graciousness in not giving up on me. Judith Mok, Michael O'Loughlin and Sara O'Loughlin provided me with a sounding board and venting space for the weariness and silences of a writing life, and some mystic devilment to boot.

Noelle Campbell Sharp allowed me residencies at Cill Rialaig on the magic mountain, and her introduction to me of Seán Ó Conaill's folktales was the initial spark that made me understand the healing power of stories. As always, in Kerry, the enigmatic Ger O'Connell, now an accomplished landscape artist, unlocked some mysteries and presented many more, and was an integral part in my understanding of how the characters and the land could be one. The people of Ballinskelligs have been so welcoming and generous. If there is any similarity to people who lived there, it is purely coincidental as this is a work of fiction, but I hope I capture something of the phenomenal spirit of the always impressive and somewhat elusive Kerry people, who have not only protected so much of our culture but have kept it living and vibrant.

As always, my sisters in the arts, the Banshees, Helena Mulkerns, Imelda O'Reilly, Caitríona O'Leary, Elizabeth White and Darrah Carr: we're still all here on this planet creating art and opening spaces for it to breathe and thrive.

The poet Kevin Williamson who is always willing to make pilgrimages to the edges of time and space. To Irvine Welsh, a loyal friend who manages to keep it all real and still be the most productive writer I've ever known.

To my daughters, Jasmine and Jade, both creative brilliant women. Yet I hope you both always make space in your life to create.

To Afshin, who curates all my news for me daily and assures me we are millionaires – it's just in everyone else's pockets.

To Valerie Sabbag, my neighbour and friend and fellow seeker. Without your counsel, advice, listening skills, humour and shenanigans, I wouldn't survive the valley of Silicon. Thank you for agreeing to bubble with me during Covid. And to Lisee Sabbag for creating a killer website for me and making me look more professional than I feel!

To Donna Collins and Rick Williams our parallel family: away from all our families, you make California seem more like home, and your support at all my events and readings has been duly noted! Our group texts with Christine and John Walker kept us connected even in the midst of lockdown. Thank you, Christine, for being a creative partner when I need someone to take a risk. To Alka Raghuram, the painter and filmmaker, you still remain one of my keys to continuing this life as an artist. To the poet and painter Kofi Fosu Forson: we grew up in New York together as emerging artists and your magnanimous spirit and talent make sure we never give up our calling despite so many obstacles. Here's to future collaborations.

Finally, I never really had suburban high school teacher in my plans but sometimes life gives you exactly what you need. And I needed a paycheck. Having a full-time teaching job and still trying to write meant there was no balance in life. Patti Dalton, for constant sage advice and for making me laugh even at the hardest times and choosing me to be godmother to Saoirse. Also, Robert Javier, for your commitment to racial justice and equity and killer cocktails. Amy Gibson, who changed the course of my teaching by introducing me to the world of ELD and our wonderful migrant students, and whose calm guidance always grounds me as a teacher. David Bigelman, for passionate conversations on the nature of teaching literature and parenting teenagers. Preeti Mayuram, for our weekly lunches, which create such a joyful space in the work week. Stephanie Fujii, for opening her home to us all for much-needed celebrations. Onette Zabinski, for keeping it real and giving me insights for free and allowing me to badger her about her own writing. Phyllis Flanagan, for putting up with me crashing into her office whenever I need it. Chary Salvador, for providing me with space to talk things out – you have the finger on the button for equitable teaching practices that mean something in real life – and for tolerating me when I walk away with all your coffee cups. Timna Naim, the moment I saw them roller blade through the yard in fiery leggings I was worried they'd be too cool to stay and inspire the students and staff, but they have so far: keep making your art while teaching, I know how demanding that is. Also, what a relief it was to finally find Jesus! Specifically, Jesus Ramirez, who makes me laugh, tells me stories and even one morning gave me a stolen bicycle straight from the courts! Curtis Lee, sorry there's no Curtis in this book as requested, maybe the next – no promises. We started teaching at the school on the same day as teaching partners, and your wry tolerance for my chaos and your wicked sense of humour ensured I was able to stay the course.

I read many books while researching this book. The key texts were:

Down Down Deeper and Down: Ireland in the 70s and 80s (2010) by Eamonn Sweeney

The Plantation of Ulster: The British Colonization of the North of Ireland in the 17th Century (2011) by Jonathan Bardon

The Great O'Neill: A Biography of Hugh O'Neill Earl of Tyrone, 1550–1616 (1942) by Seán Ó Faoláin

Lethal Allies: British Collusion in Ireland (2013) by Anne Cadwallader

Unquiet Graves – The Story of the Glenanne Gang (2018). A documentary film by Seán Murray which has done stellar work to understand British state collusion in the systematic murders of native Irish people.

In Search of the Irish Dreamtime: Archaeology and Early Irish Literature (2016) by J. P. Mallory

The Irish Tradition (1947) by Robin Flower

Tyrone Folk Tales (1996) by Doreen McBride

Origins of the Magdalene Laundries: An Analytical History (2010) by Rebecca Lea McCarthy

Over Nine Waves: A Book of Irish Legends (1995) by Marie Heaney

Dublin's Little Jerusalem (2002) by Nick Harris

There are ancient folktales included in the text, and they are in italics because they are taken directly from the book I had as a child: Ella Young's *Celtic Wonder Tales* (1910).

I am indebted to the storyteller Seán Ó Conaill and his editor, Séamus Ó Duilearga, who came to Bolus Head to gather all that ancient wealth of stories into Seán Ó Conaill's book: *Stories and Traditions from Iveragh* (1981). I acknowledge storytellers everywhere in the world who are open and willing to tell a tale and listen and keep the land alive with the telling – we die untold, untold we die.